the Berlin Deception

Deception

by Jeffrey Vanke

ISBN-13:   978-1463702717
ISBN-10:   146370271X

Cover design by Mark Ching.

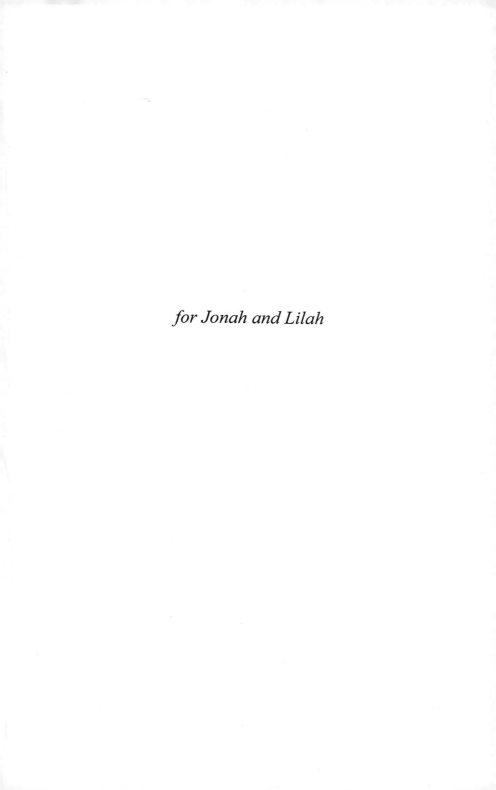

for Jonah and Lilah

Robert Vansittart
Foreign Office, Retired

London, November 1954

Dear Winston,

Congratulations on your eightieth birthday! The whole world celebrates with you.

Two decades ago, Adolf Hitler killed thousands of German protestors and threw thousands more into concentration camps. Our Government scarcely protested. You called him a murderer.

Hitler assured Germany's neighbors of his good intentions. Our Ministers called him peaceful. You called him a liar.

Hitler demanded that British Governments exclude you from their Cabinets. They followed his wishes and said it was for the sake of peace. You warned that peace with Hitler was impossible.

When Hitler expanded his arms in 1936, our Government said Germany had a right to defend itself. You said Hitler wanted war and must be stopped.

When France fell in 1940, our appeasers wanted to surrender. You swayed the Cabinet against the appeasers. Only the full force of your leadership saved us all.

At least we had Becker back in '36. If only the Cabinet had minded Becker's report, we could have stopped Hitler there and then. Thank God for Becker's other success.

Your devoted servant,
Van

Diary

Deputy Führer Rudolf Hess

5 February 1936

The Allies could crush us if they knew our secret. But if they stay put, Nazi Germany will be secure for the ages!

I've never seen the Führer so nervous. The next month will make or break the Third Reich.

CHAPTER ONE

Berlin 1936
Friday, February 7

"Shameful." The old man barely mouthed the word.

John Becker saw him and shared the sentiment.

The man sat at the back of the crowded subway car and shook his head almost imperceptibly. "Shameful."

Becker turned to the two SS guards bullying a middle-aged Jew at the front of the car. The silent passengers fidgeted, their winter clothes too much for the subterranean warmth. Melted snow thickened the humidity with the smell of wet wool. The train's steady rumble did nothing to distract the passengers from the only conversation on their car.

"So are you a Jew, or aren't you?" seethed the short, thin SS lieutenant, scowling through his small steel spectacles.

Both SS guards wore crisp black uniforms. They were so pitch black from head to toe that Becker couldn't make out the first crease in their shirts. Their pointed caps featured the trademark silver death's head skull-on-crossbones medallion in the center of the headband. The SS uniforms were utterly chilling, even without the men who wore them.

"Don't stand so close to proper Aryans!" shouted the thuggish hulk of an SS corporal.

The Jew shifted a couple feet back into his corner.

"How does it feel to have Jewish blood coursing through your veins?" hissed the officer.

Becker's blood boiled as he stood in the middle of the car, but his face was impassive. This sort of thing could be happening now to his adored childhood nanny, Esther. That thought enraged him even more. He hated that he could do nothing here. He knew he would do his part soon.

Becker glanced back at the short old man.

"Unbelievable," the man whispered to himself incautiously, dangerously.

"*Ja*, you Jewish pig, how does it feel?" shouted the towering SS guard up front.

Becker watched the short officer stare in icy silence. The Jew struggled for the dignity to return the stare. The sadistic Nazi's glare forced him to avert his gaze.

"Thick-headed Nazis," muttered the old man in the back, loud enough for Becker to hear.

Becker sensed a collective gasp. He watched nearby passengers shuffle nervously. Sweat began to bead on many faces. The train windows fogged up even more. The smell of collective perspiration was stifling.

Passengers at the old man's end watched the short SS officer turn his head toward them. Had he heard the old man? The possibility hung in the air like a suffocating smog.

The old man bowed his head toward the floor, frightened to death by his indiscretion. He closed his eyes and began to tremble.

The Tempelhof underground line stopped, exchanged a few passengers, and resumed course. Fresh air temporarily relieved the stale conditions inside the car. But new passengers instantly sensed and joined the collective paralysis. The SS officer's stare identified the old man as the center of the disturbance.

Finally the officer released his glare and turned to face the closed doors in front of him. Even the Jew joined the collective exhalation. The old man stopped shaking.

"What do you mean, 'Thick-headed Nazis'?!?" shouted a young man in the back.

The SS guards turned, paused, and stomped from the Jew to the old man.

"*Ja*, What is that supposed to mean?" barked the tall corporal as he jerked the man out of his seat.

Silence.

Self-gratified silence from the young informer.

Self-righteous silence from other passengers, chins upturned, offering their moral support to buoy the SS men.

Anxious silence from some, heads turned away in impotent embarrassment.

And gaping, terrified silence from the frail old man.

The clanking and screeching steel wheels of the train fell on deaf ears all around.

Without warning, the tall guard's fist cracked the old man's jaw.

The man crumbled to the floor, heaving in pain. Between two pairs of sparkling black boots, he spat blood and broken dentures onto the floor.

"You can come tell us what's on your mind," mocked the officer.

Both guards jerked the man's slight frame upright, and dragged him out the opening train doors at the next stop.

Another draft of fresh air.

Becker watched the Jew breathe a sigh of relief mixed with melancholy. Even the young informant seemed shocked by the fruits of his effort, which still littered the floor before him. He faced the slightest signs of disgust from a few bold passengers. Others, mostly young riders, nodded their approval.

Becker's blank face masked his revulsion at what had become of his birth country.

He was taller than average, still athletic at thirty, with thick sandy-blond hair and blue-gray eyes. John Becker, born Johannes, was returning to his boarding house this Friday evening after a company training session off-grounds. With his long, tan trench coat, he wore the dark yellow scarf his mother sent him from London. His gray felt fedora matched nearly half the men's hats in Berlin. He wore the hat low on his face, nearly touching his upturned coat collar on one side. He knew it looked a little odd, but he liked to shield his face from view.

Next to him stood Maria Geberich, a co-worker whose commute overlapped his own. Maria looked English, Becker thought. Her cheekbones were prominent but slightly lower and flatter than many Germans'. Her dark brown hair and large dark eyes seemed out of place in Nordic Berlin, as did her smooth, pale white skin. She was also on the shorter side for northern Germany. Unlike most women of the day, Maria never wore her hair up. She always let most or all of it fall to her shoulders. Today, some of it was pulled behind a large hair barrette she wore in place of a hat. Maria's hips and chest were womanly, but not excessive. She was healthy, lovely, beautiful, and thirty years old, exactly Becker's age. She looked good in anything, and best in black, which she wore today, including her black coat.

Becker still wondered why she wasn't married. She remained a mystery to him after more than a year of close observation at work and at all sorts of odd hours outside her apartment. Why did she keep to herself so much? She repeatedly rebuffed his advances. Becker wasn't used to that. Yet she was regularly flirtatious. Becker understood some people's isolation. But he was missing something about Maria.

Around Maria as much as anywhere, Becker had to maintain his apolitical persona. He would need her when the time came, but he didn't want any risks before then. So he expressed no opinion of the brutality they had just witnessed, and he avoided her eye contact.

At the next stop, one young passenger gently pushed the broken dentures out the open door with his foot. Two more stops passed. Each stop freshened the air and brought a wave of new passengers to relax the tension.

Maria uneasily and softly resumed their conversation. "We'll miss you this weekend. Our office parties are a real treat, don't you think? They make working in the Kristner mailroom a unique experience. The Carnival party in particular is such a splendid affair, with all those Rhineland games and dishes. A real treat of Catholic revelry here in dour Lutheran Berlin." She lowered her voice for the last part and looked around to see if anyone was offended.

"I'm dreadfully sorry to miss it, Fräulein Geberich. Maybe next year." He hoped not. After fifteen months in Germany, he was eager for the go-ahead from London. He was running a holding pattern until London ordered him to strike and then pull out of the country.

Suddenly, Becker sensed he was being watched. He turned, and sure enough, a tall woman in her fifties had boarded in the back of the subway car. She wore a long, dark blue overcoat and a black hat. She stood just on the edge of earshot. Worse, Becker thought he recognized her as they made eye contact. She evidently strained to remember the connection as well, somewhere in the distant past. She had to be some family friend from the Black Forest region.

Becker moved slightly to his right so that Maria turned to him and farther away from the woman. Now the woman had little chance of understanding Maria. Becker could control his own volume and speech.

"Next year, Herr Becker?" Maria continued. "Carnival isn't the only occasion when we have a party, you know. Hopefully you won't keep running off to Prague *every* time we all get together?"

"Hopefully not." Becker kept a peripheral watch on that strangely familiar woman. He did not need his identity blown by some incidental encounter on the underground.

"Why do you go so often to visit your aunt, anyway? That's a long trip for just a weekend."

Dammit, why does she have to pry like this, at just such an exposed moment? Isn't our train change coming soon?

Becker peered out the open underground doors for the name of the station – Stettiner Bahnhof. Then he glanced sidelong to confirm the continuing menace of the friendly-looking familiar woman in blue.

Four more stops until they changed lines, he thought, and until a pause to this conversation.

"My aunt helped my mother raise me while my father traveled so much in his job as a railroad inspector." He offered his well rehearsed biography, ready to embellish it if necessary.

"In Prague?"

"No." Becker was irritated at Maria's very public inquisitiveness. He had tried for months to no avail to cultivate a more private relationship. She pushed him into group settings every time he tried. She was attractive and intriguing, worth the effort, and not just for professional reasons.

"I grew up in Hanover," he said. "When my uncle retired, he moved back to his native Prague with my aunt. They lived in the German quarter, and she stayed there after he died. She has no children and just a couple of friends in Prague. She was like a second mother to me, and I've tried to visit her often since my uncle died."

This was too much for the mysterious woman to be hearing. Some of it matched his real biography, and some did not. It could only stimulate the stranger to recover her memory before he found his. Becker might have to exit the train before planned. He hesitated to draw Maria's attention to any irregularities.

Three more stops.

Becker and the familiar woman in blue kept catching each other's eyes. The connection far predated his service, and that was bad. In younger years, Becker had traveled in Germany among old family and friends. They knew he had become a proud Englishman. Identification now, especially in front of Maria, would ruin his mission and endanger his life. Captured enemies of the Third Reich faced torture before execution. Some of them were strung up by piano wire, which took its time in slicing through the victim's neck.

Now several stops after the brutal beating, the car's commuters slowly resumed reading, or blank underground stares.

Then a new passenger took a position near the silent Jew. Becker watched the passenger back into a corner. But rather than retreat into his own little space, the new man darted his eyes from one passenger to the next. Becker recognized the trademark behavior of a detective or a secret agent.

Becker watched as the agent sensed the tension in this underground car. The agent seemed both puzzled and curious. His eyes quickly followed all the furtive glances toward the fresh bloodstains on the opposite floor of the car. When the agent noticed this grim sight, he cracked a slight grin. With that hint of sadism, Becker knew he had a bad guy on his hands, probably Gestapo. Becker had so far avoided the agent's eye contact. Now he turned his head slightly more toward Maria, and dropped the Gestapo agent from his sight.

Automatically, Becker reviewed his situation. So far, no suspicious answers to Maria, no nervous voice, no harm done. Yet the dangers were stacking up. He faced unwanted questioning from Maria; an unknown familiar face from the past; and an evil Third Reich agent within earshot. Becker could not wait to escape this train.

"Don't you ever get away from the city yourself?" he asked. Becker planned to push Maria through the conversation for the last three stops.

A long pause ensued. As Maria looked into the distance of her own thought, her mood suddenly changed. "Rarely. Not for a very long time have I had someone to visit anywhere but this city. I was born in Bonn, and when my parents died in a house fire, I moved in with my older brother in Berlin, who had a civil service job here."

Becker started to remember. That familiar woman was a childhood neighbor of his mother's. He'd met her briefly some fifteen years earlier. He struggled to remember her name.

A smile of recognition swept over the familiar woman's face at precisely the same moment. Becker noticed it and knew he had to escape, even if the woman meant him no harm.

He glanced as casually as possible toward the front end of the car. There stood the Gestapo agent, with his gaze locked on Becker in a tight spot.

This was it. Becker could not have his false biography collapse before Maria's eyes. Nor could he allow her to be shocked at his Englishness in view of the Gestapo. Becker had to walk – or run – for his life. Next stop: Friedrich Strasse. Almost there. The smiling, dreaded woman approached.

Not seeing the woman in blue, Maria returned Becker's questioning, "And how did you land in the big city?"

Becker cut off the conversation as the underground train stopped. "I just remembered I need to buy opera tickets for next weekend. I'll need to step out here." The underground doors opened. "I'm terribly sorry to cut you off so abruptly." He backed out of the doors.

Too late. The woman in blue was right there, in the shuffle of hundreds of passengers crowding on and off the underground. "Herr Becker, I believe it is?" she asked barely above a whisper.

Maria looked surprised at Becker's acquaintance with the unknown, older, attractive woman.

Becker finished his good-bye to Maria and ignored the stranger. "I'll see you on Monday." He exited the train and almost ran toward the staircase and the smell of fresh wet snow above.

The woman in blue followed her curiosity and rushed out the open train doors. Becker saw her with a quick glance to his rear. That glance earned him the warning that he must beat a quick retreat. But it cost him a much greater obstacle to his get-away.

The Gestapo agent had moved to the threshold of the subway doors and was still watching Becker. When Becker looked backwards nervously for the agent, their eyes met. The agent's whole body leaned forward to start a running.

Damn! Becker's canter became a gallop out of the underground station. *Here I am a few blocks from Gestapo headquarters, being chased by one of their own!*

Becker knew he shouldn't have looked directly at the agent. But the man had moved to the subway doorway, away from where Becker had expected him. Now the Gestapo man had to know that Becker had identified him on the train. So he had to know that Becker had something to hide.

"*Halt! Halt!* Stop that man!!!" shouted the Gestapo agent.

Becker dashed up the crowded stairs and around the first landing. He wanted to beat it out before the shouts of "Halt!" could inspire some Nazi enthusiast in the crowd to hold him back. For a moment, he got tangled up with some commuters coming down the stairs in front of him. Once he reached the top, he would have to vanish instantly.

Becker leaped up several stairs at a time. He removed and dropped his mother's yellow scarf, too distinctive in a chase. Becker felt the rush of adrenaline, but he controlled it and even enjoyed it. It allowed him to observe his surroundings as if others were frozen in time.

He saw light snow falling and melting on the street. He heard the massive swastika banners snapping above the street in the strong breeze. He looked up to see the banners even more striking in spotlights than by daylight. All around him, the roads and sidewalks crowded with Berliners headed home at five-thirty this Friday evening.

Becker could run for it. But right next to the government district teeming with swastika armbands, he ruled that out. He could keep climbing to the elevated railway. But he risked getting cornered if no train were there. What was left? Slow street traffic passed the underground's exit.

Just in front of him, Becker saw a streetcar pulling away. In a short sprint reminiscent of his Cambridge days, he reached the accelerating tram and leaped onto it.

Scrambling aboard, he managed a quick look backwards. The Gestapo agent snapped his head up and down the street, eager to find his prey. Becker climbed into the tram, catching his breath. He leaned around a tall passenger just enough to look back and see his hunter staring at the tram!

The Gestapo agent searched frantically for a car. After two failures to hail moving cars, the agent opened the front passenger door of an occupied taxi. He berated the protesting passengers and assumed the cab's command. It took off after Becker's streetcar moving southward on Friedrich Strasse.

Across the intersection with Unter den Linden, the traffic became more chaotic, delaying the Gestapo agent's taxi. But Becker's tram was also slowed, and Becker watched the cab slowly close in on him. He would get caught if he stayed here. So when his tram moved behind another one ahead on the tracks, Becker jumped off.

He knew his jump was visible to his pursuer. He bent down to hide behind passing cars. Then he shuffled quickly to the next streetcar in front. He got some odd looks for his crouched posture, especially when he suddenly and athletically leaped toward the departing streetcar. Had the Gestapo agent spotted this last move? Becker guessed that the angle shielded him from his hunter's sight lines.

Yet a minute or two into his new ride, Becker noticed excitement among the rear passengers. "Look at that car!" shouted one.

No! Becker stood on his toes and looked over everyone's heads. He identified the top of the pursuing cab. It drove down the street along the tram tracks. Becker moved toward the back of the tram for a better view, leaving a couple rows of passengers to shield him.

The Gestapo's cab was so far back in the crowded traffic that another car pulled in front of it, onto the faster lane of tram tracks. Becker could see his Gestapo hunter in the front passenger seat waving wildly at the driver. The cab approached dangerously close to the car in front of it, whose driver refused to budge. The Gestapo agent flailed his hands around in such an impatient frenzy that he reminded Becker of Hitler newsreels.

Then Becker saw the cab driver try something bold. Next to Becker's tram tracks were the opposite tracks, for oncoming streetcars. The cab driver drove around the slow curve to the right, blind to oncoming traffic. He quickly jerked his cab left onto the oncoming tracks. Becker saw him angle his head to the left, looking for any oncoming tram or car. The cab jerked back behind Becker's tram. Becker shot his own glance to his right and behind, to see if any tram were approaching from the other direction. No such luck. He felt trapped and thought about jumping onto an unsuspecting car on the right.

The cab accelerated into the oncoming tracks to the left, with the Gestapo agent visibly yelling nonstop. His driver gained on the tram, and began overtaking it. From within the tram, Becker scanned his memory of the surrounding streets south of Potsdamer Platz. He was going to be trapped before the next stop!

The cab approached the front of the moving tram. The Gestapo agent rolled down his window to wave for the driver to stop. But at that moment, an oncoming tram appeared around the corner, just seconds from a head-on collision with the Gestapo's taxi.

The cab's right side was blocked by Becker's tram. The driver's only choice was to swing a leftward u-turn into oncoming automobile traffic. His masterful skid found a gap. Then he braked in place to wait for the intervening tram to pass. As soon as it had, the driver cut another sharp u-turn, back onto the tram tracks toward Becker's streetcar.

Becker saw the cab approaching again, now a half-block behind. He had only a minute or two left. Looking out the window, he strained to identify his precise location: Ufer Strasse, just before crossing the Landwehr Canal bridge.

The canal. Its shadowy pathways were superb for hiding. Becker watched the Gestapo's taxi approach his streetcar for a second time. As the cab overtook his tram on the left, Becker seized his moment. He pulled open a right-side door, and jumped from the moving streetcar. One woman passenger screamed. The tram plowed ahead.

Becker rolled into his fall on the street, only bruising his knees, before dodging a car just in time. He ran across the busy road, past honking horns and headlights. He saw the tram stop abruptly a block ahead. Time was short. The Gestapo agent would search the streetcar and learn about Becker's jump.

Becker clambered down the street's retaining wall to the broad path by the canal. As soon as he reached the walkway, he heard the Gestapo agent screaming, "Halt! Halt!" on the street above. Becker heard car tires keep driving through the snowy wet street. Next came a single gunshot and more commands for the traffic to stop. Now tires skidded and stopped. Only seconds remained until the agent would arrive at the bridge right above.

Becker looked at the canal going under the bridge and panicked. The cobblestone path ended here – his intended escape route under the bridge did not exist! Anyone looking down from the street above would see him where he stood, and for several hundred feet down the canal path. Becker could risk dashing down the path, but his shoes would clap loudly against the flat cobblestones. If he did not find cover in time, he could be shot in the back.

Then there was the canal itself. A recent thaw had melted most of its ice, though a few large, thick pieces still floated in the dark water. Submersion would kill the most robust man within minutes.

He should not have counted on hiding under the bridge, thought Becker. He should have hopped onto a passing car above. Now he had another split-second decision to make.

A half-minute later, the Gestapo agent scrutinized the canal path from the bridge above, waving his gun around aimlessly. No one was in sight. The breeze rippled across the canal surface. The traces of Becker's careful entry into the water were gone.

Several feet under, he swam away in black silence. The freezing cold quickly tightened his muscles. It ached to his bones. It assaulted his heart and lungs and brain. The escape had worked. Now Becker had to survive it.

CHAPTER TWO

Becker barely surfaced under the bridge, his eyes just above the water line.

Behind him was silence, no sign the Gestapo agent knew he was in the icy canal. Becker lifted his mouth out of the frigid water and quietly exhaled a forceful vapor cloud that blew away in the breeze.

Ahead, the abandoned canal channel offered a promising landing point. Becker was beginning to lose sensation in his hands and feet. The chill circulated to his core. His stomach knotted and ached while he treaded water. Becker's ability to think was shutting down, an early sign of hypothermia. No matter what, he could not stay in the water. He took a deep breath and sank beneath the surface to complete his swim.

On the far side of the bridge, Becker emerged from the water and grasped at the sharp angles of the canal's stone walls. He did not bother to look for danger. He could not survive in the glacial water, even if arrest awaited.

Becker climbed and perched on a ledge above the canal. Water splattered from his clothes onto the stone surface. He smelled the urban canal's grime warming in his nostrils. Only when he pulled himself straight up did he check his surroundings in the shadows of streetlights.

Becker half-expected Nazi armbands all around. Instead, he faced only the cold night and the sounds of moving traffic on the bridge above. He looked back under the bridge. He could not see the path where he had entered the water, where his Gestapo hunter might now be standing.

Fast, Becker thought to himself in English for the first time in months. *I must make it to that apartment before my body temperature drops too low.*

Several miles from home, Becker had to seek warmth at closer quarters. Soaking wet, he was just as cold out of the canal as in it. He had to stay hidden on side streets, walking just fast enough to keep him warm, but not so fast as to arouse more suspicion.

At Friday evening rush hour, a fair number of cars and people kept even the side streets and sidewalks busy. A few people turned at the sound of Becker's squishy shoes. They all quickly steered away.

Becker looked at his coat and noticed the canal water already freezing into an outer layer of ice. He moved almost automatically, with little of his usual alertness. His cold brain did not want to think.

Months of studying and walking Berlin's streets paid off. In less than ten minutes Becker stood before the doorbell. He rang, and a full minute passed with no answer. One long, shivering, threateningly frigid minute. He rang again, and again no stirring of a response.

"My goodness, Herr Becker!" exclaimed a female voice, approaching from behind, more surprised than loud.

Becker summoned up all his energy as he turned to face Maria, not to account for his current state. That would be easy to concoct. He had to explain why he knew her address. "I fell into the Landwehr Canal. As soon as —"

"Do not bother with stories, Herr Becker." She put her hand on his icy back and guided him forward. "Get inside."

Becker felt relieved, and unexpectedly emotional in gratitude for the assistance Maria was offering him in his endangered condition. He relaxed his guard even further, and followed her into the ground-floor apartment, and then to the washroom.

He barely noticed the washroom's colors of white and dark yellow. As he stood in his wet clothes, Becker's whole body shook with debilitating cold. Maria drew a warm bath.

Back near the canal, the Gestapo officer twisted one gloved fist in the palm of his other hand. After finding and following dripping water from the canal's edge to the nearest sidewalk, he lost the track in rush hour foot traffic. It had taken him ten minutes to find his prey's exit spot from the canal. Now the chase would have to slow into a methodical search. The officer fumed twin clouds of nasal breath into the cold. Then he pulled his lips into a thin, determined grin. He knew what to do next.

An hour-and-a-half later, a strengthened Becker entered Maria's sitting room in the white cotton men's bathrobe she had laid out. Why did she have that, he wondered. Becker's wet hair, now dark brown, was combed neatly across his scalp.   The robe's v-neck revealed Becker's chest muscles and hair.

Becker noticed the windows fogging from his wet clothes steaming on the radiators.   The wet wool of his pants and tweed jacket overpowered the aroma of black tea on the table.

The typical furniture of sofa, chairs, and small tables made good use of the space.   Their wood was stained dark, with deep red upholstery somewhat faded with age.   The walls were white, with small picture frames.   The lampshades spread a soft yellow across the room.

The room had a phonograph but no radio.   Maria's record collection numbered in the hundreds on several shelves.   From across the room, Becker couldn't make out what kind of music.

The three small pictures were nature paintings.   They were worthy of a small-town museum, or better.   They looked like professional copies of masterful still-lifes and landscapes.   Not cheap.

Becker was impressed.   Maria was no ordinary mail clerk.   A woman with such cultural interests should have been a teacher or a librarian, or at least a secretary at an art museum.   But not a mail clerk.

He wanted to explore Maria's politics, though he knew that had to wait.   From the start, he'd found her mostly apolitical, perhaps slightly disgusted with all the blustering of the Nazi regime.   She probably had nosy neighbors already wondering what he was doing here tonight.   He didn't need to push the politics on this visit, hopefully only the first.

Instead, Becker wanted to lighten his imposition tonight with some humor.   He had a sense of what made her laugh at work, but he didn't know how she would respond under the present circumstances.

Maria had tea waiting for him.   She sat with excellent posture, legs next each other, and holding a teacup and saucer in her lap.   They were the best Meissen porcelain, with a simple blue pattern of flowering vines.

Becker was amused at his situation.   For almost a year, he had conspired to a closer relationship with Maria.   She was an important, innocent step to his mission's success.   But after all her cool rejections of even a coffee-shop friendship, Becker's present moment of vulnerability finally opened the door.   He had never stooped to self-injury to get Maria's hospitality.   Now here he was.

And there she was, in casual clothes he had never seen on her.   The flattering thin tan cardigan made her all the more attractive.   Her dark hair tumbled over shoulders that were broad for her short height.

After more than a year working together, even joking sometimes, Becker had a firm basis for informal conversation with Maria.

However, his strange present circumstances presented a challenge. He liked to break the ice with humor.

"I was just wondering," Becker smiled as he sat down, "how badly I had to hurt myself to get your attention."

Maria laughed, covering her mouth in a half-hearted coy gesture. But she looked straight at Becker with unembarrassed dark brown eyes. What was it about Maria, Becker wondered. She seemed to choose spinsterhood. Yet she could be quite alluring when she wanted to. It didn't make sense.

"Oh, I'd say you need to hurt yourself about this much," she pointed toward him with her whole hand. Then she folded her arms across her chest and cocked her head back a little. She smirked at his awkward attempt to explain himself.

"So I threw myself in the canal," Becker joked.

She laughed again, without covering her mouth this time. "No, be more creative . . . . You . . . were thinking too hard how to feign injury when you accidentally tripped and fell in. Was that it?"

Becker was a little surprised that she carried his joke forward.

"Good," he grinned. "But how about this? I was drifting on a large sheet of floating canal ice for a quiet ride by myself, when the ice broke and I fell in."

Maria raised her eyebrows and nodded in appreciation. "I could even believe that one with you. I really could."

"Seriously . . . you must be wondering how I got soaked and ended up here." So far neither of them mentioned the chase from the underground.

"You don't owe me an explanation, Johannes," answered Maria, shaking her head. "I'll just claim a first-name basis, if you don't mind," she smiled.

Becker smiled back, and added half-jokingly, "I've been trying to get on a first-name basis for months!"

Maria did not suppress a broader, knowing smile. "Am I curious? Of course. But I do not require an account of why you so abruptly . . . left the underground, shall we say, and one half-hour later ended up at my doorstep draining the Landwehr Canal from head to toe."

Becker was impressed with her forthright dismissal of whatever confabulation he was prepared to tell. Here was some of the Maria missing from fifteen months of daily contact. She showed more delicacy, more experience, and more self-possession than she normally let on. He knew he mustn't lie. But he certainly could not tell the whole truth, either. So he chose one sliver of it.

"I have a good memory. In my spare time, I spend many of my weekends walking around Berlin. Once, many months ago, you told us about a traffic accident by your window. It was the worst that Arnold Strasse had ever seen, you said. I recognized the name of the intersection, and I remembered it. A couple of hours ago, my brain was freezing as I looked at the street signs. I recognized your street, and came straight here."

Maria gave Becker a brief, serious look that spoke what neither of them would say aloud. He must have been fleeing something, since he avoided public assistance. In 1936 Berlin, that meant the Nazis.

They sipped hot tea silently for several minutes, before talking about various colleagues in the Kristner mailroom.

"Fräulein Geb– . . . , er, Maria," Becker smiled after his intentional error and self-correction. "I hope next week you'll give me a colorful account of this weekend's party? What stunt do you think Schwarz will pull at the office party this time?"

Georg Schwarz was a buffoon. He was also the only Nazi Party member among their colleagues. They liked to make fun of him. Some of their colleagues were strong Hitler supporters, but even they made fun of Schwarz. His personality defined him much more than his party membership. Still, it was risky for Becker to make such jests alone with Maria. It was a test.

"It's always something, isn't it?" Maria shook her head and laughed a little. At the same time her eyes were dead serious as they stared back at Becker. Someone listening in would never imagine the look she gave him.

Good, he thought. She's willing to play along and make fun of the resident Nazi. But she's trying to show she knows what serious business it is.

"The funny thing is," she continued playfully, "he doesn't seem to care all that much. A little, yes. But I get the impression he's more proud of his drunken antics than embarrassed. Sure, I'll let you know how the party goes."

Their conversation stretched more than an hour. They surveyed their colleagues, one by one, at work and play. Maria could have turned the conversation to why a man Becker's age suddenly showed up working at Kristner just before Christmas 1934, but she didn't. She and the others were certainly surprised when he got the job one Monday morning. Kristner was an engineering firm with a broad range of clients. At the time they hired Becker, they were trying to land their first big Wehrmacht contract. For that reason, the Kristner managers were very careful about their hiring decisions, especially in the mailroom.

Becker brought with him an excellent reference and a stable record of employment at Karlsrat, a small German import business that sold out to a bigger firm. Or so Kristner thought. Karlsrat really did exist, and it really did sell out to a competitor. But Becker never worked there. The competitor was Jochen Becker & Associates, Ltd., Becker's uncle in London, who easily arranged it.

The conversation finally paused, somewhat awkwardly. Maria pointed out that Becker's clothes must be getting dry. Becker took the cue and excused himself to the washroom to dress in the warm, damp garments.

On his way out the door around nine o'clock, he truly was at a loss for the right words. "I don't know how to thank you."

She smiled softly, lips unparted. "It's good that I came home. Enjoy your weekend in Prague, Johannes."

Becker doffed his hat. "Good night, Maria." What does she mean, "came home," he wondered? Where else was she going to go? He had never observed anything but a regular solitary lifestyle in her routine.

As Becker walked into the night, he thought about how unexpectedly smoothly the whole visit had gone. She took him in unannounced, wet, and shivering to death. She let down a little of her veil, even called him by the first name. She went along with making fun of the bumbling Nazi Schwarz. But he knew there was still more to learn about Maria Geberich.

Becker avoided the underground on the way home to the Lande boarding house. The Gestapo might be lurking down there for him. Instead, he walked about half a mile on side streets to a secondary stop on the elevated rail, the S-Bahn. On a Friday evening, many Berliners still roamed the city's streets and rail lines. The short rail ride to Friedenau left him a mile-long chilly walk home in his damp clothes.

The wind had stopped. But it was colder, and Becker's damp clothes were freezing up again. He watched his steps on the snow-blown paving stones, two-inch rough-hewn stone cubes that covered the streets and sidewalks of much of Berlin. He lifted his eyes to check the street sign: Eisbrunnen Strasse, about fifteen minutes from home.

"I'm tired of waiting for him, Mama," Nadine Lande insisted to her mother Anna. The two of them sat in their kitchen, a strangely cramped space for so large a townhouse. The dark blue tablecloth and cabinets accentuated the white napkins and walls. Becker's seat sat empty.

"I'm going to eat," declared Nadine. Without saying grace, she took her first bite.

Anna gave up. After half an hour delaying on behalf of her boarder Johannes Becker, she let her sixteen-year-old eat. Just that morning he said he would be home for supper. She stared at his plate. She had to admit it was his fault. Only once before, almost a year ago, had he missed supper unannounced. Still, she felt rude and inhospitable to start without him. In her home village, they never ate until all invited guests had arrived.

After fifteen months, Becker was more than a boarder to Anna Lande. He was the object of her unspoken affections. She hoped he hadn't guessed. The more she loved him, the more austerely she treated him. Yet most nights, she fell asleep thinking about him. She wanted to wait and eat with Becker.

During the past year, the widowed Anna had her hands full with Nadine. More than ten years had passed since the death of Nadine's father. Her adolescence was going to be hard enough for Anna, an elementary school teacher.

To make matters worse, the Third Reich told school children they owed a greater loyalty to the Führer than to their own parents. Anna had once delivered that message in the classroom herself. Even when she used to have more enthusiasm for the Nazi regime, she had trouble with that particular instruction in her classroom. It just didn't pass her villager's code of family respect.

Other teachers, though, laid it on thick. Millions of German children tried to prove themselves better Germans than their parents. Nadine's turn had come. The girl was becoming the sort of brainwashed snitch who might turn in her own mother to the Gestapo.

Anna had ceased praising Hitler. She rarely mentioned him at home any more. Sure, the Führer made Germany strong and proud again. Yes, he brought them all jobs. All the things she used to praise were still true. But now Anna understood its darker side. She used to dismiss it as propaganda by those who were jealous of Hitler's popularity. More and more, though, Anna watched the Third Reich blacken her daughter's heart, her own flesh and blood. She should have listened to her villager's instincts all along. She never should have voted for the Nazis. She regretted taking her daughter two years ago to scream their lungs out among the delirious faithful at a Hitler parade. She risked paying for it with her only child's soul. There was only one more thing she could try on Nadine, but Anna wasn't quite ready for that.

For ten minutes, Anna quietly watched Nadine eat. Finally she joined her daughter. They ate their meal in silence. Anna occasionally looked at her daughter, but Nadine kept her eyes down. Nadine finished her water. Then without asking to be excused, she brusquely left the table for her room upstairs. Anna watched her go.

"It's time." Winston Churchill spoke on the phone from Chartwell, his country estate southeast of London. His large study was over eight centuries old, part of original the house.

At the other end of the line in London was Robert Vansittart, Permanent Undersecretary of the Foreign Office. As the highest-ranking civil servant in Britain's foreign affairs, Vansittart had vast access to classified information.

Vansittart also supervised a private intelligence agency called the Z Organisation. Fascism was on the rise in Europe, yet British governments refused to raise defense and intelligence budgets. The Depression, they argued, strained budgets enough. Besides, they insisted, hadn't the Great War been a waste?

Churchill disagreed. But for most of the 1930s, he was isolated from power. After two decades in and out of Cabinets, his once promising career was now a shambles. He was called a foolish warmonger. From the backbenches of Parliament, Churchill criticized the neglect of Britain's defenses. To fill the gap, Vansittart and Colonel Claude Dansey founded the Z Organisation in 1932. They shared some of its fruits with the official Secret Intelligence Service. But the Z Organisation retained its autonomy from the SIS.

"You want to activate Agent Z?" asked Vansittart.

"That's right," replied Churchill.

Everyone in the Z Organisation had a number. Dansey was Z1. John Becker was simply "Z." The whole organization had been founded with him in mind. He still had no equal.

Becker was a private intelligence weapon even before the Z Organisation existed. In 1925, Becker's twentieth year, Dansey spotted this young man who had taken full advantage of his affluent, unconventional upbringing. Becker's Uncle Jochen gladly indulged his nephew's passions for mastering anything that interested him – athletics and chess; guns and languages; flying and electronics. The list went on and on. Under Dansey's tutelage, Becker's hobbies became his training. Within eighteen months, he was ready for service. Uncle

Jochen, a patriotic naturalized Englishman, gladly subsidized John's missions. During long sojourns in London, Jochen kept his nephew employed at the family import business.

Dansey presided over the Z Organisation. He reported to Vansittart who, in turn, shared his intelligence information with Churchill. All this was even legal. As a former Cabinet Minister, Churchill still possessed his old security clearances. His political rivals in Westminster never knew enough to have them revoked.

"I presume you want to move quickly?" Vansittart asked.

"Top priority," replied Churchill. "Hitler could move any week now."

"We'll have to move fast to contact Z," said Vansittart. "Becker has his monthly rendezvous tomorrow afternoon in Prague. There's just enough time to get Dansey there. We'll fly him from Rome to Budapest tonight. Nazi spies would notice an arrival in Prague. We don't think they're watching Budapest. Dansey can take the midnight train. That'll put him in Prague just after noon tomorrow."

Two hours past suppertime, Becker neared his Berlin residence on foot. The wintry night grew colder by the minute.

In more than a year at the Lande residence, Becker had watched Nadine and Anna transform. The girl became a young woman and a near-hysterical Hitler fanatic. The widowed mother was cornered and cowed by her daughter's Nazi enthusiasm.

Anna had recently told Becker about the parents of a child in the primary school where she taught. They were arrested by the Gestapo when their ten-year-old told his teacher they'd been joking about the Nazi leadership. Afterwards, the boy lost his mind and had to leave school. Becker could hear the fear in Anna's voice, although she tried to hide it. Nadine was already warning her mother about loyalty to the Führer.

This wasn't the same Anna Lande who had first rented Becker a room. Back then, she was full of the usual bluster about the Führer's greatness for German morale and strength. Despite this, he took the room. He had to endure the Hitler fanaticism. Anywhere he turned in the Third Reich, he heard the same thing. Becker could not respond that the surge of German morale was built on hate, . . . that jobs came because Hitler imprisoned workers who declined his job offers. Becker hated what Hitler was doing to Germany. He scorned the German masses who drank it in. Even some long-time family friends in southwest Germany had changed. Becker thanked God he had been raised in England instead. Hitler brought out the worst in Germans, individually and collectively. All Becker could do for now was smile and nod.

Becker approached the house at almost ten o'clock. He found Anna where he expected her, awake reading in the living room. Nadine still had her light on upstairs. Becker closed the front door behind him, long after his unannounced suppertime absence. There was the agile Nadine, already atop the stairs in her pink winter pajamas. There was something reproachful and challenging in her posture.

Her mother Anna approached the entry hall downstairs in her white blouse, brown sweater, and gray skirt. She showed no disapproval at all. A year ago it might have been different, Becker knew. Despite Anna's best attempts to hide it, he could see the affections she had developed for him.

Nadine was nearly the spitting image of her mother. Tall and blonde, broad-boned and muscular, mother and daughter both epitomized the Nazi Aryan ideal. Their blue eyes and dark blonde eyebrows were nearly identical, though Nadine's nose was slightly larger and her lips were thinner and harsher than her mother's. Anna Lande had the looks of a movie star, though not the look of one. Her expressions were pragmatic, not flashy.

Standing at either end of the staircase, each with perfect posture, mother and daughter simply stared at Becker in silent curiosity.

"I'm sorry I missed supper. I got distracted by one of my long walks." His tone told them that was all the explanation they were going to get. Becker wasn't sure whether they noticed his damp clothes. He thought not, and he could blame a certain degree on the snowfall anyway. The shirt and pants should be fully dry after the night on his radiator.

It was especially the girl's curiosity he wanted to avoid. Recently, she was showing an increased interest in his affairs, and a willingness to pry.

Her mother Anna, though, presented no problem. She always respected her boarder's privacy. In the first months, she'd approached him mostly in business tones. But for quite some time now, she was clearly drawn to him, though she tried her best to hide it. She seemed shy and prone to blushing, in some ways more withdrawn around him than at first. For Becker's part, he kept his distance. She was certainly attractive. But a relationship where he lived would be too complicated. She seemed increasingly kind toward him, after the initial months of pure business in boarding him. Becker knew to expect no probing from Anna tonight.

"Good night, Frau Lande," he said.

"Good night, Herr Becker."

"Good night, Nadine," he said at the top of the stairs to the stubborn teenager. She barely budged out of his way. She turned her chin down in a half-impudent, half-coquettish grin, and skipped away.

Becker entered his small, sparse room. Within minutes his light was out. He had to wake up early for the train to Prague.

CHAPTER THREE

Saturday morning, February 8

The officer sat in his office at Gestapo headquarters, poring over a map of where his chase had ended near the canal. He meticulously plotted out a schedule for investigating many surrounding blocks, one at a time, throughout the weekend and the coming week.

Bloody hell! Only twenty yards away, Becker recognized the familiar woman who had almost blown his identity yesterday. Here in the great hall of Anhalter Bahnhof, the crowd of bustling train passengers provided him only moderate cover.

He finally remembered her name, Waltraud Rieger. She was an old friend of his mother's. A nice woman, but out of touch with his family. Her current political allegiances were therefore unknown.

There she stood between him and his Prague train. Becker had only minutes to catch it. If she saw him now and made a commotion about yesterday's chase, she could attract unwanted attention. She might even shout for the police.

Suddenly, Waltraud looked down from the departures schedule. She started walking through the crowd, straight towards Becker! He held his dark brown trench coat tight to his body, his hands in his pockets, and he whirled around as fast as he dared. He wore different outer garments today, darker shades than yesterday, having discarded the coat and hat from yesterday's chase on the way to the station.

With his back to Waltraud, Becker walked straight out of the train station. He pulled his dark gray fedora lower. He listened carefully for any accelerating footsteps behind him.

When he hit the station exit, he turned his head back just enough to see two things. First, Waltraud now walked down her train platform. She hadn't seen him. Second, the station's massive clock face showed that he had six minutes. That was enough time to walk around the station and reenter from the opposite side, right next to his train. Passengers running for their trains were not an unusual sight. But Becker didn't want the attention if he could help it.

He entered the train station on the far side and heard a last-call boarding whistle. A throng of passengers disembarked from the opposite side of the platform as his departing train. What poor scheduling, he thought. The crowds pushed him away from his train at the last minute!

He glanced at the station clock. *Good*, he thought, 08:42, three minutes to spare.

"*Guten Morgen*," said the conductor. Good morning. He seemed to be almost guarding the stairs into the train car.

Becker's heart started. He searched the eyes of this suspiciously friendly conductor to the Czechoslovak border. Nothing to worry about, Becker concluded.

"'*Morgen*," he replied, as he climbed aboard with his small weekend travel bag.

"Off to visit some Volk-Germans trapped under Czech rule, are you?"

Without a pause, Becker affirmed, "That's right." He climbed aboard.

The trip was scheduled to take six hours. Becker's second-class compartment had all eight seats filled. A two-year-old boy sat on his mother's lap. One old man probably hadn't bathed, or even changed clothes, in weeks. Becker cracked the window open to the cold air, to no one's complaint.

Within minutes, Becker settled into his book, Karl May's *The Treasure of Silver Lake*. In public, Becker had to read popular stuff that matched his pose as a mail clerk. Karl May was certainly that. The Germans loved their own author of the American West. May's books easily survived the notorious Nazi book-burning of 1933. Besides, Becker liked Karl May.

When the train left its stop at Dresden, only half an hour remained to the border check. Security would be tight. Becker couldn't focus his mind on reading anymore.

He knew the fear was irrational. If the Gestapo hadn't tracked him home during the night, they weren't going to identify him on this train. The Gestapo agent from yesterday's chase had not seen him well. Still, every advancing hour could produce a break for a Gestapo investigation into Becker's identity. German border agents kept lists of names for immediate arrest. It only took one phone call from Berlin.

After yesterday's chase, Becker resolved to carry his Luger Parabellum handgun at all times. Of course, if he were thoroughly searched at the border, having the gun would be a problem. Becker had decided it was worth the risk.

Becker looked out the train window and gazed at the beautiful Elbe River and Sandstone Mountains.

Then the train stopped at the border. First the German authorities scoured the departing faces for anything amiss. Becker returned to his book and acted bored, even annoyed with the required delay. He didn't get a second look from the Germans.

The Czechs were more scrutinizing. They suspected one man of being a Nazi agitator, trying to stir up trouble among the German minority in Czechoslovakia. They rifled through every square inch of his belongings. The little boy in the compartment started crying.

Becker's turn was next, another young German traveling alone. He gave them the usual story about visiting an aunt. They believed it. They always believed it.

He tried to enjoy the landscape when the train recommenced its journey. But his mind wandered furiously. The boy whimpered and fussed constantly now. Would the Gestapo agent care enough to track him down? In front of other underground passengers, both Becker and Maria had called each other by name. Was that before or after the agent boarded? Before, Becker was sure of it. But other passengers might provide the names, if they could be found, and if they could recall them. Neither Becker nor Maria usually traveled on that subway line, which would help obscure things. Still, the Gestapo had its ways. They had found Clara. He didn't want to think about that.

What about his mother's old friend, Waltraud Rieger? Might she inform the authorities? Becker doubted it. First, he had a vague intuitive recollection of her. She did not seem like a natural Nazi sympathizer or informer. Second, the time to turn him in was yesterday evening. The Gestapo would have arrested him in bed in the middle of the night. Becker lived in Germany as himself, his residence registered with the police, as required by law.

Still, Becker kept thinking about it. He tried to remember when his family had last been in contact with Waltraud, and how much she might remember about him. The only time he'd met her was on their last family trip to Germany in 1925, when he was nineteen. He doubted his mother had any substantial correspondence with Waltraud after that. But Waltraud knew that he had adapted enthusiastically to England.

He began life as a German boy, raised in the village of Kirchdorf, in the Black Forest of southwestern Germany. His school preached German nationalism. Young Johannes Becker was proud of his country. The Kaiser, the Army, the Navy, the whole lot. He learned both to admire the British Empire and to resent it. In his home, on the other hand, his parents spoke fondly of his uncle, Jochen Becker, an expatriate settled in London. They admired England – its power, its culture, its democratic tradition that outshone Germany's aristocratic rule and sham parliament. The eight-year-old Johannes heard all this and understood some of it. He was both proud to be German and fascinated by England. Then came 1914, the Great War. England was an enemy. Johannes's mother Amalie seldom spoke about her London in-laws. His father Reinhold was off fighting the English and visited rarely.

Four years later, right before the Germans surrendered, the news arrived. Johannes' anglophile father was killed by English gunfire. The twelve-year-old directed his grief into hatred of England. His mother Amalie directed her sorrow into hatred of the Kaiser and his cronies for starting the war that made her a widow. This was too much to explain to her son.

The war was scarcely over when young Johannes began to doubt the official explanation – the Army blamed Germany's sudden loss on sabotage by enemies from within. The Jews, to be precise. Jews had stabbed Germany in the back, the story went.

If Johannes loved anyone half as much as his mother, it was his Jewish nanny Esther. No propaganda could even begin to turn him against her. When the German Army tried to scapegoat the Jews, Johannes lost faith in his schoolhouse patriotism. He flooded his mother with questions. She just as eagerly answered them.

And a few months after the armistice, the widowed Amalie Becker left Germany with Johannes. They packed a few prized possessions and sold the rest. They moved to London and into the home of Jochen Becker, Johannes' uncle. Jochen lovingly accepted the role of surrogate father that Johannes projected onto him.

Uncle Jochen's import business had made him a very rich man. His holiday homes included one in Jamaica that was his nephew's favorite. Johannes got to travel there almost every year.

Johannes now went by John. He thrived in English schools. Despite British social barriers, the Becker family found the country open enough to newcomers and hard work. The Beckers developed the allegiance of successful immigrants, practicing English at home, even abandoning German Lutheranism for English Methodism, a minority sect less formal than the Anglican Church.

Thirteen-year-old John made new friends fast. He lost contact with old ones in Germany. His earlier raw, juvenile hatred of the British for killing his father evolved into bitter resentment of the German Army for contriving the war in the first place.

At Cambridge University, John Becker was instantly popular. He found his study of modern British thinkers fascinating, in contrast to the last century of German philosophers. During these years, Becker settled into an unshakeable patriotism for his new land.

When he began his intelligence training with Colonel Dansey, Becker assumed a lower profile. He left university for a term, and when he returned he kept to smaller groups.

Just before his recruitment into the Service, the swaggering nineteen-year-old Becker visited his old country. He boldly defended England against the resentment of old family friends. His mother was proud of his polite defense of their adopted country. Their old friends just shook their heads at the incomprehensible conversion. By the end of the visit, people in the small town referred to him as "the Englishman."

It was during this visit that John Becker met Waltraud Rieger. If she remembered anything about him, it would be his ardor for England. He had to hope now that Waltraud did not pursue him.

Becker blinked and actually noticed the landscape he'd been staring at from the train. He remembered yesterday's flight from the Gestapo. His thoughts turned to the state of Nazi Germany.

It was bad enough losing a father to a senseless war. That sacrifice was supposed to be for the German Fatherland. Becker hated how Hitler's Nazis perverted that sacrifice even further. He had read about the Nazis for years. When Hitler came to power in 1933, on a wave of popularity and bullying, Becker instantly loathed the regime.

His mother still kept in touch with a few friends, especially Esther. His former nanny was now sixty-eight. She was developing arthritis in her knees and ankles. And the Nazis made her life harder every year. She had to go farther to find stores open to Jews. Then her landlord ended her lease. The only new place she could find available for a Jew was up a steep flight of stairs. The thought of Esther's sufferings enraged Becker.

He tried to return to his book but couldn't. He could endure a chase like yesterday's and keep his cool, even sleep well afterwards. But always, after some time passed, he experienced intense memory flashes that he could not shut down. Something about the border check had triggered this frenzy of memories and thinking.

Becker relived his chase and the ice-cold swim from yesterday. He remembered his last close call on this mission, eleven months ago. He still felt responsible for that failure, even though McBride assured him he shouldn't. The British Service had approved the risk. In retrospect, Becker thought he never should have endangered Clara that way. Clara, his colleague who became his lover for four sweet, intense months. Clara, who at the same time endured the affair with a German officer that got them keys for their break-in to Army Headquarters. They almost pulled it off.

Their escape was near miraculous. But the Gestapo identified Clara and nearly caught her. London had to pull her out. That night was the last time Becker saw her, without even the chance to say goodbye.

He still envisioned her clearly, her red hair dyed light brown, her green-gray eyes, her long muscular legs. The year since then had been all the lonelier for the comradeship and love lost. It wasn't just the sex. He loved Clara profoundly. Clara understood him better than anyone ever had. He was still falling in love with her when she fled. Their separation was hard and strange. Their commitment had never been exclusive. It was unclear what it was at all.

The Service allowed the two lovers to exchange letters out-of-country, when Becker went to his Prague briefings. But no visits. The Nazis had too many eyes in Czechoslovakia for that. Clara was still back in London, not yet stationed on a new mission.

Berlin would have been less dreadful with the old cabaret world in full swing. He would have cherished Berlin nightlife in the days of Lola Montez and her many imitators. But the old acts had fled abroad or disappeared into the corners of Hitler's Germany.

Becker wanted to complete his mission, return to London, and be reunited with Clara on a well deserved vacation. But he rarely allowed himself to fantasize about that – it was too painful.

Every week alone in Berlin Becker hoped might be his last. He eagerly awaited word to reactivate his mission. He knew Hitler was provoking the Allies again recently. He had a sense that today's meeting in Prague would put his mission in motion. He guarded himself against hoping for it too much. But he was almost sure of it.

For over a year, he'd lingered in Berlin for love and hatred both. He loved England. He hated the rabid German nationalism that destroyed so many lives, including his father's. Hitler was even worse than the forces that had orphaned him in the World War. Becker wanted vengeance on the militant Führer and generals of the Third Reich.

CHAPTER FOUR

Colonel Dansey arrived in Prague at ten minutes before one o'clock. He flight to Budapest and the train to Prague had run smoothly.

Dansey explained the situation to his field director, Michael McBride. Agent Z was being activated. Churchill had decided it was time to blow Becker's cover and get what he could. Otherwise, if Hitler's next move succeeded, there wasn't much Britain could do for years after that.

Dansey looked every bit of his sixty years. A confirmed bachelor, he looked like an average educated man his age. Behind his gentlemanly receding white hair, full moustache, and black round glasses was a man of initiative and persistence.

Dansey had been running his part-time spy ring for almost a decade, dating back to Becker's first mission. For too long, Secret Intelligence worried only about Bolshevik Communists and didn't see the fascists as much of a threat. Dansey knew otherwise. Finally, just a few months ago, London arranged to incorporate Dansey's network into the Secret Intelligence Service. Dansey knew that his part-timers were professionals, and that the official service was an amateurish mess. So he still liked to run his own show. Besides, London was teeming with Nazi appeasers, not least the head of Secret Intelligence himself, Admiral Sinclair.

Hence Dansey's pleasure, almost relief, when Churchill took him into confidence two months earlier. Churchill was the most powerful Englishman yet to recognize Hitler's true aim to conquer the whole of Europe.

Churchill had once wanted to believe Hitler had limited ambitions. It took Dansey two meetings and strong circumstantial evidence to convince Churchill that Hitler was lying, that the Führer intended to pursue the full range of conquest laid out in *Mein Kampf*. Now Churchill was hot for a fight.

But he knew the British people were not, at least not yet. Hitler was dangerous, and he would get more powerful with every month and year that Britain stood by doing nothing. And nothing was precisely what most of the public and politicians wanted to do. They ignored the facts. Churchill, on the other hand, confronted them. England had to stop Hitler with some moderate sacrifice now, before the only option would be another world war. Churchill would have to convince the public, and leverage himself into the prime minister's office.

Dansey sat in McBride's office, and the two men awaited Becker's arrival.

Michael McBride ran the Prague branch of the Merchants Royal, an old British import-export business. McBride was short and stocky, fifty-years-old, his thick hair almost white but for the few flecks of orange that remained. His middle-class London accent carried only a trace of his Northern Irish parentage.

At the Prague branch since 1929, during the worst years of the Depression, McBride presided over a staff reduction from twenty-eight to nine employees. His office windows overlooked a few desks and a lot of free space on the open floor below. The large windows at the far end provided the only light they had. McBride's office lights were out. The streetside shades were drawn. He'd had his office checked for hidden microphones just that morning.

In the dim light, Dansey was first to end the small talk. "What do you think, McBride? Is there any chance Becker still feels some loyalty to Germany, even if he hates the Nazis? The man, after all, still speaks German with his mother most of the time."

"Becker feels loyal to Germans," replied McBride, "in the sense that he wants to help them cast off the Nazis. But there's no question of Becker going rogue. He has a mission and he plans to carry it out. You haven't seen him since he last left London, have you?"

"No," said Dansey.

"If you think he hated the Nazis before, you should see him now."

McBride's office was only blocks away from Prague's Woodrow Wilson Train Station. As usual, Becker took a cab all the way into the Old City, and a second one back out again. He'd never noticed himself being followed, but he always took this precaution. He enjoyed the short tour of Prague's stunning medieval stone architecture. He even made a point to take a slightly new route in and out each time. Back near the train station, it was always the same. Becker instructed the cab driver to drive the length of Antonín ulice, one street over from the Merchants Royal address, and drop him off at the end.

The winter air was cold and wet, just above freezing. Becker unlocked the entrance of a nearby apartment building. From there he followed narrow passageways and courtyards until he entered the utility closet of yet another apartment building. In the closet wall, a second door had been cut. Becker unlocked the bolt, entered another utility closet on the other side, re-bolted the door behind him, and emerged at the bottom of the stairs that led to McBride's office.

"Welcome back, Becker," said McBride. They were standing waiting for him. "You remember Colonel Dansey."

Becker was impressed. This meeting was not to be routine. "Pleased to see you again, sir," Becker extended his hand and looked into Dansey's eyes slightly longer than normal. Dansey's glasses and the low light made him hard to read.

"The pleasure's mine." Dansey had a strong handshake and scrutinized Becker as well.

Becker had first met Dansey in a meeting at his Uncle Jochen's import business. From the age of sixteen, Becker worked there part-time. At first, neither he nor his uncle knew about Dansey's role in British intelligence.

When Michael McBride requested a meeting out of nowhere, citing mutual acquaintance with Dansey, neither Becker nor his Uncle Jochen knew what to make of it. McBride worked for a competitor. In that first meeting, in October 1925, McBride said he was representing Dansey to employ John in Berlin in a joint venture with Jochen Becker.

Then McBride steered the conversation to fascism and communism and the general turmoil in Europe. McBride was especially interested in Becker's allegiances to Germany versus England. He wanted to know if Becker wished to live in England forever, that sort of thing.

Yes, in fact, Becker did prefer England. He hated the German military and much of its government. It was very dangerous for Europe that the Germans hoped to reconquer territories lost in the Great War. Becker mentioned losing his father in the war, and feared there might be another war some day.

McBride expressed his regrets, nodded, and agreed. At the end of their long lunch, McBride came back to the joint venture. He said he would explain the rest in a second meeting, and in the meantime, Becker and his uncle were to keep the proposal in strictest confidence. They did.

A week later, McBride laid it all out. Colonel Dansey and others foresaw a need for a better spy service than Britain currently possessed. They'd begun to look for young talent that could easily be trained and kept in reserve. Becker was the first and most obvious candidate approached. He excelled at everything he attempted. Though wealthy, he was not ostentatious. He seemed capable of living for periods of relative privation. After his training, Becker would simply wait to be sent on his first mission.

Becker was enthusiastic. So was his Uncle Jochen, who agreed to employ John off-and-on as service to their adopted homeland required. Jochen would even subsidize John's missions when needed. Young Becker agreed, temporarily withdrew from university, and began his training.

That was several missions ago. In 1934, after an extended term back in Uncle Jochen's business, Becker was approached again by McBride. Becker's next assignment, if he accepted it, was in Berlin. He would take a clerical job with Kristner Engineering in Berlin, and try to obtain critical defense information for Dansey's British spy network. Kristner could expect to receive state contracts when Hitler began the rearmament campaign he was threatening. Becker would monitor what he could. The work would be fairly routine.

However, McBride continued, the main point of this mission lay elsewhere. Becker wouldn't push the Kristner spying too far. His primary value would rest in preparing to steal German military secrets. Colonel Dansey knew Becker was the best man for a break-in, the only way to obtain what they wanted. Afterwards, he'd have to flee the country immediately. But as McBride explained, Becker wouldn't go for the military secrets until Dansey ordered it. Dansey's Z Organisation would wait for Winston Churchill's word on the best moment to seize the one-time opportunity of Becker's break-in.

McBride acknowledged to Becker that the extended mission in Berlin would be a sacrifice. As usual, Becker was free to decline the mission.

As always, he accepted it immediately. He loathed the Third Reich and considered Hitler terribly dangerous, to England and all of Europe. Becker was eager to help.

As always, Becker's mother was sorry to see him go. He always told her these long trips abroad were for business. Uncle Jochen confirmed this cover story. Still, Amalie Becker wept streams of tears. Her only child was leaving for the wretched capital of Hitler's Reich, home to her native Black Forest's hated Prussian overlords. John had better write often, she ordered him, and visit when he could. Becker cried too, and promised he would. Two weeks later, in November 1934, Johannes Becker was sitting behind a mail desk in the Berlin headquarters of Kristner GmbH.

"Please make yourself comfortable," said McBride. Becker handed McBride an envelope. McBride paused, then put it in his jacket pocket. They all sat down.

"You've traveled from London?" Becker asked Dansey. There was no sense dancing around the upgraded importance of this meeting.

"Rome, actually. I haven't been to London since the new year."

"How's the atmosphere there? You know, with the government scandal in December over appeasing Mussolini."

"Decidedly mixed," answered Dansey. "Churchill is getting more attention, but not enough. Prime Minister Baldwin and his heir apparent Neville Chamberlain, they still lead the appeasement retreat across Europe."

Becker heard Dansey's enthusiasm for Churchill, which he shared.

"If Chamberlain were prime minister," McBride added and turned on his Irish accent, "he couldn't even handle the Catholics in Northern Ireland, much less the fascists in Europe."

They all laughed.

McBride returned to his regular British accent. "It's a damn good thing those IRA terrorists are so disorganized."

"My Uncle Jochen always said Chamberlain couldn't even handle the businessmen in London," Becker risked. "Better just to give him a Cabinet portfolio."

More laughter.

"Quite right," Dansey joined in. "He thinks the whole world operates like the men's club up in Birmingham. 'So we have a deal? Very good. No – no need to fuss with contracts. I'm sure you're good for your word, Herr Hitler!'"

Short uneasy laughs. The stakes were high.

"The problem is, Chamberlain's got a lot of friends," said Dansey. "We're only eighteen years out of the last war. Over a million Brits perished – most of them young men. Most families lost one or more sons, brothers, husbands, fathers. They're not ready for another fight. Chamberlain's leading the retreat from strong defenses to head-in-the-sand pacifism. New King Edward VIII is even worse, smitten with Hitler's Nazis. Chamberlain and the prime minister keep Churchill isolated. That's why I'm here. We need to supply Churchill with hard evidence that Hitler's up to no good."

Becker absorbed the news from London, especially this last bit. The Nazi press reviled Churchill, even though he'd been out of office for years.

McBride looked to Dansey, who gave the nod. "Your mission is being activated, Becker. Within a matter of months, or even weeks, Hitler may move. Churchill needs time after he receives any vital information. He can't seize the reins in a day."

Becker's pulse accelerated. Finally! And if he made progress with Maria, it wouldn't have to be as impossible as last time. For a better outcome, Becker needed quick, easy access to Maria's brother, Rupert Mencke. He had to risk alienating Maria completely. He no longer had time for subtler approaches. At least her men's bathrobe showed she wasn't entirely closed off. Becker had started to wonder whether Dansey should have sent a woman to work on Maria instead.

"I think you know what's at stake," Dansey said. "There *will* be another war. The longer we wait, the worse for us." Becker nodded in agreement. He'd seen enough of Hitler's regime to know where things were headed.

"Hitler is threatening to move his Army into the German Rhineland, right next to the French border," Dansey continued. "As you know, Germany is supposed to leave the Rhineland demilitarized forever. If Hitler fortifies the Rhineland, he will be exceedingly difficult to stop in the future. He claims he's got all kinds of new divisions ready. We think he's bluffing, and we want you to find out. Churchill wants to call Hitler's bluff."

Becker looked at McBride studying him.

"We think it's only a matter of weeks," added Dansey. "Ideally, we'd like your results within a fortnight."

Becker watched Dansey watching him. He braced himself for the challenge ahead. With or without Maria's help, he would escalate his risks on an almost daily basis. He would produce results no matter what, either the German Army facts and plans for England . . . or himself as a victim of the Gestapo's counter-espionage efforts. There was no time for caution and second chances. Becker saw Dansey relax and smile slightly as he sensed Becker's resolve.

Dansey continued, "Churchill has asked for weekly updates on your progress. More often if possible. It's that important. You're the best we've got. And almost the last."

"Almost the last . . . ." Becker nodded and looked away. Becker thought about the torture. He imagined every possible sadistic act they could exercise on him and plotted how to endure it. Known cases of capture made the possibility more real.

"There's more," added McBride. "The Nazis found out that Agent Z is in Germany. Fortunately, they don't know who you are. But they figure you were involved with last year's Wehrmacht break-in. Security there will be tighter than ever."

"How?" asked Becker.

"The leak must be back in England, but we don't know where," said McBride. "One of our double agents picked up the news in Germany."

"Have you ever read *Mein Kampf*, Becker?" asked Dansey.

"Of course. It's everywhere in Germany. For fifteen months, I've had plenty of free time on my hands. I've even brought it to my meetings here once or twice."

"Good," Dansey replied. "I hired some Viennese psychologists to tell me if Hitler has changed much in the twelve years since he wrote that. He hasn't. He wants it all, and he thinks he can get it all. And he actually expects Britain to accept his plans – he takes Europe, and we stand by our empire and send the supplies he demands. It's our job, Becker, to show our naïve king and all his subjects how dangerous Hitler is. Every month that passes, the balance tips toward Hitler's favor. Get us whatever you can."

Becker knew what Hitler's Germany was capable of. The beaten old man on yesterday's underground train was just one example of the millions of victims that Hitler would lay low. For the sake of Europe's long-suffering innocents, Becker wanted it stopped. He did not want the next generation of children to lose their fathers as he had.

"I'll find a way," Becker assured them.

Becker said nothing of his chase the previous day. He didn't want to alarm them.

"Does Fräulein Geberich still work in the office?" asked McBride.

"Yes," answered Becker.

"Good," replied McBride. "Be damn careful. You're the only agent I've been meeting in this office. Still, after the interrogations of the ones we've lost, the Gestapo certainly knows about me. We've created yet another way out of the building, which we'll show you in a few minutes. If you need to meet again, leave a chalk mark behind the geranium boxes at that apartment where we once met across town. Do that any Saturday afternoon, and I'll meet you in the same apartment the next morning at ten o'clock. Back in Berlin, I'm creating a new drop site for you and your remaining colleague. I know it's dangerous, but he may need to leave a message for you to forward, if he gets only part of what he's looking for."

A drop site was especially dangerous now, Becker thought. What if they caught one of them, and extracted the location with their hideous tools, and then sat there waiting for the other one?

"It's in the Café Hildegard at Savigny Platz," McBride continued. "It's a busy place. Check it once or twice a week, at the busiest times of day. In the lavatory, there's small sign with a joke: 'Attention passengers. The train on platforms one, two, three, four, five, six, and seven has arrived sideways.' Not bad, eh? It's a hearty little joint, I'm told. The joke is framed and hanging on a cork wall. Also in that frame – unknown to the proprietors – is a blank sheet of paper."

McBride lifted a briefcase from his desk. "Here are blank sheets of identical size. Here is a bottle of phenolphthalein. It's colorless on acidic or neutral paper, applied with a toothpick or something like it. When you spray base ammonia on it," McBride sprayed one sheet, "it turns pink."

Slowly the letters "A B C" appeared on the sheet, barely legible in the shadows of McBride's office. McBride tore the page to shreds.

"Stay away from the old drop sight in the Grunewald Forest," said McBride. "The agents we've lost didn't know about that site. But it's better to be safe."

Becker had his own little stash at the Grunewald site. Should he hide it elsewhere? He didn't ask.

"If you ever need to meet, the exchange is this: 'Have you eaten yet?' and 'Not since yesterday.' Any questions about all that?"

Becker gave one shake of his head.

"There's one other thing we'd like for you to be on the lookout for," added Dansey. "It's unrelated to your mission. But it could be important to us later on. Heinrich Himmler's SS continues to rise. If you ever see one of his elites with the Death's Head ring, try to identify him and tell us at your next meeting. We're charting their networks."

"O.K., let's back up," said McBride. "Kristner's arms contracts. We got your January drop-off. Any news since then?" Becker laid out the latest information he had committed to memory. It was basically a continuation of contracts McBride already knew about, moderate quantities of electronics supplies for tanks and airplanes.

When Becker finished, he looked at McBride and thought about the imminent conclusion of his mission. He knew he might never see

McBride again. If the two-week deadline got close, Becker would have to take some long-shot chances.

He let out one long exhalation and put his hands on his knees to stand up. "I guess this is it."

"One last thing, Becker," Dansey added. Becker remained seated. McBride winced and looked away to the floor, as he reached into his jacket pocket.

"McBride didn't want to tell you this now, but we made a promise, and we're going to keep it. . . . Clara is dead."

Becker's heart rose to his throat. He closed his eyes and lowered his head. He strained and sweated. His hands shook.

"I'm so sorry, John." McBride's own voice cracked as he held Becker's shoulder with one hand and handed back the envelope, Becker's last letter to Clara.

"Howwww . . . ?" Becker whispered, as he opened his glassy eyes and half-lifted his head.

"She turned a Soviet diplomat for us," Dansey continued. "Stalin's assassins caught him and killed them both."

So she hadn't been just convalescing in London. She'd never written of her London assignment. Of course she couldn't. Clara.

"She made us promise we would tell you at the first chance, if she ever got hurt," said Dansey. "It happened two weeks ago. Never made the papers. We're awfully sorry."

CHAPTER FIVE

Sergeant Rupert Mencke stayed at Army Headquarters after his boss left. Major Friedrich Hossbach often kept Mencke working late, even on Saturdays like today. Mencke still hoped his stepsister Maria would invite him over for dinner this evening. But if she hadn't called by now, she wasn't likely to.

Mencke was Hossbach's trusted secretary, a career non-commissioned officer. Hossbach told him everything, Mencke thought. And Hossbach saw a lot. He was Adolph Hitler's personal liaison to the German Wehrmacht.

As the trusted secretary, Mencke felt entitled to look at Hossbach's personal notes. At least he did when the major wasn't looking. Hossbach had learned shorthand for the liaison position, which Mencke could read. The notes were thorough, often verbatim. They were much more colorful than the official minutes that Mencke typed.

He'd been waiting all day to read Hossbach's personal notes on yesterday's big meeting. The Führer had all the top brass in a top-secret conference. It had to be something good, Rupert knew. Finally Hossbach was out of the office. Rupert picked up Hossbach's journal.

Friday, 7 February, 16:45. Pre-meeting. Führer Adolph Hitler, Deputy Führer Rudolf Hess, Major Friedrich Hossbach.

My arrival interrupted a private conversation between the Führer and his Deputy – something about Operation Cathedral, a secret second prong that the military would never know about – only the two of them and their Dublin connection, whatever that means.

Hitler: The time has come! The Chiefs of Staff know why I've called this meeting. The generals are afraid to move our forces into the German Rhineland. We know the Allies could stop us if they wanted. But they won't! [shaking fists in air] They won't!

Hess: *Jawohl, Führer unser!*

Hitler: Why should any part of Germany be undefended? We can't just leave the Rhineland unguarded! Besides, the Allies don't care about the Treaty of Versailles anymore. How can our great nation be hemmed in by such nonsense as Versailles?!? It's a denial of history. I never signed that abomination!

Hess: That's right!

Hitler: Germans will rise up and lead the world for centuries to come. Yet these planning years are dangerous, Hess. Our Army is still weak. Once we rebuild it, we will be ready to strike. But until then, the Allies could destroy us. Our generals know it, and they're paralyzed. That's why we're in charge, Hess!

Hess nods and smiles enthusiastically.

Hitler: After this meeting, your task will be to convince the generals and make sure they're ready. We must acknowledge the difficulties they will raise, while projecting the utmost enthusiasm and optimism. I will provide the political will. You will work out the details. Because we will it, we shall succeed! If France and England believe our boasts of dozens of full divisions, they will stand aside. . . . Our intelligence insists they will. We have to take the risk sometime. We just have to. . . . Oh, this whole bluff is the greatest burden I have ever carried! If the Allies oppose us now, we'll be finished within days. Yet we must seize the moment!

Arrival of Chiefs of Staff.

Meeting, 17:00. Führer, Deputy Führer, Maj. Hossbach, the War Minister, the Commander in Chief of the Army, the

Commander in Chief of the Navy, the Commander in Chief of the Air Force, and the Foreign Minister.

Hitler: Gentlemen, the time has come.   Germany must reoccupy the German Rhineland before the Allies do.

Commanders stare in skeptical silence.

Hitler: It is our own country, and they tell us we cannot protect it? [getting agitated]   Once we remilitarize the Rhineland, our defenses will be secure.   In the future, once we are ready, we will pick battles on our own terms!   Soon Germans can fulfill their destiny as the master race over all!

General von Fritsch: Herr Führer, I think we are all agreed on the necessity of fortifying our own sovereign territory in the Rhineland. It is part of our country. I am concerned, however – begging your pardon – that we not risk war with the Allies. We have only started rearming. Our forces are a fraction of theirs.

Hitler: Your concerns are most valid, general.   We must avoid an armed conflict, which we cannot win. Don't worry, though.   Those decrepit, decadent French lack the fighting spirit. And the Nordic English are too intelligent to side with France's decline against the vitality of the Aryan race. The ground is ripe for Germany to blossom! During the next three weeks, Deputy Führer Hess and Major Hossbach will arrange the necessary details with the Army. We are about to reverse the humiliation of postwar occupation. And this is but the first step–

Sergeant Mencke heard footsteps down the hall.   He stopped his reading and returned the journal to Hossbach's desk.

"When is Colonel Dansey due back?" asked Churchill. He met at his London flat with Robert Vansittart, his ally in the Foreign Office.
"Dansey is on your schedule for Monday," said Vansittart. "He's got his meeting this afternoon with Becker."
"Good," said Churchill. "I want frequent updates. We could never demand this kind of mission from anyone else. . . . Becker comes from

an extraordinary family, you know. His uncle built their import company from nothing. The uncle makes fine conversation, too. By far the best German I've ever known, except he's so English now that one could scarcely call him German. Our John Becker is even more talented and driven than his uncle. The one time I met him, he was impressive and composed, an unusual combination for a young man of his talents."

"I haven't had the pleasure of meeting either man," said Vansittart. "We need John Becker's news for Paris as well. The French think they already have the right numbers. They think Hitler's army is nearly as strong as theirs, so they're afraid to act. But French estimates just have to be wrong. There's no way Hitler has rearmed so much in only one year. He does have dozens and dozens of divisions. But it doesn't add up. It doesn't seem like he can possibly have them fully armed."

"How specific is our current information?" asked Churchill.

"Not very, unfortunately," answered Vansittart. "Hitler boasts of enormous strength. We think it's poppycock, but we can't prove it. If we're right and we fight back, a short battle could sweep the Nazis from power. But if we fight and Hitler's numbers are real, it would be a second world war. There's no telling who would win. Or whether the Bolsheviks could use the war to take over all of Europe. Without solid information, the risks are immense."

"How long does Dansey give Becker to pull it off?" asked Churchill.

"You said a matter of weeks, sir," replied Vansittart. "Dansey and I narrowed it down to two. Within two weeks, we'll have what we need, or our best agent will die trying. My money's on Becker. But it's not safe money. The Gestapo will make it perilous."

"Two weeks are a long, long time," said Churchill. "Keep me posted. . . . Let's be in touch with the new French government. Tell them we mean business. Reassure them that Prime Minister Baldwin's appeasers aren't the only option in London. Sooner or later, the appeasers will fall from power. Unfortunately, Hitler's next threat is sooner. If he moves on the Rhineland, we ought to stop him. If Hitler's bluffing, we can take him! We can hound that bastard across the Rhine, back to Berlin, and all the way to hell."

CHAPTER SIX

At the stroke of midnight, John Becker was making love. It began satisfying, slow, and lovely. He felt his lover's chest arch up beneath him, and he opened his eyes.

His lungs froze in horror. Gone was his lover's body. In its place, staring back at him, were the empty eye sockets of a grinning skull. Suddenly the skeleton's hands gripped his neck and shook his body violently up and down.

Becker jolted onto all fours and opened his eyes for real, half in nightmare, half-awake. He still couldn't breathe. He stood on his knees in bed and clutched his throat and chest. He felt like the wind had been knocked out of him, without the first gasp of air. Then it came, and he collapsed face-first onto his bed, heaving and panting. At last he could think. Beloved Clara was dead.

He couldn't remember or recognize where he was. He closed his eyes again. But the image of the skull returned and he opened his eyes to the disorienting room. Still breathing heavily and sweating, he finally recognized it – Aunt Sophie's apartment in Prague.

Six hours later Becker woke up for breakfast with his great-aunt. He and his mother were her closest relatives. She enjoyed his regular visits since his return to Germany fifteen months ago. He always checked that she had everything she needed. She always insisted he accompany her to Sunday morning's first mass, and he always obliged. The rest of their conversations dwelt on family stories two and three generations old. He took great care in saying good-bye, probably the last time for a long while.

By late morning, Becker was on the train back to Berlin. His mission was now most urgent. He would have to take greater risks. And he already faced increased danger from Friday's chase. He sat on edge for every routine police encounter from the German border to Berlin. True, he was just one more criminal of sorts in a city of millions.   But something told Becker his Gestapo hunter wouldn't forget about him so easily.

Gestapo Colonel Kurt Wächter was often at work Sunday mornings. This weekend he had more than enough reason to be there. When his telephone rang, he glared at it, annoyed at the interruption.

"Wächter," he answered.

"Kurt! I knew I'd find you there. How much longer are you going to work today?"

"Hans! We haven't talked in days. A lot has been going on." Wächter was glad to hear from his childhood friend. After two days of frustrating dead ends, he needed a break. Furthermore, he wanted Hans's opinion of a rumor he'd heard.

His friend Hans Kolke was full-time Waffen-SS. Colonel Kolke worked in the Nazis' own private army.

"You're telling me," said Hans. "Of course you've heard that England's Agent Z is supposed to be back in town. I'm sure you Gestapo men are ready to chew him alive. After the way he and that woman broke into Army Headquarters last year and almost got away with the goods."

"You heard the news about Agent Z?" replied Wächter. "They need to keep such things under tighter wraps. We intercepted that information in a Soviet communication from London to Moscow. The Gestapo is on high alert. But the only thing we know about him is that Agent Z speaks German like a native. We don't know his name or alias or what he looks like. We don't know whether he arrived in Germany last week, or if he never left – I suspect the latter, by the way. No offense, friend, but you guys at Waffen-SS shouldn't be in on such information."

Wächter and Kolke had a friendly rivalry to see who could rise up through the SS ranks the fastest. Currently, they both held the rank of Standartenführer, equivalent to colonel in the army. Both were recent recipients of the cherished Death's Head ring.

Since Wächter worked in the Gestapo, the secret police, he couldn't wear his uniform in public. But he almost always worse it at Columbia Haus, Gestapo headquarters. Wächter loved the black SS uniform.

"I'll be done at the office shortly," Wächter answered his friend. "And I've got some field investigation this afternoon. But I could use a break. My work this afternoon isn't far from your apartment. Shall I come by there in a bit?" Kolke lived alone in the Kreuzberg district.

"Sure. See you in about half an hour?" asked Kolke.

"Sounds good," replied Wächter.

Wächter had just washed his hands, literally, of the morning's bloody interrogations. He didn't do the dirty work himself. But it was impossible to stay entirely clean in there. He liked to threaten the men with sexual assault, not just by truncheon.

With women prisoners, he carried out such threats about half the time. But he'd only do that before the women were beaten up. He got mad at the technicians – that's how he thought of them – when they beat up a woman before he had his way with her. They learned to check with him first.

Wächter put his hand on his chin and leaned back from his solid oak desk in his new swiveling chair. The walls of his mid-sized office were white and bare. His shelves were impeccably arranged. His desktop was nearly bare. The office had tall windows facing the courtyard, which nearly reached the ten-foot ceiling. Outside was a cloudy, dark winter morning. Wächter looked at his reflection in the window.

Thirty-seven-years-old, Colonel Wächter still turned the heads of women fifteen years his junior. At least until his eyes scared them. A slim six feet tall, Wächter had light brown hair that seemed soft next to his cold, ice-blue eyes. The eyes seemed beautiful and expressive from an angle, he'd been told. But when Wächter looked straight at someone, his eyes seemed penetrating and mean. His dark brown eyebrows angled inward and accented the sinister effect of his gaze. His long, thin, elegant hands and fingers impressed everyone – a career cop with the hands of a pianist.

Wächter loved his Gestapo work. He loved the Nazi Party for lifting talented men like himself quickly through the ranks. A long-time party member, he'd never anticipated the personal promotion he would achieve once the Nazis seized power. In 1933, he immediately left the Berlin police, to work for the new Secret State Police, the Gestapo. He now gave orders to his old superiors in the police force. Not bad for an illegitimate pauper from the slums.

Wächter returned his thoughts to Friday's case. He couldn't stop thinking about the tram chase. It was keeping him up at night. He was obsessed with it.

Only by coincidence did he get drawn into chasing the suspect. Wächter's specialty was political enemies. He supervised investigations and interrogations, not chases.

The novelty of a chase had exhilarated him. He'd once excelled at such things. The escape maddened him to no end. He had no leads. What would become of his soaring career if he failed in basic legwork?

Gestapo agents were already mocking him through Columbia Haus. His own subordinates were spying on the police spies, and they'd reported this to him yesterday. He wished he could have some answer to the case before Monday morning. Any answer. But he knew he wouldn't.

And he couldn't justify devoting all his official time to this case either. That's why he was working so hard this weekend. He had no good reason to set other work aside in favor of a man running away to avoid two women in his life meeting each other. That happened all the time.

Yet Wächter was a perfectionist. And there was something about the way this fugitive had looked straight at him.

Wächter had analyzed the tram chase dozens of times. It was late Friday afternoon. He had just boarded the U-Bahn subway. A male passenger looked like he was caught with his mistress and suddenly exited the train. Wächter followed. So did the woman who caught him.

The man made a mistake. The last time he looked around, he didn't even bother to look at the woman in blue. The man was worried about Wächter. He must have noticed Wächter's automatic detective eyes on the underground. That was the only way Wächter could explain why he worried the escaped passenger. The man pegged Wächter as a plain-clothes agent of some kind. The chase was on.

The man jumped on a tram. Wächter followed with a cab in rush-hour traffic. He lost sight of the man and guessed he'd switched trams. He guessed right. After nearly getting killed by an oncoming tram, Wächter stopped the fleeing tram, but too late. Other passengers reported the fugitive's jump into traffic. Wächter searched the surrounding area. But in rush hour, the man could have fled by foot or car in any number of directions.

Wächter knew he couldn't pick the man out of a lineup, not reliably. The eye contact at the Friedrich Strasse Station had lasted only a split-second, from thirty yards away. He'd lost the mysterious suspect. He reassured himself he would have caught an amateur.

This conclusion was his investigation's only progress: He was dealing with a professionally trained agent. Wächter hadn't divulged this to anyone. He didn't want the investigation reassigned to Counter-Intelligence. He wanted to show he was capable of finishing the job himself. He wouldn't let it go. Furthermore, a successful capture would boost Wächter's reputation. An unsolved chase would hinder it. Wächter was obsessed.

During the weekend, Wächter could only prowl the neighborhoods where he'd lost the fugitive. On Monday, at precisely 5:13 P.M., Wächter would take his investigation to the same U-Bahn train where it started at See Strasse. He would ask various passengers what they had seen or heard of the man who fled the underground.

Wächter tapped the long fingers of his left hand on the desk. It was the one nervous habit he allowed himself, and only when he was alone. No coffee, no cigarettes, no alcohol. Only discreet finger-tapping. He watched his elite Death's Head ring bob up and down.

Wächter decided to distract himself by inspecting his own uniform. For this very purpose, he kept a mirror on the back door of his office closet. He was proud of his uniform and the accomplishments it stood for.

No black cloth in Germany was darker than Kurt Wächter's crisp SS uniform. He looked up at the pointed cap on his head. Then he took it off to admire the Death's Head skull and crossbones in the center of the headband. The skull looked over the viewer's left shoulder rather than straight at him. It overlay the flattened crossbones, which receded in a three-dimensional effect. This wasn't some tacky pirate flag. It looked real. Wächter had preferred the earlier jawless skull, but he liked the new skull enough. He grinned back at it. Then he replaced the cap and glared at himself in the mirror.

It was time to go. He changed into his street clothes and had a Gestapo chauffeur drive him to Kolke's apartment. A few inches of snow had fallen since last night. Wächter worried the sidewalk slush might sully his uniform. Then he remembered he wasn't wearing his uniform anymore, only imagining it. He laughed at himself.

Kolke and Wächter resembled each other somewhat. Wächter even wondered whether they might be half-brothers. He never specifically asked his mother whether Kolke's old man might be his father, too.

Hans Kolke was tall, dark blond, with blue-gray eyes. But in contrast to Wächter's refined face and hands, Kolke's were muscular and intimidating. He used to work as a bricklayer, and his hands looked like they could snap a brick in two.

"I'd offer you a real drink," said Kolke. "But since you scorn the good things in life, here's some water."

"Thanks," said Wächter.

Wächter proceeded to tell Kolke all about Friday's tram chase. Kolke even shared his belief that the suspect was a resistance agent of some kind.

"All day yesterday I prodded around the surrounding neighborhoods," said Wächter. "Nobody reported anything unusual, at least nothing helpful to me. If the suspect jumped some car's sideboards to the suburbs, I'm wasting my time around here. But I'll keep trying for awhile."

"What do Susanne and the children say," asked Kolke, "when you work like this on a Sunday?"

"The two girls don't care. And Paul's too young to want his father. Sure, Susanne complains. But she'd rather spend the weekend at her parents' house, anyway."

"You going to have a fourth one any time soon?" Kolke inquired.

"I don't see why not," answered Wächter. "Susanne says she's not interested, but I'm not giving her a choice."

Kolke laughed darkly.

"Do you even know how many children you've fathered across Germany?" Wächter teased his friend. Kolke boasted of at least two children by the wives of unsuspecting husbands.

"I don't keep up with enough of the women to know!" Kolke slapped his thigh and laughed loudly. "You should try my method sometime. You get just as much racial propagation with none of the trouble."

"Who says I haven't?" replied Wächter.

"I know you," said Kolke. "You'll pay for a whore, Wächter, but you're too cold to seduce another man's wife. A man has to believe his own bullshit to pull it off. But you, Kurt, you take yourself too seriously. You can tell cold lies but not warm ones. That's why you're married and I'm not."

Wächter smiled. Kolke was right. They'd had this conversation countless times, usually after Kolke divulged his latest exploit.

"There's something else I wanted to tell you," started Wächter. "I overheard a rumor last week in the halls at Columbia Haus. It's about Himmler."

Kolke perked up. Heinrich Himmler ran the entire SS, from the Gestapo to the paramilitary Waffen SS. The SS was the Nazi state within a state. Himmler lorded over it all.

"It turns out, 1936 is the thousand-year anniversary of King Heinrich's death," said Wächter. "You know, the one who founded the First German Reich. I'm sure you already know that Himmler is immersed in medieval German lore. Wait till you hear the latest – Now Himmler claims he's the reincarnation of King Heinrich! He's even having people call him King Heinrich. Can you believe it?"

For a moment Kolke was speechless. "I'll be damned. . . ."

Wächter wasn't religious. He believed in a supreme Aryan being who made Germans the dominant race. He believed this was clear in medieval history, and even earlier. But he wasn't working so hard in the Gestapo in order to turn Himmler into some kind of demi-god. Wächter served the German People, and the Führer Adolph Hitler.

"Now Himmler wants to take over Quedlinburg Cathedral, where the king is buried," continued Wächter. "He plans to deconsecrate the cathedral, take it away from the Catholic Church. Here's the best part: Himmler wants to resurrect King Heinrich's knights, with a new Order of the Death's Head. Those of us who aren't married yet – that's you, Hans! – will be encouraged to consummate their wedding nights on the graves of our ancestors."

"The Order of the Death's Head?!? That's us!" shouted Kolke, looking at his own Death's Head ring.

"What do you make of this reincarnation business?" asked Wächter judiciously.

"Who the hell cares?!?" insisted Kolke. "I'll screw my wench on a tombstone as well as anywhere else. The Führer will keep us focused on what's important. Himmler can believe whatever he goddamn wants. *Ein Reich! Ein Volk! Ein Führer!*" One Empire! One People! One Leader!

"That's all that matters," continued Kolke. "Let Himmler believe his nonsense. I'll even kiss his sword. If that's what he wants, so be it. He's for Germans, against the Jews, and all the rest. That's what counts. Don't take it too seriously."

Wächter nodded. Kolke put him a little at ease.

"Listen, Kurt. No matter what Himmler believes, no one's going to take him too seriously. The Führer is the Führer. Himmler might be at the top, but he's just one of us. You're worried he might warp the Third Reich with his hocus-pocus. Never in a thousand years!"

Kolke laughed and Wächter joined him. His friend was right. Himmler's fantasies couldn't endanger anything. The Führer had already set Germany down its predestined path to glory, the thousand-year Third Reich. And Himmler was exceedingly efficient in his more worldly pursuits.

At that moment, while Wächter was looking out the window to a nearby U-Bahn street entrance, he noticed something familiar. A man was exiting the otherwise empty stairs when he bumped into someone entering the stairs to go down. They bumped because the man coming up was on the left side, thinking he had the stairs all to himself.

Of course! thought Wächter. The same sort of thing happened when his fugitive fled up the stairs at the Friedrich Strasse station last Friday evening. But then, the stairs were crowded with people moving both directions. The mistake wasn't one of an unexpected commuter. It was one of reflexes. Under stress, the fugitive took the left side of the staircase. No country in Europe walked and drove on the left side . . . except Great Britain. The fugitive was English! Maybe he . . . . Wächter remembered that Agent Z was back. Just because Wächter's fugitive was English didn't mean he was the infamous Agent Z. What a coup *his* capture would be! Wächter didn't let himself get too hopeful. And still he hoped for it.

Wächter hid his excitement. Even Kolke didn't need to know this now. Wächter would save the news until he needed it. The intelligence coup would be all the more glorious for its surprise. Certainly General Heydrich would praise him, probably Himmler, maybe even the Führer himself!

"Tell me, friend," said Kolke, "where are you prowling for your fugitive this afternoon?"

"There's a little neighborhood center around Arnold Strasse," said Wächter. "I didn't get to that one yesterday. It's a little farther from the canal bridge. But it's close enough to bother with. I'm going to get that bastard if it kills me!"

CHAPTER SEVEN

Monday, February 10

A sinister smile swept over Colonel Wächter's face. Before him was the same 17:13 underground train to Tempelhof, with many of the same passengers from Friday. Wächter knew in his veins he would find some vital trace of the missing Englishman.

The underground car was not nearly as sweaty and stuffy as during the old man's beating on Friday. But it remained too warm for the winter coats, and several passengers tugged uncomfortably at their clothes.

Wächter began questioning passengers where Becker had stood on Friday. Were they on this train last Friday? Did they remember a man and woman talking in the middle of the underground car? Had the witnesses overheard or seen anything in particular?

"Oh, most definitely," answered a small old lady. "But I can't seem to put my finger on it. I'd know him if I saw him, though, that's for sure."

Wächter glared at her. She opened her mouth again but said nothing. He enjoyed intimidating people like this. He let his silence do its work. She omitted the old man's beating. Maybe she presumed he'd seen it. He certainly knew about it.

"Are you kidding?" intervened her tall, stocky acquaintance. "That woman couldn't stop nagging him – 'Herr Becker' this, 'Herr Becker' that. The poor fellow! It's no wonder he couldn't wait to get off the train." Her tone was alternately mocking and earnest.

Yes! Wächter's thin lips smiled broadly. *Becker.* His English spy had a German name and might even be German.

"And what did they discuss?" he asked.

"Their whole lives, it seemed like," replied the old woman. "He was missing some party to go visit his aunt in Prague for the weekend."

"Oh, yes," remembered her short friend. "He was from Hanover, he said."

Two men across the aisle nodded their heads as the ladies exhausted their memories. A few other passengers seemed to remember Friday's odd couple, but couldn't offer any details.

"Did you catch the name of the woman?" Wächter asked eagerly. Becker was a common name, just a start.

The two ladies looked at each other, straining to remember. "I'm sorry," answered the short one. "I don't even remember that he used it."

"Gentlemen?" Wächter turned to the men across the aisle.

"Sorry, sir," replied one of them. "We were not nearly as close as the ladies."

"Did any of you see these two before last Friday? Were they regular riders?"

Everyone shook their heads.

Wächter thanked them all and took their names and addresses. They seemed honored, he thought. He would let someone else bring them in tomorrow for physical descriptions of the suspects. He himself couldn't pick Becker out of a lineup of identification photos. This Becker had kept his trench coat collar upturned on Wächter's side of his face. Only Becker's eyes registered in Wächter's memory. Surely at least one of these passengers could pick him out, though.

Wächter took a seat and waited. His outward appearance was calm. Internally, he was excited. His own success aroused him. He thought of his wife and his regular call-girl Sonia in the same moment. *Later*, he told himself.

The next stop was Friedrich Strasse. Wächter disembarked to retrace Becker's steps to the streetcar. Berlin had thousands of Beckers. At least that ruled out four million others. After a long weekend with no leads, Wächter was glad for his progress. He was also frustrated not to have the woman's name. Investigation into police records on all the Beckers could wait until tomorrow. Today's trail was too hot to relinquish.

Becker had the feeling he was being tracked. Last Friday's chase had left enough clues to his identity. He and Maria had even named each other in front of strangers. He could only hope they were too shaken by the old man's pummeling to remember his conversation with Maria.

When he wasn't thinking about imminent arrest, he thought about his activated mission and the stakes involved. Colonel Dansey made those quite clear. If Hitler were lying and had only the shell of an army, then Britain or France could drive the murderous Nazi from office. But not only did both Allied governments lack the will. They also lacked the sure knowledge that Hitler was bluffing. Becker hoped to have the answer within a week.

All day at work Monday, Becker and Maria acted as if Becker's rush-hour chase had never happened. They exchanged no more words than the regular, "Have we received the engineer's report, Fräulein Geberich?" or "Could you please walk this message to the workshop foreman, Herr Becker?"

At the end of the workday, Becker delayed his departure. He found Maria stalling, too. Then she accompanied him toward the U-Bahn as usual. They normally boarded the underground at Wittenberg Platz, a fifteen-minute walk from the office. Their regular Friedrichsfelde Line was a different underground line than that of last Friday's chase. Still, Becker thought it best to avoid the subway altogether. That morning he had walked the two miles to work.

The clear night sky cooled the air. Soon it would be freezing again.

Becker and Maria silently followed their routine path to the underground station. The evening temperature was cooling off from the February sun, but still in the thirties. It was risky enough for Becker just to stay in Berlin, not to mention ride the U-Bahn. Maria had to know that, he thought. He would escort her to the station, but no further.

Five minutes into their walk, she stopped abruptly and faced him. "You cannot be serious, Johannes." She was back to the more intimate first name. "You are already dangerously close to the station."

Becker nodded slightly to confirm his agreement.

"And so am I," she continued in her energetic whisper. "You put me in danger, too, when you fled . . . not that lady, but the Gestapo. Did you think about that, Johannes? Now you now have no choice but to escort me home by foot! Even there we must be careful. My landlady noticed your visit last Friday. She asked about you. She's certainly looking for your return. I'm being watched at home now, thanks to you."

"I'm very sorry." Becker was genuinely apologetic. He was also impressed by Maria's assertiveness. It wasn't exactly out of character, but it was new to him. He liked it.

"Special surveillance is something I most certainly do not want," she concluded. "Now be a gentleman and offer me your arm, Johannes Becker!" she added coyly, no longer whispering.

What in the world? Becker asked himself. *A year of aloofness, and now she's asking me to pay her a visit? What is this concern with surveillance?* This was critical. If Maria was already being watched, even followed, he was in great danger.   The Gestapo would automatically track any man she got involved with.

"Gladly, Maria Geberich," Becker offered his arm.

Maria steered him down a side street, away from the U-Bahn station, toward her home a mile away.   Becker and Maria posed as a couple to onlookers.   They were crossing a threshold of friendship possible only in murderous dictatorships – mutual trust of one's life. Neither knew the other's dangerous secrets.   But they each knew the other had secrets, and that was danger enough.

"You're innocent, you know.   Why should you be so concerned?" he asked softly.

Maria glared up at him in response, still walking. He saw that she resented the question and wouldn't answer. Fine, he thought. For now, anyway.

"Try to relax and enjoy yourself," she said. "It's the best way."

Cars and people crowded the streets and sidewalks around them.

"All right then," he said. "Where were we? You were telling me about your move from Bonn to Berlin."

"Actually, before you dashed out of the U-Bahn, I had just asked you how you ended up here, if you recall. I already told you that I moved to Berlin after I was orphaned. My older brother lived here. He was my natural refuge. . . .   But if you'd like, we can forget the last minute or so. . . ."

Becker knew she meant the woman in blue.

"My brother and I both attended Catholic schools back in Bonn," she continued, "his for boys and mine for girls. Right before my father died, he went into debt to buy the newsprint shop he ran. So there was no money left for me to attend private school in Berlin. The stark Lutheran atmosphere of Berlin depressed me. At sixteen, I was too old to make it feel like home. I still dream of moving back to Bonn or Cologne. But my brother Rupert is the only family I have. He'll stay in Berlin forever. Anyway, after school and training, I went to work at Krämers.   A few years ago I switched to Kristner, at a friend's suggestion.   It's a much nicer place to work, frankly."   Her tone expressed a finality to the story.

The end? thought Becker. *No personal life, no man in view for this attractive woman, now pushing spinsterhood?* Becker's intuition told him there was more to the professional story as well. He could have asked what friend suggested Kristner and why. His bosses in London knew about Kristner's defense contracts. They had no record of Maria's work at Krämers. Her start at Kristner "a few years ago" was exactly when Hitler came to power. Coincidence? The more Becker learned about Maria, the more mystery he sensed about her.

"Did you ever consider leaving?" he asked. "Berlin, that is?"

For several paces in silence, Maria looked straight ahead, at nothing in particular. "Look at me," she stopped at an intersection. "I'm not going to lie to you. But we will both be better off if we don't share each other's . . . particular situations. I don't need to know why you show up out of nowhere for a dusty little desk job. You don't need to know why I . . . live my life as I do. Understood?"

"Understood." Becker backed down for now. He'd approach her past more subtly another time.

"Good." She nudged him forward, and they continued in silence.

Who wouldn't want to get out of Berlin, out of Germany, since the Nazi takeover three years ago? thought Becker. Eminent Jews and others, from Albert Einstein to Thomas Mann, left the country immediately. Had Maria's decision to stay been politically motivated? Or was it completely personal? She was far too compelling a woman to have no personal life.

Nearing her own neighborhood, Maria broke the silence. "Wasn't Herr Janeck in an awful mood today? The poor fellow. He was already homesick. . . . Oh, that's right – you were making a delivery at the end of the day when he got a call about his brother's accident. It seems serious. He's headed home to Cologne."

"Well, that explains it," Becker replied. "I thought he looked exceptionally dour. I just guessed it was from missing the Carnival season back home. You Rhinelanders sure are a different breed."

Becker actually felt more akin to Rhinelanders and their spirited holidays than to many Prussians of Berlin. Just last week at work, he'd told Maria as much. But the specific Rhineland traditions were in fact foreign to him. They offered a reasonable topic for conversation on this walk.

"The more so from abroad," answered Maria.

Abroad? What was she getting at? Becker knew that Germany used to be three dozen different countries, only two generations ago. Some people still talked of the different parts as foreign lands.

"Listen," Maria changed the subject.

Becker was supposed to be the spy in control of the situation. Without knowing Maria's goals and motivations, he saw they shared hostility to the Hitler regime. She seemed a good judge of his own dangers. But he relied on his own judgment, too, at every turn of Maria's guidance.

"We have both just altered our routines," Maria continued holding his arm. "And not just for today. We need each other for appearances. And it needs to seem real. I think you understand me." She squeezed her head against his shoulder in a lover's gesture.

Becker nodded, "Mm-hm."

"Excellent!" Her tone dropped all seriousness and reverted to the seemingly carefree Fräulein Geberich he had known before.

Pedestrian traffic around them was steady. They were nearly anonymous. Few people had seen Becker's face clearly on the train last Friday. They had heard the names Becker and even Geberich, though. Danger might not have followed them down this street. But it awaited him somewhere, he was sure. It was only a question of whether the Gestapo cared enough to pursue him.

"Why don't you take me this way, to the coffee shop near my apartment?" she added cheerfully.

She was a good flirt, Becker observed. He wasn't even sure himself whether any of it was sincere.

He watched her as they walked. The Service had identified her as the object of his intended seductions. When he met her, Becker was pleased to find her attractive. He now remembered that first impression. Her unfolding sophistication and mysteriousness made her all the more alluring.

Maria was the key to quick access to the German Army documents. Without her, his mission would be much harder, not impossible, but even more dangerous. He had to remind himself that his emotional attraction must not obstruct his mission.

His profession was very solitary, not only sexually, but also personally. He had lost fellow British agent and lover Clara twice – once a year ago, and now forever. Maria was different, German, unknown. He simply could not afford to fall in love with her of all women.

Becker escorted her down the street, toward the café. They were escorting each other, really, since she knew the way. When they were about to cross the street to the café, Becker recognized a face on the inside – the Gestapo agent from Friday's chase!

"No!" he whispered to Maria. He stopped her from crossing, and directed her to continue straight ahead. "Walk like you're a grandmother."

Becker pulled her into a hunch. They slowed to an elderly pace. Becker lowered his apparent height by almost six inches. Without stooping very much, he just made his height disappear into the joints of his body. His and Maria's aged posture mismatched their younger faces dramatically. But the Gestapo agent was behind them. Becker gently guided Maria with the skill of an experienced ballroom dancer. She adjusted her step accordingly. She followed his lead just as quickly and invisibly as he asserted it.

"We must get off the street immediately," Becker whispered again, camouflaged with a smile.

"Follow me," Maria replied.

Becker saw out of the corner of his eye that the Gestapo agent was calmly exiting the café, slowly replacing his fedora. All Becker could do was walk the other way and hope.

"Under no circumstances must we face the other way." He continued to whisper in gentlemanly flirtatious gestures that his words belied.

Colonel Wächter stood still on the sidewalk and took a deep breath of evening air. He turned his large eyes down the street. He saw the backs of an old couple walking arm-in-arm. Too old and too short, he thought.

By now, Wächter knew the scene of Becker's escape fairly well. On Sunday and again this morning, Wächter had prowled the surrounding blocks. His suspect had vanished quickly. Wächter deduced that Becker must have known the area, perhaps even lived in it.

Wächter had asked a couple dozen shopkeepers and other locals if they had noticed anyone behaving unusually Friday evening. He didn't have anything promising yet. But he would ask many more. There were scores of people for Wächter to question, across a dozen neighborhoods. Yet he still had his political interrogations to tend to. It would take some time for him to explore this neighborhood thoroughly, mostly on his own time.

As Becker and Maria strolled onward, neither of them afforded a rearward glance. They didn't know if they were still in the agent's sight. Only when they began to circle around the block did Becker strain his peripheral vision to see if they were being followed.

"I think we're clear," he said. He walked upright again and resumed the pose of a lover's escort.

Fake flirting in a dictatorship full of enthused would-be informants. The hardest kind of acting, thought Becker.

"So why do you call your Carnival Monday, '*Rosenmontag*'?" Roses Monday, asked Becker in a conversational tone.

"Your question betrays a foreignness," Maria quickly replied. She continued the game of smiles with a playful tilt of her head.

I know my native country well enough to know that "Rosenmontag" can be foreign to a native German, thought Becker. *I mustn't let her catch me on a bluff.*

"No Rhinelander would need an explanation," she continued. "Actually, it has nothing to do with roses. It's an old variation of 'frenzied Monday,' '*Rasender Montag.*' Your home province of Hanover must be closer to its English relations than to its Catholic compatriots to the south."

Another taunt? wondered Becker. There was no way Maria should be able to guess his Englishness. Yet she left so much open, he couldn't be sure. On the one hand, he trusted her instincts more with every passing moment. On the other, he had less and less sense of what she really cared about or stood for. For now, that mattered little. London was desperate for the German Army documents. Maria's help would raise his chances significantly. He had to take risks . . . great risks.

"Or perhaps Rhineland Germans are the odd ones, foreigners in their own Fatherland?" teased Becker.

Maria smiled at this jest. "It may well be . . . ."

Becker felt the Gestapo danger behind them with every cell in his body. He was relieved when they saw Maria's building at the corner of Arnold Strasse.

He paused. "A proper escort home must have its proper conclusion," he said.

"Oh?" she looked disappointed.

"I am expected for supper at my boarding house. As I was last Friday. A second unannounced absence would be just too impolite."

Suspicious, more like it, he knew she must be thinking. Their two commuting patterns were disrupted by Becker's chase. But he had to maintain as much routine as possible. How much he wanted to stay and visit with Maria.

"That is clear," she observed. "But perhaps next time you should plan better!" Maria smiled as she raised her eyebrows in interrogation.

"Perhaps I should!" answered Becker with a courteous nod of enthusiasm.

They stopped outside Maria's building. Maria casually turned her head upward and offered Becker her right cheek for a formal parting kiss. Part of their couple act. Becker gladly obliged. Without another word, he bowed and tipped his hat to her. He resolved to conclude tomorrow night's escort more pleasurably for them both.

He pointed his head low to hide his face under the brim of his hat and beat a quick retreat from Maria's neighborhood.

CHAPTER EIGHT

Minutes later, the phone rang in a small townhouse in the Wedding district of Berlin.

"Mencke," answered a male voice.

"Hi Rupert!"

"Maria!" Rupert Mencke was always glad to hear from his stepsister.

"It turns out tomorrow night's not good for me," said Maria. "Some of us from work are getting together. Can you come over this evening instead?"

"Certainly!" he answered. Rupert smiled at Maria's unexpected call.

"You haven't eaten yet?"

"No," he replied.

"Great," she said. "Try to be here by seven o'clock. I'll cook something for both of us."

"I'll be there in about half an hour," he replied.

Rupert Mencke was a sharp contrast to his stepsister. They were close in age, his thirty-one to her thirty. But he loomed over her. Her dark hair and eyes were nothing like his fair features. His broad muscular frame, over six feet tall, seemed oddly matched to his gleaming blue eyes. Not the ice-cold blue eyes of some northerners, but a soft blue-gray. His short hair was sandy blond. He would have looked younger than his age but for his cropped moustache, in the fashion of the Führer. Rupert had been a Nazi Party member for six years. He was unmarried, though he'd been with the same girlfriend for three years.

Rupert loved his stepsister. He still felt the pangs of the unrequited love he had declared to her in adolescence. He knew their relationship would always be that of brother and sister. Still, he was always jealous of any male acquaintance she had.

Several times in the past, Rupert had helped Maria financially. At the time, she was always changing jobs or lacking one. That Krämers job hadn't worked out very well. He was glad she had settled down in the mailroom job at Kristner Engineering for the past three years.

It was a quarter to seven when he arrived at Maria's flat. They sat down to a meal of baked ham, pickled asparagus, and fresh bread, with a Riesling wine.

"*Guten Appetit!*" said the hostess.

"*Danke schön,*" he replied.

After a bite, Rupert gave his usual compliments. "It's a nice meal you've made us," said Rupert. "Thank you for inviting me!"

He took a few more bites and leaned back in his chair. "Mmm! Thank the Führer we have enough meat and wine! Things were so bad just a few years ago."

"I'm grateful he returned us to prosperity," acknowledged Maria. "Some of the Nazis could be a little more gentlemanly about it, though."

"Exactly so!" Rupert agreed. He was eager to press some common ground on the subject of politics. He was confident she wouldn't turn him in for expressing mild reservations about his own party . . . especially since he didn't believe them. He was only trying to placate her. She probably knew as much.

He knew she had fond memories of Jewish friends from childhood. She once complained to him about the regime's anti-Semitism. For his own part, Rupert hated Jews, or what he thought he understood of them. He and Maria had long since stopped talking about it.

Rupert wanted to believe that his sister appreciated the rest of what Hitler was doing for Germany. Sometimes, though, he wasn't so sure what she thought, about anything. She remained mysterious to him after all these years.

For the rest of the evening, they enjoyed warm conversation and avoided any topic remotely political.

Anna Lande looked forward to Herr Becker's company at supper tonight, as always. He was young and handsome, charming yet sincere and modest. She loved him. He was unattached. But she would never pursue romance with him.

It wasn't that Anna thought herself unmatched to Becker's attractiveness. She knew she looked good for forty – a trim body, excellent skin, shoulder-length blond hair she kept curled, brilliant blue eyes, and full-bodied red lips. Rather, the widow Anna had enough on her hands with her rebellious adolescent daughter. Nadine needed her full attention.

Sixteen-year-old Nadine grew more contentious by the day. Anna hoped Becker's presence at supper would take the edge off. Nadine liked him. She behaved better when he was around.

Anna savored cooking. At least the pan-roasted potatoes obeyed her. The small kitchen's door was closed to the rest of the house. The suburban alley door was open, making the kitchen cold and invigorating.

The whole kitchen was no more than ten-by-ten feet. Three walls were covered by white wooden cabinets. On the plain wall was a calendar.

The rest of the house remained free of cooking smells that might go stale later. Anna kept her home smelling as fresh as its surfaces were clean. She let in so much outside air that she wore a scarf indoors most of winter.

She heard Becker come in and climb the stairs to his room. As usual, he and Nadine would stay in their rooms until she called them for supper. Anna wondered what exactly was going on in Nadine's room, directly above. Her daughter's first boyfriend, Martin Lodt, was visiting again. The past two months, Anna had watched Nadine develop an air of adolescent cheekiness and womanly confidence. Anna worried less about what might be going on upstairs than about Nadine's choice of boyfriend.

Martin's father, Gustav Lodt, was a druggist. He was also the neighborhood's open secret, Gestapo block leader for Maricfel Strasse. The Lodts lived just three townhouses away. Anna couldn't stand the father or the obnoxious son Martin. He only worsened Nadine's domestic disrespect.

The girl's soul was already seduced by school propaganda, Hitler Maidens, and every other facet of Nazi government. At least she wasn't smitten by the Lodt boy. Anna could see that Martin had not captured her daughter's heart. Still, the boy was expressly not invited to supper tonight or most nights. Nadine usually asked. Tonight she hadn't. Becker would be joining them. Anna smiled.

Supper was almost ready. As if on cue, Martin's steps could be heard jogging down the stairs and out the front door. Two minutes later, Anna opened the kitchen door and walked to the bottom of the stairs. "Suppertime!" she called.

Becker's door was directly opposite the top of the stairs. Anna saw Nadine standing to the side, waiting for him to come out. Her daughter's interest and curiosity in Becker increased by the week. Nadine was gaining experience with her boyfriend Martin, and this emboldened her behavior toward Becker.

Becker came out and pulled his door shut behind him. Anna watched him catch Nadine's half-bold, half-embarrassed stare. He smiled politely and gestured for her to go downstairs first, to their usual places at the small kitchen table. They all wore sweaters for the cold.

There wasn't much to the "evening bread" supper in the Lande home. Around eight o'clock, Anna usually served a mix of bread, cheese, and cold cuts. Occasionally, like tonight, she cooked something warm and simple to accompany those. She offered no dessert. She always served tea. Becker once joked she'd given him an addiction. If ever he missed his two or three cups before bed, he woke up with a headache.

Nadine took her place at the tiny kitchen table in silence. Becker followed. "Good evening," he tipped his head to his hostess.

"Good evening, Herr Becker," answered Anna.

Anna folded her hands in her lap and bowed her head for grace. Her open eyes looked at Becker to suggest he lead them. Nadine placed her palms on the table and held her chin high and eyes wide open, which Anna ignored.

Becker obliged. "God is great, God is good, let us thank him for this food. Amen."

"Amen," whispered Anna, and glanced sternly at Nadine.

"The potatoes smell great," he complimented her.

"Herr Becker," started Nadine, "will you be dining with us this week or what?"

Anna kicked Nadine under the table without looking at her. In the afternoon Anna had lectured her daughter to be discreet about Becker's comings and goings, including his odd lateness last Friday. They needed the rent money, she pleaded.

He deserved privacy from an insolent snoop, Anna thought to herself. She could never love him openly. But she'd take good care of him when she could.

"Thank you, Nadine," answered Becker. "Yes, most nights I will. Not tomorrow, though."

Nadine raised her eyebrows in curiosity and looked ready to question him.

Anna cut her off. "But Wednesday?"

"I believe so, yes," he answered.

"I hope so. You see, my two cousins will be in town from Munich. It would be wonderful to have you join us for supper Wednesday. Unfortunately, that's the only evening they can spend with us, since–"

"Liesl and Gertrude?" interrupted Nadine.

"Don't interrupt, dear. Yes, them. They are coming for some war widows meeting. They insist they can only stay two nights, Tuesday and Wednesday. And they're only free for supper on Wednesday."

"They're the ones who used to live upstairs from the Führer's apartment in Munich?" asked Nadine.

"Right," answered Anna.

"They always have something irreverent to say about the Führer. They'd better watch out," warned Nadine.

Anna stared coolly out of the corner of her eye. She'd have to warn her cousins about Nadine's Nazi fanaticism. They hadn't seen each other in three years. Some of their stories, especially about Hitler and his niece, might set Nadine off. The girl's sanctimonious impulsiveness was dangerous. Suddenly, Anna wished her cousins weren't coming, for their own safety.

"They don't have any children, do they?" asked Nadine.

"No, neither one does. They both married during the war, and were widowed with almost no chance to have a baby. Sad, isn't it?" Anna smiled lovingly at her daughter.

Nadine ignored it. She was having nothing of reconciliation.

"Mama," Nadine asked, "why didn't you and Papa have more children?" Nadine knew the answer – she had asked the same question several times during the past year.

Anna always answered this question patiently, as if for the first time. "Well, my treasure, first there was the war, when we scarcely saw each other for four years." Anna and Erich Lande were married just days before Germany entered the First World War against Russia, France, and Great Britain. "And then we had such a hard time in the years after the war, that we stopped with you, at least for awhile."

Nadine seemed more impatient with the story this time, Anna observed.

"Then just when times were getting better, in 1924," Anna continued, "your father came down with diabetes. As you remember, he wasn't well the last three years before he died. He was unable to have any more children."

Anna watched Nadine, who seemed to consider her father's impotence for the first time.

"You mean, Mama, you wanted to have more children, but you missed your chance?" Nadine grilled her mother.

Anna paused. She had not faced follow-up questions on this subject before. "I was happy with you, Nadine. I wanted just you, at least for awhile. And then, it was too late to do anything else."

"And Papa, what did he want?"

"He wanted more." He wanted a son. Anna did not want to tell her daughter how upset Erich had been when his first child was girl. "But we had so little money. So we waited."

"You mean it's your fault?"

Anna's eyes studied her daughter, frowning reproachfully at what her adolescent daughter was becoming, Hitler-Maidens and all.

"Don't you know how many sons the Fatherland lost in the war? For God's sake, Mother, you lost your own baby brother! You owed it to Germany, you owed it to your family, to grow the Aryan race!"

Anna sat staring, jolted and dumbfounded. "Nadine Lande," Anna was gathering steam for a stern rebuke, "even at your age, your father would have whipped you, to talk to your mother this way!" Anna rose, her left fist clenched at her side, her right index finger hammering away at Nadine.

"Do not you ever, *ever* speak to me in that tone again. Doesn't your school teach children to respect their parents?!? Do you hear me?!?" Anna spoke sternly and firmly, but she did not shout.

Nadine glanced at Becker and looked momentarily embarrassed. She turned to her mother and answered coldly, "They teach us our duty to produce abundant German children for the Führer. I for one will do my duty."

"Go to your room," glared Anna. For a moment she wondered about Nadine's activities with Martin. "And think about your duty to your mother, young lady."

Nadine stood pridefully from the table, lifted her chin into the air, gleamed self-righteously at Becker, and marched upstairs to her room.

Anna exhaled a long sigh. "I apologize for my daughter's shameful behavior."

"You have nothing to apologize for," he reassured her vaguely. It was still impossible for Anna to guess John Becker's political views.

The two of them sat silently through the rest of their supper. When Anna began to clean up, Becker offered to dry the dishes. She thanked him and accepted. She scrubbed the dishes ferociously and avoided conversation.

To each of Becker's attempts at small talk, she responded with barely more than a grunt. Usually she cherished these moments alone with Becker. At the moment, though, she barely held herself together. She was on the verge of dismissing him when he gave up and just dried the dishes.

"That's the last one," she said. "I can do it." She took the dishrag from his hands. "Thanks for your help."

Becker paused, then said, "Good night." He turned slowly and walked out and up to his room.

Anna thought about what the Third Reich was doing to her daughter. Suddenly she was interested in her cousins' stories, which had previously angered her. When Gertrude and Liesl last visited Anna in mid-1933, Anna was still very impressed with Hitler. The two cousins had lived near him for years in the 1920s. They were less impressed. When they launched into the story about Hitler's niece, Anna made them stop. She refused to believe such things. Now she might. She was curious. She hoped they would tell the whole story this time – but not around her daughter. Nadine could get them all arrested and sent away forever.

CHAPTER NINE

Tuesday, February 11

Becker looked cautiously in all directions as he left the Lande house. Something told him he hadn't totally escaped the Gestapo on Friday. It was now Tuesday morning. A less cautious man might consider himself off the hook. But Becker's sixth sense felt them scouring Berlin for him. Even so, Becker still had to complete Churchill's mission, to determine whether the English statesman could call Hitler's bluff and crush the Nazis before they got too strong.

For Becker, every outing was now a life-or-death risk. Every day turned the screws tighter. The simple morning commute tapped his strength. The walk itself was easy, even welcome. But for almost an hour he had to watch all around him on crowded streets, while seeming not to.

It had to be worse for Maria. The Gestapo agent was lurking in her neighborhood. She'd been on the U-Bahn with Becker last Friday. He had even spoken her name there. She, too, had to walk more than two miles to work in the early morning darkness. He realized she had walked yesterday as well, without telling him. She's a stoic, he thought. When Becker saw her enter the Kristner mailroom at eight o'clock, she looked flushed and invigorated by the walk.

The mailroom was small for its dozen workers and stacks of mail. The basement space was half underground, with little daylight. The overhead lights cast an unnatural brightness.

Dust was swept away early every morning. Wooden desk surfaces were polished every week. At Kristner GmbH, even the mailroom sparkled. Mail trucks unloaded their cargo at the end of the hall, at the top of a half-flight of stairs. One side of the mailroom was usually piled high with letters and packages, incoming and outgoing.

Two employees stood all day sorting. Each of the others covered one section of the building and roamed much of the day. Becker's section was the financial division. This got him access to documents on defense contracts.

He never transcribed the documents. Just reading them was a challenge. He stole glances when he walked the halls alone. He skimmed with extraordinary speed, memorized what he needed, and reported it to London.

That morning, Becker and his colleagues were sorry to hear the office news. Janeck's brother had succumbed to his injuries and passed away during the night. Janeck would remain in Cologne for the week. Everyone observed how tragic it was, but no one was very close to Janeck.

Becker felt physical pain whenever he learned of someone losing a family member before their time. He had lost his father at age twelve. His pity for Janeck was deep and sharp.

Half an hour later, Becker realized the opportunity in Janeck's extended absence. When everyone seemed busy, he walked to the office phone book and looked up Janeck: Wittmann Strasse 121, Flat 68. Of course Becker knew the street. He knew virtually every street in Berlin. This one was a mile from his lodging at the Lande residence, safely distant but relatively convenient. And Janeck had a car he'd left in Berlin. Perfect, thought Becker.

Far from Becker, Sean Russell's pub wasn't crowded that afternoon. Besides, the regular clientele knew to leave Dublin's IRA boss alone. Russell wanted privacy.

The Catholic man from Belfast who called himself Andrew wanted to hire IRA guns. Russell knew they both hated England. Andrew wasn't in the IRA, and Russell wondered about that. On the other hand, Russell was tired of IRA restraint against England. It didn't matter who put out the contract. He was excited to strike again.

Andrew had invited Russell to get confirmation of his credentials from the IRA in Ulster, and Russell checked him out. He didn't want to get blown by some undercover English operation. Andrew was indeed known to have participated in the war of independence against England in 1921. More recently, he ran a small crime ring in Belfast, including some cooperation with the local IRA.

Russell set this afternoon for their meeting. No one at the pub must hear about it in advance. He instructed Andrew to walk straight through the pub without speaking to anyone.

The IRA boss smoked alone in the small, dark, back room when the man from Belfast appeared in the doorway. Andrew wore a simple cap, as Russell had instructed. Anything fancy would draw too much attention in Dublin. Russell's own cap lay on the table, next to two tall beers. Russell's beer was already half-empty. Neither man spoke a greeting or even nodded.

Russell took a drag from his cigarette, then held it between his fingers. His green eyes stared at Andrew. The stranger took a seat, put his own hat on the table, and sipped the beer.

"We need an assassin." Andrew cut to the chase. The Ulster accent fell harsh on Russell's Dublin ears.

"That's what you say," answered Russell. "We got 'em. What's the job?"

"Winston Churchill."

Russell's jaw dropped. "Jesus, Mary, and Joseph!" he whispered. "But why? He's all washed up."

"That doesn't concern you." Andrew stared at him. "What's your price?"

"How soon you want this done?" asked Russell.

"The sooner the better," answered Andrew. "Three weeks maximum. How much?"

"For that? We'll have to blow our best man in London. That'll cost you. . . . Two thousand pounds. Up front." Russell named a high price. A lucky Dublin worker might make 300 pounds a year.

"Half up front, half when it's done," said Andrew.

Russell shook his head. "All up front. Or no deal."

"Two thousand up front?" The Ulsterman leaned across the small table. Russell could smell onions on his breath. "You guarantee three weeks maximum?" asked Andrew.

"Yes." Russell didn't know if he could. What choice did he have?

"Fine. Two thousand up front. But then I'll have to pay you another five hundred afterwards, to make sure it gets done. Twenty-five hundred total. Do a good job, and we might do business in the future."

Russell's eyes widened, astonished. This man didn't come to negotiate. He came for efficiency. What was his purpose? For that kind of money, it didn't matter. "Deal."

Andrew pulled out his billfold, counted out twenty hundred-pound notes, and slid them across the narrow table. "How soon?"

"It depends on Churchill's schedule," answered Russell, sliding the money into his jacket. "Our man in London has his best chances when Churchill's in a social mood. We might not need three weeks. Maybe not even three days. It depends."

"Drop a line once it's scheduled." Andrew handed over a phone number. "We're eager for the confirmation. You'll get the rest of the money within twenty-four hours of completion. Just follow your routine. A stranger will hand it to you in a newspaper. . . . Like I said, the sooner the better."

At the end of the afternoon, most of the mailroom staff left promptly at five o'clock. Two stayed late to finish a mailing. Georg Schwarz was the only Nazi Party member on the staff, but more a bumbling blowhard than a threat. Herr Franzoser was the office manager.

Among the rest who left, Becker and Maria lagged behind, walking together as usual toward the U-Bahn. Once their colleagues were out of sight, Becker solicited Maria's arm. Becker knew it didn't matter if the others saw. But if they did, they needed to see a certain amount of modesty.

"Shall we?" he asked Maria.

"Yes, of course!" she replied.

"Well then, first allow me an explanation of the sudden scare in your neighborhood yesterday." Becker spoke softly under the busy street noises.

Maria replied only with the nod of her head as they walked past the subway entrance toward.

"Coming out of the café was the very same man –" Becker paused while they passed someone walking the other direction. "The man who chased me out of the underground last Friday. I'd never seen him before. I don't know why he pursued me."

"But you knew you did not want to be pursued?" Maria cocked her eyebrow.

Becker stood at the red light for a moment without answering. The corner was crowded, and he wasn't sure how to answer. He gestured toward the crowd and waited until they were half a block away from Wittenberg Platz.

"Right," he answered. He turned to Maria as they kept walking. "Now that we're speaking the unspoken, let me ask you this. Did you happen to notice what happened to that woman who recognized me, after she got off the train?"

Becker couldn't tell Maria that the woman in blue knew his background, including his settlement in England.

"I didn't see much," Maria answered, "though I tried. The woman trotted just a few steps in your direction before giving up. Then she tried to re-enter the underground car. But the doors were already shut. That's the last I saw."

"How about the man chasing me? Was he alone?"

"As far as I could tell," answered Maria.

That's a relief, thought Becker. If Maria was telling the truth. He sensed she was. He'd watched her for over a year.

Becker's ability to sense a lie was extraordinary. Colonel Dansey tested his recruits for this skill with a slew of seasoned business negotiators. Becker later learned that he was the only one ever to score perfectly on Dansey's test. A few others had identified every lie, but they had also misidentified some truths as lies. Becker saw straight every time.

It seemed that his mother's old acquaintance, Frau Rieger, had simply waited for the next subway train. There was no second Gestapo agent on hand to question her. Subsequent non-events reinforced this interpretation. If she had talked to the police, Becker would be in a Gestapo torture chamber by now.

"Herr Becker!" Suddenly, an unidentified man's voice called him from close behind. Becker was surprised he hadn't heard the approach. He started and then froze in his tracks. He and Maria exchanged nervous glances. They didn't know if they had just been overheard.

"Herr Becker! I need to have a word with you please!"

The would-be couple relaxed as they recognized Herr Schwarz. He was out of breath from running to catch them. His heavy body didn't look accustomed to running.

"Good evening, Fräulein Geberich. Excuse me. Becker – Herr Janeck called earlier from Cologne, while you were on delivery rounds. He specifically asked for you to tend his cat. Franzoser sent me to catch up with you; he forgot about Janeck's request until now. The rest is all written down. Here." Schwarz handed over a sheet of paper with Janeck's address, along with some keys. "It sounds like the poor cat must be starving by now."

Becker wondered why Janeck would have singled him out for this favor. Perhaps he just didn't want to impose on the family men. Becker and Janeck were the sole bachelors in the office.

A very bad week for this, thought Becker. *Hitler is poised to undermine France. Churchill is desperate for vital information. Now I'm supposed to feed a cat. Fantastic. At least now I won't have to pick the locks if I need to hide out there.*

"I didn't know you were so charming with pets!" joked Maria.

"Say, are you two headed for a drink?" asked Schwarz. "How about I join you?"

Maria and Becker exchanged glances.

"Frankly, Schwarz, Fräulein Geberich and I were just walking along," said Becker.

"Excellent," said Schwarz. "I'll join you. I know a great little place some distance away. It's a brilliant evening for February, wouldn't you say? And the walk will do us all some good!" Schwarz started walking in their direction.

Becker reluctantly resumed course. The office staff familiarity struck again. He made fun of Schwarz's rudeness. "Perhaps your wife doesn't hold your arm any more when you go for walks, just the two of you?"

Schwarz missed the point. "Café Charlotte, that's the place."

"Are you sure that's right?" asked Maria. "I'm familiar with it, and it doesn't seem like your kind of place. I hear they still serve Jews there. I even heard a rumor the place is secretly owned by a Jew. Sounds fine to me. But to a dutiful Party member like you, Schwarz?"

Schwarz looked surprised. "Well . . . ," he stammered.

Neither Becker nor Maria offered any encouragement. They both smirked at Schwarz as he stumbled over Maria's challenge.

"Uh, I suppose we could, uh, go somewhere else," said Schwarz.

"No, no, Herr Schwarz," laughed Maria. "Café Charlotte is a wonderful choice. Who knows what cosmopolitan delights lay in store there! Why, I hear their secret Jews look just like the rest of us Germans."

Schwarz looked back and forth from Becker to Maria. Each smiled broadly, almost laughing at Schwarz's discomfort.

"You know," Schwarz said, "I really ought to get home to my wife. I'll be home too late if I keep heading here in the wrong direction. Uh, have a good evening."

"Good evening," answered Becker and Maria in unison.

Schwarz turned awkwardly back toward Wittenberg Platz.

"You made that up about Café Charlotte?" asked Becker.

"Never heard of the place," smiled Maria.

After walking several minutes hand-in-arm, Maria was the first to interrupt the silence. "He could have heard us. That conversation must not resume out in the city like this."

Becker didn't think they could have been understood from behind. He'd been careful to watch all angles. He was a professional. Still, he affirmed Maria's general note of caution. "You're right."

"The only safe place for us to continue is at my apartment," she added dryly, with no romantic suggestion.

Maria dropped the playful romance act as soon as the door shut behind them. She directed Becker as if giving orders. "I'll take your coat and make us some tea. You may have a seat in the sitting room."

Before going to the kitchen, Maria followed Becker and put on a record.   When the music started, she turned up the volume. "Neighbors," she whispered. "Every time one side finishes, please turn to the next from this set." Becker could read "Mozart" from where he sat, and he heard the first strains of Piano Concerto No. 23 in A major.

"Except, please skip anything in a minor key," added Maria. "Music in a minor key is too sad for apparent lovers, don't you agree?" Maria's tone remained stern and matter-of-fact. "Play only sonatas in major keys."

Becker replied with a nod and a grin, to witness such skillful construction of the setting. He sat in the modestly furnished room. Again he admired the paintings and the record collection. Again he wondered why she lived alone and worked as a simple mail clerk.

More importantly, he needed to push for her cooperation with his mission. He needed Maria's help to access her stepbrother Rupert's Army office. He wondered how far he could take it tonight.

CHAPTER TEN

Maria was strangely silent when she brought out tea for her guest Becker. For a few minutes, they sipped in silence. Maria seemed to be deep in thought. She occasionally scrutinized him squarely, as if in a job interview.

This visit was her idea. Becker would leave her the initiative.

"You will not tell me everything about yourself, even if I ask. That's fine." Maria was direct. "You called me by name in the crowded U-Bahn. We're lucky the Gestapo hasn't tracked that down. You have implicated me. I acknowledge it was unintentional. Still, you must allow me a question or two."

"Of course," he replied.

"Did that woman in blue know more about you than I am going to learn? Did she know enough to endanger you?"

Becker was under strict orders not to reveal his English identity. He was permitted to seek collaborators in spying for the weaknesses of Hitler's Army. But not at the cost of revealing his masters.

"Yes," he replied.

"Thank you for answering me. You're clearly in some dangerous business. You probably have a way out. But you show up for work this week as if the noose were not slowly tightening around your neck, as it surely is. I can only guess what you're up to. I suppose that once you get what you want, you'll cut loose. Or you will have to cut loose soon in any case, before it's too late. Or you won't make it. But you have a choice."

Maria paused. "I, on the other hand, do not have a way out. I couldn't get a visa if I tried."

Becker sensed this last statement wasn't exactly true, that somehow Maria thought she *could* get out of Germany if she tried. This wasn't Stalin's Russia.

Maria continued, "And now I'm drawn into your affairs. You sprung from our U-Bahn conversation into a chase with the Gestapo. There were witnesses. . . . I have things to hide from them, Johannes."

She paused. Becker said nothing.

"So before I carry on with this facade of courtship," said Maria, "I need to know this: Will you share your place of refuge, when it comes time to seek it? Will you get me out of Germany? Can you do that?"

Becker admired how cleverly Maria prefaced the question. He had to acknowledge nothing except his fugitive status. Of course he would help her.

He had planned to leave her an innocent bystander in his spying business. Even if she were willing to collaborate now, he regretted involving her more explicitly. It could ruin her life . . . or end it.

Even if she escaped Germany, she would have nothing left. Except him. He would enjoy playing her white knight, but not forcing her to need him. He didn't want to prey on her vulnerability. Either way, he needed her cooperation. If she wanted escape from Germany, he would deliver her himself.

"Yes," he promised.

"If I am a very good actress," Maria responded with a wry smile, "I could myself be a Gestapo agent ready to arrest you tonight."

Becker's eyes froze on Maria as she put it so bluntly. He felt his eyes drying for lack of blinking. Had he misread her so completely? Somewhere there had to be a liar who could beat him. Maria? No, he affirmed to himself, she wasn't Gestapo. But her suggestion was chilling.

The 78-rpm record stopped mid-sonata. Becker dutifully got up to turn it over, and returned to his seat.

"The fact is," she resumed, "I know with certainty from your chase whose side you are *not* on. And I recognize that you cannot, at least not yet, hold the same certainty about me. For the moment, please allow me to be presumptuous about your motives . . . and frank about mine."

Becker finished his tea and put down his cup and saucer. Maria filled the cup. Becker prepared to listen.

"It's possible your urgency relates to something you hope to discover at Kristner," started Maria. "But I doubt it. If there is anything of real value to you there, you've already found it. After fifteen months, you certainly couldn't expect that another couple of weeks – or however much time you've left for yourself – are going to produce anything worth risking your life for."

Maria's eyes searched him for confirmation.

Becker expressed nothing.

She looked alternately between her teacup and Becker's face. "You are clearly no friend of the Hitler regime. You have surely noticed some of my hostility to the whole business. Despite my caution on other matters, I choose not to hide my disgust with the wild anti-Semitism they belch forth and stir up. . . . Appalling. . . . Just a minute, I'd like to show you something."

Maria retreated to her bedroom for a couple of minutes. She emerged with a framed photograph of a smiling young man. "That is my brother."

Becker was perplexed. He knew Maria's stepbrother Rupert Mencke by sight. Rupert was the Wehrmacht secretary with access to high-level documents. This was not Rupert.

"Rather, that was my brother. Max." She stared at the photo with a bittersweet smile. "He was a Socialist. He hated the Nazis. He even fought them in the streets. When the Nazis used their new offices in 1933 to murder all the Communists, Max vowed to oppose the new regime. He didn't have a chance. Within days he was arrested and executed."

Becker winced in pity. He folded his hands together under his chin. He held his silence, but his face showed Maria his sympathy. She paused only a brief moment to look at him. A tear ran down her right cheek. She continued with a shaky voice.

"They arrested me, too," said Maria, "for nothing besides my relation to Max. The first I knew for certain of his arrest was when I saw him during my own interrogation. He had been beaten to a bloody pulp."

Maria's voice broke and she paused and inhaled. She regained her strength. Her voice now reflected anger at the events she recounted.

"When they started to unleash the same treatment on me, in front of his swollen eyes, he volunteered to confess everything, to reveal all persons, meeting places, everything . . . if they would let me go. So I got my reprieve. But I had to watch him absolutely weep as he informed on his closest friends and colleagues. Of course they lied. They weren't finished with me. I was automatically suspect because of Max. It could have been worse, but I still bear the cigarette burn scars on my neck."

Maria pulled back her long, thick, dark brown hair for Becker to see the twisted round, pink scars. Many of them blotted an otherwise beautiful ivory neck. He had never noticed them before, although he had observed her unusual custom of wearing her hair down at work. He realized he had not once seen Maria pull her hair back.

"I . . . I'm so sorry." Becker first furrowed his brow in shock and anger, then looked at her with sad, compassionate eyes. He sensed there was even more to the story. "I never would have guessed." He knew Hitler's goons did this sort of thing all the time. But to see it face-to-face was different, especially with an innocent woman.

Now Maria's earlier silent stares made sense to Becker. She'd been deciding whether to distance herself from him or to lean more on his protection. Now that she had implied her allegiances, Becker had mixed feelings about it. On the one hand, he could be safely out of Germany within days, if he successfully obtained the Army documents. Mr. Churchill could use the Wehrmacht's secrets to take power in London and crush Hitler.

On the other hand, Becker was sorry to upset Maria's life. He still hadn't asked for her help to use Rupert, though Becker had promised his help to get her out of Germany. Whatever came of all this, she would have to leave her home, start over from scratch. She hadn't sought this out. He had accidentally endangered her on the U-Bahn. Still, she seemed strong in her resolve to escape Nazi Germany.

Becker was less certain of her feelings towards him. He guessed she was herself uncertain. She still held her hair drawn back during the pause in conversation.

Becker reached from his chair to stroke Maria's wounds. She slowly let her hair down and pulled her head back just out of his reach. She shook her head gently.

Understood, Becker showed with a nod of his head. He leaned back into his chair. Not yet.

"I have never been in any active resistance against the Third Reich." Maria reduced her voice to a whisper under the music. "But I have friends – those that remain – from the heyday of Weimar Berlin, who might be. . . ."

Maria sighed. "I really miss those times. Berlin was hard to like at first, before I found my niche among admirers of the avant-garde. Then the Nazis came and shut it all down. I digress. Sorry. . . ."

"In short," she continued, "I hate what the Nazis have done to my brother, my friends, my life. I can try to help against them. Tell me what you want from me. But also tell me how I'm going to survive it."

Becker knew she wasn't referring to romance. He saw how perceptive she was about his professional agenda. She was so forthright about it. Under a murderous dictatorship, there was no use beating around the bush after she trusted him with her denunciation of the Nazis.

Becker was sorry Maria had been cast as a pawn in the spy game. He wished for something else, almost anything, to define his relationship with her. But the truth was unavoidable.

If he was so lucky to have her full collaboration, then he would treat her like a partner. Her brother's position in the Army was precisely what he needed to exploit. Yet before he could get a word out of his opening mouth, Maria continued.

"I half-suspect that your chief interest in me lies in my brother's position in the Wehrmacht."

She really has a knack for this.

"You already know, if you've paid any attention in office conversation, that my brother Rupert works as a secretary for the General Staff of the Army?"

"I do remember that fact," Becker replied, with no effort at surprise.

"Well, he's not very important. But they know he can be trusted. He handles some very, very important documents."

"You had one brother killed by the Gestapo, and another lives to work with top security clearances in the Wehrmacht?" asked Becker.

"Unbelievable, isn't it? Rupert was only our stepbrother. That must be the only reason why they don't mistrust him at his job. That and they're reassured that I came out clean from a Gestapo interrogation. They know Rupert despised Max, and that we're related only by circumstance."

"So when you were orphaned, which one drew you to Berlin?" he asked.

"That was Max. They both happened to live here already. Max followed the Communnist Party. Rupert followed his family roots, moving in and out of Berlin with the Army. The two boys hadn't gotten along at home in Bonn. They never saw each other in Berlin. Not once. They followed each other's lives only through me."

Becker was fascinated to learn these utterly unknown details of Maria's background. He was frustrated that the Service in London didn't even know about Max, much less Maria's brief internment. What else didn't they know about Maria Geberich?

"We didn't grow up with Rupert, you know," Maria continued. "At least mostly not. Our father died in the war, and mother died of the Spanish flu in '19. Rupert's parents needed the foster care money, so they took us in as strangers. The house fire later on, those were

Rupert's parents who died. So I'm twice orphaned. Without Max all along, I don't know how I could've survived it all. . . ."

"Rupert, too, has always adored me," added Maria. "He welcomed me into his family immediately. I was thirteen at the time. Rupert was fourteen and Max was seventeen. Rupert was terribly jealous of my affinity for Max. But he helped us both when we first came to his family. I love Rupert for that, and for the good that is in him. . . . But my politics and friends were always closer to Max's. He and I were both inspired by our father. Papa was a quiet Catholic socialist. He adored Pope Leo XIII. . . ."

Maria returned her gaze from a blank spot on the wall to Becker. "In Berlin, Rupert became harder to like. I'm not sure I like him now. But I still love him as my brother. He swallowed that Nazi *Scheisse* through-and-through. We mostly avoid discussing politics. . . . There you have it, Johannes. Rupert is all that's left of my little family tree."

Becker wondered what other tragedies Maria could manage to divulge in one evening. No wonder she was so hard to read. She'd learned self-reliance early and hard. Becker knew the trauma of losing his father in childhood. Millions of Europeans their age did. Maria had suffered many times more – two sets of parents and a brother.

"You haven't had it easy," he said.

Maria shook her head slightly. "I suppose it could've been worse," she replied.

After a long pause she asked, "So what do you want from Rupert?"

"Not from him directly, but through you," Becker answered. "How much do you know about his office?"

"Oh, I've visited him there many times. I know where he keeps his in-office keys. I know where they keep the important documents. I think he has a key to that file, but I'm not sure. I've even been to the office after hours."

"How hard do you think it would be to break into that office?" asked Becker.

"At night?"

"Yes."

"Very hard," she replied. "Not impossible, but it would take a lot of preparation and luck."

"Today is Tuesday," said Becker. "Do you think we could get in by the weekend?"

"By 'we' you mean that I am to use Rupert, and to endanger him insofar as his carelessness would have facilitated the break-in?"

"Possibly, although it could be done without necessarily revealing whose office key had been used . . . provided the key found its way back to Rupert unnoticed. But the risk to your brother is there, yes, that cannot be denied."

Maria stared silently across the room. Then she turned her eyes, but not her head, to Max's photo, smiling from beyond the grave.

"I cannot intentionally bring harm to Rupert," she said. She continued to look at Max. She paused, and then exhaled a sigh of further resolve. "But I'm willing to take the risk." Maria lifted her eyes to Becker's. "Promise me you'll try to shield Rupert from blame."

"I promise," he said. This was a half-truth, and Maria probably knew it.

Rupert Mencke might not need to go down with a weekend break-in to Major Hossbach's office. But Becker owed more to his mission than to anyone's life, including his own. He certainly felt no sympathy for some Hitler fanatic in German uniform. Maria was making this harder extracting promises. It would be easier not to worry about his fate. But Becker would honor Maria's wishes, if he could.

"The earliest I can arrange is Saturday night," said Maria. "Will that do?"

"It will have to," answered Becker.

"I'll give you more details later this week."

"We can't meet tomorrow evening, but after that I should be free," said Becker.

"All right. We'll come here after the office closes on Thursday. Or perhaps we could go feed Herr Janeck's cats together?" Maria joked about Becker's unwanted burden.

"Your resistance friends, or possibly resistance. . . . Any of them still live here in Berlin?" asked Becker.

"One or two, yes," answered Maria.

"You know how to find them?"

"I think so," she said.

"We need two Wehrmacht uniforms."

"Two?!?" Maria exclaimed. "First of all, I don't know where I'll find the first one. Second, you don't mean to have *me* marching in that uniform, do you?"

"Would you come with me, if I needed you?"

"I wouldn't know what to do. Oh dear. I'll have to think about it. But I'll ask about the uniforms – two of them."

Sparing Rupert Mencke was a stupid risk, thought Becker. With Rupert's stolen uniform, it would be much easier. Once Becker got

Rupert's keys and the office layout from Maria's memory, he could get everything he needed.

But Becker would either have to kill Rupert, or tie him up for the Gestapo to find later. Yet that would spell Maria's doom as well. He'd have to find another way. It was so much harder being a good guy in this spy game, thought Becker.

Maria put down her teacup and saucer. For several minutes she slowly rotated her gaze between Max's photo, Becker, and some empty point across the room.

Then she slowly and deliberately pulled her hair back again with her right hand, to expose her scars. She reached across her lap with the other hand. She took Becker's hand and drew his fingertips slowly to her neck scars.

Becker leaned forward just enough to follow Maria's lead. At first he allowed his fingertips only the most delicate pressure on Maria's scarred neck. She closed her eyes. He stared at the neck that he barely felt. He could almost see the light between his fingertips and Maria's scars, so slight was his touch.

That pose seemed to last countless moments.

At last Becker left his chair almost imperceptibly. He moved his lips toward the curve where Maria's neck met her shoulder, at her lowest scar. He felt moved by Maria's confidence in him. He was aroused by the sensuously relaxed expression on Maria's beautiful face. He ignored the arousal and cherished the intimacy.

To meet his advance, Maria held her shoulders still and tilted her head in the opposite direction, baring and lengthening what was still a beautiful neck.

Becker approached her from a kneeling position upward, steadying himself on her armchair. At last his mouth met her neck. He was as still and deliberate and soft as if kissing a sleeping baby's forehead. Then as unhurried as he had moved to her neck, Becker withdrew again to his own chair. He watched Maria savor the moment, unmoving, eyes still shut, lips slightly parted, holding her breath.

"Thank you," she whispered through her exhalation. She opened her eyes and turned to Becker. She looked exhausted. Her right hand released the thick tresses to drape her scarred neck. She smiled. "I'll see you tomorrow."

Avoiding the U-Bahn, Becker walked the two miles to Schöneberg. He felt good about the evening's progress.

Maria's help would give Becker more flexibility for a successful break-in at Army headquarters . . . flexibility he hadn't had a year ago, with Clara. He wondered if Clara's same impatience had led to her recent demise.

Becker and Clara, espionage duo and incipient lovers, almost pulled it off in 1935. In the middle of the night, they got through locked windows with ease. Guard dogs were appeased with food scraps and Becker's natural touch with animals. Then Clara shot the dogs with tranquilizers.

Becker hadn't anticipated the second round of German shepherds. Before he could reassure the dogs, Clara anxiously fumbled for the tranquilizer gun. The dogs sensed fear and attacked them both.

Becker let both dogs latch onto him, to clear Clara's escape. She ran ahead of him to the basement and their backup escape route through the sewers. He held the dogs at bay. He would have shot them right away, but one dog's bite was sunk into his flesh right above his holster. The teeth would have torn Becker's fingers to shreds.

Then the sound of Clara's running stopped. She didn't want to leave without him. "Z!" she shouted from the basement. "Z!"

Without further warning, two Wehrmacht guards came running from the far side of the building. They were much closer to Clara's shouting than to Becker's snarling German shepherds. One guard shined his flashlight directly into Clara's face while the other ran toward Becker.

With Clara's escape blocked, Becker started running toward her, dragging both dogs with him. When the first dog's bite slipped from Becker's side, he withdrew his Luger.

Becker and the second guard fired at each other simultaneously. As Becker fired, he ducked his face into one dog's back. It worked. His German opponent momentarily tried to avoid the dogs. Becker dodged the bullet, and now the German lay dead.

Just before Becker could kill the other guard, holding the flashlight like a bull's eye, the guard jumped through a doorway. If Becker had been alone, he would have hunted him down. This Wehrmacht guard had both seen Clara's face and heard Becker's code name.

But they couldn't know if more guards were on the way. Becker had to get Clara to safety. He grabbed her arm and pulled her with him into the sewer.

German officials never got closer to them that night. Clara had a secret second apartment, where she and Becker washed and talked and slept.

In the morning they made love, unrushed, their imminent separation unspoken but deeply felt. The lovemaking ended in quiet tears from them both.

Next they cut and dyed Clara's hair before she departed for Sweden. That was the last time Becker saw Clara.

After that night, Becker knew Army security would be even tighter. Another break-in like that would be out of the question, at least for a long time.

It was now a year later. Maria knew her way around parts of the building. Becker and McBride had avoided approaching her the first time. This time, Becker was pulling up stakes, and it was worth risking Maria's antagonism. Her stepbrother Rupert, loyal to the Army and the Nazis, handled precisely the documents Becker needed. Somehow Becker must take advantage of the connection to improve his chances. Towards the end of the week, he would assess the possibilities. Then he would determine his exact approach.

Becker turned his thoughts forward to the trivial task of feeding Janeck's cat. He easily found Janeck's apartment building on Wittmann Strasse, a long side street. The key to the building entrance worked fine. Next he had to choose from four unlabeled stairwells on the courtyard. Only after climbing several stories in two of them did he find the right place, Flat 68.

Becker found Janeck's entry light switch easily enough in the dark. In the dimly lit hallway, the cat wasn't shy at all. It immediately approached Becker's legs with repeated purring.

Janeck's apartment was an assault to Becker's sense of smell. It was warm and stuffy. There was a slight scent of unwashed human sweat. Janeck probably hadn't opened the windows all winter. Food scraps rotted in the trashcan. A half-full cup of coffee and cream was already growing mold on the kitchen counter. Over it all was the smell of stale cigarette smoke. Janeck was a chain smoker, and his flat reeked of it.

The cat food was hard to find. Becker didn't have any specific directions there. It wasn't in any obvious cabinet. While looking, Becker automatically took note of the apartment's layout and personal artifacts.

And there it was, a stack of food cans on the kitchen table, so obvious that Becker was ashamed for not spotting it instantly. One top of the stack was a note explained the cat's name was Rosa, and how much food she needed how often while Janeck mourned his brother in Cologne.

One can sat to the side, on top of some papers.

"*Sopade*," read the title.

Sopade!   The underground Socialist resistance network in Germany.   Its Prague headquarters were just blocks from Becker's weekend visit to McBride.

Sopade!

Janeck – or someone – had certainly left these documents for Becker to discover. They could not be missed under the cat food.

Still, Sopade was a codename. Agent Z certainly knew it. But unless Johannes Becker read the documents more closely, his mail clerk persona would have no reason to recognize their significance or to suspect anything. He left the documents untouched.

Janeck had always protested a certain apathy whenever politics arose in mailroom conversation.   Now his apartment betrayed something very different. But why? After all, Janeck's message and flat key had been delivered to Becker by Schwarz, a Nazi Party member. Schwarz wasn't clever enough for intricate trickery. But he was loyal enough to be a Nazi errand boy.

Who put these documents here, and why?

Becker thought it was probably Janeck. But maybe it was someone else. In either case, he didn't know what to make of it.

Is this a trap? Why was I singled out for this?

He instinctively looked over his shoulder toward the door, his escape.

Becker looked straight into the handgun held by Wolfgang Janeck.

CHAPTER ELEVEN

"Herr Janeck! What a surprise! I thought – "

"Good evening, Becker." Janeck's voice was a little nervous. "No, I never had a brother. I've been watching from across the courtyard. Thanks for feeding Rosa. You took long enough . . . to find things."

Becker saw Janeck's fear. His instinct told him Janeck was not Gestapo. Becker kept his hands and face still, but darted his eyes around the hallway behind Janeck.

Janeck chuckled. "No, Becker, I'm alone. I really am in the Socialist resistance. This isn't a trap. The trouble is, they're closing in on me. I've got to leave the country."

Me, too, thought Becker.

"You hide your real self well, Becker. I still don't know who you are. But you came strutting into the Kristner mailroom looking for more than a job. I could see that. I've watched you. I've even spied you skimming finance documents in the halls."

"I was just cur–"

"*Ja, ja*, everyone on the mail staff is just curious. Good excuse. I don't believe it, Becker. Be more careful about your skimming, is all."

They both heard footsteps in the stairwell. Janeck jerked his head nervously and closed the door.

Becker believed Janeck so far. He decided Janeck's gun was for defensive purposes only. He left his own gun in his coat while Janeck looked away.

"Just one of the neighbors," Janeck mumbled to himself. "Here's the thing, Becker. We need a replacement for me, someone on the inside. You don't have the usual background, longtime Socialist credentials. But you're well placed, and we're running out of people. My guess is you're on the same side. You can even have my car."

Janeck fished out his car keys and threw them to Becker. He still pointed his gun with his other hand. "I can't take the car with me."

Becker caught the keys and stared back blankly.

"So what is it, Becker? Will you do it? Time is short. I need to get out of here. If you need to think about it, do that. I or someone else will find you again in a couple of days."

"I don't know what you're talking about," lied Becker. "Whatever it is, I'm not interested. I'll feed your cat, Janeck. But please get your other stuff out of here. Otherwise, I'll have no choice but to—"

"Report me. Right. No choice, of course." Janeck kept his gun trained on Becker. "Let's feed the cat." Janeck didn't move.

"At gunpoint?" Becker raised an eyebrow.

"Sorry," chuckled Janeck as he lowered his gun.

Becker opened a can of cat food, and put it in one bowl and some fresh water in the other.

Janeck snatched the Sopade documents from the kitchen table. "If you change your mind, Becker, leave my bedroom window shade exactly halfway open. . . . Those Nazi bastards are closing in on me. Be careful in my flat. Once I walk out of here, I'll be gone through passages you don't know. Don't try to follow me. Or turn me in. But I don't think you will."

Becker watched the sweat collecting on Janeck's temples.

"*Auf Wiedersehen*, Herr Becker. Until next time."

Janeck slipped his gun into his coat pocket, backed out of his flat, and fled down the stairwell.

Becker wanted to get out of here fast. He listened for Janeck's steps to reach the stairwell's exit. Then Becker fled Janeck's flat.

He walked a zigzag home, making sure he wasn't followed. His encounter with Janeck was strangely distracting from his other concerns. What were the full repercussions of Janeck's move? he wondered. All night, Becker's brain and dreams churned the possibilities.

"Good morning, Standartenführer Wächter." It was Wednesday morning, not quite eight o'clock.

Colonel Wächter looked up from his desk at Gestapo headquarters. He left Berlin Chief of Police Jörg Arndt standing for a moment. The soft light of dawn filtered indirectly into the office. Wächter hadn't turned on any lights.

"Morning," came his gruff reply.

Wächter had once served in the ranks of the Berlin police force. Now a Gestapo officer, *he* gave the commands to Chief Arndt.

Wächter enjoyed the role reversal. He loved the Third Reich for allowing talented men like himself to rise quickly.

Wächter scowled at Arndt. The chief of police was a breathless, overweight man. Wächter, the thin, rising Gestapo officer in his thirties, despised the aging chief, a relic from Germany's less glorious past.

"Have you finished the Becker project?" Wächter brusquely inquired.

He expected complete results. Twenty-four hours ago, he'd ordered Arndt to produce files on every Becker in Berlin by Wednesday morning.

Wächter knew this was straining his credibility in Columbia Haus. He didn't care what the regular police outside thought. He hadn't told anyone that his fugitive might be Agent Z. They all just thought Wächter was obsessing about a regular adulterer that got scared and escaped him. Wächter knew differently.

Maybe it wasn't Agent Z. But the man was probably English. And he had shown great skill in the chase and escape. He was worth Wächter risking his reputation by throwing all these resources into the investigation. Wächter had no doubt the fugitive was worth it. The risk was that Wächter wouldn't catch him to prove it.

"As you know, . . . *sir*, there are thousands of men by that name in this city," answered Chief Arndt. "I have here most of the lists you ordered. The full files are being unloaded from my car downstairs right now."

Wächter smiled wryly when Chief Arndt called him "sir." Then he quickly straightened out his face again. He stood up, leaned forward, and snatched the lists.

"About one-quarter of our police districts were unable to complete their lists until this morning," Arndt continued. "I will forward those to you by noon today. By then, every district in the city will have listed every registered resident named Becker. As I'm sure you remember from your work with us, we don't let people go unregistered."

"I remember plenty of people slipping through the cracks," snapped Wächter.

"Things have changed, you know!" Arndt shot back. "The Führer made it much easier to catch vagrants. . . . Like I said, you'll have the rest by noon. After that, I'll be sure to get any updates to you."

"Daily. I want them daily," barked Wächter. Both men leaned toward each other across Wächter's desk. Wächter knew he couldn't harm the chief of police. The missing fugitive was his problem, not

Arndt's. But the chief couldn't do anything to Wächter, either. So they stood there blustering at each other.

Half of Gestapo headquarters knew about his failed chase last Friday. Every one of them thought Wächter was obsessing excessively about it. Wächter had a reputation of success. He wanted this stain removed immediately.

What was more, the covert British fugitive could prove a real prize. Wächter had to keep his conclusion about British nationality a secret. If he told them, they would surely move the case to Counter-Intelligence, out of his hands. Since he endured some mocking today, he ought to get the glory tomorrow, he reasoned.

"Yes, sir," begrudged Arndt. "Daily."

"And the hotel reports?" asked Wächter.

"They're in there, by district," said Arndt.

"Any leads there?"

"A couple of Beckers, but not much," answered Arndt.

Wächter nodded his head and sifted through the papers in his hands. He sat down and ignored Arndt for a moment.

"Dismissed." Wächter relished giving that command, the more so to senior police officers.

Wächter wanted to read all the district summary reports together at once. So he'd wait until he got them by noon. This morning he could pursue another avenue.

If only those foolish ladies on the subway could remember the woman's name, he thought. *Perhaps I'll try to jog their memories.*

Wächter kept on his civilian clothes and left his office.

From an empty grocer's store in Dublin, Sean Russell made the call to Andrew, his client from the Belfast underworld. Andrew wanted to know when Churchill's assassination was scheduled.

"Hello?" answered Andrew.

"Next Wednesday, the nineteenth. At a concert at seven-thirty," said Russell. "I'll let you know if the plan changes."

"I understand," said Andrew, and hung up.

He picked the phone right back up and called Wolf, the man who'd hired him. Wolf wanted Sean Russell to think Andrew was the contractor, when he was just the go-between.

"Hello?" Wolf spoke with an English accent.

"We've got an update," said Andrew. He wondered why an Englishman wanted Churchill killed, but he didn't care. The pay was excellent.

"Well?" asked Wolf.

"It happens at a concert next Wednesday evening, the nineteenth," reported Andrew.

"Anything else?"

"That's it," said Andrew.

"Good work," said Wolf and hung up.

Half an hour later, while Andrew walked down a busy Belfast street, he felt a sudden shove from behind and fell right in front of a speeding beer truck. Wolf ducked into an alley and was gone.

No connection remained to the contractors for Churchill's assassination.

An easy atmosphere prevailed in the Kristner mailroom on Wednesday morning. No one mentioned Janeck's brother. The morning sunlight caught just the right angle into the basement windows. Moods were light, even jocular.

Not Becker's. All night he had thought and dreamed about Herr Janeck's visit. Why did Janeck choose Becker? He sensed Janeck was telling the truth. He could rely on that. But what was the full story? Becker couldn't stop thinking about it, even at work with Maria.

The mailroom staff made small talk while they collected their morning's deliveries. None seemed eager to abandon the rare winter sunlight for Kristner's corridors above. Franzoser allowed their delay. He liked keeping his staff happy. He liked his staff, Becker knew. He was a rare manager in these strange times.

Georg Schwarz wasn't a typical Nazi. He was of average height, aged fifty, somewhat overweight, with slightly drooping facial features. He was usually jovial and friendly. Occasionally he became indignant about something, reminded people of his Party membership, and threatened vague consequences. Even he knew such threats rang hollow. Delivering office mail seemed to lie at the outer reach of his talents. No one took him very seriously.

Schwarz took his turn procrastinating the morning's work. "Hey Janski, has your wife gotten over her weekend hang-over yet?" Schwarz asked.

"Most certainly," answered Janski, one of many Germans of distant Polish descent. "In fact, just this morning she was asking the same thing about you," retorted Janski, to chuckles all around.

Schwarz laughed self-consciously. "Well, I expect she would think twice before trying to drink me under next time," he trailed off.

"Schwarz, you should pick on your own sex next time," chided Herr Schmidt. "To think, accepting a drinking challenge from a woman!"

Schwarz scowled and shuffled some papers on his desk. He looked like a parody of himself pouting.

"I'm just so glad that your Nazi Party, Herr Schwarz, has refocused our Fatherland on higher virtues than drinking contests." Frau Cassels joined the fray.

"My National Socialist Party is our National Socialist Party!" answered Schwarz. "It's not my fault if you choose not to join!"

"A German is a German, Schwarz," Manager Franzoser weighed in.

"That's funny coming from you, Herr Franzoser, since your name means Frenchman!" joked Janski to the boss.

"But some Germans are purer than others," insisted Schwarz, in a transparent jibe at both these colleagues. "And don't even start, please, Fräulein Geberich, with your claptrap about how Jews are Germans, too."

Maria glared and paused for a moment. "Your time will come, my dear Aryan colleague, when you will have to answer to your maker," she said. God was about the only safe way left to challenge Hitler in Germany, and only indirectly.

"Fortunately, my dear Catholic colleague," answered Schwarz, "no one has to answer to your popish idolatry in the Führer's Germany, or in the hereafter."

"Calm down over there, you two," Franzoser half-suggested, half-ordered.

Workplaces across Germany were constantly disrupted by lower-ranking staff members using their Nazi Party membership to challenge authority. Franzoser was sensitive to Schwarz's Party position. But since Schwarz was such a blowhard, he posed less of a threat than the legions of unknown informers that penetrated every corner of the Fatherland.

"Notwithstanding Janski's jest," continued Franzoser, "we're all in this together. I consider myself thankful the Führer has revitalized our economy so quickly. The Allied terms after the war were criminal to our country – billions in reparations, huge chunks of territory and compatriots lost, no army to speak of. The Führer has cast off those shackles. He delivered us from evil! *Heil Hitler!*"

Everyone, even Maria, joined in the obligatory salute and cry, "*Heil Hitler!*"

Becker hated being pinned into this, but he went along. He didn't need any suspicion over his loyalty. He thought about the boss leading the office in this. It was ironic that Franzoser, the most French-hating German he knew, was named "Frenchman."

Franzoser himself appreciated the irony. "I curse the Catholic France that stole from my Protestant ancestors. They stole billions from us after the World War. They still want to hem us in. Every day I thank God for the Führer revitalizing German strength and independence."

Franzoser suddenly seemed to notice himself offending the Catholics who worked for him. "Of course, by Catholic France, I mean zealous Catholics, not that Catholic Germans are in any way inferior Germans. I certainly hope the Führer militarizes the German Rhineland before the French occupy it again."

That was precisely the problem that now confronted Churchill, Becker knew. Churchill needed to know immediately if and when Hitler planned to move. And he needed to know whether German forces could handle an Anglo-French attack, as Hitler boasted.

The vital information that Becker sought would help Churchill immensely. This might be the perfect time to stop Hitler – if he was bluffing. And Churchill had more taste for fighting back than anyone.

"But Herr Franzoser, I beg your pardon," intervened Frau Cassels. She used the respectful tone that Franzoser allowed his employees for challenging him. "Don't you think it's too risky to provoke the Allies in the Rhineland?"

"Life is full of risks, my dear lady," answered the boss. "It would be risky *not* to fortify our own territory."

"But the French invasion in '23 destroyed my family's savings, and the lives of so many," said Frau Cassels. "The Führer has made life so good for us again. Why do we need this?"

"My dear Frau Cassels, you need to understand the realities of foreign affairs. If the Führer doesn't stand firm, what's to stop a sudden French attack, like in '23? Some in France wish they had not left in 1930. They want to come back."

"I see." Frau Cassels more gave up than conceded.

"I just hope that it all works out for the best," added Fräulein Derder, in support of her friend. "I lost a fiancé and two brothers in the war. My mother does not need to lose her grandsons in the next generation."

"Oh, it will work out for the best," answered Franzoser. "The Führer is a genius, and a patient one. He knows how to protect Germans for time immemorial."

"I would like to see him protect all Germans right away," said Frau Alleswohl, "including Germans separated from Germany by the Allies. Not least my cousins in Poland, who complain bitterly of their treatment by Polish authorities. Curse those Slavic beasts!"

The hatred in Frau Alleswohl's voice gave pause even to Schwarz. She sent chills down Becker's spine. The conversation halted abruptly, as several workers looked around their mail stacks to contemplate the day. The sunlit mailroom suddenly seemed like the least desirable place to be. Becker observed these reactions with fascination. Germans overwhelmingly supported Hitler, but many of them did not want to contemplate the ugly consequences.

"What do you think, Herr Becker?" asked Franzoser. "You seem a serious sort. But you never let us know what you think about the great issues of the day."

Becker knew what the rest did not. Hitler firmly planned to remilitarize the Rhineland. His colleagues viewed the idea as more hypothetical.

Franzoser hardly seemed to be hoping for dissent from Becker, unless to smack it down. To come to Frau Cassel's aid would be imprudently chivalrous. Becker wasn't sure how to react, so he played it by instinct, watching Franzoser's reaction to every word.

"I don't trust the French," said Becker. "That makes me anxious about the Rhineland, whether we arm it or leave it exposed to France. I'm glad I don't have to make the decision. Thank God it lies in the able hands of the Führer. May his wisdom protect us!"

"So you don't have a position?" persisted Franzoser. All heads turned curiously to Becker, the quiet colleague who rarely spoke an opinion about anything.

"I agree the German army must secure the Rhineland," answered Becker. "I trust the Führer to lead us wisely," he lied.

Franzoser looked satisfied.

Becker preferred to lie than play dumb. That was too hard in long-term settings, where his intelligence was appreciated. Instead, he played informed and reflective, yet indecisive.

Becker saw Maria watching him apprehensively from across the room. He allowed his eyes to meet hers only briefly. He sensed a tinge of nervousness in her, but only because he was looking for it. The others probably couldn't see it. She seemed in good control of his secrets.

"The sooner, the better," insisted Frau Alleswohl. She wanted German aggression now.

"Don't worry," reassured Herr Schwarz. "The Führer will not abandon your kindred in Poland or anywhere else. He will lead all Germans to our united destiny!"

"It's a shame they won't all be together in time for the Olympic games in Berlin this summer," said Alleswohl. "I heard there are some great German national athletes in Czechoslovakia who refuse to participate under a Slavic flag."

Becker had not heard this one. He very much doubted it. But he found the rumor an interesting one.

"Have you seen the stadium they're building?" asked Schwarz, to no one in particular. "It's absolutely splendid."

"*Heil Hitler!*" rang out two voices at the front door.

Two SS guards flung out their salutes and an SS officer entered the room between them. Their voices in hailing Hitler lacked Franzoser's buoyancy. They were dry and mean and menacing. So were their pitch-black uniforms.

Becker immediately recognized the man from the underground – the demonic Nazi who had hauled off the toothless old man.

The officer was short and thin, with a handsome angular face, and short brown hair barely showing under his uniform cap. He slowly walked into the room, holding his hands behind his back, scanning everyone through his steel spectacles. He patiently scrutinized everyone. He'd take his time with whatever purpose brought him here.

Were they here for Becker? His desk was far from any doors. The windows were well closed for winter. There would be no quick escape. If he had any chance, it was probably after being escorted out.

Becker tried to steady his eyes while his mind raced. He dared not share any knowing looks with Maria. The officer was scanning for precisely that sort of odd behavior. Becker hoped his eyes did not betray his pounding heart.

"*Heil Hitler!*" shouted Schwarz as he leapt up from his seat and thrust his arm into the air, after an awkwardly long lag since the guards' own thunderous entrance.

"*Heil Hitler,*" saluted everyone else anxiously, while they stared at the officer. Even Franzoser was unenthusiastic.

"Yes," said the officer. "It will be a splendid Olympic Games." This was his only acknowledgment of Schwarz's nervous eagerness to please. "Interesting that you should be discussing that just now."

"You, there," the officer pointed at Becker.

It's still too soon to make a break for it, thought Becker.

"Yes?" said Becker.

"You seem like the athletic type. From a competitive point of view, how would you predict our national team's performance this summer?" He slowly sauntered toward Becker.

"Well, sir, our boxers are especially strong."

"Our boxers. Yes, yes. . . . Does your faith in the German race go only so far as the raw fight?"

"Oh no, sir. Not at all. I daresay we will find successes in all kinds of events."

"I see you have an affinity for boxing. Very interesting." The officer slowly pivoted around to look at the rest of the office staff. They stared back dumbly.

"And you there, my dear Frau," he looked at Maria's right ring finger, where Germans wear their wedding bands. "Rather, Fräulein. Do you follow athletics?"

"No, sir. I'm sorry, I don't," said Maria.

"That's all right. But certainly you must have an opinion on whether it's a good idea if ladies participate in the games?"

"If the authorities see fit and some ladies want to do it – God knows, not I! – then I don't see why not." Maria was beginning to lose her composure under the pressure. Small beads of sweat began to form on her forehead.

"What good do you think it could serve?" asked the SS officer.

"Well, uh, besides encouraging ladies to challenge themselves," stammered Maria. "Uh, it can promote greater health and fitness among the whole population."

"Including the sons and brothers of these athlete-ladies, to prepare them to serve the Fatherland?" The SS officer bore down hard on Maria.

"Yes, sir, of course." Maria averted her gaze back to her desk after answering this last question, as she tried to calm herself.

"Fräulein Geberich." He knew her name! Maria jerked her head back up. She was visibly stunned. She blinked her eyes, near tears.

Becker held his breath. They weren't here for him at all. Poor Maria! She knew from her tortured interrogation three years ago what now faced her.

"Your brother Max advocated ladies' athletics as some sort of liberation," said the officer.

Maria's colleagues gasped collectively at the direction this was taking. The officer took no note of them.

"The Führer views athletics as a means of strengthening our future mothers," he continued. "What view do you take?"

"Both, if I may, sir," answered Maria.

"Hedging our bets, are we? Fräulein, we've turned up one of your old . . . associates, a lady athlete as it turns out. She couldn't help but remember your friendship in her . . . discussions with us." The officer looked around the mailroom. He smiled fiendishly at that line's chilling effect.

"We found her so interesting that we want to talk with her friends, as well. Please come with us."

Maria moved with all the numbness of someone taken very ill. She fumbled at her desk before remembering to collect her coat and hat.

Her colleagues stared in stunned silence. Even Schwarz's mouth hung open in shock. They heard every rustling of Maria donning her coat, as if the act were a wailing cello solo, and not near-silence itself.

"*Heil Hitler!*" shouted the guards, piercing the deadened silence of the mailroom. They exited immediately after the officer and Maria.

For two full minutes, no one spoke. No one worked. A couple of them shifted a piece or two of mail in unfocused stupefaction. Fräulein Derder cried a little, and Frau Cassels offered her a handkerchief. Herr Schwarz looked both agitated and stunned. He made no attempt at his usual Nazi Party commentary on what had transpired.

Damn! Becker thought to himself. *Damn! Damn! Damn! Maria does not deserve this!* His mind raced and raced to think of how he might rescue her. Nothing. He wondered what was the real story behind her arrest. Had she already made inquiries to obtain Wehrmacht uniforms? Was that the act that got her in trouble? Or was it just coincidence, some friend of hers suddenly in trouble? Or something completely different?

Perhaps Maria was already involved in some illegal resistance that Becker didn't know about. If it was coincidence, the timing was terrible, for Maria and Becker both. From their conversation the night before, Maria was now compromised. She had offered to help Becker infiltrate German military secrets. If she were otherwise innocent, last night's visit with Becker could destroy her.

Becker looked at the clock. Of course, he was now in danger, too. He began to think in terms of hours of safety, not days or weeks.

Sooner or later, Maria would almost certainly tell the Gestapo about him. How could he save her? He wracked his brain.

Franzoser finally broke the silence. "Ladies and Gentlemen, we can only hope that Maria has done nothing to compromise herself and that she will be back with us shortly. In the Führer's Germany, justice will surely prevail. We can all take heart in that."

Fräulein Derder now broke down into sobs. Her friend tried to console her. "The poor thing, the poor thing!" Derder kept repeating.

"Herr Franzoser?" Becker asked.

"Yes?"

"I would please like to place a phone call to Fräulein Geberich's brother on her behalf, if I may."

Franzoser raised his eyebrows. Any sort of active sympathy for the recently detained was bold, perhaps worse. "Well, of course." Franzoser's tone was skeptical, even suspicious.

"Thank you," said Becker.

Becker picked up the receiver. "Operator? Yes, I'm looking please for the Army Liaison Office."

After a minute, again, "Yes, hello, operator, I'd like the Army Liaison, please."

Becker's co-workers looked on in depressed curiosity. Most of them knew that Rupert Mencke was a secretary there. But Becker spoke with unusual authority.

"Hello, Liaison Office? . . . Yes, I'm looking please for Herr Rupert Mencke. . . . Oh, you are Herr Mencke? Good, I've found you."

The conversation absorbed the whole Kristner mail staff.

"My name is Becker. I work with your sister, Maria Geberich. . . . Well, the thing is, sir, I just wanted to let you know that she has, well, been taken in for questioning by the SS. All they said was that a former colleague of your sister's was in trouble and had named your sister."

Becker paused to listen to Mencke.

"No, sir, I'm sorry I don't know anything more. I just thought you should know. And I thought, you know, with your Army connections you might be able to . . . see her." That was euphemistic enough, Becker thought.

"Yes, sir. Goodbye, sir." Becker replaced the phone. His colleagues looked at him in wonderment of his initiative and firmness. Even Franzoser seemed impressed.

For the rest of the day, Kristner mail deliveries were slow. Maria's colleagues worked and walked in shock. When closing hours finally came, they somberly left the office and went home.

Despite the scheduled dinner party with Anna Lande's cousins, Becker walked home slowly. He was curious about their scandalous stories of the younger Hitler in Munich. But he could scarcely think about that.

Becker analyzed his situation. He considered and reconsidered all the possibilities. Was Maria already in active resistance before he enlisted her? He doubted it. But it was possible. He thought the most likely reason for her arrest was that she had already pursued the Army uniforms he had requested. That was the worst possibility for her, and for him, because her guilt would be indisputable and all his fault.

Becker asked himself whether to return to work tomorrow. Even staying the last hours today had constituted a risk. If the Gestapo were successful with Maria, his cover would be blown within days or even hours.

He asked himself whether this was the moment to begin operating from hiding. It would be much harder to work that way, to get the Army documents he needed. Yet any hour could bring the fatal knock at the door, at home or at work. Just returning to his boarding house tonight was a great unknown. Should he do the prudent thing and turn away from Maricfel Strasse before it was too late?

Becker chose to hold his course.

CHAPTER TWELVE

Becker slowed his pace on the cobblestone sidewalks. He quietly approached his residence under the cloudy, dark skies of the winter evening. He looked around for anything unusual.

The Gestapo could be waiting for him at Maricfel Strasse. Maria might already be dead. He shook his head in guilt and sorrow at her arrest.

As Becker reached the Lande townhouse, his heart jumped at every sound – car doors closing, house doors swinging open, pots and pans banging in kitchens. He noticed nothing unusual outside. He heard women's voices laughing inside the house – Anna and her cousins.

But up there, in an unlit third-story window, he noticed a quick movement. Anna Lande didn't even use her top floor! Becker contemplated whether to enter. He could still walk away and abandon his cover . . . or at least he thought he could. He wondered if this were his last free moment on earth.

He looked through the tree branches to the starry evening sky above. He sniffed the small bunch of flowers he'd bought for the little dinner party. He took a deep breath of crisp winter air and warily opened the front door.

"Good evening, Frau Lande," he said. He looked into the narrow kitchen, his fedora hat in one hand and flowers in the other. No sign of the Gestapo down here.

"Oh!" said Anna. "What nice flowers you've found in the middle of winter!" Anna seemed genuinely surprised at this typical dinner guest gift. "Thank you very much!"

"My pleasure," said Becker. "It sounds like your cousins are already here?"

"Yes, they arrived about half an hour ago. They're in the living room, on the other side of the kitchen service window here, listening to us right now." Anna smiled as she teased them.

She raised her voice. "Girls, why don't you say hello to Herr Becker?"

"Don't get up, ladies," insisted Becker. He trotted through the hall and around the staircase to the living room. Liesl and Gertrude were standing by the sofa.

"Very pleased to meet you, Frau . . . ?" he asked.

"Anders," answered Liesl, the shorter brunette.

"Hausen," answered Gertrude, the tall grayish-blonde.

"I look forward to a splendid evening with you!" Becker took their hands in turn and bowed to each woman. "Please excuse me for a moment." Anna's cousins nodded their heads and sat down on the sofa.

Becker ostensibly went to hang up his coat and hat and to freshen up for dinner. What he wanted was to explore the top floor.

As he neared the top of the first flight of stairs, he heard footsteps above! He sprung into his own room across the landing and eased the door shut behind him. Quickly he reached under his jacket and pulled out his Luger handgun. His bedroom light was still out.

Becker stood behind his door and held the doorknob. If anyone tried to enter, he would jerk the door open and then closed. He should have plenty of warning. He'd tried the upper staircase when he first moved in. Almost all its stairs squeaked terribly.

There it was! The stairs squeaked, slightly. The stalker took several steps at a time. He had to be a small man not to make more noise. Next Becker heard a door open and close quickly. He saw a brief light coming under his door . . . from Nadine's room.

"The flag raised high," she sang, "The rows in tight formation . . . ." That murderous Nazi anthem.

Becker opened his door. His hand rested on his gun in his pocket. He looked into the hallway. Nadine continued singing behind her closed door. She was his stalker from the third floor.

For the moment, Becker didn't care if Nadine meant something sinister with the Horst-Wessel Song. He remained beyond the Gestapo's grasp at least a few hours more.

Becker replaced the gun to his dresser and returned to the living room. He sat in the armchair next to Liesl's end of the sofa. Nadine remained in her room.

"So what brings you to Berlin?" he asked the cousins.

Liesl, closest to Becker, answered. "We had a great opportunity to come to Berlin and visit our cousin Anna."

"Opportunity?" asked Becker.

"Yes," answered Gertrude. "The Reich is hosting a week-long convention for young war widows, those of us who spent only a few married weeks with their husbands and never got to have children."

Liesl laughed. "My cousin Gertrude means, we were young when we were widowed. Look at us now!" They both laughed.

Liesl is too modest, thought Becker. She looked barely older than thirty. She and Gertrude were both very young in the face, very spirited. He knew they had to be almost forty, but it was hard to believe in Liesl's case.

"Rudolf Hess spoke to the convention today," added Gertrude. "He said it was a shame we had never had children, but wouldn't we like to help raise the children of others? For the sake of expanding our population. He wants us to work in new orphanages."

"I wonder whose children they are?" asked Liesl.

"That's the third time you've asked that," said Gertrude.

"Don't you think it's important?" asked Liesl.

Nadine entered the room. She wore a black dress with white flowers, black stockings, black shoes, and a tight-fitting red sweater. Her blonde hair was freshly curled, and she wore a modest amount of make-up. She sat between Liesl and Gertrude.

"Hi Nadine," said Liesl.

"Of course it's important," Gertrude answered Liesl. "You see, Herr Becker, Hess has us thinking. And I mean all of us – thousands of war widows our age, all in a dither this afternoon. He says he wants us young enough to see infants into adulthood. And childless, so we can dedicate ourselves to the task."

"I really wish I could have had children," regretted Liesl. "Our cousin Anna is so lucky, at least she had a baby before her husband died." She smiled at sixteen-year-old Nadine and pinched her cheek.

"Once we lost our husbands," continued Liesl, "we had no other chances. Millions of men died in the war, all of them our age. Two-thirds of the boys in my high school class didn't come home. . . ."

"Who needs a husband?" interjected Nadine. "I mean, good Aryan babies are born every year to unwed mothers. Of course it's not ideal. But it serves the Fatherland."

"Young one," started Gertrude, "watch yourself! You have no idea how hard it is to raise a child. Don't go off and try it alone."

"How would you know?" snapped Nadine.

From the kitchen, Anna listened to her daughter provoking their cousins. She opened the service window to the living room. "Herr Becker, could you please lend me a hand for a moment?"

Becker walked around to the kitchen.   Anna rolled down the wooden-flats shutter on the service window.

The living room conversation got heated, with Nadine debating Gertrude and Liesl on theories of parenting.

Anna lowered her voice for Becker.   "I'm sorry about my daughter's behavior recently."

"Not a problem," replied Becker.

"Yes it is, I'm afraid," said Anna.   "I'm glad you knew her a year ago, before she got so testy and provocative.   Hopefully this is just a phase, not some kind of permanent brainwashing by . . . ."   She trailed off.   She knew that Becker understood her.   It was dangerous enough just to imply it.

He looked a little surprised, Anna noticed.   But he didn't seem upset that Anna was badmouthing Nazi propaganda.   He neither encouraged her nor discouraged her from continuing.   Anna didn't think Becker cared much for the Nazis, especially the racist stuff they pushed on Nadine in school.

At this point, Anna was too worn down to hold up her guard to everyone.   She used to like the Nazis' can-do attitude.   She'd even voted for them.   But in the past year, Anna had changed her mind completely.   The trouble was, she had no one to confide in.   She didn't know who might turn her in.   She thought Nazi propaganda was responsible for most of her troubles with her daughter.   She was near her wit's end.

She wanted to enlist Becker's help.   If he didn't respond favorably to this first part of the conversation, she would back off.

Finally, Becker replied.   "You haven't seemed to be getting along well the past couple of months.   She would've been a challenge at this age anyway, you know."

"It's been nearly unbearable," said Anna.   More than once she had considered sending Nadine off to live with Katerina, Anna's sister, in the Bavarian countryside.

"I always thought I was prepared for my child's adolescence.   But this . . . this . . . ."   She looked toward the living room and lowered her voice to a whisper.   "This utter nonsense in my daughter's head should not be tolerated!"   Anna was afraid.   She could be arrested and sent away for those words.   Her eyes pleaded for Becker's mercy.

"It sounds like they're chatting away nicely, now."   He changed the topic.   Indeed, the living room conversation had grown more amiable.

"Yes, but who knows how dinner will go," said Anna.   She wondered whether to continue this conversation with Becker.   She wanted to ask him to exercise some authority on Nadine. To do so, he'd have to enter dangerous territory. So much of Nadine's teenage defiance was cloaked in Nazi propaganda. Even indirect confrontation could get Anna or Becker in trouble.

Anna stared at Becker. He looked back at her. But she couldn't read his eyes. He certainly didn't rush to the Nazis' defense. But Anna wasn't confident he was fully on her side, either. At least not enough to say so. She didn't blame him, but she was disappointed. She sighed and dropped the subject.

"Nadine!" called Anna. "Could you help me set the table, please?"

"Gladly, mother," answered the Nadine, unexpectedly politely.

Anna looked at Becker and raised her eyebrows in surprise. Becker raised his shoulders to show he didn't know what to make of it, either.

Nadine gave Becker a coquettish smile as she pressed past him in the narrow kitchen doorway. He returned to the living room. Anna turned to the stove and rolled her eyes at Nadine's behavior. She didn't like Nadine bothering her boarder in any way. But this wasn't the moment for a lecture.

"How shall I arrange the places, Mama?" asked Nadine.

"Pour water and white wine for everyone," answered Anna. "Use the porcelain and crystal from the china cabinet. Put the two of us on the kitchen side. Other than that, it doesn't matter. We can all see each other in a circle anyway."

A few minutes later, Nadine returned from the dining room. "Everything's ready! May I help bring in the food?"

Anna paused, suspicious of Nadine's sudden courtesy. She hadn't seen Nadine like this in months. "Certainly, thank you."

When the table was ready, Anna walked into the living room with her hands together in front of her chest. Her apron was off, and she felt elegant in her long, dark purple dress. "Dinner is served!" she smiled.

As they settled into their seats, Anna looked at her daughter and said to all, "Let us pray." She watched Nadine roll her eyes.

Then Anna bowed her head. "*Alle guten Gaben, Alles was wir haben, Kommt O Gott von Dir. Wir danken Dir dafür. Amen.*" All good things, all that we have, comes oh God from you. We thank you for it. Amen.

"Amen," murmured the others. Then they took their spoons to their soup bowls.

"The leek soup is marvelous," said Becker.

Anna knew Becker had no choice but to compliment her. She felt flattered anyway. "Thank you."

With small talk and hungry sips, the five of them finished their soup and moved to the main course.

"The roast chicken tastes every bit as good as it has smelled for the past hour," said Gertrude. "Wouldn't you agree, Nadine?"

Nadine seemed surprised by the question. Caught with a large piece in her mouth, she could only nod yes.

"And your spätzle is better than anything we have at home in Bavaria," added Liesl. Anna remembered learning to cook the stove-roasted potato pasta from her late mother-in-law, a native of northern Germany.

"Mama's spätzle is the best anywhere!" interjected Nadine.

Now Anna was stunned. What had gotten into her daughter? This wasn't the same Nadine of the past six months or more.

"Why thank you, Nadine," smiled Anna to her daughter. "It's your grandmother's recipe." Anna watched Nadine's face transform into sweetness at the memory of her beloved Oma.

"Mother," added Nadine casually. "My friend Susanne is going with her parents to the Harz mountains for the weekend. They invited me to go along. It would be wonderful to go. What do you say? May I please go with them?"

Anna paused her eating. So this is why Nadine was behaving so well, she thought.

"What about little Karl and Almut? You and I are supposed to babysit them Friday night."

"Oh, Mama," replied Nadine. "You can manage them by yourself, can't you?"

"Perhaps, though you promised your help before I agreed to keep them. . . . More important, what about your grades? They've been suffering recently."

Anna wanted to be discreet about this in front of her guests. But it was Nadine's choice to ask a delicate question in their company. "Shouldn't you better use the weekend for some studying?"

"I can study during the trip," said Nadine.

"Hmm." Anna thought about it and looked at her daughter.

"No, Nadine, I don't think that would be a good idea."

"But mother . . . ."

"If things improve at school by the next report, then perhaps you can take such a trip."

"Then it will be too late!" Nadine was scowling. She unveiled her resentful mood. "Ski season is almost over! I'm getting my very first chance to ski, and you're going to ruin it for me? You . . . You . . . I hate you!"

"Nadine Lande!" Anna shouted and raised her hand to smack her daughter. Nadine's eyes widened in surprise.

"*Never* talk to your mother that way. Ever. Now apologize."

"Sorry," mumbled Nadine. Anna lowered her hand.

"Your Papa would be ashamed of you. So would your Oma."

The memory of Nadine's father and grandmother remained Anna's last resort. Nadine had adored them both, in relationships untainted by current concerns and conflicts.

"Completely ashamed," repeated Anna.

It worked. Tears welled up in Nadine's eyes. "I just wanted . . . ," she barely kept her composure, "to do something exciting for a change." She broke down crying, "It's not fair . . . ."

"I apologize, everyone," Anna said above her daughter's sobs. All three of the others shook their heads reassuringly, in support of Anna. She felt stronger and calmer in their presence.

Nadine looked around, stopped crying, and pulled herself into an upright posture. She wiped off the tears with her napkin.

Anna took charge. "For that, Nadine, you will spend the weekend not only in Berlin, but in your room. Do I make myself clear?"

"Yes, mother," answered Nadine softly. She didn't look at her mother. Anna sensed Nadine was already plotting something.

"Now let's please enjoy the rest of our meal," said Anna.

For five minutes they ate in silence.

"Nadine, darling, will you please make the tea?" With the others here, Anna had deeper reservoirs of patience with her daughter. She addressed Nadine lovingly, as if her daughter had been nice all evening.

"Yes, mother," answered Nadine, and she went to the kitchen to heat the water.

Anna noticed that both of her cousins had emptied their wine glasses for the second time this evening. She hesitatingly refilled them.

"Thank you," said Liesl. Gertrude nodded the same sentiment.

"You know, Anna," said Gertrude, "last time we visited, I never got to finish telling you that story about the Führer."

"Not now, please, Gertrude," said Anna. "You've been drinking." She had warned her cousins about uttering indiscretions in front of her Hitler Maidens daughter. If they drank too much, their tongues might show no restraint.

Anna was scared. She was also curious. She very much wanted to hear the story. But if it spoke ill of Hitler, Nadine's response would be unpredictable. Anna suspected her daughter may well report Gertrude to the authorities. Becker was an unknown, too, though he didn't seem the informer type.

"Nonsense!" said Gertrude. "There's no harm in repeating what the Munich newspapers all published."

"What's more," said Anna, "my daughter is still too young to be hearing that sort of thing."

Anna was certain Nadine was listening from the kitchen. She was desperate to cut off Gertrude.

"Gertrude will just tell the facts," said Liesl. "It's all right."

"If you don't want to believe it, that's fine," said Gertrude. "But you can't stop me from telling you."

Anna was defeated. She sat back nervously in her chair to listen.

"As you know – but you don't, Herr Becker – I'm a maid in the apartment building where the Führer lives when he comes back to Munich," Gertrude started.

"Now, these are very nice places. Very many, large rooms. Very expensive. Nice enough, in fact, for multiple residents per apartment. In the late twenties, Adolph Hitler moved in. Some of the neighbors liked that. Others didn't. He was on the margins of German politics at the time. Of course, they're all thrilled to have him now, whenever he stays at his place in Munich." She took another long drink of wine.

"Anyway, soon after Herr Hitler rented the place, this young woman moves in. About twenty years old. She's got her own rooms, their maid told me. Her name was Geli, short for Angelika, Hitler's niece."

The hot water whistled in the kitchen. A moment later, Nadine returned to the table.

Anna saw that Nadine had left the steeping tea in the kitchen. Perhaps Nadine was so distracted by Gertrude's story that she forgot it.

Nadine sat down, captivated, leaning over the table to hear about the Führer's personal life.

"It was never clear why Geli moved from Vienna to live with her Uncle Adolph in Munich," said Gertrude. "Their maid guessed Geli liked living in a different city. A lot of young Germans, after all, move around at that age. But the maid saw why she stayed for two years. Her uncle absolutely adored her. They hung out with other top Nazis. Those men lavished attention on her. She didn't have movie-star looks, but she more than made up for it in other ways. Tall, wavy dark brown hair, broad faced.   She sparkled like you wouldn't believe!   Just riveting.   She was the center of that little social world for two years."

Anna watched Nadine.   The girl looked star-struck with envy for Geli's life with the Führer.

Gertrude finished her third glass of wine.   She clearly enjoyed telling this story.

"I can see you're fascinated, Nadine," said Gertrude.   "You should have seen it.   We never saw Herr Hitler so happy as in those days when Geli lived in Munich. . . .   But there was a darker side to all this."

This is what Anna feared.   Nadine furrowed her eyebrows.   Anna knew her daughter would not tolerate any hint of a flaw in Hitler's character.

"Herr Hitler adored his niece.   That much was fine.   But it went farther.   He was enraptured, smitten . . . in love.   Geli returned his affections.   My employer . . . ," Gertrude giggled.   "My employer . . . ," Gertrude and Liesl both giggled.

"This is the best part!" said Liesl.

"My employer said she heard Geli screaming her uncle's name in the night: 'Alf! Alf! Yes! Oh, Uncle Alf!'"

Anna glanced at Nadine, whose eyes bulged and mouth gaped, uncertain what to make of this.   Anna lifted her hand over her eyes and massaged her temples.   Trying to stop her cousin would only drag out the story-telling.   Better to keep quiet and let her finish, thought Anna.

Liesl and Gertrude laughed and laughed.   Becker sat there like a statue.

"More than once, mind you," continued Gertrude.   "And from Herr Hitler's personal room!"   The two cousins laughed again.

"For awhile, Geli had a lot of fun in Munich.   She enjoyed life with her uncle and other men twice her age."

Suddenly Gertrude's face went dark.   "But of course it couldn't last.   A young spirit like Geli wasn't going to spend all her youth on an older man.   Herr Hitler wasn't going to tolerate anything else.   He became insanely jealous.   Geli had an affair with Herr Hitler's chauffeur.   The man was lucky to escape with his life."

Gertrude had called Hitler murderously jealous.   Anna watched Nadine squint her eyes in displeasure.

"It got worse.   Geli wasn't happy anymore.   Even the maid upstairs, I could see that.   She was ready to move on."   Gertrude hoisted the last drops of wine into her mouth.

"Herr Hitler became more the jealous lover than the happy one. Their maid told me he and Geli had awful arguments, yelling at each other and carrying on. She decided to move back to Vienna. He said he wouldn't let her. She said he couldn't stop her. . . ."

Gertrude and Liesl sighed at the same moment. They suddenly seemed stone-cold sober. Gertrude leaned over the table and whispered harshly, "The next day she was dead. Shot in the chest with Herr Hitler's own gun."

Nadine gasped.

"It's all true, young cousin," Liesl said to Nadine. "The Munich papers covered it extensively at the time. Some insisted Herr Hitler did it. Others claimed he was up in Nuremberg at the time, that it was suicide."

"In any case," said Gertrude, "she was dead. Herr Hitler left town for days. The other big Nazis were very worried. But after a week or two, things quieted down. Herr Hitler snapped out of it. Mark my words, he loved that girl like no other. The maid says he still keeps her picture in his bedroom. I've never seen him so happy since then, not with Fräulein Braun or anyone."

"Gertrude thinks it was suicide," said Liesl. "I'm not so sure. . . ."

Anna's eyes closed at the indiscretion. She opened them to see Nadine's face burning with anger, her thin lips pursed to near invisibility.

Twice Nadine started to speak and stopped, trying to find the right words. Then she stormed off to the kitchen.

The four of them looked at each other across the table.

Anna didn't know what to say. Finally, "Liesl and Gertrude, what's it like, being around so many other war widows just like you, widowed very young right at the end of the war?"

"Frankly," chuckled Liesl, "it's not much different than going grocery shopping in the late afternoon back home – the widow's hour, we call it. Except that here at the convention they're all on the younger side. There are so many of us widows, and many of us are childless. So when women with children or husbands are greeting their families at home, we childless ones are out doing our grocery shopping." Gertrude nodded and laughed.

Nadine returned with some cookies she'd baked earlier, and five cups of tea already poured.

Anna had taught Nadine to pour tea at the table, so it would be its hottest. She looked past this small failure of her daughter's. Nadine distributed the cups around the table, and put the cream and sugar in the middle.

"My goodness, this tea is strong," Gertrude said to Nadine. "You're developing quite a taste for bitterness, aren't you?"

For a moment Nadine just stared back coldly. Then she said, "The sharper flavor makes me feel warmer on a winter night like this one."

Anna looked into the darkest cup of tea she'd ever seen. "I think I'll put sugar in mine, if you don't mind," she said. She then passed the sugar to her guests, who each added some.

"Auntie Liesl," started Nadine, "What is your opinion on why we lost the war?"

Anna noted the aggressive tone. She was sure her daughter now hated Liesl for calling the Führer a murderer.

"Mother says it's because the Americans were too much for us," said Nadine. "That's not what they teach us in school, though. They say it was the Jews stabbing Germany in the back. What do you think?"

"Frankly, Nadine, I wasn't paying much attention at the time. I was devastated when my Harald died three months after our wedding."

Liesl sounded more defensive than mournful, Anna noticed, as if she recognized her imprudent smearing of the Führer.

Gertrude piped up enthusiastically. "We could have beaten the Americans! They had no business arming the English, anyway. We lost the war because we lost the will to win. It's as simple as that. You should've seen the defeatism everywhere right before we surrendered. Once our soldiers got polluted with that Socialist claptrap, all was lost. Damn Jews!"

Anna winced. "Gertrude!"

"My apologies, Anna. But you and your husband were always wrong about why we lost the war."

Anna saw Nadine smiling to find an ally against her.

"See mother, I told you so!" Nadine basked in her evening's one triumph. "I almost asked our teacher about your different views on the war."

Anna was shocked. She wondered if Nadine understood that such a thing could get her mother sent to a concentration camp. Was Nadine threatening her?

Anna turned to see Becker's reactions and was surprised. He was barely paying attention. He blinked his eyes over and over again, and seemed to be highly distracted.

"Herr Becker, are you all right?" she asked.

"Yes, yes, thank you. . . . I seem to have gotten something in my eye."

"If you need to excuse yourself, you won't offend us." Anna was perplexed and worried.

Becker considered her offer. He had nothing in his eye. He was suddenly incredibly sleepy, as if . . . . He looked at his teacup and then at Nadine. She tried to suppress a smirk. Becker's head was swimming. He could barely keep his eyes focused.

He stood up and steadied himself on the back of his chair. "I do think I ought to tend to my eye. It seems to do better when I blink it shut. It was a lovely meal." He looked at Anna. "Thank you. And thank you for the company, everyone. I'm very sorry to excuse myself like this." He managed to nod his head at each of the others before walking what he hoped was a straight line out of the dining room.

Becker held the staircase rail tight as he climbed to his room. *Sleeping powder*, he thought. *The girl must have put some in my tea.*

His thoughts were a scattered collage of the dinner's conversation. He struggled to remember all the details of Gertrude's story from Munich. Near the top of the stairs, the sudden recollection of Maria's arrest at work jolted him awake, but only for a matter of seconds. He stumbled straight into his room, closed his door, and fell into his bed.

CHAPTER THIRTEEN

Thursday, February 13

Heavy knocking on his door startled Becker in the middle of the night.

"Herr Becker, are you in there?" Anna called.

His brain was so doped up, Becker had no idea how long she'd been knocking. It was loud.

Becker saw Nadine's outline in the dark, kneeling on the floor beside his bed. She leaned over to whisper, "Have you nice dreams, Mister Becker?"

The question and his name were *in English*!

"Who knew we had an Englishman under our roof all this time, dreaming his English dreams?" Nadine asked in German.

Becker tried to think while he watched Nadine's silhouette. He was so disoriented and so deeply fatigued from whatever sleeping powder she'd put in his evening tea.

Anna's knocking continued.

"What is it that's got your mind on England?" asked Nadine softly.

Becker started to respond, but his mind produced only English words. He didn't answer.

"Herr Becker?" Anna called again from outside his door. "Nadine is gone."

"Who are you, really?" asked Nadine.

"Herr Becker?" Anna knocked constantly and loudly.

"Perhaps I should report your English to the police?" whispered Nadine.

"I'm coming in Herr Becker, if you're in there," warned Anna. He heard the doorknob turn.

He blinked his eyes and was shocked by the morning sunlight. Nadine had been a dream.

"Herr Becker, you're still here! Nadine and my cousins are already gone for the day. What in the world has gotten into you? You are definitely late for work. This is so unlike you. Are you sick?"

Becker struggled for words as he batted his eyes into consciousness.

"Uhh . . . ," he mustered only a sound.

"Oh dear, you don't look well at all," said Anna. "In all your fifteen months here, I haven't known you so much as to cough. Oh my, you slept in your clothes!" He still lay on top of his covers.

"What time is it?" he asked.

"Already 8:30," she answered.

"Ughhh . . . ," he groaned.

"Shall I call your office and tell them you're sick?" offered Anna.

"No . . . please don't," he insisted. He didn't know why.

"Really, you need more rest," she said.

Becker started to sit up to prove he could. But he felt immediately dizzy and rested on his elbows.

"You see, you need rest," said Anna.

"Please?" He nodded toward his condition of being in bed.

"Oh yes, of course." Anna left him on his bed, easing the door shut behind her.

Becker's mind started to wake up. He pieced everything together. Nadine's tea. Her visit to his dream. His mission. Maria Geberich. . . . Maria's arrest.

Maria. What could he do for her? Nothing. Her brother was the one with connections. Becker had already called him yesterday.

Becker cursed himself. He could have played on Maria's connection to her stepbrother Rupert without her knowing it. That would have been harder for him, and it might still have endangered her in the end. But instead, he'd explicitly implicated her. Under torture, she'd incriminate herself, and him of course. At least he was momentarily free. She was doomed. Becker's sore head was bursting with regret.

So how long did he have? The Gestapo would probably move fast on her, so they wouldn't lose any leads. At most it was a matter of days. Then again, Becker was lucky to have slept through the night, without the fatal knock at the door.

Becker felt the conflict within himself. His mortal instincts told him to go into hiding immediately. His heart and mind told him to report to his job later this morning. Staying put was riskier. But disappearing would call immediate attention to himself, perhaps risking his mission unnecessarily. If his mission failed, Churchill would have nothing on Hitler. The Third Reich would survive. His Nanny Esther's people would suffer even more every year. Who knew how far Hitler would go to hurt the Jews? If Becker's luck held and he held off the Gestapo a few more days, he might expose Hitler's Achilles' heel. Otherwise, the dark side of Germany, which had taken his father's life years ago, would strengthen and thrive.

Becker knew he would hold firm. As long as they didn't come for him, it was best to stay in place and keep a low profile. He gave himself until Saturday night to get the Army documents. If they found him before then, he would try to escape. If he didn't get the documents by then, he would go underground and risk the attention that would draw.

Maria's arrest was tragic for her. It was merely inconvenient for him . . . so far. He would gladly sacrifice anything but his mission, even himself, if it could save Maria.

He pulled his legs to the floor and sat up. This position cleared his mind some. *I can still make a day of it*, he thought.

With a new pair of pants on his legs, but yesterday's shirt still on, Becker cracked open his door to the hallway.

"Frau Lande?" he called downstairs.

"Yes?"

"Will you please call my office for me?" he asked.

"Gladly," she said. "What shall I tell them?"

"Say I was ill during the night. I've recovered enough to come into work later this morning. The number's written by the phone, next to 'Becker at Kristner.'"

As Becker pushed his arms through his clean shirt, his hand felt a folded piece of paper. He pulled it out and opened it.

"Have a good day, Mister . . . Becker???" it read in English.

No! Nadine's visit wasn't just a dream! Becker felt around all his clothes and in his bed for any other notes. He didn't find any.

Nadine had heard him dreaming in English. Saying what? That was crucial.

He put the note in his pocket. He surveyed his meager belongings. They had definitely been rummaged through during the night. Was Nadine simply curious, or would she report him?

Becker quickly checked his hiding spot in the floorboards under the bed. It was untouched. The coat lining with false papers wasn't tampered with, but it was impossible to say if someone had felt the papers.

As he put on his shoes, he could hear Anna taking the blame with Herr Franzoser for letting her boarder sleep late. He admired her. Even in a generation missing millions of war dead men, her character and her looks could easily have allowed Anna a second husband. Yet she chose to dedicate herself to her daughter.

Becker listened closely to Anna's side of the conversation to see if she sensed something wrong at his work. If Maria had recently cracked under Gestapo interrogation, they could be waiting for him at work, or even on their way to his lodging on Maricfel Strasse.

Becker sensed nothing unusual in Anna's conversation with Franzoser. But that didn't mean much.

Although she had already eaten, Anna sipped tea with Becker as he ate his small breakfast. She had taken a holiday from work for her cousins' visit, though she barely saw them.

"I apologize for Nadine's behavior last night," said Anna.

What was Anna talking about? Becker's mind was still slow. Had Nadine told Anna about the drugging? No, Becker remembered their spat about Nadine's weekend plans.

"You mustn't apologize," he said. "You've done a great job raising her on your own, under the circumstances."

Becker was thinking of Nadine's Nazification. How could anyone raise a child under a regime that taught children to spy on their parents?

"You needn't say that, but thank you," she answered. She seemed close to tears.

"How did things go with her this morning?" he asked.

Did Nadine tell you about me speaking English? he thought.

"Fine, actually. We all four sat around and talked about nothing much besides Nadine's gymnastics class at school. She really likes it."

"Since your cousins arrived, I haven't seen much of Martin," said Becker. "Is he still in the picture?"

Anna shrugged. "As far as I know."

Nadine's boyfriend wasn't around as much this week. Martin Lodt's father was the Gestapo block leader for Maricfel Strasse. If Nadine wanted to tell anyone about his English dream, it would be Martin. But only if they were still on good terms. Becker wanted to know.

"Has Martin ever bragged to you again about his father's favor with the Gestapo?" asked Becker.

"I'll bet he uses that on all the girls." Anna shook her head. "Even if it's true, it's ridiculous to go around talking about it. Certainly

Nadine sees that. They're supposed to be the *Geheime* Staatspolizei!" the *Ge*-sta-po, the *secret* state police.

She and Becker actually managed to chuckle over that. Herr Lodt was a quiet man, but on the clumsy side, and too proud to keep a good secret. He must have boasted to his son, Becker thought. The whole street knew Lodt was the local Gestapo block leader . . . as well as the druggist, Becker now remembered. That's where Nadine must have gotten the sleeping powder.

"To tell the truth," said Anna, "I don't think the father's position matters much to Nadine. I don't quite know what she sees in the boy. He's cute enough, but not nearly as strong-willed as my Nadine."

Becker smiled. "Who is?"

Anna smiled back and raised her eyebrows slightly. "Some are. . . ."

Becker just held his grin. With his brain clogged, he couldn't risk any more nuance.

Anna looked at the closed kitchen door and service window. "Herr Becker, may I ask you a favor?"

With Maria in SS hands, and now the charade of Janeck's cats, Becker wasn't really looking to do favors. In three days, he hoped, he'd be out of the Fatherland.

"Of course," he answered. No harm asking.

Anna started a little speech that looked rehearsed and spontaneous at the same time. "Nadine is going to get worse, more dangerous, before she gets better. Or before she moves out, whichever comes first. I can avoid political conversation just as well as you can, Herr Becker." She nodded at him knowingly, but he refused to acknowledge this. "Except that as her mother, if she's insistent, I cannot avoid it."

"Yes, I've noticed her pushing you harder recently," he said.

"So I just wanted to ask, when you're around, if you would please help me keep the conversation on other topics? This is very presumptuous of me, I know, but–"

"I'll try to help," he assured her.

"My Nadine provokes me into dangerous comments. Probably she only wants the power of blackmail over me. But she doesn't understand how quickly such a thing could get out of her control . . . could even orphan her."

Anna was admitting to no heresy against the Third Reich. But the possibility was within her, she was saying. This was an enormous trust to place in Becker. He felt both honored and burdened. He wouldn't be around much longer to help.

He nodded silently to acknowledge the depth of Anna's danger.

He couldn't mention his own danger from Nadine. This morning's departure from Anna's house might be his last, if he ran into trouble. Anna evidently knew nothing about his English dreams.

That was another facet of Becker's dilemma. If he didn't return to the Lande house, Anna might worry enough to call the police. He didn't need that. On the other hand, at home this evening, or even at work this morning, he might find the Gestapo waiting for him. He could be dead sooner than Maria.

This ongoing dilemma was easily the hardest he'd ever faced. There were risks on both sides, going underground or going to his desk job. The danger faced him from at least two sides – what Maria knew about him, and what Nadine knew about him. Becker knew his brain was still struggling to wake up. He felt like he was still hours from a normal state of mind.

"Thank you for waking me up this morning," said Becker. "I apologize for your inconvenience."

"Not at all," she said. "Do take care!"

He stood up to leave. "This evening I'll miss supper. I need to help a colleague with a family death. I won't be home until late, but I'll see you for breakfast tomorrow."

If I manage to spend another night in this house, he thought.

Becker didn't trust his own decision-making with his head still drugged. Going to work could land him on the executioner's block. He wanted to wait a couple of hours before deciding whether to risk it.

So he took a detour. He was supposed to check his new drop-off spot once or twice a week. It was already Thursday.

The sky was clouding over when Becker left the house. He walked in light snowfall to the nearest elevated rail station at Innsbrucker Platz. There, when he thought no one was watching, he threw away the English note Nadine had left in his sleeve. He tore out the word "Becker" and left it in his pocket.

By the time the S-Bahn got to Savigny Platz a half-hour later, snow was falling heavily. When Becker stepped off the train above the street, the frosty winter wind seemed to blow his sleepiness away. He felt fully alert.

Outside the station entrance downstairs, Becker allowed himself to forget his dangers for a moment. He enjoyed walking in the heavy snowfall.

Becker adored snow and how it seemed to purify the world. Ever since moving to London at age twelve, he'd missed the deep snowfall of the Black Forest hills. For a minute or two, the snow at Savigny Platz revived his spirit as much as his brain. It reminded him of a more pleasant Germany, now lost to the world.

Suddenly a different chill hit Becker – the eerie sense of being watched.

Becker shifted his eyes around the square as subtly as possible. He noticed a man watching him from the far side, dressed in a long black coat and a broad-brimmed black hat. Becker pretended not to notice.

The Gestapo was everywhere all the time, he reminded himself. The man might be looking for anything.

Becker walked directly to Café Hildegard and ordered a coffee. A slight turn of the head and a further shift of his eyes showed no sign of the man in black. Becker headed to the toilet.

In the tiny, stinking, poorly lit water closet, Becker relieved himself. While standing there, he looked for the joke about the train. There was a framed joke, but not about a train. "What do you call a man who doesn't withdraw? . . . Daddy." Becker wondered what kind of clientele this was aimed at.

The joke's paper size and color matched the blank sheets McBride had given him in Prague. Becker wondered why any British agent had picked this place out of hundreds of possibilities.

He fastened his trousers but left the toilet unflushed. He removed the framed joke. The bathroom door had no lock. He had to act quickly. Behind the frame was the promised blank sheet of paper, and Becker removed it.

Footsteps approached the unlocked water closet. Becker held the opened picture frame in his hands. He would be in a tough spot if even a perfect stranger walked in on this. He suddenly made strained grunts of constipation. The footsteps stopped in response.

Becker quickly replaced a blank sheet in the frame, camouflaging that sound with more grunts. He held the old blank sheet to the dim light bulb. It had a message! He folded it quickly and put it in his jacket pocket. He took some toilet paper, rubbed it between his hands, and flushed the toilet.

Just when he turned the sink water on, the door opened.

"Everything all right in there?" asked the unseen voice behind him. There was no mirror.

Becker turned to face a gruff, unshaven man, probably not even a customer. Just someone stopping by to use the toilet. The man looked too disoriented to hold a job, much less to be a Gestapo agent. Becker relaxed a little.

Back in the café, Becker retrieved his coffee. He had a straight view outside but saw no sign of the man in black.

He contemplated whether to risk returning to work. If he didn't, the police would surely investigate him. They may or may not link him to Maria. If his disappearance accelerated her interrogation, the Gestapo might be waiting for him at Army headquarters. Then it would be almost impossible for him to carry out his mission.

The Army was one of the few German institutions that Hitler didn't completely dominate. Becker hated it anyway, for taking his father away from him in the Great War. This hatred was older than the Nazis. With fresh coffee in his veins, Becker seethed in renewed anger at that old injustice.

Yes, he would go to Kristner and risk his life there, rather than worsen his chances at the Army break-in. He finished his coffee, paid, and exited to the snowfall.

Becker tried to avoid looking obviously toward the man in black. Twenty yards from the café, he stole a glance while crossing the street. The man had vanished. Nor was there any sign of him on the cold, windy S-Bahn platform.

Becker felt weighed down with potentially incriminating evidence in his pocket, the hidden-ink message. He had the phenolphthalein spray in another pocket. A smart frisking would find both the paper and the small bottle. If he got arrested, he didn't want those on him.

Before he got to Kristner, he would find a restroom where he could decipher and destroy the message.

Colonel Wächter was impatient. It was taking days to sift through the thousands of Beckers in Berlin. What if the man neither lived in Berlin nor had stayed in a hotel here? Or if he lived under a different name?

He'd inquired of the London field agent how common was the name Becker in England. It was too common to pursue that track, he'd learned.

On Tuesday and Wednesday afternoons, Wächter had ridden the same underground train again, looking for more witnesses. He tried other cars of the same train. He tried the train two minutes earlier; the one three minutes later. No new witnesses.

He still hadn't told anyone his suspicion. His fugitive was probably English, and perhaps even the infamous Agent Z. Counter-Intelligence would snap the case right out of his hands, and he didn't want that. But short of sharing these thoughts, he was facing the beginnings of scrutiny for his obsession with this case. As long as he did the rest of his work as usual, he believed, they'd give him free reign to spend extra time on the Becker investigation.

Wächter had wasted his time yesterday trying to get more information out of the U-Bahn witnesses he already had. They couldn't remember anything more than they'd told him on Monday.

But he gave four of them orders to visit his Columbia-Haus office on Thursday, at one-hour intervals. Then he spent Wednesday afternoon preparing the line-ups.

Wächter was careful to avoid false leads. He wasn't interested in solving the case for appearances only. That was no way to build a career, and no way to protect the Reich. Wächter wanted to find his man.

Precisely 4,330 persons named Becker lived in Berlin. Of these, 1,417 were adult men under the age of sixty, his secondary list. Wächter figured his Becker was under forty, which limited it to 542, his primary list.

More than five hundred faces were too many for most untrained witnesses to sift through in one sitting. Wächter used his instincts to pick the 50 most likely suspects. All four of his witnesses would look at those. The remaining 492 he divided into four groups, one for each witness.

For good measure, he added 23 photos of political criminals already arrested and executed by the Gestapo, men whose photos looked particularly suspicious. If any of Wächter's witnesses were prone to false identification, Wächter wanted that focused on decoys, not false leads.

Indeed, early in the morning, the two male witnesses picked a different decoy each. Wächter angrily pointed out the error and sent them off in turn.

Next, the first female witness didn't felt confident identifying the fugitive from the photos provided. She named five possibilities.

The other lady, his last witness of the morning, said she couldn't identify any of the photos. Wächter pressured her to come up with a short list. She seemed to pick ten at random.

The first lady was his most reliable witness, and she wasn't much good for now. Wächter put her five choices on top of the pile. But he didn't put much stock in them.

It was nearly ten-thirty when Becker arrived at Zoologischer Garten, the closest elevated rail station to Kristner. He was anxious to see if the mailroom had any word of Maria.

First he had to get rid of his hidden-ink message. He walked into a sizeable café at Wittenberg Platz, ordered another coffee, and sought out the toilet.

At a table near the back sat Georg Schwarz. Why wasn't *he* at work? Becker cursed his bad luck. Schwarz was already smiling in recognition.

Becker knew the encounter was coincidence. Schwarz was too clumsy to trail anyone undetected. The Nazis would never assign their loyal Schwarz to such a task.

Still, Becker didn't like seeing Schwarz here. He could ask Schwarz about Maria, but he didn't want to seem suspiciously anxious about her. Association with the guilty was treacherous in Nazi Germany.

"What's with the casual stroll into work this morning, Becker? Catching up on the day's news?" Schwarz motioned to the newspaper under Becker's arm.

"And good morning to you, Schwarz," replied Becker. "I felt awful this morning. It was probably something I ate. I'm feeling much better, but I do need to dash in here."

Becker entered the men's room. Schwarz must be using some office errand as an excuse to dither in a café, thought Becker. He saw that Schwarz had already been to the mailroom this morning. Schwarz made no mention of anyone looking to arrest Becker. That wasn't the sort of thing Schwarz was capable of hiding, either.

Thank God!

Becker felt his muscles relax as if he'd had more of Nadine's sleeping powder. But his mind remained clear. It seemed the Gestapo hadn't found him yet.

This also meant Maria had not yet confessed to Becker's plotting. That could mean she was still all right. Or it could mean she was very resilient even under severe pain.

Becker chose the second of two toilet stalls and locked himself in. He removed his trousers, sat down, and pulled out the message and the spray. Within moments the text appeared.

"Two messages," read the heading.

"1. Churchill target of assassination," followed the first part.

What?!? This was completely unrelated to Becker's mission. Why was he learning about it? There were any number of ways to get that information back to London. Not least, his unknown counterpart British agent could travel with the message himself.

Then it made sense to him. Hitler was preparing for another world war, right under the Allies' noses. The only Allied statesman who recognized this was Churchill. Even though Churchill was out of power in London, Hitler feared him.

Assassinating Churchill was part of Hitler's planned double strike, Becker understood. First, Hitler would remove the only foreign leader who threatened to mobilize against him. Second, Hitler would remilitarize Germany's Rhineland frontier, making it much harder for France to contain his future ambitions.

There were others in France and Britain who saw that Hitler wanted another world war. Only Churchill had the political power to hope to do something about it. If ever Churchill were killed, Britain would be finished, Becker knew.

A dozen years ago, Hitler had written in *Mein Kampf* that Germany ought to conquer Europe while avoiding war with Britain. Without Churchill, Hitler would get just that. Chamberlain and the other appeasers would avoid war at any cost, including the enslavement of Europe and their own dastardly surrender to the German Führer.

Becker shuddered at the prospect. He had to save Churchill!

At that moment, someone entered the men's room and went to the urinal. Becker remained in place and shuffled his newspaper open. He placed the message between the pages and continued reading it.

"Wednesday Feb 19, concert 19:30," it read.

Today was Thursday, February 13. The assassination attempt was six days away!

"Becker, are you all right in here?" Schwarz suddenly called from the restroom entrance.

That damn snoop, thought Becker. "Yes, I'm fine, thank you. I shouldn't be much longer."

"You sure you don't need anything?" asked Schwarz.

Becker thought Schwarz sounded concerned and suspicious at the same time.

"No thanks, I'm fine." *Leave me the hell alone!*

"I wonder what was the story with Fräulein Geberich?" said Schwarz. "Oh, that's right – you haven't heard yet."

Maria! Becker cared about her news as much as the shocking information in his hands.

"Can a guy take a shit in peace, please?" Becker half-joked. He had to get Schwarz out of here. Waiting five or ten more minutes for Maria's news wouldn't change anything.

"Yes, of course, sorry," said Schwarz. "Just wanted to check on you, you know."

"Well thanks," said Becker.

"Wednesday Feb 19, concert 19:30," he read again.

Churchill must have plans to attend a concert that night. There had to be some reason for Becker to get this information. Obviously, his anonymous colleague in Berlin was relying on Becker to relay the information to London. But why?

True, visitors to the British Embassy and other offices were routinely followed by the Gestapo. But couldn't his colleague find another way to get the warning out?

"2. Rendezvous requested. Sunday, 2 P.M., Angel's Hill," read the message.

That's interesting, thought Becker. McBride had told Becker to stay away from the old Grunewald Forest drop-off site. This other agent didn't seem to have that update. Was it safe to go? Becker wanted to be out of Germany by then, anyway. He'd think about this later.

As quietly as possible, Becker tore the message to shreds. Once he saw they were all flushed away, he hid the phenolphthalein bottle behind a loose bathroom tile. Then he exited to the café.

"You all set, Becker?" Schwarz asked eagerly.

"Fine." Becker tried not to sound irritated.

He sat down to his coffee. He wanted to hear about Maria.

CHAPTER FOURTEEN

"The new prisoner is English?!?" asked Wächter. His heart raced at the prospect.

The prisoner wasn't Becker himself. Wächter had seen the new man on his way into Columbia Haus before dawn. He didn't think he could identify Becker by sight, but he ruled out this second Englishman. Counter-Intelligence would snap up this new prisoner if they knew he was English. Wächter wanted to keep the prisoner under his domain, Political Enemies.

He still hadn't told anyone he guessed Becker was British. He constantly worried they'd steal that case from him, too, if they thought it involved a British spy. Wächter wanted full credit for Becker's capture, which he expected soon.

"Yes, Standartenführer Wächter," answered Sergeant Schumacher, Gestapo interrogator. "He's definitely English."

"He told you that?" Wächter asked.

"Not directly," answered Schumacher. "It's the language he screams in."

"English. . . . Very interesting. . . . Do you have anything else out of him yet, Scharführer Schumacher?"

"No, sir. We only started on him at nine o'clock this morning. Less than two hours."

"Tighten the screws," said Wächter. "All the way. No sleep for him tonight. Don't involve anyone besides your unit, and report directly to me. I want the transcript and a summary report at the end of the night. And tell the technicians to make sure he's still alive and conscious. I'll be in at dawn to finish the job myself."

"You said there's news about Maria?" asked Becker. He sat with Herr Schwarz at a café at Wittenberg Platz.

"Well, I had to leave while Franzoser was still on the phone," said Schwarz. "So I don't know much about it. Just that she was released this morning and won't be at work today."

Becker smiled from ear to ear. He heaved a sigh of relief. It was fine for him to look happy now. Schwarz was supposed to think Becker was courting Maria.

"Poor Maria," said Becker. "At least it's over. But she had to spend the night with them? I hope she gets some rest today."

"Surely Herr Franzoser can tell us more," said Schwarz. "You almost done with your coffee?"

Becker left his cup half-full. "Finished. Let's go."

Together they walked the ten minutes to Kristner GmbH. It was exactly eleven o'clock when they entered the mailroom.

"Good morning, Herr Franzoser." Becker reported to the boss. "I'm terribly sorry I'm late. I was awfully sick during the night, but I seem to be mostly well now. It must have been something I ate. Again, I apologize."

"Good morning, Becker." Franzoser's tone was dry, neither supportive nor skeptical. "I'm glad you're better. I'm also glad you're here."

Becker held his breath.

"We've got tons of mail today. With Geberich still out, I need everyone else I've got. . . . I trust Schwarz has updated you?"

"Only the basics, Herr Franzoser," said Schwarz. "I missed most of it."

"That was Fräulein Geberich's brother on the phone earlier. She was released this morning and is now resting at home. She'll be back at work tomorrow. I never realized her brother was so well connected."

Franzoser caught himself. "Of course, she is innocent and was going to be released so quickly anyway. It was obviously a misunderstanding. Still, good thinking to call the brother yesterday, Becker. He said to be sure to extend his special gratitude to you."

"Thanks for the update," said Becker.

"My pleasure," replied Franzoser.

The rest of the day Becker delivered mail back and forth from the finance department to the mailroom. Each time he returned, he wondered if arrest awaited him, if they'd finally found him. Each time he was relieved they hadn't. This tension alone exhausted him.

Another problem turned over in his head all day.

Two days ago, he and Maria had planned to meet Thursday evening, tonight. In the interim, she'd spent the night with the Gestapo. Although she had been released, the Gestapo might be trailing her.

Furthermore, the Gestapo agent from last Friday's tram chase was lurking around Maria's neighborhood. Becker thought it best to avoid the neighborhood himself, if he could avoid it. Phoning Maria was out of the question – her phone was probably tapped now. The lesser risk would be visiting her apartment, if necessary.

At the end of the day, Becker watched the clock tick in the mailroom. He didn't have any more mail runs. He only needed to wait until five o'clock. Please, he thought, don't let them arrest me in the last minutes of the day. The clock struck five o'clock, church bells rang down the street, and Becker was the first one out the door.

As he exited Kristner into the cold, cloudy evening, Becker remembered something. On Tuesday, Maria had joked about feeding Janeck's cat together tonight. Perhaps she would think to meet Becker at Janeck's apartment? Janeck's flat suddenly seemed somewhat safe by comparison to Maria's.

He decided to try it, at least for a first plan. She'd been to an office party at Janeck's place once, he remembered. She knew where it was.

If Maria were being followed, at least Becker could choose the ground of their meeting, somewhere the Gestapo wasn't expecting. There were enough ways into Janeck's apartment complex for Becker to find an escape if needed. If Maria never showed up, then he'd risk visiting her at home.

The walk to Janeck's flat took about thirty minutes. When Becker arrived, he saw no sign of Maria. There was no café on this small street where he could wait for her.

Janeck's apartment did not face the street, Becker remembered. He could not just go in and watch for her. Lingering on the street was too dangerous. He would just have to listen for her to ring the bell.

But the bell buttons bore only cryptic numbers, Becker observed, not the apartment numbers. He could try to mark Janeck's somehow. But he had no way to identify it among the dozens present.

He'd have to break the building's main entrance lock. Then Maria could just walk right in, if she thought to try. Incapacitating the lock was easy. Becker had to pause for a few minutes while two residents entered the building. Then it took him less than ten seconds to break the lock.

His next problem was to break into a streetside flat to watch for Maria. At the end of the workday, there were still plenty of empty apartments in the building. They'd be filling up fast, though. Becker had to choose one, pick its lock, and try his luck.

The individual door locks were harder to manage than the front door. He chose one apartment and started at its lock. Instantly, a tiny dog began barking. Becker had to find a different apartment.

He found another quiet door, one flight up, and took a full minute to pick its lock . . . no dogs barking, no people talking.

Becker couldn't know whether Maria would come, or when. He needed a place to hide if the occupants came home before he saw her. He hid in the curtains. If the lights came on, though, his silhouette would be visible from the street. He pulled the blinds almost shut.

For thirty minutes, Becker watched every entry through the broken door. There must be hundreds of flats in this apartment complex to generate so much foot traffic, he thought.

Then a locksmith approached the door. Maria would be locked out. Becker would have to risk meeting her on the street.

But within two minutes, the locksmith sifted through his toolbox and shook his head at the door. He looked at his watch and walked away. The building door remained unlocked.

After thirty minutes more, a man and woman entered the flat where Becker hid. They seemed not to notice the picked lock.

Becker quickly turned his feet sideways to the wall, almost hidden by the curtain's bottom edge.

After the hallway lights came on, neither husband nor wife seemed interested in the sitting room where Becker waited. From the kitchen came sounds of cooking, and newspaper pages turning. Becker kept his vigil for Maria.

He gave himself twenty more minutes. When the flat's occupants finished cooking, there would be fewer noises to cover his escape.

From the kitchen came the husband's voice. "It looks like the fight over us in London is really heating up."

"Oh?" answered his wife.

"Their new King Edward is a real admirer of the Führer. But that viper Winston Churchill hates us. He fails to recognize the greatness of the German race. He should be glad for the success of his kindred Aryans, that ungrateful bastard!"

Suddenly Maria appeared on the sidewalk below. But she was leaving the building, not entering it!

Becker wondered how he'd missed her. Maybe she'd gotten here before him? Or maybe right afterwards, before he reached his present perch above the street.

He had to catch her immediately. His entire escape route from this apartment was out of the kitchen's view. In quick, long, silent strides, he made his way to the door.

A crackling noise threatened to unveil him. It came not from the floorboards, but from his ankles, stiff from standing still so long. Becker kept moving and listening to the pots and pans. He seemed unnoticed when he opened the front door and pulled it shut behind him.

"Good evening, Herr Schau," came a voice walking up the stairs. Becker ignored it and flew to the ground floor to catch Maria.

If she were being followed, Becker would be seen chasing her down the street. He had no other choice. He invented a cover. He was only twenty seconds behind her when he hit the sidewalk and called down the street.

"Maria, I'm sorry! I shouldn't have said that. I'm sorry you were sick. It's just I was mad when you didn't answer the phone last night, even though you knew I was waiting. Really, Maria, I'm sorry! Will you please forgive me?"

Maria stopped and listened. Then she turned around and stared. After a long pause, she strode decisively back to the penitent lover played by Becker. She kissed him on the mouth, lingering as they embraced each other . . . their first kiss.

"Oh, Johannes!"

"I'm so sorry, Maria."

He offered his arm, put his key in the broken door, and opened it for her. There was no sign of anyone following Maria.

They paused their conversation while they walked through two courtyards and up the stairs. Becker thought Maria looked very serious, but not exactly worried. She seemed physically unharmed from her detention. He was eager to hear her story.

Maria burst into tears the moment they closed Janeck's door behind them. She sobbed and clutched at Becker, dropping to the floor in a flood of emotions.

Becker went down on his knees with her, and embraced her tightly while she wept. For many minutes they kneeled facing each other, Becker rocking them slightly. Maria's sobs ebbed into sniffs and then silence.

"The worst part of it," Maria started, "was that I never knew how it would end. It felt like a death sentence. Then all of a sudden, early this morning, I was free to go."

Becker just held her and looked at her.

"Don't worry," she said. "They didn't learn anything. They were very gentle with me. Even my bed was very comfortable. At first, I wasn't so sure. They left me alone in a cold cell for hours and hours. Maria shuddered at the memory.

"But after that, I got nothing but the most humane treatment, including a very nice dinner. The only interrogation I got was about whether I liked my job fine. Did I want a better one? they asked. Of course I told them I was perfectly satisfied at Kristner. I would never want their favors." She started crying again.

Becker stroked Maria's head and shoulders while she spoke. She paused for a few minutes and rested her head on his chest. They still kneeled on the floor. Then she pulled her head back to continue.

"My brother Rupert said you were the one who called him. He got Wehrmacht Headquarters involved in my case, he said. That might have made a difference, although those Gestapo men hate the Wehrmacht officer corps. Who knows. It does seem strange that I started in such a barren cell before moving to a room that was quite nice. . . ."

Rosa the cat approached and purred as she rubbed against them.

"Sometimes I had the impression they might be looking for a reliable, high-level secretary," said Maria. "Sometimes I thought they were waiting for me to trip myself up. But the patient interrogator approach – like Dostoyevski's Porfiry, you know? – that's not their style. They're brutal."

"You're well read for a mail clerk," said Becker.

"So are you," she smiled. "It's just a job."

"That it is."

"Let's feed the cat before I tell you the rest," said Maria. They stood up and walked into the kitchen. "What's his name?"

"Her name is Rosa," answered Becker.

Becker poured the cat food into a bowl and started filling the water dish. "You ought to know more about our colleague Janeck," he said softly.

"Oh?" she asked.

"I ran into him here on Tuesday."

"What?!?" she exclaimed quietly.

"That's right," he said. "The whole story about the brother was fake. He was waiting for me to come."

Becker decided it was time to search the flat. Since Maria had collapsed into his arms at the entryway, he had initially neglected to check the place out.

"Excuse me a minute, please," he said.

The apartment was small. Becker took only two minutes to examine every space possibly large enough to conceal a person. They were indeed alone.

"Like I was saying, Janeck was actually here on Tuesday. He claimed to be part of the Socialist resistance. He said they wanted to recruit me."

Becker didn't want to tell her about Janeck's gun. He didn't want to worry her any more than he had to.

"Did you believe him?" she asked.

"I did," Becker answered. "He was by himself, and he seemed awfully nervous."

"What did you say?" Maria asked.

"That I wasn't available," he said. "His main point was that he's now a marked man. His apartment won't be safe for long. I'm going to leave out lots of food and water for Rosa tonight. We shouldn't come back."

Maria nodded.

"There," he was satisfied at the large buffet for the cat.

Next Becker reached for Maria's hand and led her into the small sitting room. They sat next to each other on the sofa.

Maria changed the subject. "You remember that female athlete the SS man mentioned yesterday?"

"I remember the whole thing, yes," said Becker.

"She was an old associate of Max's. She hasn't seen me in three years. She seems to have remembered, in her . . . tortured interrogation, that Max had a sister. For that, I got to spend a night with those creeps."

"Was there anything else to it?" he asked.

"My detention? Not that they told me."

"Would you rather have nothing to do with stealing the Army documents on Saturday?" he asked. "I'll understand completely."

Maria looked Becker in the eyes. She was more serious and resolved than ever.

"Count me in. I'll take my chances. I hope it does some good somewhere. And then I'm really looking forward to getting out of this country. I've had enough. I'm ready to start over, even learn a new language if I need to."

"I'll help you get out anyway," he said. "You don't have to take more risks."

"Even so," she replied. "I want to help on Saturday."

Becker wanted to ask about the uniforms, if she had made any progress on them. He wasn't sure how to put the question delicately to someone who'd just spent the night with the Gestapo. "Is there any chance—"

"The uniforms?" she asked.

He nodded.

"Sorry," she answered. "I never got to that."

"That's O.K.," he assured her. "It's too late to pursue it further. You're surely being watched, at least at a distance. We'll do without."

Becker didn't say that he planned to rely on Rupert's supplies. He still would try to avoid implicating Rupert in the break-in. Since her arrest, he would tell Maria only what she absolutely needed to know.

"I do have some progress to report, though," added Maria. "Your contact with Rupert about my arrest has made things a lot easier. He is very eager to host us for lunch at his place on Saturday, to express his gratitude."

"Perfect!" he said.

"Isn't it? Remember though, Johannes. Rupert stays safe. Are we clear about that?"

"Insofar as we stay safe ourselves, yes, absolutely," said Becker.

"Do you remember his address in Wedding?"

"Yes," he answered.

"We're to meet there at eleven o'clock for lunch. Oh, and one more thing. As you may have figured by now, Rupert is a little jealous about me. There must be no hint of further intimacies around him," she added.

"Got it." Becker smiled as he leaned over to kiss her.

Maria closed her eyes and turned her face and mouth up to meet Becker's. Their kiss was slow and long and still. Becker then pulled Maria to his chest. He held her there, while they listened to each other breathing.

Becker was the first to interrupt the moment. "For appearances' sake," said Becker, "in case you've been followed, you need to stay at Janeck's flat just the right amount of time. Neither too long nor too short. Sooner or later they're going to tear this place apart."

Becker thought to himself, *They did not arrest Maria and keep her overnight for nothing. Whatever they're after, they'll keep looking. Even if they're not following her, they've got her in their sights.*

"Another thing," said Becker. "Janeck left some incriminating documents here. I made him take them away. But I need to search the whole apartment more thoroughly for anything like that that remains. If someone searches the place after we leave, it needs to be clean. I'll start looking around. You should rest."

"No problem." She smiled weakly and lay down on the sofa.

Becker thought she looked half-asleep. The past day's stress had to be unbelievable.

Maria kept her eyes half-open while she watched Becker search the apartment. His first move was to crack open a sitting room window for fresh air. From there, he took time to explore every visible cavity of the flat. He was quick and methodical.

After awhile he reported, "So far, I haven't found anything. I've only got the bedroom left."

"I think," said Maria, "sadly for me, it's time to go. Alone."

"But—" started Becker.

"No," she interrupted. "It's too dangerous for you to escort me home. Someone decided to arrest me. Someone different let me go. The first someone might still be tracking me. You've got to let me go alone."

"No, really, I insist—"

"No, Johannes. Thank you, but no. I refuse to endanger you further. Remember that I want you to survive. You can punish these cretins. Besides, you're my ticket out of here. You can let me walk home alone with a clean conscience. It's for my sake as much as yours."

Becker just stared at her for a moment. "If you insist."

He was skeptical this was best for Maria. He still felt like he didn't know the whole of her, either. Like there was always something more to the story.

She stood up and they briefly kissed good night. It was the kiss of a well worn, endeared couple. A few days facing great dangers together made them close.

"I'll see you tomorrow at Kristner," she said. "And Saturday at Rupert's."

"Looking forward to it!" he answered.

"Good night," said Maria.

"Good night," he replied.

Becker took another half-hour to search everything in Janeck's apartment, including the mattress. He didn't find any more incriminating papers. But there was a small cache of weapons hidden behind the bathroom tiles. He left those in place.

His thoughts turned to the plot to assassinate Churchill. Maybe he should give up his mission to make sure he got the news to London? At least that would save one man . . . the one man with enough strength and conviction to lead Britain in the fight against Hitler that would surely come, sooner or later.

Hopefully, though, if he stayed, Becker could find a fatal weakness in Hitler's Army. That could save millions.

To save one man. To save the masses. Becker wanted both.

CHAPTER FIFTEEN

Colonel Wächter arrived at Columbia Haus in the pre-dawn darkness. At this hour, Gestapo headquarters were as sparsely populated as the streets, except the prison section. Gestapo interrogators worked around the clock.

Wächter checked his office on his way to the interrogation chamber. The typed report lay on his desk.

INTERROGATION record, 13-14 Feb. 1936
Subject: Tom HARDAM
Nationality: English
Report: Fri., Feb. 14, 05:00, Sergeant S. SCHUMACHER

Tom HARDAM's interrogation has proceeded in three phases. The first three hours, significant duress was applied. The subject provided his name and confessed to being a British spy. He named a drop-off location at Café Hildegard. Our agent arrived at the drop-off at 11:40 in the morning. Between Wednesday evening and then, a second British spy picked up a message from HARDAM. Before we could determine the message contents, HARDAM fainted.

The subject remained unconscious or semi-conscious for eight hours, until 20:00. Standartenführer WÄCHTER then amended his instructions – sleep deprivation but no more serious injury during the night.

For the past nine hours, the subject has been uncooperative. Except for two falls, attributed to fatigue, he has remained standing naked on cold cement. He earned one broken finger for each fall.

Wächter entered the dimly lit, cold interrogation chamber. Hardam stood in the middle, three feet behind a steel chair with leather restraints. Hardam was naked except for the handcuffs behind his back. His eyes were swollen half-shut. He turned them listlessly to look at Wächter for the first time.

Wächter dismissed the night shift interrogator with a nod. The two brawny assistants remained in the background. A single light bulb hung over the empty steel chair. Next to the chair was a table strewn with bloodstained tools, and buckets of water, some of them steaming. Wächter kept his silence for five minutes, glaring at Hardam and pacing in front of him. Hardam breathed noisily, with much effort, through his broken nose and teeth.

"I'm here to relieve you, Hardam." Wächter spoke matter-of-factly, slightly rushed. "I'm not the next shift. I'm the last shift. We don't want it to be a long one. I'm an impatient man. How you spend your last hour or two, that's up to you. What do you say we make it more pleasant?"

Wächter knew that after any amount of torture, most prisoners believed this lie.

Hardam stared back mutely.

"Let's review the facts," said Wächter. "Name: Tom Hardam. British spy. Caught in possession of documents from military counter-intelligence. You obtained these through Dora Hengel, personal cleaning lady of Deputy Führer Rudolf Hess. You haven't confessed that, but Dora has. You seduced her as your lover. Like you, she will die this morning. You have murdered her."

Wächter's monotone could have been reading radio program listings. He had introduced himself in this manner to dozens of prisoners. This time, though, his heart raced with excitement – an Englishman! Who knew what fruits this conversation might bear. Wächter would reveal his agitation momentarily, but not yet.

Wächter paused. Hardam just stared back through eyes too swollen to express anything.

"Now be reasonable, Tommie. Tell me – what was in the message you left at Café Hildegard? What else do you have for us?" asked Wächter.

Hardam closed his eyes for a few seconds. When his standing body started to waver, he opened his eyes and stared dully at Wächter. He said nothing.

Wächter stomped up to Hardam's face and changed his tone completely.

"Listen here, Tommie. I will personally crack your skull on the floor, if I need to. But only after inflicting so much pain you'll beg me to kill you. Out with it – everything! Right now!" Wächter shouted.

Hardam stared back blankly. Wächter snapped his fingers, and one of the guards approached Hardam from behind.

"Ahhhh!" Hardam dropped to his knees, as the guard crushed his right shoulder with a massive club. Hardam crouched and heaved in pain.

"Stand up!" Wächter lifted Hardam by the hair. Hardam fell back to his knees. Wächter motioned to the guard. The guard's thick, muscular fingers seized Hardam's cuffed hands and snapped a third finger broken. Hardam sucked more air but didn't scream. Then he stopped breathing.

"Breathe, you bastard!" ordered Wächter. "You think I'll let you pass yourself out?!?"

To the guard he continued, "Tickle him!"

The guard gave Wächter a dumb look.

"You heard me right – Tickle him! Under the arms, mostly."

The guard obeyed.

"It makes them breathe again," said Wächter.

It worked.

Wächter continued, "Now strap him in the chair and get your tools ready."

The two guards uncuffed Hardam, lifted him, and strapped him in.

Hardam constantly winced in the pain of his shattered shoulder.

All right, thought Wächter. *I don't want to make him unconscious again. I want this done with.*

"Talk," he ordered. "Tell me everything I'd want to know."

Hardam's encrusted lips began to bleed when he opened them. "Cathedral . . . ," he groaned.

"What?"

"Cathedral . . . code for Churchill. . . . Assassination . . . next Wednesday."

Wächter was stunned. He was torturing an English spy to get top-secret *German* information?!?

"You know this from the trash bin?" he asked.

"Yeah," muttered Hardam.

"This was the drop-off message?" Wächter would read any hesitation as preface to a lie.

Hardam answered immediately. "Yeah."

"Does Dora know about Operation Cathedral, as you call it?"

"No," said Hardam.

"Who else knows about the drop-off spot? Who was supposed to pick up your message?"

"Not many. . . . Don't know. . . ."

"Are there other drop-off locations?" demanded Wächter.

Hardam named three others.

"Any more drop-off spots?" asked Wächter.

"No."

"Any rendezvous planned?"

Hardam paused again. He's not very good at this, thought Wächter. Most of them know by now to spit it all out. He slammed his fist onto Hardam's shattered shoulder. Hardam sucked air through his teeth but didn't scream.

Wächter had to be careful. Hardam was close to losing consciousness again. Wächter threw a bucket of cold water into Hardam's face and waited for Hardam to stop choking on it.

"When's the rendezvous?" demanded Wächter.

"Sunday afternoon . . . two." Hardam started crying.

They always cry when they give up their colleagues, thought Wächter.

"Where?" he asked. He held his hand high, ready to strike.

"Angel's Hill, Grunewald Forest."

"Now let's talk about Agent Z," said Wächter. "What can you tell me about him?"

Hardam looked surprised. Wächter could see this meant something to him. At the same time, Hardam didn't seem to have any current connection with Britain's top agent. The Gestapo knew the man was in town. But they didn't know who he was, or why he was there.

"What do you know about him, Tommie?"

Hardam choked through his tears but held his tongue.

Wächter lifted his fist above Hardam's shoulder.

"That's all, I swear . . . ," pleaded Hardam. "I'll make stuff up. . . . Please kill me," he begged.

Wächter wandered to the table and sifted through its tools.

Hardam's eyes bulged for the first time since Wächter's arrival. "Invent . . . sign anything . . . kill me. . . ." Hardam tried again to hold his breath and pass out. He wept so hard he couldn't manage the trick.

Wächter stepped back toward Hardam. Suddenly he lifted his right leg and slammed his boot down between Hardam's legs on the steel chair seat. Hardam convulsed in pain and vomited on Wächter's boot. He was barely conscious.

Hardam whispered something Wächter couldn't understand. Then he whispered it a second time.

At the risk of Hardam vomiting on his face, Wächter put his ear next to Hardam's hanging head.

The dying prisoner whispered, "Becker."

Becker! Wächter stood and smiled from ear to ear. *Agent Z! The man he'd chased from the subway!* This afternoon he'd have a short list of suspect Beckers without alibis for Thursday morning, when someone had retrieved Hardam's Café Hildegard message. Wächter almost forgot about Hardam.

At that moment Hardam made a show of spitting in Wächter's direction.

Wächter was so enraged he jumped at Hardam's neck and pushed the chair over backwards. Wächter fell with him. This made him doubly furious. Hardam was knocked out. He probably knew more about Becker and wanted to draw Wächter into killing him first. Now Wächter was furious at himself.

Wächter stood and washed his vomit-stained boot with a bucket of water. Then he threw some scalding hot water into Hardam's face. Hardam sputtered, barely conscious and blinking while his face welted.

Wächter nodded to the guards to lift the chair upright. Hardam's head keeled forward in unconsciousness.

"Take him out of the chair," ordered Wächter. "And lay him down gently on the floor."

Wächter watched as Hardam breathed unevenly, unconscious, face-up naked on the cold concrete floor. Wächter's blood boiled at the insolence of Hardam's spitting.

His foot prodded Hardam's arm away from his body. Then he slashed his steel-tipped boot into Hardam's side, over and over, cracking his ribs, shoving them into his innards. After a minute of this, a panting Wächter stepped back and looked at the bloodied corpse.

Sean Russell greeted the dawn ferry from Liverpool. "Welcome home, Paddy." Russell's breath billowed into the cold gray morning.

Patrick O'Hagan cut a short figure descending from the boat. He carried only a small bag of extra clothes. His cap kept the thick fog from soaking his hair. He looked at Russell with dark brown eyes that matched his hair.

"Thank you, Sean." The two IRA men embraced.

"We've got a warm breakfast for you up at the pub," said Russell.

The two men walked from the docks into Dublin, straight to the small back room of Russell's pub. The proprietor brought them hot coffee, eggs, and corned beef in abundance.

O'Hagan rubbed his hands together in delight. "This is just the thing after a freezing February ferry ride. Thank you, Sean."

"Not at all."

The two men ate. Russell answered O'Hagan's questions about friends back home.

Finally O'Hagan brought up the business of Churchill's assassination. "It couldn't be easier, Russell. You know I work in Queen's Hall."

Russell shook his head. "You've already told me everything I need to know, Paddy. I only needed that for confirmation purposes. Find a new place to live. I don't even want to know where you live or how to reach you. I'll wait to read about the assassination in the papers."

Russell pulled out an envelope from his jacket. "Here's a hundred pounds, Paddy. Find your new flat as soon as you get back to London this evening."

"This evening?" asked O'Hagan. "I thought I got to spend the weekend in Dublin?"

"Sorry, Paddy. We need you back in country before anything goes wrong. Then lie low. We won't contact you. Once you step back on that ferry, accept no communications as genuine. The assassination order is irreversible."

Winston Churchill rang up his foreign policy ally, Foreign Office Undersecretary Robert Vansittart.

"Hello?" answered Vansittart. "Do you know what time it is?"

"It's the crack of dawn. You mean you're asleep already?" Churchill laughed at his own joke. He sat in his tuxedo in his London flat. "I've spent the night rallying anyone who will listen to the anti-Nazi cause. . . . Do we have any news yet from our man in Berlin?" asked Churchill.

"I wish we did," replied Vansittart. "No, nothing from him yet, I'm afraid. . . . God, how I'd love confirmation that Hitler's bluffing. They'd surely make you prime minister then, Winston. You could rout the Nazis before they really do get too strong. We could even get the new French government to come along with us. Foreign Minister Flandin sees things more clearly than anyone on our own Cabinet, I'm afraid."

"Let me know at the first sign of news from Berlin," said Churchill.

"As always," replied Vansittart.

"Good night, Vansittart. You should get out more." With another laugh, Churchill hung up and went to bed.

As usual, Wächter showered down the hall. He had much more blood on him than usual. His heart still pulsed in fury at Hardam's insolence.

Wächter put on his immaculate black uniform. From the prison section of Columbia Haus, he marched to his office and picked up the phone.

"Get me Chief Arndt, Berlin police. . . . Arndt? Standartenführer Wächter here."

"Yes, Good morning, sir," replied Arndt. "We've stricken seven names from the lists, as having recently moved out of Berlin, although—"

"I'm not calling for trivial updates," said Wächter.

"We still have hundreds of Beckers in the main age category," said Arndt.

"Still in the hundreds?" replied Wächter. "That's unfortunate, because it's going to take up a lot of your police resources."

"How's that?" Arndt was clearly irritated.

"It looks like our Becker was on the prowl yesterday mid-morning," continued Wächter. "He picked up a message before we could catch him at it. So here's what I need: Find out which Beckers have alibis for the entirety of Thursday morning."

"Sir, are you aware–"

"Yes, I know that will take hundreds of man-hours," said Wächter. "Today. I need this done by the end of today. It's now eight-fifteen. That gives you about eight hours."

"That's just not possible, sir," replied Arndt.

"What do you mean impossible?!?" exclaimed Wächter.

"I'd have to drop so many routine matters," said Arndt. "The police force would come under a lot of heat. I can't do that without very high authorization, sir."

"Higher up? I'll give you higher up! Stay on the line."

Wächter set down the receiver and went out to use his secretary's phone. He motioned her out of the room. Then he asked the operator for the upstairs office of General Reinhold Heydrich, head of the Gestapo.

"Good morning," Wächter spoke to Heydrich's secretary. "Standartenführer Kurt Wächter speaking.   I please need Obergruppenführer Heydrich.   An interrogation over here has yielded a security breech of the utmost urgency."

"I'm afraid he won't be out of a meeting until ten o'clock, sir," she answered.

"I don't care if he's in a meeting," insisted Wächter.   "I need Heydrich now.   You can tell him that I'll stake my career on the importance of the matter."

Wächter beamed as he thought about how his star should rise from this break.   Not only had he identified a major security breech.   He was about to close it by capturing Agent Z!

"Just a moment, sir," she answered.   Wächter heard irritated conversation in the background.

"Wächter, what is it?" demanded Heydrich.   "This better be exceptional."

"General Heydrich, sir, I've got an English spy on the loose who knows about something called Operation Cathedral."

Wächter played his trump.   He told them Becker was British.   He hoped they wouldn't reassign the case to Gestapo Counter-Intelligence downstairs.   Wächter was so immersed in it.   They just had to let him keep the case.

"Operation Cathedral?" said Heydrich.   "Never heard of it. Where'd he get this?"

"From the home of Rudolf Hess," answered Wächter.

"I'll be damned," muttered Heydrich.   "Come up here right now."

"Yes, sir," said Wächter.

On his way out his told his secretary, "Tell Chief Arndt on my phone to hang up and stand by for General Heydrich's call."

Wächter ran upstairs.   Heydrich's secretary nodded him forward to the general's office.

"*Heil Hitler!*"   Wächter presented himself.   "Obergruppenführer Heydrich!"

"*Heil Hitler!*" Heydrich saluted.   "What the hell is going on?!?" He was even younger than Wächter.   Otherwise he looked similar – tall and thin, with angular facial features and a severe expression, brown hair and blue eyes.   What a mean mouth, Wächter thought.   He admired Heydrich's quick mind and self-confidence, his personal success, his harsh discipline.

"We're tracking down a British spy sir," said Wächter.

"Your evidence for this?" asked Heydrich coolly.

"At first, just the fact that he veered to the left side of a walkway under stress," replied Wächter. "Admittedly that's not much." Wächter eagerly watched Heydrich as he dropped the big news. "This morning we interviewed one Tom Hardam, a captive British spy. He ratted out a colleague named Becker. That's precisely the name that witnesses report of my fugitive from last week. Becker's our man."

Wächter saw that Heydrich was satisfied. He hadn't even delivered the biggest news yet.

"You know," continued Wächter, "that Britain's Agent Z is back in Berlin. Hardam knew who Z was. It's Becker."

Wächter trapped himself and he knew it. He was raising enormous expectations. He was staking his entire career on capturing Agent Z. So be it. The Reich had Becker within its grasp. It was Wächter's duty to pursue this opportunity as hard as possible, whatever the personal consequences of failure.

For the first time ever, Wächter saw a look of surprise on Heydrich's cool face. Wächter hoped as much as anything that Heydrich wouldn't reassign the British case to Counter-Intelligence, away from him. He wouldn't make a direct case for it unless Heydrich raised the question. So far, Heydrich didn't.

"My investigation is well underway," said Wächter. "If I may sir, I'd like to save the details until later. We urgently need your intervention with Chief of Police Arndt to deploy hundreds of officers today. We have a good lead, and we need to check alibis on over five hundred Beckers in the city. But Arndt won't do it on my authority."

"Absolutely." Heydrich picked up his phone and demanded Arndt's office.

"Arndt," answered the chief.

"This is SS Obergruppenführer Heydrich. Thank you for considering your other duties. I order you to drop them. Do what Standartenführer Wächter instructs. He speaks on my authority. Have I made myself clear?"

"Yes, sir," said Arndt. "Absolutely, sir. Immediately, sir."

Heydrich handed the phone to Wächter.

"No later than five o'clock," said Wächter. "Got that, Arndt?"

"If I have to track them down myself, sir," replied the police chief. "Yes, sir."

Wächter relished the fear in Arndt's voice. "I'll be hearing from you today, then. Good-bye." Wächter hung up.

Heydrich asked him, "What do you know about Operation Cathedral?"

"An assassination plot against Churchill, set for next Wednesday. We've got a British spy on the loose in Berlin right now who knows about it."

Wächter watched Heydrich mull it over. He realized even Heydrich hadn't known about this. Then Heydrich nodded to himself with a plan.

"How many of your people know about this?" asked Heydrich.

"Four interrogators and myself," replied Wächter.

"You tell those men immediately, they will be arrested if word of this leaks," ordered Heydrich. "Do not speak of it, even amongst yourselves. Destroy any record of it in the interrogation. If the Gestapo didn't know about this, it should remain that way. Do I make myself clear?"

"Yes, sir," replied Wächter.

Wächter wondered if he, and now Heydrich, knew too much. Even among devoted Nazis, forbidden knowledge could be fatal.

"Inform me immediately when you capture Agent Z," ordered Heydrich. "*Heil Hitler*," Heydrich dismissed Wächter.

"*Heil Hitler.*"

CHAPTER SIXTEEN

Friday, February 14

"Do you speak any English, Herr Becker?" Nadine asked him in German at the breakfast table. "I'm having problems with English at school."

Anna Lande heard something coy in her daughter's voice. She'd been pressing her daughter to study harder. But Nadine sounded more provocative than solicitous.

"I was wondering," continued Nadine, "if you could help me with my English this weekend?"

Anna looked at Becker. He seemed unusually reserved. It didn't last long, but it was there.

"As a matter of fact," he answered, "I speak it fluently. Our next-door neighbors in Hanover had an English mother. They spoke English at home, even during the World War. When I played at their house, which was all the time, I spoke English with them."

Anna thought Nadine looked deflated. Why didn't Nadine like Becker's answer? Wasn't she looking for an excuse to play her adolescent games with their boarder Becker while she was grounded this weekend? It was strange that Nadine seemed disappointed in Becker's answer.

"I'll be gone all day tomorrow, I'm afraid," Becker said to Nadine. "Day trip with a friend. It's not clear yet whether I'll be around on Sunday. If I am, I'll be glad to help."

Anna knew her daughter could get annoying. This couldn't possibly be Becker's first choice of how to spend Sunday afternoon, thought Anna. What a good soul he was, she thought. She glowed in undeclared love and admiration. If Becker were still around in a few years, maybe . . . .

"By the way, Frau Lande," Becker turned to Anna, "I should tell you I've got a borrowed car parked on the street outside. I'll have it till

Sunday.   A colleague of mine had to leave town for a family emergency. He asked me to take care of his cat. To help, I get to use his car."

Herr Janeck's small black Opel 4/20-PS was perfectly anonymous, thought Becker. Over a hundred thousand in the 4-PS line had been manufactured and were still in use, not counting hundreds of thousands of other Opel models on the road.

Anna turned to look out the alley window. "It wasn't necessary to tell me about the car. But I appreciate the notice."

"Did your cousins enjoy their visit?" he asked.

"Yes, very much, they said," replied Anna.

Anna watched Nadine stare at her plate. Last night, right after the cousins' departure, mother and daughter had a terrible argument about Liesl and Gertrude. This morning, Nadine held her tongue.

Becker stood up to leave for work. "Have a good day, both of you. Bye." He nodded politely.

"Bye," Nadine replied.

Anna simply nodded her head, and Becker left. Anna watched Nadine and chose her moment carefully. She needed to let Becker get safely away from the house, but not too far. About twenty seconds after he had left the kitchen, Anna stood up and walked calmly to the front door. She stepped into the cloudy winter morning and closed the door behind her.

"Herr Becker!" she yelled and waved down the street. "I forgot to ask you a favor." She saw Becker turn and she trotted to meet him, before he could get too close to the house. The cobblestone sidewalk was slippery with powdery snow. When Anna stood in front of him, she looked to make sure no neighbors could hear.

"Well, not exactly. . . ." Anna spoke softly. "That bit was for Nadine's benefit. She doesn't know yet. . . . We're leaving town this afternoon. I'll be back Sunday evening. You won't be seeing Nadine again for awhile. I'm taking her to live with my sister in Bavaria. A little countryside isolation will do her some good right now. You should have seen the fit she threw last night about Liesl and Gertrude and their story of Hitler's niece. Nadine is absolutely furious at them for that. She's out of control. So I'm sending her away. Last Christmas, my sister Katerina offered to keep her. Now I'm taking her up on it. Nadine doesn't know any of this yet."

Anna looked back at the house. There was Nadine watching them from her bedroom window on the second floor.

With her daughter gone, Anna could look forward to more time with Becker. She knew that, and felt guilty about it. That was the only reason she kept Nadine in January. She didn't want to send her daughter away for even the slightest self-interest. Even now, with the decision made, Anna swore to keep her distance from Becker upon her return to Berlin.

Becker knew he would be gone forever by the time Anna got back from Bavaria.

He replied, "Hopefully the country life will bring her into balance. I know it was hard decision for you."

"Yes and no," said Anna. "But it's a relief to have made it."

"Well, good luck with all that," he said.

"Thank you," said Anna. "I'll see you Sunday or Monday."

"Have a safe trip. Good-bye!" Becker lifted his fedora in courtesy. Anna waved. After Becker turned his back, she returned to the house. Nadine was no longer in the window.

"Mama!" cried Nadine from the doorway. "It's Aunt Katerina on the phone. She's hysterical but won't say what it is. Come!"

Anna ran to phone in the hallway. "Katerina?" Anna's sister didn't even have a phone. It had to be serious. Nadine looked on.

"Anna! Anna! It's awful." Katerina sobbed uncontrollably at the other end of the line.

"What is it, Katerina? What?" Anna's heart pounded.

"Liesl and Gertrude – They've been taken away by the SS! They're gone, Anna, they're gone! We may never see them again!"

Anna's mouth dropped. Nadine? Nadine!

Katerina continued, "They were waiting for them at their apartment this morning, when they got back to Munich from Berlin. Oh, Anna!"

Anna was in tears. Her mouth trembled as she stared at her daughter. Nadine's eyes widened and then she dashed upstairs to her room.

"Katerina! Katerina! How horrible! I should come down there. I was going to . . . . That's what I'll do. We'll arrive by train tonight. I'll call from the train station when we get there. How awful! . . . I'll pack up right away. I'll see you tonight. Good-bye, Katerina." Anna hung up.

"Nadine Lande!!!" Anna stormed up the stairs and ripped Nadine's door open. Her hands trembled as much as her voice. Tears streamed down her cheeks. "What have you done?!?"

Nadine's eyes darted around the small room. She alternated between smirking and looking scared. "What?"

"You know what! Liesl and Gertrude, that's what! What did you do? Whom did you tell – that Lodt boy?"

Nadine smiled impishly. "I didn't do anything. They're the ones who did it."

Anna crossed Nadine's bedroom and smacked her daughter hard.

Becker decided to drive Janeck's car to work, or at least nearby. He carried his own passport in his pocket, as well as a blank passport for Maria, ready for her photo. It was risky to have the blank passport. But he wasn't sure he would return even tonight to the Lande house on Maricfel Strasse. He still carried his Luger under his shirt.

When Becker entered the mailroom, Maria wasn't there yet. This would be her first time back since her arrest. He was anxious to see her safe arrival. Every second seemed like an hour until she arrived. Finally she did, her face flushed from the long winter walk.

"May I?" Becker helped with her coat. Several others smiled to see Maria again.

"Of course, thank you!" she answered.

"We're all very glad to have you back." Becker acted as if they hadn't seen each other yesterday evening. "What a dreadful error they made in taking you in!"

"Thank you," replied Maria. "Let's not talk about that, please."

"My apologies. . . . How does a boring day at the office sound?" he asked.

"Great!"

Chief Arndt set the whole Berlin police force in motion to find the right Becker . . . the Becker without an alibi Thursday morning. The chief summoned all precinct captains to a short emergency meeting at headquarters at 08:45. The captains were ordered to schedule meetings with their staffs back in their precincts at precisely 09:10.

At 09:15, all the detectives and on-duty officers in the Schöneberg precinct crowded into the conference room. The detectives read over the respective lists of Beckers just handed to them. Which ones had alibis for Thursday morning? The preliminary results were due at 15:50 that afternoon. Any final results were to be submitted by 16:15. Gaps were frowned upon. Mistakes would be severely punished. The pressure was on.

Detective Andreas Sturmbach had thirty names to investigate. They all lived close to each other in one section of the precinct. But on a Friday, most of these men would be scattered at their jobs across the city. Detective Sturmbach's duty was to track down all thirty men today, to identify all failures to produce alibis, and to mark especially suspicious ones. He was encouraged to dispatch regular officers for follow-up inquiries if time was short. In the event of no conclusive information, Sturmbach had to be damned sure that he could document his best efforts to learn more.

Sturmbach was further informed this was not a regular police affair. It was a matter of state. The entire Berlin police force buzzed with rumors. Today in Berlin, every man named Becker was a political suspect.

Sturmbach laid out his plan. He would telephone Becker employers scattered across the city. He would telephone the homes of unemployed Beckers. There would be follow-up phone calls and visits. He'd be lucky to finish it in one day.

If he didn't finish half the names by 12:15, he was instructed to call for help. He was expected to check out five alibis an hour – one every twelve minutes. Some of the employer information was bound to be outdated. Because of the scope and urgency of the assignment, regular officers were on standby for assistance.

The first name on Sturmbach's list was Adelbert Becker. Sturmbach called the church where Adelbert was groundskeeper. Adelbert had been fired, they explained. He probably didn't live in the same place anymore, either. If all thirty names were this complicated, Sturmbach was in for one tough day. He immediately assigned a regular officer to make inquires into Adelbert Becker's whereabouts.

The next fourteen names were easier. Detective Sturmbach finished them by 11:30. One was disabled and unemployed, and spent his days at home; Bernhard Becker had no alibi, but that was his routine. Among the first fifteen names, two others also had unsuspicious non-alibis. Of four more Beckers to have changed jobs, one proved especially difficult to track down; ultimately, Ferdinand Becker turned out to have moved to Breslau.

The field report on Adelbert came in at 11:45. The post office had a forwarding address. His new landlord reported that Adelbert Becker now managed a nightclub. Adelbert usually slept through the morning. So he went on the list without an alibi, but as a matter of course.

Half the list was done, ahead of pace and without gaps.

Next on the list: Johannes Becker, born August 11, 1905. Address: c/o Lande, 68 Maricfel Strasse. Employer: K. Kristner Engineering, GmbH. Supervisor: A. Franzoser. Detective Sturmbach telephoned Johannes Becker's work supervisor.

"Hello, Albrecht Franzoser?   This is Sturmbach, Andreas Sturmbach. Do you remember me? We went to Georg-Wilhelm Primary School together."

"Andreas Sturmbach? That's really you? I can't believe it! I never heard about you after the war, and I feared the worst. It's great to hear your voice!"

"Yours, too, Franzoser. We'll have to catch up sometime."

"So what can I do for you?" asked Franzoser. "Where are you now?"

"I'm a detective in the Schöneberg police precinct. I need to talk with you about one of your employees."

"Sure, hold on just a second." Franzoser closed his office door.

"This is very curious, Sturmbach," Franzoser spoke softy so he couldn't be heard by his employees. "We just had the SS in here a couple days ago. They arrested someone on staff, a woman of all people, though they released her right away. Anyway, go ahead."

"Well, this is no woman," replied Sturmbach. "Man by the name of Johannes Becker."

"Yeah, he works here. A very solid, reliable fellow. Is he trying to work in some kind of security service? I'd hate to lose him. But he would serve the Fatherland well."

"Actually, no. I called to ask if there was anything unusual about his activity yesterday morning, Thursday."

Franzoser fell silent.

"You still there?" asked Sturmbach.

"Yes. . . . Yes, there most certainly was. This guy had an impeccable attendance record. Then he calls in sick yesterday morning – food poisoning or something. A few hours after that, he strolls in looking fine. Very strange."

"That's very interesting. I'd better have a chat with him. I'll do it in person. I've got some other work to tend to. I should be there by three o'clock. Will that be all right?" asked Detective Sturmbach

"Of course," said Franzoser.

"Absolutely no word of this to anyone."

CHAPTER SEVENTEEN

A little after three o'clock in the mailroom, Franzoser approached his employee. "Becker, could I have a word with you please?" he asked.

Becker sensed some nervousness in the boss's voice. He also watched Franzoser turn to watch Maria's reaction. She happened to be in the mailroom between deliveries. She was staring at Franzoser. When the boss's eyes met hers, she snapped her anxious gaze away.

Becker looked above Franzoser's office door. The clock read 15:15, three-fifteen. Just like yesterday, Becker was counting the minutes until five o'clock. Every appearance at the door caused him to jump, fearing they had finally come to arrest him.

"Certainly." Becker followed Franzoser to his office.

Franzoser sat at his desk but did not offer a seat to Becker. "Director Campenhausen asked for you by name. It seems he has a special package for you to hand-deliver. He says to bring your coat and meet him in his office."

Becker grabbed his coat and hat. He walked down the hall to the paternoster elevator. He loved stepping onto this open-front, perpetual-motion elevator. He stepped off at the top floor. When he entered Campenhof's offices, he was motioned through by the director's secretary.

"Good afternoon, Herr Becker." Campenhof sat in a massive office, mostly empty, with wide windows. The director looked young for his position, although Becker knew he was upwards of sixty.

"Good afternoon, sir," replied Becker.

"I have these documents to go to the Defense Ministry right away, before the weekend. Franzoser has long boasted that you're the most professional man he's got. And the best dressed." Becker didn't think he was particularly well dressed. But he knew his mailroom colleagues often wore old clothes for the dusty work.

Director Campenhof continued, "This is a very important courier run. That's why I've selected you . . . even over Franzoser."

Becker knew from spying on company mail that Kristner was vying for another big defense contract. "Yes, sir. I'm honored." He took the small package.

"I'm sending you with my driver. You are to enter the ministry and personally hand these documents to Procurement Officer Lothar Riklew. Not to his secretary or anyone else. To Riklew. Is this clear?"

"Absolutely, sir," answered Becker.

"Good," said Campenhof. "I'll tell Franzoser this is your last job for the day. If you finish early, you're free to leave."

"Thank you, sir!" said Becker.

"Now be speedy about it."

"Yes, sir," said Becker.

He took the paternoster elevator back to the ground floor and saw the clock on the opposite wall. It was 15:22. As he walked through the building's entrance lobby, he saw a uniformed police officer ask at reception for Franzoser and Becker.

Oh no! And what about Maria?!? Becker had to get out of here immediately. He turned his head away and almost ran to the waiting driver. As they drove away, he looked out the back window and made sure no one was following.

"Gone?!?" Detective Sturmbach stood in Franzoser's office, despite the invitation to have a seat.

"I'm sorry, Sturmbach," replied Franzoser. "A bittersweet reunion I've provided, I know."

"What am I going to do?!? What are the chances he'll be back by 16:15? That's the latest I can phone in my updates." Sturmbach had fully accounted for his other twenty-nine Beckers with an hour to go.

"He won't be back that early, if at all," said Franzoser.

"Maybe you can help," suggested Sturmbach. "What happened yesterday morning, exactly?"

"Only what I told you," answered Franzoser. "His boarding house matron called to report him sick. She said he'd come in late. And that's what he did, seemingly fit as a fiddle."

"Do you know this woman who called?" Sturmbach asked.

"Not at all," Franzoser answered.

"So the phone call could have been from anyone?"

"I suppose."

"May I use your phone?" asked Sturmbach.

"Yes, of course," replied Franzoser.

Detective Sturmbach gestured toward the door. "I please need to ask you to step outside. At least all your staff is off delivering mail. . . . Thanks." Franzoser closed the door behind him.

Sturmbach called his precinct headquarters. "Peters? Sturmbach here. I need your help. I've got a live one here: Johannes Becker. We need to find the woman who owns his boarding house. Frau Anna Lande, it says here, 68 Maricfel Strasse. Send one of our guys to the house. Look her up. If she works, send another officer to her workplace. We need her immediately. Ask her what she knows about Becker's whereabouts yesterday morning. I'll call you for updates at 15:50, and again if necessary at 16:10. This gets highest priority. Bye."

Sturmbach hung up and opened the office door. "O.K., Franzoser, can you step back in for a moment?" Franzoser came in and shut the door. "You told me the SS was in here earlier this week. What was that woman's name?"

"Geberich," answered Franzoser. "Fräulein Maria Geberich."

The detective wrote it down. "Now, tell me who sent Becker on his errand this afternoon."

"Director Campenhausen, upstairs," answered Franzoser.

"Can you put him through to him on this phone? Thanks."

"Campenhausen," answered the director.

Sturmbach explained who he was and what he needed. Campenhausen gave him the name and phone number for Lothar Riklew. Sturmbach left a message with Riklew's secretary to call him at Kristner.

"I need to keep using your phone here," Sturmbach told Franzoser. "I'm sorry to be commandeering your office like this with no explanation. Remember, not a word to anyone. They're bound to be curious out there. Tell them you have no idea why I'm here."

"No problem," said Franzoser. "Help yourself to whatever you need." He left Sturmbach alone in the office again.

At ten till four, Sturmbach called the precinct. Peters reported that Anna Lande had suddenly called in her absence from teaching school today, to leave town for an alleged family emergency. She could not be reached.

Sturmbach reread Johannes Becker's papers in front of him. He stared at the photo.

Riklew still hadn't called him back. Sturmbach picked up the phone to call him again, trying to intercept Becker at the Defense Ministry.

As Becker rode along, he thought about the ironies. The documents in this sealed package could be a goldmine for London. He was supposed to read any sensitive defense documents he could get his hands on at Kristner. But this was not the moment to risk it.

He'd been trusted by Kristner with this sensitive delivery. But he was a British spy who just missed arrest and doom by leaving the building on this assignment.

It's too bad, he thought, that this delivery isn't to the Army Liaison office instead of the Defense Ministry. In just over twenty-four hours, he would be attempting to read and steal top-secret Army documents. He needed to confirm the fatal weakness in Hitler's army. With or without it – if Becker survived the attempt – he had to communicate the information to save Churchill's life.

The ride from the Kristner Building to the Defense Ministry, from near the bustling Ku'damm to the government district, took only ten minutes.

Inside the Defense Ministry, Becker had to pass through a main checkpoint, where he was expected. On the third floor, too, Officer Riklew's secretary expected him. Becker read the nameplate on the door.

"Herr Riklew will be back in a minute, Herr Becker. Please have a seat."

"Thank you."

"Oh, there he is already. . . . Herr Riklew, here's an urgent message from the Berlin police force."

What?!? Becker's pulse accelerated.

"Thank you, Frau Wintzer. . . . Herr Becker, is it?"

"It's a pleasure, Herr Riklew. Here is the package from Director Campenhausen."

"Thank you, Herr Becker. That will be all. . . . Frau Wintzer, put through that call, please."

Becker fled at the fastest unsuspicious speed possible, exited past the building's entry checkpoint, and all but ran to the waiting chauffeur.

On Becker's ride back towards Kristner, traffic was slower, but not too bad. As he neared the Kristner Building in the chauffeured Kristner car, he saw a clock – one minute past four o'clock. He had to stay far away from the building, from that police officer inquiring after him.

He said to the driver, "My car is parked a few blocks away, near Spichern Strasse. Would you mind dropping me off there? I'm free from work for the rest of the day."

"No problem, sir."

At four minutes past four, Becker got out of the company car, next to Janeck's car. "Thanks for the ride."

Detective Sturmbach was waiting for the company car at the building entrance. He watched the car drive past him and park, its back seat empty. He ran to the driver before he was even out of the car.

"Berlin police. Any word on Herr Becker's whereabouts?"

"I dropped him off at his car, a couple of blocks that way." The driver motioned vaguely up the street. "He's headed home, I guess. Certainly not coming back to work today."

"Where, precisely, did you drop him off?" Sturmbach's voice was exasperated.

"Two-and-a-half blocks up Spichern Strasse, on the left," answered the driver.

"Thanks." Sturmbach stood paralyzed. His watch read 16:15. It was time to call the precinct office with his update of Johannes Becker's story. He raced back to Franzoser's office and called Peters.

"It's Sturmbach again. Here's what I've got. Write it on my list for the captain, and give it to him right away: 'Johannes Becker, no alibi, and a mysterious absence from work for Thursday morning only. Investigation ongoing.'"

Next Sturmbach tried to track down the driver who had dropped off Becker. It was too late – the driver had already left on a new assignment, and wasn't expected back for an hour.

Ten minutes later, Sturmbach pulled a piece of paper out of his pocket: "Maria Geberich." In his last-minute haste, he had neglected to mention either Maria and the SS, or Anna Lande's sudden disappearance. It was too late now. The report was surely on its way to Chief Arndt's office, and from there to who knows where. Sturmbach kept the omissions to himself and returned to precinct headquarters.

Colonel Wächter sat at his desk, watching the clock tick the seconds past four-fifty. Chief Arndt had arrived five minutes ago with four assistants. At the desk of Wächter's secretary, they organized and collated the last straggling reports from across the city.

At precisely 16:59, one minute before five o'clock, Arndt re-entered Wächter's office. Sweat streamed down the chief's jowls. He placed the reports on Wächter's desk.

"Never in my three decades of police service have I witnessed anything like today," said Arndt. "We assigned hundreds of men to this case, we neglected more than one hundred new cases received today, and we had six auto accidents rushing to get this information here on time. . . . So here you are. The papers are in order of precinct sections, as each detective submitted his own report. Out of 1,417 adult male Beckers in Berlin, 85 could not be found; we'll keep looking for those; they are marked as temporarily without an alibi on Thursday morning. Another 117 were tracked down and lack alibis for most or all of yesterday morning. However, of those 117, a full 103 are usually alone on a Thursday morning anyway. But the other 14 of those 117, these 14 men lack alibis and were suspiciously absent from routine activities. . . . I'm sure you're disappointed in the 85 not found yet; I know I am. But I think you'll find the rest quite thorough."

Wächter ran his thumb up the edge of the stack of papers. "Is there a summary sheet of the 14 suspicious cases?" he asked.

"Near the top, yes," answered Arndt.

"Leave your home phone number with my secretary on your way out," ordered Wächter. "I want to be able to find you if I have any questions."

"Yes, sir." Arndt stood for a moment waiting for a more formal dismissal. It didn't come. The chief turned and left.

The untraced 85 Beckers really bothered Wächter. They would surely include a higher incidence of anti-social characters, he believed.

But there were these interesting fourteen suspects. Even that was an intimidating number to investigate on such short order. Wächter looked at the list of their names. Then he pulled out his alphabetical list of Beckers from Chief Arndt earlier this week, which included full address information.

When he cross-checked Johannes Becker, he noticed something interesting. This was the first one whose address read "care of." Wächter cross-checked the others. Johannes Becker was a boarder, more temporary than the other thirteen, and therefore more suspect. There it was: "Johannes Becker, c/o Lande, 68 Maricfel Strasse."

Wächter looked at today's report on Johannes. Conducted by Detective Andreas Sturmbach. Wächter phoned the Schöneberg precinct.

"Sturmbach," he answered.

"Colonel Kurt Wächter, here. Gestapo. I need to ask you about the report you filed today."

"Certainly, sir," replied Sturmbach.

"What do you know about the Lande household, host to Johannes Becker?" asked Wächter.

"The strangest thing, sir," said Sturmbach. "Since Johannes was absent from work on Thursday morning, I wanted to check his residence for any alibis. I had my office call Frau Anna Lande at work. There it was reported that she had suddenly called in absent today. Allegedly some kind of family emergency has taken her to Bavaria for the weekend. She and her sixteen-year-old daughter, Nadine, seem to be gone."

"Why the hell wasn't this on the report, Sturmbach?!?" fumed Wächter. He might otherwise have missed Johannes Becker, but for the "care of" address. Wächter loathed sloppiness in police investigations. How glad he was he worked for the Gestapo now.

"I'm sorry, sir," said Sturmbach. "I did mark him as suspicious, sir."

"Is there anything else related to this case?" demanded Wächter.

"Yes, sir," replied Sturmbach. "Earlier this week in Johannes Becker's office at Kristner Company, the SS briefly detained a woman by the name of, let's see here, Fräulein Maria Geberich. I don't know anything else about that case. And that's all I know about this Johannes Becker character as well."

"Who told you about Maria Geberich?" asked Wächter. He was fundamentally suspicious of any unmarried woman over twenty-five. They ought to be creating little babies for the Fatherland, thought Wächter.

"Her boss, Albrecht Franzoser, also at Kristner," answered Sturmbach.

"When you are explicitly told, Sturmbach, that state security is at stake, you are compelled to provide the most thorough report," said Wächter. "I am going to file a complaint with your precinct captain."

"I'm sorry, sir. Yes –"

Wächter slammed down the phone. He opened the file he had been maintaining on Becker since the tram chase a week ago today, before he even knew the name.

One of the old ladies he'd queried on the same U-Bahn train on Monday seemed the most competent among his witnesses. He picked up the phone again and had his called connected.

"Moldauer," answered her tired voice.

"Frau Moldauer, it's Standartenführer Wächter again, investigating Herr Becker from the U-Bahn last Friday. I thought you might be able to help me with a new lead."

"Yes?" she replied, energized.

"It's possible I have the name of the young lady talking with our man Becker. Will you tell me if you recognize it? If you don't, that's all right. Just say so."

"I'll try," she said. "I'm not sure I'll recognize it. But let's try."

"Geberich. Fräulein Maria Geberich."

"Yes! Geberich – that's it! That's definitely it! Oh, I'm so glad you found it, Herr Wächter!"

"Yes," Wächter smiled wickedly. "So am I. So am I. . . . Thank you very much for your help, Frau Moldauer. I've got to work on this now. Goodbye."

"Goodbye," she said.

Wächter opened his phone book. There she was: Maria Geberich, 116 Arnold Strasse.

CHAPTER EIGHTEEN

At five o'clock, Maria left work for the weekend. A half-mile into her walk home through bustling Berlin, she gasped in surprise.

"Good evening!" Becker sat behind the open window of a parked car. He was parked far from the Kristner Building. He thought he was safe.

"Oh! You scared me! What beautiful flowers, thank you." She hesitated to reach for them and continued in a much softer voice, "Is anyone following me?"

Becker glanced in the rear-view mirror at the rush-hour sidewalk in the winter twilight. "I don't think so."

"You have to get out of here, Johannes."

"I know," he replied. "Will you ride with me?"

"All the better," she answered.

Becker waited until the doors closed them in the car, and he rolled up his window. "How much did you see?" He started the car and pulled into traffic. That was safer than lingering parked on the side of the street, he thought.

"The police came after you left," she said.

"Only the police? Not the SS?" he asked.

"That's right. And they weren't looking for me. Judging by the way Franzoser kept looking at your desk, it's you they're after."

"I saw the cop asking for me in the lobby at Kristner. They've found me. A week almost to the minute since the chase, and they've found me."

Becker was also thinking that Nadine might have led to this, not the Gestapo. Maria knew nothing about Becker's British masters. He couldn't tell her about Nadine and his dream in English.

"There's no way I can go home," he said. "At least not tonight. I don't know if you should, either. You're doubly jeopardized. First, you were talking with me when I ran from the Gestapo. Second, our . . . ." Becker paused didn't know what to call it, because it was still evolving. "Our walks this week."

Becker reflected further on the few facts he had. "But this was the regular police, not the SS or Gestapo. Very interesting. They haven't linked you to me; they didn't ask for you. There are other ways they could track me down besides the tram chase last Friday." That was all the elaboration she needed on that topic.

"On the other hand," he continued, "after the drama of your arrest on Wednesday, Franzoser might have mentioned that to the police. It wouldn't take much to get them back on your case. I'm so sorry for the trouble I've caused you." And he was, even if her connection should make this weekend's break-in easier.

As he drove, Becker kept changing streets and checking his mirrors to see if they were being followed. It looked like they were clear.

"I won't go home, then," she said. "I was already scared to. But with no sign of you at five o'clock, I didn't know what to do. I'm staying with you until this is all over, Johannes." She managed a thin smile in the face of their grim danger.

Becker thought aloud. "We can hide out at Janeck's place until tomorrow. He did say they might come for him any day. But next to my place and yours, Janeck's looks relatively safe tonight. What do you think?"

"I don't see any alternative," she answered.

"Janeck's it is, then. Is there anything you need from your apartment? For tomorrow's meeting with your brother Rupert? Or for that matter . . . ever again?"

"Mother of God, what have I gotten myself into?!?" she exclaimed. "Max. My brother's photo. It's the only copy. I just don't know. What do you think? What would you do?"

Becker wanted her to stay safe, away from her apartment. It was better for her. And it would help his chances to conclude his mission.

But more important, he was responsible for any danger she now faced. And she was volunteering to help him. He would honor her wishes and deal with the consequences.

"It's extremely risky," he said. "I wouldn't do it."

"I don't know," she said. "At least drive the car towards my apartment while I think about it."

Becker obliged, prepared to turn away at the slightest hint of danger.

They rode toward Arnold Strasse in the heavy Friday evening traffic.

"What about my passport?" she asked. "Will I need it?"

"It would help," he replied. "But we can do without it."

"I think I'm looking for an excuse for risking the photo," she confessed.

"What would Max want you to do?" he asked. Becker was now driving down Arnold Strasse. His heart raced and his eyes darted around the street near Maria's building.

"Well put," she said, barely holding back tears. "All right. . . . I won't do it."

"Turn toward me – Look at your apartment!" he said.

"The light's on! Someone's in there! . . . Now it just went off."

"Now look forward," said Becker. "They might have someone in the street looking for you."

"But no one's coming out. They're just going to wait there in the dark until I come home, that's their plan." She started crying. "Get me out of here, Johannes. Get me out of Berlin. Get me out of this country. . . . Oh, Max, my lost brother! Goodbye, Max!" She broke into sobs.

Becker held Maria's hand for a moment before switching into higher gear. "I'm sorry. I'm very, very sorry."

Across town in Schöneberg, at half past five o'clock, Standartenführer Wächter banged on the door at 68 Maricfel Strasse, the Lande residence.

After thirty seconds with no answer, Wächter went to the kitchen door on the side. His gloved fist broke the glass. He let himself in, followed by his trusted assistant Sergeant Schleunert. Wächter turned on the lights and saw nothing in particular, just a regular middle-class family home, scarcely heated, as if recently abandoned.

He glanced at the empty rooms downstairs and then walked to the bedrooms upstairs. In the upstairs hallway, all the doors were shut. Wächter opened the first door, in front of him. It held only a few scattered belongings, including one pair of men's shoes. Wächter was sure this was Becker's room.

"Schleunert!" Wächter stood aside while Schleunert tore the room apart. He dumped the desk contents on the floor, and then hurled the desk out of the room, followed by the mattress and bed frame. Next he tore Becker's belongings from the wardrobe, and stood aside.

Wächter rubbed down the interior of the wardrobe for any false walls. He climbed the desk chair to check the top. Then he and Schleunert sifted through Becker's desk contents and clothes on the floor. Nothing unusual.

"Let me see that coat," demanded Wächter.

Schleunert handed it to him.

"You see the stitching on the lining? It doesn't look right." Wächter pressed the thick coat against the wall and felt around the suspect spot. Still not satisfied, he took out a knife and sliced through the lining and coat all the way to the wall on the other side.

A few papers fluttered to the floor.

"Well, well!" said Wächter. This was his man! Johannes Becker. Wächter was elated. In less than ten hours, with the entire Berlin police force at his command, he'd done it! He'd found Agent Z!

Among the documents on the floor, Becker's face stared up from a French passport in the name of "Adolphe Beauregard."

"Let's see what else we can find," said Wächter. "Get the wardrobe and rug out of here. I want the place bare."

Schleunert pulled the wardrobe out of the room. When he let it fall to the floor, the height of it went past the top stairs, and the whole thing crashed to the floor below.

Good, thought Wächter, *that'll get the neighbors talking!*

Then Schleunert carefully rolled up the carpet and shoved it out as well.

"Rip up that mattress and search it," ordered Wächter, "while I look through the desk contents on the floor."

Schleunert had the mattress in shreds within minutes. "Nothing here, Standartenführer."

"Now go tell the immediate neighbors that Herr Johannes Becker is a wanted man. Any sighting of him is to be reported immediately to the local police. Next go to the district police station and give them the update. We've found our Becker! But first, use the phone downstairs to call Columbia-Haus. Tell them to send two more deputies immediately to search the rest of the house."

Next Wächter started tapping the walls and the floor in search of hollow places. He paid particular attention to where the bed had been. And sure enough, a floorboard there seemed loose. Wächter picked up a letter opener and pried up the loose floorboard. Underneath were stacks of cash. He pulled up the bundles and leafed through German marks, French francs, and Swiss francs.

Agent Z! Wächter was thrilled with his good fortune.

Becker and Maria entered Janeck's building and walked across the courtyard. At this early evening hour, residents were buzzing around the place. When Becker and Maria climbed the stairwell to Janeck's flat, they both avoided eye contact with one woman coming down.

Becker didn't like this slight encounter. There were only four flats above Janeck's. He and Maria were strangers here. The woman had to be wondering who they were and what brought them here.

Becker waited until the woman was out of the stairwell before pausing at Janeck's door. He unlocked it, and he and Maria entered quickly. As soon as the door shut behind them, Maria dropped her flowers in Janeck's dark hallway. Becker held his hat in his hand and was about to pick up the flowers when Maria clutched him. She pressed her head into his chest and was silent. He embraced her around the shoulders. Her fingers nearly bruised his biceps, she gripped him so hard.

"I'm so afraid," she said.

"We'll make it," he promised. He believed they would, but he knew the next two days would be hard and unpredictable. "We'll get through this."

Rosa the cat purred as she approached them and stroked her back against their legs.

"This place scares me," she said. "Janeck said they'd come tear it apart any day now. And who knows what Janeck's really up to."

Becker remembered Janeck's promise to ask one more time for help. That request hadn't come yet, from Janeck or through anyone else. He expected to find some clue here in Janeck's flat. Janeck's immediate concerns were not his, except for the refuge of this apartment.

"He's a mystery to me," said Becker. "But I think if his danger were so imminent, he would have fled immediately and wouldn't have stuck around to find me. We're probably safe here."

"Maybe it's not as bad as Janeck said," she said. "But after the past few days, this place just adds to the stress."

"I'm sorry," he said while he held her shoulders firmly in his hands. "I'll do my best to make it comfortable."

Maria held still for a moment and then let him go. She reached towards the wall and turned on the hall light.

"I have to call my brother Rupert to confirm our lunch tomorrow," she said, "before he tries to call my apartment and wonders where I am."

"Sounds good," he said.

The cat followed Maria to the phone in the small sitting room. Becker followed her. They both sat on the sofa, with three feet empty between them.

"What if the phone is tapped?" she asked.

Even with the lights still off, the room felt crowded. It was smaller than Maria's sitting room. And unlike hers, Janeck had this placed stuffed with small furniture, cheap wall hangings, papers, and books. Becker was reminded of how dirty the apartment was. By now, old cat litter joined the bouquet of unemptied ashtrays and dirty dishes.

"Assume it's tapped," he replied. "Just keep the call as straightforward as possible, and avoid names."

Maria dialed her brother's home in the Wedding district northwest of downtown.

"Hi Rupert! . . . Well, I'm glad I reached you before you went out. I'm going out tonight with my girlfriends from work, and– . . . . No, don't worry, I won't tell them anything else about my detention. They all know about it, though. You know that. It happened right in front of them. . . . Anyway, so I wanted to call you first since I won't be home, just to make sure we're all set for tomorrow. . . . Great. Then Herr Becker and I will see you tomorrow. . . . Oh, one more thing. I'm getting my hair done earlier in the morning. You know, the hairdresser down my street. Do you think you could come pick me up there at ten-thirty? I've given Herr Becker your address and he'll meet us at eleven. . . . Good, thanks. See you tomorrow! Bye."

"Good thinking about the hairdresser," said Becker. He opened the flat's windows to let in fresh air.

"Thanks. He would be a little jealous if you gave me a ride, which wouldn't start things off well. Take care about that tomorrow."

"All right. Our story will be that we haven't seen each other since work on Friday?"

"Right," she replied.

"Got it. Now for the matter of your hairdresser. How much do you trust her?"

"She is very discreet, and loyal to her regular customers. She tells us about special shopping deals and such, but only when no one new is around. What's more, she's seen my neck scars, of course. Every time. But she never asks about them. She makes sure no one else sees them. She's been wonderful to me."

"That's the best we can ask," he said. "By tomorrow morning, the Gestapo might have asked every merchant in your neighborhood to be on the lookout for you. In fact, if they missed opening hours today, they might be prowling around those places tomorrow exactly when you plan to meet Rupert. It'll be treacherous. Do you think your hairdresser will be more than discreet? I mean, will she conceal you if needed?"

"She would try it in a way that made her look innocent, I think. I don't think she would risk getting sent to a concentration camp. But she'd do everything short of that."

Becker was concerned. This wasn't the first place he would have chosen for Rupert to pick her up. Berlin was crawling not just with formal Gestapo agents, but also informants of all stripes. The Gestapo excelled in placing snitches in public places like a hair salon. It was going to be more than tricky. It was going to be dangerous. But the call to Rupert was done. Anything further might arouse Rupert's suspicions. He dropped the issue.

"Since the Gestapo is watching my flat," said Maria, "I guess we're stuck here tomorrow night, too?"

"It looks like," he replied. "It turns out that everyone else at my boarding house will be gone for the weekend. But with the police after me, I can't go back there. Especially not with you, since they weren't looking for you today. And yes, we definitely need the place for two nights. We won't be leaving the country until Sunday."

"Are we really going to come out of this weekend alive, Johannes? Or are you dragging me into some sort of suicidal mission?"

"One knows not what yet may pass," he replied.

"Ludwig Uhland," smiled Maria. "Faith in Spring." She recited the poem by Ludwig Uhland:

> *The gentle breezes are awakened,*
> *They sigh and waft, day and night,*
> *They give life at each turn.*
> *Oh dewy scent, oh new tone!*
> *Now, poor soul, be not afraid!*
> *Now must it all, all turn.*

Becker quoted the next verse:

> *With each day the world more fair,*
> *One knows not what yet may pass,*
> *The blossoming wants not adjourn.*
> *The farthest, deepest dell does bloom,*
> *Now, poor soul, forget the pain!*
> *Now must it all, all turn.*

"May our own world indeed see a fairer tomorrow," said Maria.

"Yes. And with us still in it. In answer to your question," Becker lowered his voice, "Lives will continue to be lost in the fight. But I don't intend them to be ours, or Rupert's. Our business tomorrow and the next few days is dangerous and essential, but not suicidal."

They sat some moments in silence.

Suddenly, the flat's front door was unlocked, opened, and shut again. Someone was standing in the hallway!

Maria and Becker exchanged terrified glances. They both sat frozen in place. It was possible the intruder didn't know they were there. Slow footsteps approached the open door to the sitting room. The lights were still out in there. But they were plainly visible by the hallway light. From their positions on the sofa, Maria would be seen first, then Becker.

Becker put his hand on the Luger under his shirt. The floorboards were far too noisy for him to move to ambush the intruder. They were sitting ducks.

"Fräulein Geberich," greeted Janeck's voice, just out of Becker's sight in the hallway. "I thought that was you I saw coming in." He took two more steps and leaned against the sitting room doorway.

Janeck was average height, heavy, and out of breath. His fedora was bent low over his face and he wore a long dark trench coat. His right hand gripped his gun, pointed almost straight down his side. A silhouette worthy of the movies, thought Becker.

"Good evening, Becker." Janeck turned on a floor lamp next to him. He pointed at Maria with his free hand and gave Becker a questioning look.

"It's all right, Janeck," said Becker. "She knows."

"Yeah, I'll bet she does. More than I do, about you anyway. You've got your own agenda, whatever it is. . . . Any chance you've had a change of heart about serving the Socialist exiles?"

"I'm afraid not, Janeck." Becker sensed that Janeck respected him. The feeling was mutual.

"What do you want?" asked Janeck. "Money? A false passport? I can get you any number of things."

"Nothing," replied Becker. "I won't do it. I can't do it. You keep tracking me down, and you say they're tracking you down. That means you're putting me in danger. Please stop, if I may ask." Becker wasn't in a strong position to make demands, sitting on Janeck's sofa. "If you want your car back—"

"Keep it," replied Janeck, before Becker could fish out the keys.

"Much appreciated," said Becker. Next he decided to trust his instincts about Janeck's sincerity. Becker always knew if someone was lying. He wanted Janeck to leave them alone.

"I'll be frank about something," said Becker. "Access to your flat has proven invaluable to me this weekend."

Janeck looked at Maria and raised an eyebrow.

Becker shook his head. "As a matter of survival. Broadly speaking, let's just say I'm sure you'd approve."

Janeck frowned in thought. "You'd be more effective working with my organization than on your own. But you're stubborn. So be it. . . . Remember, I don't know how long you can hide out here. Franzoser thinks I'm coming back on Monday."

He turned off the lamp and started backing out of the doorway, the gun still in his hand. "They might come looking for me on Monday . . . or sooner. Beware!"

CHAPTER NINETEEN

Saturday, February 15

Becker and Maria slept poorly in the fear and stench of Janeck's flat. They left the place before dawn to escape it.

The smell of the morning's snowfall invigorated them instantly. The next three hours they sat in two successive cafés, where freshly ground coffee was heaven on earth. Even fresh cigarette smoke around them was hardly noticeable after spending the night among stale ashes.

Now the coffee chitchat was done. They faced the perils of re-entering Maria's neighborhood. They knew the Gestapo was waiting for her to return home. Becker drove Janeck's Opel to the far end of Arnold Strasse.

"I don't know your street from this direction very well," he said.

"Just leave me at the corner here," said Maria. "Not too close to my flat. I can get to the hairdresser's from here."

"Even for ten o'clock on a Saturday morning, the traffic seems light," commented Becker.

"This is usual, even without snow," she replied.

Becker pulled the car over, and Maria started to open the door. Becker grabbed her arm, and she turned back to return his gaze. "Please be careful, Maria. They might have the whole neighborhood looking for you by now." The next half-hour was perhaps the most dangerous they would face today, he knew. Maybe more dangerous than breaking into Army headquarters tonight.

Maria nodded and got out.

Becker pulled the car away, looking at Maria in the mirror. She was bundled thick against the snow in her coat and bright red hat. The hat was beautiful on her. It was too prominent, but it's what she had worn to work on Friday morning.

Maria walked briskly as the snow overflowed the cobblestone cracks and indentations. Her hidden face was unrecognizable from more than a few yards away. Soon all Becker could see were puffs of breath rising from the walking bundle.

They were supposed to meet in an hour at Maria's brother's house. In the meantime, Maria might get arrested on her street, in which case he'd never hear from her again.

Ursula Scherer the hairdresser looked up from her work to see who was entering her hair salon.

"Good morning, Frau Scherer," said Maria. "Good morning," she added to the only other client.

"Good morning," answered the unknown client.

"Good morning, Frau Mencke," said the hairdresser.

Ursula saw the surprise in Maria Geberich's face. She kept her calm in repeating the family name of Maria's stepbrother, not the usual Geberich. "What can I do for you today, Frau Mencke?" Ursula caught Maria's eye in a mirror that the other client didn't see. She pointed her head toward the dangers of the street outside. She thought she saw Maria beginning to understand.

Maria paused a few seconds and finally nodded. Then she answered, "Just the basics, please. A couple of inches off. I'll have to go without the curlers for now, since my brother's coming to pick me up for lunch in a little while."

"Gladly," replied Ursula. "If you'll wait here for a couple of minutes," she pointed at a chair, "I'll be right with you."

Ursula turned to the first client. "Does that look fine?"

"Good as always." The first client's compliment was matter-of-fact, but by Berlin standards almost too gushing. She turned her head in the mirror and then stood up and paid. She put on her coat and hat and approached the door. "*Auf Wiedersehen*, ladies."

"*Auf Wiedersehen*," they answered together.

When they were alone, Ursula changed her tone abruptly. "What are you doing here?!?" she whispered emphatically.

"Getting my hair cut," replied Maria.

"No!" said Ursula. "You have to get out of here. If I get caught with you in here, it will be the end of me. How did you get here? They're looking all over for you."

"The whole neighborhood knows about that?" reflected Maria. "That's not good. What is it now, ten o'clock? I've got to make it another half-hour. . . . Please! This is where I'm getting picked up, precisely because I can't go home. Please let me stay here!"

Ursula just stared at her regular client Maria for a few moments. "If I let you stay," she started, "then this conversation didn't happen.

I'll keep calling you Frau Mencke. But if you get caught, you're on your own, you understand?"

"Understood," replied Maria.

"All right, all right . . . ," Ursula mulled over the problem she had on her hands. "A couple of inches you say?"

"Right, thank you," said Maria. "I cannot possibly thank you enough, Frau Scherer."

"It's just a simple haircut!" Ursula winked nervously.

During the short haircut, two more clients came in. One of them was one of Ursula's regulars. She had an appointment that Maria was intruding upon. She voiced her displeasure and kept glaring at Maria.

Ursula ended Maria's haircut with an unsolicited wash, to give her a reason to sit and wait until ten-thirty, for her hair to dry. Maria accepted the wash as if she had requested it.

Ursula kept looking at the clock – 10:18, 10:22, 10:24. She started sweating. She desperately hoped Rupert Mencke would show up soon. She wasn't sure how much more of this she could take. In any event, she knew she'd never see Maria again. She'd never been so eager to be rid of a loyal customer.

At 10:30, on the minute, Rupert walked in the door. Ursula had met him here once before.

"Hello, Maria!" he said.

"Hi, Rupert!" she replied.

"Good morning, ladies." Rupert greeted the others with a tip of his Army cap. Even his long thick coat was Army issue. He looked like he'd been at work this morning.

Rupert watched as Maria carefully and quickly pinned part of her wet black hair over her head and left the rest covering her neck. At no moment did she leave the scars uncovered. Then she stood up and walked to embrace Rupert. She put on her coat and hat, and he offered his arm.

"Shall we?" he said.

"Wait a minute," interjected the ruffled regular salon client. "Aren't you–"

Rupert watched Frau Scherer's face go white and wondered what was wrong.

"Aren't you Thomas Martin?" asked the client

"No, ma'am," replied Rupert. "I'm sorry, you must be mistaken."

"Oh no, the fault is mine," she answered. "Forgive me, please. I took you for an old schoolmate of my brother's."

"*Auf Wiedersehen,*" Maria announced to the salon.

"*Auf Wiedersehen*," joined Rupert.

"Goodbye," they answered together. Frau Scherer only mumbled it, and she didn't look at them.

Rupert thought that was odd. She was so sociable the other time he was here.

Brother and sister, as they saw themselves, stepped out into the gathering snowstorm.

"Are you parked nearby?" asked Maria.

"Just down the street, close to your place," he replied.

Rupert watched Maria pull her hat down low in protection against the snow. He couldn't even see her face from his height. The snow muffled their footsteps and all the usual street sounds. They walked arm-in-arm without speaking, listening to the near silence. Half a block away, they entered Rupert's car and drove away.

Rupert drove slowly in the snow. "Have you been all right since I took you home on Thursday?"

"Yes, fine, thanks," answered Maria as she put her red hat in her lap. "The people at work have been very gracious. They could have shunned me there after my SS detention. Instead, they've been doubly nice. I'm lucky. In a lot of places, I'd be completely ostracized by now, or even fired. . . . By the way, they all saw Becker call you on Wednesday. They're pretty impressed that you seemed able to help me so quickly."

"Who knows with the SS," he said. Rupert's SA faction of the Nazi Party had lost power, in favor of the SS snobs, as he saw them. They were dangerous snobs, he knew.

"I don't know what those SS bastards wanted with you. It's true my boss, Major Hossbach, holds a lot of sway as the Führer's personal military liaison. . . . This week, I even got to see the Führer up close. He had a meeting with the general staff. In fact, after lunch today, I have to go help Hossbach type up the notes. He likes to finish a week's business before Saturday night and Sunday dull his memory. He gave me special leave for our lunch, to be a good big brother and all after your rough week. Afterwards, instead of going to the office, I'm headed to his house in Dahlem. . . . You remember the place, right? I took you to a reception there once."

"Oh, yes, I think I do," replied Maria. "A beautiful villa with a wonderful garden, as I recall."

"That's the place," he said.

"Sounds like a lovely place to spend a Saturday afternoon," she said. "Even in the snow."

"It sure is coming down thick now. Do you think this Becker fellow is good with directions? The landmarks will be unrecognizable after much more of this."

Rupert realized that for the first time in his life, he wasn't jealous of a man Maria knew. Becker's phone call had quite possibly saved his sister. Perhaps this was the right man for Maria, after all these years. Rupert never thought he would want to see Maria attached. He hadn't even met Becker yet, only spoken to him on the phone. But he had the urge to encourage Maria to be with this man.

"He'll find it all right, I think," said Maria. "He's quite resourceful."

"That's certainly true," Rupert spoke in admiration.

Traffic thinned as Rupert drove out of Berlin's business district toward his neighborhood in Wedding. He pulled up to his narrow townhouse and parked on the street.

Inside, they both removed their coats and hats. Maria pulled her hair across her shoulders to dry. All six-feet-plus of Rupert stood tall and straight and proud in his Army uniform. They weren't even out of the hallway when they heard the knock at the door.

Rupert pulled the door open and smiled broadly. "You must be Herr Becker! Come in!" The two men shook hands.

"Thank you, Herr Mencke," answered Becker. "It's my pleasure."

Rupert took his coat and hat.

"Good morning, Herr Becker." Maria offered her hand.

"Good morning, Fräulein Geberich." Becker shook her hand without the slightest flirtation. "It's so generous of your brother to invite me to lunch."

"Not at all, after what you did for my sister this week," replied Rupert.

"All I did was pass along news to a devoted brother," said Becker.

"Excuse me for a moment . . . ," said Rupert. Then he called down the hall, "Anja, Herr Becker is here."

Anja was a short, dark-blonde with gray eyes. Her attractive roundish face looked somewhat Slavic.

"Allow me to introduce my girlfriend, Anja Strepka," said Rupert. Anja and Becker exchanged pleasantries. The two women greeted each other in familiar terms. Rupert had been seeing Anja for three years.

Rupert gestured toward the sitting room at the back of the ground floor. "Please have a seat."

Becker and Maria sat in chairs across the coffee table from each other, Anja on the sofa. The dining table was set on the opposite side of the room.

"Some tea?" asked Rupert. They all accepted.

While the water heated, the tall muscular host returned and sat on the sofa between his guests. "Herr Becker, thank you again for thinking to call me on Wednesday. It's good you called right away. Major Hossbach was headed for a quick trip to Hamburg. I got his help just in time."

"Did you give him my thanks for helping me?" asked Maria.

"Yes, this morning by phone, and I will again this afternoon in person," answered Rupert.

"You work on Saturdays?" inquired Becker.

"Not usually," replied Rupert. "But today, yes, to catch up on the week's business after Hossbach's trip." He felt proud to be so ready and devoted to his military service.

"Then I'm doubly honored that you're making time for me today," said Becker.

"I'll tell the Major you said so," said Rupert. "He's holding up his own schedule today just for this reunion with my sister and you. . . . They get so much right – wouldn't you agree, Becker? It's unbelievable they would make such a mistake, arresting Maria. All based on some former acquaintance. Maria can't help it if someone she knew long ago turned up a traitor to the Fatherland."

Becker paused. Rupert waited for his response. Maria and Anja looked silently toward him, too.

"It does make one wonder," started Becker. "They certainly know more about what they're doing than I can. And they have the Führer's trust. But how could they come to detain your good, honest sister? I can't imagine."

"Precisely!" Rupert clapped his hands once and clasped them together. "I'm sure the higher-ups will severely reprimand those responsible." He looked to the others for their agreement. No one objected.

"The water's boiling," observed Rupert. "Maria, could you please give me a hand in the kitchen for a moment? Excuse us, please, Herr Becker, Anja." Rupert closed both the sitting room door and the kitchen door between them.

Once in the kitchen, Rupert observed, "He's really nice to you, isn't he? Not too pushy, you know."

He was happy for his sister. He was sure some of her previous suitors had been nice, too. For some reason, though, he liked this one. Maybe he was getting old, he chuckled to himself.

"How long have you known him?" he asked.

"Since he started at Kristner, more than a year ago," she answered.

"Well, I certainly approve of him. Not that you need my approval, though!" Rupert studied Maria's face. He wondered how involved she was with Becker. But she could be as inexpressive as a stump.

"How much does he know?" he asked. "I mean, about your . . . career?"

"Nothing!" she snapped. "And you mustn't tell him!"

Rupert couldn't have gotten more out of her if he'd tried. He could see Becker was important to her. "All right, all right! I was just curious."

He balanced the large tea tray in one hand and opened the kitchen door for her with the other. They returned to the sitting room, where Rupert let Anja pour the tea. She then went to the kitchen to finish lunch preparations.

"Your sister tells me, Herr Mencke, that you work for the Army Liaison office," said Becker. "She's quite proud of you."

Rupert beamed.

"How do you like it?" asked Becker.

"Great, and getting better every day," replied Rupert. "Now that the Führer has renounced our arms limitations, the Wehrmacht has become such a dynamic place. These are really exciting times."

"Exciting in what way?" asked Maria.

"Of course, I can't say much. But you know, what you read in the newspapers. We're now able to expand. And we're working on a real defense of the Fatherland." Rupert stopped himself. He'd said enough.

Anja appeared with a pushcart in the doorway. "Lunch is served! We'll start with beef and carrot stew, served with toast au gratin. That will be followed by sliced pears. Finally, we will have a warm chocolate cake, served with whipped cream and coffee."

"Thank you!" said Becker. "Both of you. This looks and smells marvelous!"

Lunch conversation ranged from the raging snowstorm outside, to Rupert's short monologues on German greatness.

In the middle of dessert, the phone rang.

"Who could that be?" Rupert asked himself aloud. "Please excuse me." He carried the phone into the hallway and closed the door.

"What a lovely meal, Anja," said Maria.

"Thank you," she replied.

Rupert returned and replaced the phone on its stand. He gathered his coat and hat in the hall, and then came back to his guests. "Hossbach is concerned about the weather slowing me down later this afternoon. He doesn't want to be late for his party tonight, so he wants us to get a start on things. He apologizes to you all, as do I. But I have to go do some work for him now. . . . Maria, you may stay here overnight, if that's more convenient for you in the snowstorm. If you need to get home, I'm sure Herr Becker can take you."

Rupert turned to Becker. "Herr Becker, thank you again for helping my sister this week. We'll see each other again soon, I hope."

Then he leaned over Anja. "Thanks for the wonderful meal, my treasure." He gave her a kiss on top of the head. "I'll see you at your place when I'm done this evening. . . . Bye, everyone!"

"*Tschüss!*" they sounded in unison.

After they finished dessert, Anja took the dishes into the kitchen and began cleaning up. Becker and Maria walked across the room to the sofa.

Becker noted to himself that the water and clanging dishes in the kitchen were more than enough to allow them private conversation in the sitting room.

"This is unexpected." He spoke softly. "I could try to get an extra uniform upstairs and just stride into Army headquarters, presuming to be your brother."

"Are you kidding?" whispered Maria. "You're several inches shorter, and a lot smaller."

Becker knew it wouldn't be easy. Maria didn't understand the urgency of his mission.

"No," she said. "Here's another idea. Rupert told me something very interesting. The work he has to do this afternoon? He's typing up notes from a meeting earlier this week. A meeting with Hitler! That's the kind of thing you're after, right?"

Becker nodded. That could be a goldmine!

"Evidently," continued Maria, "they'll leave the meeting's minutes there at Hossbach's house for the rest of the weekend. I think you should try there instead of the Liaison office. Or at least try Hossbach first," she urged.

"Very interesting," said Becker. "It's worth a try. But I still want to get one of his spare uniforms. Oh, but there's a problem. More than the uniforms I need Rupert's keys, and he took those with him. . . . Well, that certainly limits my options. . . . Hossbach's house it is."

Becker thought to himself, if he found nothing valuable at Hossbach's house, he could pay Rupert an unexpected visit tonight. Then he could get the keys and a uniform, and try to break into Army headquarters during the night. But he didn't need to trouble Maria with that contingency plan for now.

After all, even with keys and a uniform, breaking into Army headquarters was perilous. He knew – he'd been there. If it were only a question of his mission, he'd have a contingency plan ready for tonight.

Yet there was the assassination plot against Churchill. Only four days remained till Wednesday's concert. What if Hossbach's house yielded nothing? He should probably postpone any more dangers and get the assassination news to London. Once Churchill was saved, Becker could re-enter Germany and tackle the break-in.

"I guess we need to get out of here, then," said Becker. "Before we get snowed in."

He and Maria thanked Anja again for lunch and walked to Janeck's black Opel on the street.

Once they were inside the car, Becker thought aloud. "I'm going to leave a lot of footprints outside Hossbach's house tonight, I'm afraid. And if this storm keeps up, it's going to be hard to make a quick getaway in the car, too."

"I've been to Hossbach's house once," said Maria. "It has multiple approaches."

"You know the place?!? That's fantastic! Tell me everything you remember."

CHAPTER TWENTY

For hours on end, Becker and Maria sat parked down the street from Major Hossbach's house, waiting for him to leave. It was freezing cold, and now it was dark, too. The car windows were cracked open so the insides wouldn't fog. Becker let snow pile up the side windows to hide them from passers-by. But the windshield he cleaned every ten minutes with a crank of the wipers. He needed clear sight lines to the Hossbach house entrance down the street.

It had already snowed more than a foot since morning. Becker knew the getaway drive would be slow. At least he'd bought new tires that afternoon. They'd also bought some automat passport photos for Maria.

"Are you doing all right?" he asked Maria.

She nodded.

Becker looked at his watch. "Half an hour since we saw Rupert leave the Hossbach house. I wonder when the Hossbachs themselves will leave for the party. It could be hours still."

Becker was bored, but well trained to concentrate through hours of boredom for that crucial moment. At times, Maria closed her eyes to rest.

"At least it's finally dark," she observed. "We won't likely be seen sitting in here now."

"Yes," he said, "but the Dahlem district is teeming with Nazis and informants." Sitting still in the cold was tiring. Part of him kept begging for sleep. It was cold enough to remind him of his hypothermia the night he'd escaped in the canal.

"You would have been safer and warmer back at Janeck's flat," he insisted.

"No," she repeated. "We're in this together. And besides, you're my only way out of this. No way are we getting separated!"

"Well, your knowledge of the path behind the house will be most useful," he admitted. "And I'm glad to know Hossbach doesn't like dogs. . . . Did Rupert say anything today about whether Hossbach's children were going out, too?"

"I wish he had," she replied. "It sounded like it was a late party, so I guess his kids will be staying home. The house probably won't be empty."

"Have you ever heard anything about a nanny, or who would stay with the kids?" he asked.

"No, sorry," she replied.

"I guess we just keep watching for the Hossbachs to leave."

Anna and Nadine stared at each other coldly across the short distance between their beds. They'd just returned from a walk in the hilly meadows by the house outside Nuremberg. One small desk lamp cast its dim yellow light on the tiny bedroom. Supper with Anna's sister Katerina was an hour away.

"You're staying here," started Anna.

"I don't get to eat?" asked Nadine.

"No, not that," replied Anna. "You get to eat. . . . You're not coming back to Berlin with me. You're staying here. You're going to live with Katerina for awhile."

Nadine's jaw dropped. She searched for words but couldn't find them.

"I would rather it not have come to this," said Anna. "I've lived my life for you since the day you were born. But you have become excessively disobedient . . . unmanageable. Life on the farm here will do you some good."

"Are you out of your mind?" snapped Nadine. "You can't leave me here! I'll run away."

"You won't get far," said Anna. "You're underage, and the authorities will return you to wherever I say."

"The authorities . . . right," said Nadine. "And you know what I'll tell them? I'll tell them you stuck me here to undermine the authorities. I know why you're doing this. It's all about Liesl and Gertrude, isn't it? It's not my fault if they got themselves in trouble. I stand up for the Third Reich, and you don't like it! So you ship me away."

Nadine was nearly screaming by this point. "Well it won't work, Mama! I'll make sure it doesn't! You . . . you . . . Fatherland-traitor!"

Anna wanted to smack Nadine like she had yesterday. But she just sat there, managing to keep calm. She'd anticipated this. Nadine was partially right about why she was being left here. Anna hoped the country life would dilute Nadine's Nazi brainwashing. But it would be perilous for Anna to admit that, even to Katerina.

"You're just making excuses," said Anna. "In fact, you have become deceitful and disobedient, just the opposite of what the Führer demands of good Germans. And what a mother demands of her child. I think you'll find that country life will restore the values you seem to have lost in the past year or so."

Nadine was now smiling. "It's too late to save him, you know."

Anna was puzzled. She raised her eyebrows to question her daughter for elaboration.

"You know very well what I mean . . . ," said Nadine. "Herr Becker. I heard him speaking English in his dreams the other night, so I listened. You know what he said?"

Anna was surprised, and curious to learn more. She shook her head and waited for Nadine to continue.

"'Get Churchill the numbers. . . . Get Churchill the numbers,' he said, over and over," said Nadine.

Anna waited for more.

"That was it, over and over for five minutes. Don't you see Mama?!? Herr Becker is an English spy!"

"You don't know that," said Anna. "His dream could mean anything. You heard him explain why he knows English so well."

Anna found herself hoping that Becker *was* an English spy. The man she quietly loved suddenly seemed larger than life. Since she'd come to loathe the Hitler regime, she was glad to think Becker was working against it. All the more reason to downplay Nadine's claim, she thought.

"Maybe he is a spy, and maybe he isn't," said Nadine. "We'll let the Gestapo find out."

"What?!?" Anna felt shock and sudden desperation.

"Before we left yesterday, I left my boyfriend Martin a note. I had especially his father in mind, Herr Lodt, the not-so-secret Gestapo block leader. I had to tell Martin why I wouldn't be home, that you were taking us to Aunt Katerina's. . . . Well, while I was at it, I told him about Herr Becker's English dream. I'm sure he told his father right away. And from there, it certainly moved up the Gestapo ranks by now. I wonder how long it took them to haul in Herr Becker?" Nadine laughed.

Anna was already standing, pacing the room in silence.

"See?!?" said Nadine. "You're worried for him. . . . You know it's true! Face it, Mama, you've seen the last of darling Herr Becker."

Anna glared at her daughter. She opened her mouth to lecture Nadine but stopped herself. Nadine would have an answer for anything. That's why Anna had brought her to Katerina's farm.

There was only one thing for Anna to do. She had to return home immediately. She could take the night train and get there by morning. She had to save Herr Becker, if it wasn't too late. No danger mattered to her any more. If the worst happened, Nadine was taken care of. Anna had to save him.

Rupert and Anja entered his home laughing, arm-in-arm, snowflakes sprinkled on their heads and shoulders. They smelled of wine and Rupert's cigarette smoke. It was nearly ten o'clock, and Rupert was looking forward to taking Anja upstairs.

"Good evening, Sergeant Mencke," came the voice from the dark sitting room.

Rupert and Anja jumped and then froze in their tracks. Rupert didn't recognize the voice, and he turned on the light. The house was turned upside down – furniture, rugs, and papers scattered everywhere.

"Ahhh!" shrieked Anja and Rupert both. They faced a man in plain clothes and pointing his gun straight at them.

"Who's that?" asked the intruder.

"Anja Strepka," replied Rupert. "My girlfriend. Who are you?"

"Gestapo." Colonel Wächter stepped under the hall light and strained to identify Anja. No, it wasn't Maria. "Fräulein Strepka, I know it's freezing outside. But will you please excuse us for a few minutes?"

Anja was sobbing. "Rupert? What is it?!?"

"I don't know, Anja," he answered. "I'll come for you in just a minute."

Rupert walked her to the front door. After closing it, he turned to face Wächter.

"Hands up!" barked Wächter.

"What . . . what is this all about?" stammered Rupert.

"Where is she?!?" Wächter looked up at the much taller sergeant, then threw his knee into Rupert's groin.

Rupert doubled over and gagged in pain. "Who?" He turned his head upward, genuinely stunned. "I am . . . an officer . . . in the Führer's Army." In his pain, he took short, staccato breaths.

"Don't give me that bullshit, you idiot! I can see you're a mere sergeant. Answer my damn question. And keep your hands above your head, soldier! Where is she?!?"

"Anja? She's right outside. . . . ."

"Your sister, you fool! Maria. Where is she?"

"I don't know. At home, I guess?" Rupert still bent over in pain.

"She hasn't been home since Friday morning," replied Wächter. "We've been watching the place for more than twenty-four hours. Haven't you seen her?"

Rupert didn't know what to say – anything to help his sister.

Wächter made one large fist with both hands and slammed it down onto Rupert's back, forcing the tall sergeant to the floor. "Answer me!"

"I saw her for lunch today." Rupert got up on all fours but kept his head down. "I have no idea what you're talking about. I brought her here for lunch from the hair salon in her neighborhood." He still coughed from Wächter's blows. "Then I left her here in the early afternoon to go work for Major Hossbach . . . *the* Hossbach, Hitler's military liaison."

Rupert Mencke's professional connection actually gave Wächter pause. He had not bothered to pull up Mencke's records. As soon as he'd identified Maria Geberich's stepbrother, he'd rushed here to pursue Becker's cooling trail.

"Where did she go?" demanded Wächter.

"I don't know. I guess Becker – that's Johannes Becker, a fine man – I guess he gave her a ride home . . . er, or somewhere else. I thought she was going home. Hell, what's going on? Really, sir, I have no idea."

"Becker?!?" exclaimed Wächter. "He was here today? What else do you know? Where do you think they went?"

"Becker's place? Wherever that is. Has he gotten her into trouble?" asked Rupert.

Wächter didn't answer.

"My sister is innocent, I'm sure!"

"Shut up!" shouted Wächter. "Schleunert, come out and introduce yourself."

Scharführer Schleunert appeared from the sitting room. He was several inches shorter than Rupert, but very muscular. Sergeant Schleunert pointed his gun at Rupert.

"Listen, Mencke," started Wächter. "You're going to stay here and clean up your place. If your stepsister comes back here, or if you have any sign from her, Schleunert will tell you what to do. He will be your houseguest for the night. . . . Now get off the floor and tell that hussy of yours to go home."

Rupert straggled to the front door and opened it.

Anja embraced him on the threshold. "Rupi, my God, I'm so scared. What's going on?"

"I'm sorry, Anja. I don't know. It's about someone I know." Rupert felt a gun barrel press hard in his back as a warning to shut up on that point. "The man says you have to leave. You know where the bus stop is. I'm really sorry, darling. Please go – get out of this mess."

Anja broke into tears again. She slowly backed away. Then she started shaking her head violently and turned to run as fast as she could.

Rupert closed the door.

"Keep your hands up," said Wächter. "No outgoing phone calls, and no funny business, you understand, Mencke? I've left your face clean on purpose. If Maria or Becker or anyone else comes here, act like it's life as usual. Do you understand? If you want everything to be all right, you do as I say. I'll be checking in on you later tonight or in the morning."

Rupert just stared back at him, hands in the air. His mind started piecing things together.

Wächter turned to his assistant. "Schleunert, if you learn anything, call Columbia-Haus headquarters."

Schleunert nodded silently, his gun trained on Rupert.

"Remember, Sergeant Mencke – Stay in line!" Wächter slammed the door behind him.

Rupert knew where Becker must be. *That scheming bastard!* And he knew what he was going to do about it.

CHAPTER TWENTY-ONE

Wächter was barely out of Rupert's house when Scharführer Schleunert gave the next order. "Turn around and put your hands on the wall, Mencke."

Rupert did as he was told.

"You have any weapons on you?" demanded Schleunert.

"There's a revolver inside my coat. And a knife on my belt. That's it," answered Rupert. Though he'd drunk almost a bottle of wine tonight, Rupert's mind felt suddenly clear. His night with Anja was cut off. His beloved sister Maria was in danger. Rupert was mad as a hornet. But he had to be patient.

Schleunert pocketed Rupert's weapons. Then he stripped off Rupert's coat and searched the rest of him.

"All right, Mencke, turn around slowly and turn off that light. . . . Good. . . . Here are some more rules for tonight." Schleunert stood several feet away, his gun still aimed ahead of him.

Rupert turned around.

"First, you're going to clean up the furniture and everything else downstairs."

And a fine mess of the place they've made, thought Rupert.

Schleunert continued. "Then I'm going to sit in your armchair, with the lights off. You are going to lie on the sofa, as if you fell asleep by accident. If anyone comes to the door, I hide in the closet, and you behave normally. If you tell anyone about me, we'll haul you into Columbia-Haus in a heartbeat. Trust me, you don't want to be the Gestapo's houseguest."

"Understood," replied Rupert.

"Good. Now clean this place up. On the double! And be quiet about it."

Rupert moved all the furniture so quickly he broke a sweat, but more from the speed than the effort. His tall, broad-shouldered strength made the lifting an easy task. Next he stuffed papers and broken dishes and anything else loose into the hallway closet. He didn't keep much of that stuff around, so this part was quick.

"All done," he announced softly. "Does that pass muster?"

Schleunert looked around. "Yes. . . . Now get in the sitting room. We'll spend the whole night in there if necessary. We wait for word from Wächter."

"May I first make some tea?" asked Rupert. "I had a lot of wine tonight."

"If you can do it in the dark. . . . I'll come with you. All those knives, you know." Schleunert pointed his gun at Rupert's back and followed him to the kitchen. There, the Gestapo guard moved into the opposite corner and watched Rupert by the blue light of the gas stove.

Rupert lifted the water just before it whistled and poured it into the teapot. "All ready," he said. "It's just got to steep a few minutes."

"Your mother let you be left-handed?" Schleunert sneered.

Rupert grinned in the dark.

Schleunert continued, "I wonder what other faults of upbringing you have."

Now Rupert fumed silently.

"Carry the tea into the sitting room," Schleunert ordered. He followed with his gun.

Rupert put the tea service on the coffee table. He sat on the sofa while Schleunert took his place in the chair.

"Are you going to have any?" asked Rupert.

"Yes," replied Schleunert.

Rupert glanced at the bulge in the rug under the front two legs of Schleunert's chair. When he was cleaning up, he'd put two magazines under each front leg. This was just enough to tilt the chair backwards slightly, without making it obvious.

Sitting on the sofa, Rupert first poured his own cup of black tea. He set down the pot and placed his cup on the end table. Then his large left hand subtly grasped the searing hot teapot below the handle. He felt the instant burns blistering the length of his palm and fingers. But he held on tight.

By the time Schleunert got a shot off, it was too late and too wide. The teapot hit his nose so squarely that Rupert could hear the bone fracture under the shattering porcelain.

A bullet hole pierced the sofa back where Rupert had been sitting. In flinging the teapot forward, he had also leaped to his right, pushing the end table and lamp to the floor.

The teapot shards clattered to the floor and the scalding hot tea steamed off Schleunert's cheeks and eyes. His chair tipped over backwards while he waved his arms around frantically, firing a second time into the ceiling. By now Rupert's burned left hand clutched Schleunert's right wrist with the gun. The chair's back slammed to the floor. Rupert was on top of Schleunert, his right elbow in the Gestapo guard's throat.

Schleunert gagged and he closed his burning eyes tight. Rupert kneed Schleunert in the groin and then moved his right arm to grip Schleunert's left one.

"You're a dead man, Mencke!" Schleunert gasped. He was no match for the much larger Army man.

Rupert twisted Schleunert's right wrist until he heard the joint cracking and the gun hit the floor. Then he jerked Schleunert's body around. He pressed Schleunert's chest into the floor and held his hands behind his back.

The rest was easy. Rupert straddled Schleunert, and his legs held down Schleunert's arms. Rupert tightened his fingers around Schleunert's neck. The dying man writhed to escape Rupert's chokehold. Then his body went limp. Rupert held firm for two full minutes more. Then just to be sure, he snapped Schleunert's neck backwards and broken.

"Right-handed, you bastard!" hissed Rupert. He'd feigned otherwise to keep his right hand free from burns for later tonight.

Rupert turned on the light and looked at the clock. A quarter past ten. *That Becker will get the same.*

Rupert picked up the phone and called the Hossbachs. No answer. They couldn't be long gone, he knew. Rupert told the operator to let the phone keep ringing. Then he got his car keys and left.

"Try not to fall asleep, Maria," said Becker. "It will be hard to wake up again, at this hour."

"You're right," said Maria. "I'm just so sleepy, cooped up in this car for hours. What time is it by now?"

"Just a couple minutes past ten o'clock," he answered. "I'll crack the window open wider. At least the snow is stopping. . . . I wonder if the snow has kept them home tonight? Rupert made it sound like Major Hossbach was very eager to attend the officers' party."

"The fresh air helps," Maria replied. "Thanks. . . . Look! Someone's finally coming out!"

"It's about time," said Becker. "They've ordered a cab to come pick them up."

"Are those their three young children with them, Johannes?" asked Maria. "At this hour?"

"Will you look at that. . . . What a stroke of luck. The house will be empty!"

Becker saw the whole family file out and into the cab. The parents carried the two youngest children, already asleep. This was evidently a family party. Then unexpectedly, the cab turned toward them.

"Watch out! Here comes the cab. Duck!" Becker pulled Maria down with him, and they watched the headlights and shadows shift across their car's interior. They stayed down another minute before rising to scan the street.

"We'll wait a couple more minutes before moving the car," said Becker. "We'll park it where that back yard path comes out on the next street, where you found it this afternoon. Then you'll wait while I break into the house."

"No, Johannes. I'm coming in with you."

"I don't think that's a very good idea," said Becker. "You don't have any practice at break-ins, and I might have to run for it."

"I'm quick on my feet," she retorted. "And besides, you might need help."

"I might. . . . Or you might. . . ." He waited for her to change her mind, but all he met was silence. "I wish you would stay here. But I can't stop you. If you come, you have to stand guard where I tell you. . . . First I need to dig this car out of the snow."

Becker had purchased a snow shovel with the new tires. After the car was clear, he drove a long block away, to the far end of the garden path. The path's near end was closer to the house, a much shorter walk through the snow. But their car would be better hidden at the path's far end. If they got caught in the house, it would be a long run through deep snow to the car. But then they'd have a better chance of escaping, with different streets available to them.

"Let's leave the windows cracked, but just barely, so they don't fog up while we're away," said Becker. "Are you sure you want to come along?"

Maria nodded with resolve.

"To our success, then!" he said.

"To our success!" she answered.

Becker leaned over to kiss Maria's cheek. She held her own kiss on his cheek and then slowly turned to meet his mouth with hers. They pulled away slowly and stared at each other in the shadows for an instant.

"Let's go!" they each said simultaneously and then gave a short, nervous chuckle. They climbed out of the car and closed the doors quietly.

No one had walked this path behind the houses since the snowstorm. Becker intentionally dragged his feet through the foot-deep snow to make Maria's walking a little easier. It was still slow-going for them both. The return would be only slightly easier. Becker remembered dreams of being chased with legs of lead. Walking here felt like that.

The clouds began to break up, and the starry night was surprisingly bright in the snow.

Becker and Maria had to pass dozens of houses on both sides with back yards bordering this shared path. And several of the houses – each about twenty yards from the path – still had people awake in the ground-floor rooms. One old woman clearly observed them, Becker noticed from the corner of his eye. She didn't seem to care, he thought.

Then on the left, Becker recognized the back of the Hossbach house from when he staked it out that afternoon. The lights were all off. He could hear the phone ringing inside. They stopped at the backyard gate. It was almost one hundred yards, in one straight shot, back to the car.

"I have to pick the lock," he whispered. "Stay here at the gate until I motion for you to come. Once we get inside the house, I want you to stand watch at the back door unless I signal otherwise. I'll try to find the office and the documents. If they are very brief, I'll read them and leave them – it's best for my purposes to leave things in place. If there's too much, though, I'll take it. Either way, we should be in and out within just a few minutes. All right – ready?"

Maria nodded.

"Wait for my signal."

Becker advanced through the back yard. His tracks in the deep snow were unmistakable. He tried the back door and found it unlocked and unbolted. Next he motioned for Maria to follow him.

Once Maria reached the door, Becker pulled it open just long enough for the two of them to pass. Maria quickly shut it behind them. The phone rang incessantly.

The interior of the Hossbach house was almost completely dark. The starlit sky and distant lights of other houses barely penetrated here. Becker pointed silently to the floor to remind Maria to stand in place.

He saw her silhouette, but he wasn't sure she could see him. He could hear the snow crunching under his shoes with every step. Their footprints inside would be as obvious as those outside.

When Becker turned to face ahead of him, he first noticed the coals and small flames in the adjacent room. They were standing in some kind of large parlor, and he could just make out an upright piano among the usual furnishings. The house breathed no sign of life besides the slow hiss of glowing coals.

As Becker crept toward the next room with the fireplace, he spied a desk. The study! He tiptoed to the doorway between the two rooms and surveyed the study.

A large desk had two chairs drawn under it, one by a typewriter and a larger one for writing. Next to the typewriter was a stack of papers. For fifteen months of spying on Kristner Engineering's mail, Becker had practiced the art of skimming for salient details. He hoped there was enough firelight to put those skills to work now. He glanced out the window to make sure no one was watching, and then he approached the desk.

The phone on the desk rang and rang. Becker thought how strange it was for a caller to be so persistent. Under the circumstances, the normal ringing volume seemed deafening to Becker. He hoped it would stop soon.

It didn't take Becker long to determine the firelight was too dim. Just making out the document headings was slow and tedious. He'd be here half the night at this pace, and of course the fire would only diminish in size. He had to risk turning on the light. He motioned to Maria to warn her that it was coming.

Becker squinted and blinked for several moments in the bright light. He could no longer see past his reflection in the window. He knew he was eminently visible from the outside. He turned back to the desk.

There it was! Front and center:

MEMORANDUM

BERLIN, February 15, 1936.

Minutes of a Meeting in the Reich Chancellery, Berlin, Wednesday, February 12, 1936, from 14:00 - 16:15

Present:
The Führer and Chancellor, Adolph HITLER
Deputy Führer Rudolf HESS
Wehrmacht CHIEFS OF STAFF

The FÜHRER began by reminding the military chiefs of staff of the remaining Versailles Treaty conditions. Germany is supposed to leave its Rhineland unarmed and defenseless. This is preposterous, he said. Germany must remilitarize its Rhineland western border.

Field Marshall BLOMBERG and General VON FRITSCH stressed the weakness of the German Army. It is a fraction of the strength of the French Army alone, not to mention any additional British forces. Germany has not yet filled the dozens of divisions created in 1935. The western Allies could easily repel an Army occupation of the German Rhineland.

The FÜHRER agreed that Germany is not in a position to hold off an attack on its western front. He insisted the Allies will not put up a fight. For several years after remilitarizing the Rhineland, Germany will lay preparations to defeat France and destroy Poland.

For now, if the Allies invaded, retreat was the only possibility. The Führer stated that German forces would retreat beyond the Rhine River and hope for the best. But he is counting on a successful bluff. He pointed out that the deception of exaggerated German strength is imperative to the success of the operation. Otherwise–

Without warning, a gunshot shattered the backyard window to the study.

"*Hände auf!*" shouted Rupert, pointing his gun straight at Becker's chest. Hands up!

The phone kept ringing.

Becker lifted his hands. He recognized Rupert instantly. He was caught red-handed.

Rupert stepped over the windowsill, clutching his gun with both hands.

"You traitor!" he shouted. "You lying, scheming son-of-a-bitch! You used my sister, risked her life. You're finished! The police are on the way. Don't think you can escape me."

Rupert walked closer and cocked his gun.

"Nooo!" shouted Maria. She ran out of the unlit parlor and collapsed at her stepbrother's feet.

"God in Heaven! Maria, what are you doing here?!? The police are about to arrive. I just killed some Gestapo goon who came looking for you at my house. Arresting Becker here is going to be my redemption. Get out of here! Take the back door! Run!"

"No!" Maria sobbed.

"Leave, Maria! Now!" ordered Rupert.

"Save yourself while you can, Maria," Becker urged her.

"No, Rupert," said Maria through her tears. "It's finished for me here. You think they'd let me live? And how do you think I'd escape Germany? I don't even have my passport on me. Becker's my only way out. You have to let him go, too. Or I won't move."

"Don't do this, Maria! There's no time. Go!" implored Becker.

"Just go, Maria," stammered Rupert. "You can make it. I'll . . . I'll save you. Just go!"

"No, Rupert," she said. "Either Becker comes with me, or I stay."

"Why, Maria? Why?" Rupert's voice cracked.

She looked at him in pity.

Police sirens were approaching from a distance.

Rupert's eyes welled up with tears. "Go," he whispered, pointing at Becker as well.

Maria stood up. Rupert realized he was losing her forever. The last of his family. Nothing held him steady in life like Maria's sisterly love. Now she was leaving.

"Go," he mouthed silently, his face close to sobs. He motioned to the back door, while he just stared at his stepsister.

Rupert lowered his gun, and Becker lowered his hands. For one brief moment they all stood there.

Maria pulled her brother's face down to kiss it. "Thank you. Goodbye, Rupert. I'll always love you."

He tried to speak, but could only bend his face down in sobs.

Becker reached for the papers.

Rupert fired a bullet that tore through them, inches from Becker's hand.

"Get the hell out of here!" ordered Rupert.

Maria and Becker dashed to the rear door. The sirens were getting louder. Rupert jerked upright into action, as the military trained him to do under shock. He escorted them to the door and pulled the parlor curtains shut against their footprints in the snow. The sirens reached the house and stopped.

When the escaping couple reached the backyard gate, they heard more gunshots. They briefly turned to look. Rupert had taken cover behind the large desk. He was firing at the police at the front door. He stood halfway to fire again. Then a shot from the house entrance sent Rupert staggering backwards. Now a cascade of bullets riddled his body, as it fell out the shattered back window into the snow.

Maria inhaled for an involuntary scream, but Becker's hand was over her mouth before it escaped.

"Wait – not yet – Run! Run like hell!" he whispered.

She just collapsed into his arms, unable to move, heaving as she sobbed into his hand.

Becker had to uncover her mouth in order to lift her. The snow absorbed enough of her weeping sound. With her on his shoulders, he dashed as fast as he could toward the waiting car.

Close to the car, he heard police shouting in Hossbach's back yard. It would not have taken them long to see more backyard footprints in addition to Rupert's. Becker looked but saw no one on the path yet.

When they got to the car, Becker opened the driver's side door and pushed Maria across to the opposite seat before climbing in himself.

The sirens started up again.

Suddenly Becker heard a bullet fly over the car, the unmistakable sonic pop, followed by the sound of the gunshot down the path. More gunshots fired, farther off-target.

The engine was still warm. Becker cranked it up and pulled out of the line of fire, accelerating slowly and carefully on the snowy road. He took the first right-hand turn. This got them out of sight before any police could see where he turned.

For what seemed like forever, Becker heard the sirens keeping about the same unseen distance from him. He wasn't sure if they guessed which way he was trying to escape. He drove as fast as he dared, zigzagging through snowy intersections, trying to lose the police.

"Oh, Maria, I'm so sorry about your brother. I'm the one who drew you and Rupert into this. I'm so, so sorry. . . ," Becker was beside himself with regret for Rupert's death. "I'm so sorry," he repeated.

Maria sat in shock. Becker raced and skidded the car through snow for their lives, and she just sat there looking forward. Finally she mumbled calmly, "It's not your fault. . . . It's not your fault," over and over again as he drove frenetically away.

Though the sirens continued, Becker didn't hear any more gunshots. Soon the sirens faded, too. They'd escaped.

Later Becker would have time to digest the extraordinary information he'd read. For now he had to get them to safety, and Maria to where she could mourn in peace.

CHAPTER TWENTY-TWO

"Come to bed, Georg – our party's finally over, the children are asleep, and we're alone!" Elsa Schwarz flirted with her husband across the small bedroom while she undressed.

"I've got it! Janeck's cat!" Georg Schwarz let a little spittle fly in his inebriated excitement. Flabby in his tank-top undershirt, his brown-gray hair a tousled mess, his face flushed red, Schwarz nonetheless felt attractive and compelling in his own bedroom.

"What?" asked Elsa. She left her slip on and sat on the bed, folding her arms over her naked chest.

"Janeck's flat!" exclaimed Schwarz. "That's where he must be."

"For crying out loud, Georg," said his wife. "Can't you stop thinking about that Becker guy for once? Why don't you leave your Kristner world alone sometime. Even if I'm drunk, do you expect me to sleep with you like this?"

"Just let me call the police first," insisted Schwarz. "I'll be a hero!"

"No!" Elsa got in bed and pulled the covers over her body. "It's your choice – sex or crime-solving, but not both."

Schwarz stared blankly for two seconds. "Here I come, my little tigress!"

They made blurry, intoxicated love on their marriage bed. Immediately afterwards, the Schwarzes fell fast asleep.

Becker parked the car two blocks from Janeck's flat. The police had never gotten close in the chase from Hossbach's house. Becker thought they hadn't even identified the car.

"I'm so sorry about your brother." He was at a loss for any other words.

"It's not your fault," Maria repeated. The occasional tear still ran down her cheek in the silences between her sniffles. "I loved him. He was the only family I had left, and he loved me to no end. This Nazi shit ruined him. With his parents gone, he lost his moral balance. He could have been a good man. He had that in him, Johannes, really he did."

"He was a kind man," replied Becker. *Kind to Maria, anyway.*

They sat in silence for a minute. That was all the memorializing that Rupert Mencke would get for now.

"What do you think?" asked Becker. "A hotel is out of the question – they'll have our names at every check-in desk in Berlin. We could spend the night in the car. Or we could risk Janeck's place one last night. I don't think they saw his car, not to mention the license plate."

"I can't take it anymore, Johannes. I just want to get out of Germany right now. Can't we just drive to the border tonight? We could be free by dawn. . . ."

Becker held her hand. "Tomorrow, yes, but not tonight. We could put your new photo from this afternoon into the blank passport right now. But anyone driving at night is automatically suspicious. We'd never make it without close scrutiny of our papers. And that we have to avoid."

"I understand . . . ," she replied. "What do I think? I think Janeck's place is too risky. But I'm a wreck. If I spend the night in this car, I'll be useless tomorrow. I need a bed. With some rest, I'll be much better. I'm scared of Janeck's place. And the stench! But I need a bed."

"I'm sure we'll both be better for a little decent rest." Becker supported her. He preferred the anonymity of sleeping in the car, but he wasn't going to tell her that. He braced himself as he restarted the car and pulled right in front of Janeck's building.

Even on a Saturday night at this time, there was only the occasional passerby on Wittmann Strasse. The usual nighttime street echoes were swallowed into mounds of snow, leaving an eerie silence all around.

Becker and Maria returned to Janeck's building as if they belonged there, walking through the building entrance and across the courtyard. Becker glanced up at Janeck's windows – of course they were unlighted. They would be even if someone were hiding there.

As quietly as possible, they climbed the three stories to Janeck's flat. Becker motioned Maria to stand out of view of the doorframe while he opened it.

Everything was in place.

When Rosa meowed, they both jumped. They were half-expecting the Gestapo and had completely forgotten about Rosa.

Becker motioned to Maria that it was safe, and they closed the door behind them, the lights still off. They hung their coats by the door and walked straight to the bedroom. Becker cracked the window open for fresh air, no matter how cold. No sooner were their shoes off than they were under the covers, with Maria spooned in Becker's embrace. Both lay quiet, awake, and troubled. Their tender silence seemed the best epitaph to the deadly evening.

Becker replayed the shooting sequence about five times in his mind. He would have gone on, but he forced his thoughts to the document he'd discovered. It was important that he think through it several times, to remember every detail past tonight's sleep.

The setting was easy to remember. So was the main point – Hitler planned to remilitarize the Rhineland, but he had nowhere near the armed forces for a fight. If the Allies chose to oppose the remilitarization, they could do so easily. That answered Churchill's question! Of course, there remained a lot of people in Britain who thought Hitler should be allowed to defend German territory. Hitler promised his intentions were merely defensive.

Becker tried to remember more about the document. Rupert's banging on the door had interrupted him before he had time to finish the document or even process what he'd read. Becker remembered mention of Poland.

That was it! Hitler clearly said he planned a future war against both France and Poland. This was exactly the information Churchill needed to justify fighting Hitler now, while he was weak.

For twenty minutes, Becker anxiously rehearsed all these details from the document. By the sixth time he rehearsed the document's points, paragraph by paragraph, he was quite sure he would remember them forever.

Immediately his thoughts returned to the vision of Rupert slumping dead outside Hossbach's study window. Becker could hear inches away that Maria's breath was still irregular and awake. They still lay curled together, wearing clothes they'd each chosen for work on Friday morning.

For another half-hour, Becker listened to Maria's restless breathing and let his own thoughts race about tonight and tomorrow. After Becker heard Maria's breathing slip into sleep, he let himself drift off as well.

Patrick O'Hagan cleaned the galleries of Queen's Hall after the Saturday evening concert. The IRA's chief hit man in London had been in place for over a decade. They were finally using him. Next Wednesday night, Winston Churchill would sit at the front of the box O'Hagan now cleaned.

When the hall was clean and ready for Sunday's matinee, O'Hagan said goodnight to his colleagues and left the building. He quickly walked around it to a basement window he'd left cracked open. He crawled in and waited until the last concert hall attendant had locked the doors.

O'Hagan returned to Churchill's favorite box seats. He looked around one more time to be sure he was alone. Then he pulled a screwdriver out of his pocket – occasionally the attendants had to tighten seats. Quickly and carefully, O'Hagan detached the seat bottom. Next he removed a long knife from his boot. He slit the back bottom of the cushion cover and cut out all the padding. He felt inside the seat to determine the size and shape of the springs. Then he replaced the padding, tucked the cushion cover into the metal frame and screwed the seat back on. He looked at his watch – the whole thing had taken six minutes.

There were two more concerts before Wednesday's. O'Hagan would not install the bomb until Tuesday night.

"Georg?" stammered Elsa Schwarz.

"Huh?" he answered. Early Sunday morning after their rowdy party, neither of the Schwarzes was in great shape.

"It's getting too bright in here," she said. "We forgot to close the shutters last night. Would you mind?"

"Ugh." Schwarz rolled over and squinted beyond his wife to the offending window, covered in frost patterns he failed to appreciate. "Just a minute." The naked Schwarz first grabbed his pajamas and made his way to the bathroom.

Stumbling back out, he shielded his eyes from the light and braced for the cold blast when he opened the windows. The shutter hinges squeaked as he pulled them shut, and he banged the securing rod into the shutter's latch. Quickly he pushed the windows back shut in the very dark, much colder room. Schwarz reached down and opened the radiator full blast.

"I feel like I'm forgetting something. . . . Can you think of it, Elsa?"

"Huh-uh," she mumbled.

Schwarz trotted to the warm bed and huddled under the covers. "It must not be important."

His cold body took a few minutes to warm up and doze off.

"Becker. . . ," he whispered. "Janeck's flat! That's it!" By now he was shouting. Elsa covered her ears with a pillow.

Schwarz leaped out of bed and dashed toward the kitchen phone, bumping into doorframes along the way.

"Operator?" he said "Yes. Get me Berlin police headquarters."

Within minutes the officer on duty forwarded Schwarz's information to Chief Arndt's home.   Arndt immediately called Wächter.

The Gestapo colonel was irritated at the ringing phone. He'd only managed to fall asleep an hour ago.   He picked up the phone. "Wächter."

"Standartenführer Wächter? . . .   Sorry to call so early.   Chief Arndt here."

"You found Becker?" demanded Wächter.

"Not exactly, but – "

"Out with it!"   Wächter was beyond impatient, after yesterday's near miss of Becker at Mencke's house, and then having Schleunert murdered, and another miss at Major Hossbach's home.

"We have a lead," said Arndt. "Wittmann Strasse 121, Flat 68, registered under the name of Wolfgang Janeck. Shall I dispatch any officers to meet you there?"

"Yes, but nobody gets killed, at least not before I arrive," ordered Wächter.

"Yes, sir," replied Arndt.

"How calm and peaceful with the snow."   In Becker's dream, Maria commented on the safe beauty of the Czech landscape, safely outside Nazi Germany. "It will be a very bright morning."

He opened his eyes and remembered where they were. Maria was looking through a crack in the bedroom curtains. He lifted himself to his elbows.

"How did you sleep?" he asked.

"Very deeply," she answered. "First I had nightmares about last night.   Then I dreamed about Rupert, sweet and innocent like he could sometimes be. . . . Now I feel very rested. Very sad, but very rested."

To Becker, the events of last night seemed like a dream. He'd slept the sleep of a drunk man, alternately deep then disturbed and unrefreshing.   That was his mind's usual response – to put stressful events on hold in dream-like memories, until he was done with something and could think through it all. Not yet. He had to get them out of Germany. Today! What a pleasant thought. This business was almost over. He looked at his watch – seven o'clock. The winter sky was still gray, beginning to turn yellow.

"You honor your brother and yourself at the same time. You never cease to amaze me, Maria."

They had to get out of Janeck's place fast, he thought. Suddenly, he had the feeling of immense danger there.

"Where next?" she asked. "What's the plan?"

"I have to pick up some false papers and money in one of two locations. Both are risky. We could manage without money." He meant they could easily steal some. "And we've got the false passport for you. But the only identification papers I have for myself are my own. And by now, I am surely on every German border guard's black list, and every train conductor's as well."

Becker knew he could get out of Germany without papers. He could steal cars, ride bicycles, and hike through forests. But he doubted he could do all that with Maria. With her, he'd have to take it more conventionally. He needed false papers.

"Either hiding spot will do. One is back at my place at the Lande residence. Probably they looked for me there on Friday, but they might not be there now."

"What about the landlady and her daughter?" she inquired.

"Gone for the weekend until late tonight," he answered.

"What was your second option?" she asked.

"In the Grunewald Forest, buried under the snow in a hole in the ground. I know the place fairly well, between two large pine trees. But it will take some digging around in the snow to find the spot."

"So which one first?" she asked.

"I haven't decided yet," he said. "Most of the money is at the house, with one of my better false identities."

"And then?"

"We take the train to Prague, under the false names, and looking . . . very different," he said. "I need to look around here for some peroxide and scissors. Let's get ready to go."

Becker got out of bed, put his shoes on, and began to look around. He pulled out a large, worn brown leather suitcase. Becker was taller than Janeck, so there was no use looking for clothes.

This suitcase is just big enough for Maria, Becker thought to himself.

With Maria still staring through the crack between the curtains, Becker took a few moments to shave.

Glancing at the bathtub in the mirror, he saw the loose wall tiles he'd found the other night.   There were Janeck's Mauser handguns. Becker decided they'd carry two of the guns on them, and keep the third in the suitcase.   The spare ammunition would go in there, too, along with the large knife.   Janeck's little armory was quite a stash.   He must have had even more to take with him, Becker thought.

Becker removed his Luger from the holster strapped to his body. He replaced it with one of the Mausers.   He kept the Luger, in his coat pocket.   He'd have to test fire the Mauser before relying on it completely.   There was more ammunition for the Mausers, so he hoped they worked well.

Becker went from the bathroom to Janeck's desk, where he found a small bottle of glue.   Then he moved to the bedroom.   "There were scissors and peroxide in the bathroom."   He packed everything into the suitcase, taking care that Maria not notice the weapons yet.

"Time to go," he said.   Already in their clothes, both of them now put on their shoes.

"Why the bigger suitcase?" asked Maria.

"It's best to be prepared," he replied.

Maria furrowed her eyebrows for a moment.   "You mean to put me in there, don't you?"

"I hope not," he answered.

She shook her head in disbelief and gave a soft laugh.   "I thought you had papers for me?"

"I do.   Like I said, the suitcase should be just for appearances." His hand was on the door handle.   He was anxious to get going.

Becker didn't bother to lock the door, and they scampered down the stairs.

When they were halfway across the courtyard, they heard police sirens in the distance.

They looked at each other in horror.

Then Becker took Maria's hand and led her running towards the empty street.   Their car was right in front of them.

The sirens were unmistakably getting closer.

Becker stuffed the suitcase into the trunk and heard the peroxide bottle break.   They jumped into the car.   He prayed the engine would start quickly.   The temperature was far below freezing.

After two cold cranks, the engine caught.   Becker was ready to buy Opels for the rest of his life.

"Duck down!" he ordered. He lowered his fedora brim as far as would seem normal. Then he pulled the car into the street to normal speed.

He was halfway down the block when the police car came around the corner, its sirens wailing, headed right toward them! The two cars were about to pass each other. Becker tried to avoid looking at the two policemen sitting in front. From the passenger's floor, Maria stared up at him like the fugitive in mortal danger that she was.

Even in Becker's peripheral vision he could see both officers in the police car turning to scrutinize him and his car. He expected them to turn and follow him, and he looked around for the best getaway.

Instead, Becker watched in his mirror as the police car stopped in front of Janeck's building. Becker took a calm turn onto the first small side street.

Four blocks away he relaxed slightly. "I think we've made it."

"Not until we cross the border," Maria reminded him.

Becker continued to drive on side streets as far away from Janeck's flat as possible. Finally, near an empty Schöneberg park, he parked on the side of the street and left the engine running.

He exhaled and stretched out his arms and fingers. "That was close. Too close. They might have been coming for Janeck or for us. Who knows."

"Thank you for helping me, Johannes. I realize it would be easier for you to abandon me now."

Becker pressed her hands in his. "I won't leave this country without you, Maria. We'll make it, together."

She smiled, looking exhausted after their close call.

"Still," he continued, "the earlier I check my two hiding places, the better. There's a back way into the Lande house. I'll try that. First I'll drive by the front for signs of Gestapo ransacking. Of course, they know my face in that neighborhood. . . . Do you know how to drive?"

"Sure," she answered. "I'm not bad in the snow . . . but inexperienced at chases, if you find that acceptable," she half-joked.

"Good. I'll stay on the floor and tell you how to get there. Then you tell me just as we reach the house whether the street is clear of neighbors for me to pop up and have a look around."

"Break open the door." Standartenführer Wächter crowded the landing outside Wolfgang Janeck's apartment with the two regular policemen. They'd have to do until Gestapo reinforcements arrived.

"Yes, sir," answered Officer Hans Haber. He first tried the doorknob. "It's unlocked, sir."

"Well open the damn door!" bellowed Wächter.

All three of them lifted their guns, and Officer Haber pushed the door open with his free hand.

"Search every corner, fast!" ordered Wächter.

Haber and his partner waved their guns around as they searched the flat in short spurts, turning over furniture and flinging open doors left and right. They destroyed all traces of recent occupancy. Or almost all.

Wächter followed slowly, hands-off, room by room.

First he checked the kitchen. Rosa purred as she rubbed against Wächter's legs. Wächter kicked violently at Rosa, but she dodged him and ran out of the apartment.

Wächter walked down the short hallway to the sitting room on the left and then to the main bedroom at the end. He tore back the sheets. There were a few long, black hairs – Maria Geberich!

Next Wächter stood at the bathroom doorway and looked inside. "Damn! You police fools were too slow! The sink is still wet, despite the dry radiator heat. Damn! Damn! Damn!"

Haber and his partner exchanged fearful looks and remained silent.

"Did you two see a phone?" asked Wächter.

"In the sitting room," answered Haber.

Wächter stomped around the corner.

"Operator, get me Columbia-Haus right now. . . . You heard me right." He tapped his foot and stroked his thumb against the holster of his gun.

"Hello, who is this? . . . Schmidt, it's Wächter again. . . . I don't need condolences right now. Just listen! I need two competent – more than competent – officers to meet me as soon as possible at the entrance to the Grunewald elevated rail station. Make sure they can recognize me. Tell them to arrive together and then identify themselves with the following greeting: 'Do you think it will snow more today?' Is that all clear? . . . Good. As soon as possible. I'll be there within twenty minutes."

"Maricfel Strasse is coming up on the right." Becker described the streets to Maria, his head bent under the glove compartment.

She turned a slow left onto the narrow, snowy residential street.

"Is anyone around?" he asked.

"Not that I can see," she replied.

"Tell me when we pass Memel Strasse on the left."

"O.K., I'm almost to it," she said. "Now we're passing it."

"All clear?" he asked again.

"Yes."

Becker slowly rose to his seat and looked down the block to the Lande house on the right. As they drew closer he observed that it looked neat. But the curtains in Anna's bedroom were drawn shut. She never did that. She only used the shutters. Certainly someone had searched the place. Maria continued driving past the house.

Suddenly he noticed someone walking at the far end of the street. He started kneeling to the floor to hide, but then paused.

"It's Anna Lande!" he whispered sharply. "That woman who just turned the corner with the suitcase. She's coming from the U-Bahn station. She wasn't supposed to be home until tonight. . . ."

Just as suddenly and closer, Becker saw some neighbors exit their garage on the right. He looked at the blue BMW they had shoveled free of snow. That Gestapo bastard Gustav Lodt! Becker immediately sank to the floor.

"Keep driving at the same pace," he said to Maria.

"He's staring at us," she reported. "I think he saw you. Now he's pointing at us and shouting something to his wife."

Next Becker could hear Lodt's voice screaming "*Halt! Halt!*"

"He's charging with a gun!" exclaimed Maria. "What should I do?!?"

"Don't look at him! Hit the gas!"

Maria slowly accelerated the car on the narrow, snowy street.

Becker heard a loud thud and thought they'd hit something. "What was that?"

"He slammed his fist on the hood as we drove past," replied Maria.

"*Halt!*" Lodt shouted again.

"He's aiming at us!" screamed Maria as she looked into the mirror. Becker heard a gunshot and then another "*Halt!*"

"He shot into the sky," reported Maria.

She continued to accelerate. "We're about the pass Anna. She's just standing there watching all this. . . . He's aiming the gun again!"

Becker heard two more gunshots. "Take the next left!"

Maria wheeled through the snow. Another gunshot followed.

"Oh no!" she shouted. "Anna just went down!"

Becker's mouth dropped and his breathing stopped. He forced himself to exhale. Anna! Why did she have to get mixed up in all this?

"Get out of here!" he shouted. "To the Grunewald Forest!"

CHAPTER TWENTY-THREE

"Here's Wiesbadener Strasse," said Maria. She drove Herr Janeck's Opel through the snowy streets. Few cars were on the road this early Sunday morning. Maria and Becker had just escaped Gustav Lodt, the Gestapo leader in Anna Lande's neighborhood. Becker remained crouched out of view on the passenger's floor.

"Which way?" she asked.

"Turn right," he said.

"Finally a big road where the snow is packed. How far to Grunewald Forest from here?" asked Maria.

"A little over a mile," he replied. He pulled himself up to his seat. "Ahead on the left we'll take Zoppoter Strasse. . . . After the shooting back there, we should consider this a marked car. We must get into the forest as fast as possible."

Becker sat poised to give directions for more turns. "Here's Zoppoter on the left, good. . . . Now take a quick right. . . . All right, pull over at the second street and I'll take over the driving. We're just a few blocks from the forest."

With the car still running, they jumped out, ran around, and switched sides.

Becker was about to get into the driver's side when he looked down the street.

"Lodt!" he shouted. "That's his blue BMW! He's found us!"

They slammed their doors shut. Driving in the snow, Becker slowly accelerated into an immediate leftward turn. He knew a turn was the only thing to slow down Lodt enough that he couldn't catch them. On the next street, the two cars drove just a few dozen yards apart.

Becker took the approaching snowy curve dangerously fast. He heard Maria inhale quickly through her teeth and hold her breath. He could almost feel her hands crushing the door handle in fear.

At the next street, Becker took a sudden left turn. He knew it was much too sharp and fast for the snow. His new tires began to slip underneath him.

Now Becker jerked the steering wheel even farther to the left. This spun the car in place like a top, right in the middle of the street. There was no crash. When the car stopped, it faced the reverse direction.

Becker had taken the turn so quickly that Lodt missed it entirely. Lodt's car skidded down the previous street, trying to stop in the snow.

Becker rolled his car forward and turned right, away from his pursuer. Lodt was still skidding in the opposite direction; Becker knew his new tires had to be better than Lodt's. He turned left, and zigzagged through a maze of side streets. Rather than go westward toward Grunewald Forest, he bore southward in his maze of left and right turns. If by chance Lodt should spot his car again, Becker wanted him to think he was driving out of town.

"The snow saved us," said Becker. "But now it's going to hurt us. This early on a Sunday morning, after yesterday's snow, we're going to leave tracks on the forest roads. It'll be better if we stay on the main roads and then walk. Maybe the paths will already have some footprints."

"I know my way around the Grunewald quite well," said Maria. "Of course I don't know where you're hiding spot is."

"Do you know Angel's Hill?" he asked.

"Know it?!? Climbing it is the highlight every time!"

Becker knew this. During fifteen months of observing Maria, he'd trailed her a few times in the Grunewald. After the first such expedition, he'd decided to create his own private drop spot nearby.

He had not forgotten the message found at Café Hildegard on Thursday. His unknown British colleague in Berlin had requested a rendezvous at Angel's Hill at two o'clock this very afternoon. Becker had a bad feeling about it, especially after McBride had waved him off the place.

Becker had information on the gaping hole in Hitler's Army. He knew Hitler planned to launch a mighty war in a few years. And only three days away, Hitler planned to have Churchill assassinated. Becker had to get his intelligence coups to London right away. It was too much to risk. He would skip the rendezvous.

Becker might be able to make it into the British Embassy on Monday, or to one of the alternate communications locations. But the Gestapo would surely have his image up at every police station. They would be watching outside all the obvious places, especially the embassy and the passport office. If he managed to get into the embassy, he could seek expatriation from there. But that would leave Maria high and dry. No, he had to cross the border to get them both out safely.

Becker entered Grunewald Forest on a main road, Hüttenweg Path. A mile into the forest, they passed under the railroad tracks. The main road ended a few hundred yards later. Becker continued on a secondary road where few cars had ventured in this snow. This driving was slow-going. He risked getting stuck.

"We have to walk from here on," he conceded as he parked on the side of the empty road.

Becker opened the car trunk and looked into the suitcase. The broken bottle and spilled peroxide were collected in one bleached corner. The remaining articles were still tucked in a side pocket. Becker lifted the suitcase and dumped the peroxide and glass into the snow. Then he wiped the inside with a rag from Janeck's car.

"That would have been a trade-off anyway," he said, "with different hair color than in our passport photos. Of course, you need to keep your hair long over your neck. So it looks like we're left with our own appearances."

Becker reached into the suitcase pocket and pulled out the foot-long sheathed knife, a Linder hunting knife. He would have preferred something smaller, but this would do. He tucked it in his coat lining pocket.

"Was that at Janeck's?" asked Maria.

"Behind the tiles in his bathroom," affirmed Becker. "So was this." He pulled out a gun and checked that it was fully loaded.

"This is a Bolo, the short-barreled version of the semi-automatic Mauser C-96. Janeck left it hidden in his flat." Becker aimed at a distant tree to get a feel for the gun, but he didn't fire. Then he offered the gun to Maria.

"No, thank you." She shook her head. "I don't want anything to do with that."

"You may not have a choice. We've got two more of them here, and plenty of bullets. I hope we don't need them. But you really ought to carry it."

Maria stood silent.

"Take the gun, Maria. They'll kill you if they find you, either immediately, or in some disease-ridden prison. If you have a chance to save yourself, take it!"

Maria slowly reached for the handle, and took it gingerly.

"The safety's on, but it's already loaded," he warned. "Hold it like this."

He showed her how to grip the gun with one hand, and with two hands and extended arms, aiming with the gun sight. Half the purpose of the gun, he explained, was to look like you were prepared to use it even if you didn't. They rehearsed a couple of draws, so she would look like she could handle the gun and fire with accuracy. Becker saved the reloading lesson for later. "Keep it in your purse."

For a moment, Maria just examined this foreign object in her palm. Then she firmly gripped the handle, before holding it delicately again, like fine jewelry. She laid the gun into her small purse.

Becker removed a second Mauser from the suitcase and put it in his left exterior coat pocket, opposite the pocket with his Luger. He returned the suitcase to the trunk.

"You know the way to Angel's Hill from here?" he asked.

"Of course," she replied.

"Here's the plan. From the footprints at the trailhead over there, it looks like a few walkers have climbed the hill since yesterday's snowstorm. Our own prints will be visible. Halfway up, I'm going to veer rightward into the trees, to approach my hiding spot from the far side. That spot is about fifty yards from the hilltop, beyond the crest above the path. While I'm doing that, you continue to the top and rest on the bench up there. When I'm done, I'll come out to meet you, and we'll come back down together. Is that all right?" he asked.

"That's easy enough, yes," she answered. "Am I supposed to be a lookout or something?"

"No," he said. "It's just a convenient place for you to wait separately."

"Why are you going so far out of your way? Are you expecting trouble?"

Becker thought about the two o'clock rendezvous. He still had a bad feeling about the place. But he needed the false passport for himself so that he could escort Maria across the border.

"No," he replied. "But this hill is used by others besides me. It's not as safe as it could be."

"Here we go, then," she said as she slipped her left hand into the crook of his right arm.

Becker remembered walking the streets with Maria like this just a few days ago. Then, they'd been able to feign flirtatious tones even in the face of danger. Last night and this morning cast a more serious pall over the romantic couple act. Now their danger deepened their bond but spoiled its playfulness.

On a normal Sunday morning, one that did not require loaded guns, the walk through the sparking white Grunewald Forest at dawn would have overwhelmed the senses. After days of clouds, the sunlit snow banks would be blinding by late morning. The air remained freezing cold. It bore the scents of new snow and fresh pinesap from broken branches. The air's crispness carried sounds well, compensating for the snow's muffling effect.

For half an hour, Becker and Maria waded uphill through the deep snow. Their conversation was limited by the exertions of the climb.

"This is where I need to exit the path northward," said Becker. "You'll continue westward to the top, where I'll meet you."

"I prefer to come with you," she replied.

"It will be a much harder walk," he said.

"Did I slow you down going to the Hossbach's last night?" she asked.

"No," he admitted.

"I'll deal with the difficulty," said Maria. "I don't want to be separated from you, even within shouting distance. Your fate will be mine." Her dark eyes looked up at him sternly.

"All right," he said. "But if you can't keep up, do you promise to turn around and meet me at the bottom? The last part from this side is really hard to climb."

"I promise," she replied.

The next forty-five minutes, they plodded through foot-deep snow, around the base of Angel Hill to its northern face. Their path climbed slowly, until they could see the tall hilltop above a steep incline. It looked like a small mountain.

"You see those two big pine trees near the crest?" asked Becker. "That's where we're headed."

"That's where *you're* headed. I'm exhausted, and we've got to go back through all this snow. I'll wait here."

"Good idea," he said. "I hope I won't be long. But I may have to dig a few times to find the spot. . . . How's your whistle?"

"My what?" she asked.

"How loud can you whistle?" he explained.

"Not very, I'm afraid," she replied.

"Well then, if for some reason you see someone following our tracks, yell up to me, all right?"

"Got it," she replied.

Becker began the steepest part of the ascent. He was glad Maria had stopped. When the steep slope began to level off, he lost sight of her.

He approached his two large pine trees and walked past them. Next he turned to face them from the ridge, twenty yards to the south. He sought the most familiar approach for guessing where between the trees lay his stone marker under the snow. It was nearly nine o'clock.

The foot-deep snow was cold and dry, and easy to sift through. On his first try, Becker hit dirt. He widened the hole at the base, trying to find his marker without digging a new hole. Right away he hit a stone. His fingers grasped for the rock's outline, but it was too big. It wasn't his marker. Becker stood up and tried to remember this large stone in relation to his marker. He picked a new spot to its right and started digging again.

"Do you think it will snow more today, Colonel Wächter?" The code greeting. Two young plainclothesmen approached Wächter at the entrance to the small Grunewald train station.

"It's about damn time you two got here!" seethed Wächter. Wächter had barely slept, and his famous impatience was even rawer for it.

"At two o'clock today is a planned rendezvous at the top of Angel's Hill," he continued. "The participants are subversives, which is all you need to know. We're going to scout out the site now and intercept the meeting later. . . . The hilltop is all the way across the forest, very close to the main road by the river. Before we drive over there, I'd like to examine the access points on this side. How good are your tires in the snow?"

"Surprisingly effective, sir," answered Sergeant Leim.

"Just issued last month, sir," elaborated Private Vogt.

"Good, then we're taking your car," said Wächter. "Give me the keys."

Wächter drove the car under the railroad tracks and turned left into the forest. After the quarter mile of developed areas, even the connector road became hard to manage. To test the forest's secondary roads, he took a short cut toward Hüttenweg Path.

Slowly the car plowed through a few dozen yards of snow. Then they heard the tires spinning.

"We're stuck!" Wächter banged the steering wheel in frustration. "Don't just sit there, get out of the car and push!"

Leim and Vogt did as commanded and moved to the front of the car to push it backwards.

Wächter spun the wheels in place, icing up his problem. His two subordinates dared not advise him. The spinning grew louder.

"Push, you fools!"

They tried to rock the car. Wächter finally coordinated his driving with their pushing.

Wächter welcomed the sound of crunching snow. The car finally inched backwards from its icy rut. But when Wächter tried to build on the reverse momentum, he spun the tires again.

"Push harder!" he ordered.

Wächter looked at the thirty yards that separated them from the better road. He yelled at his subordinates until finally they unstuck the car.

"That answers that," declared Wächter. "The secondary roads are virtually impassable. Now we'll take the perimeter roads to the far side of the forest."

Fifteen minutes later they pulled up to the western base of Angel's Hill and got out of the car. "We'll make a lot of tracks and noise climbing in this snow, men," he began. "But otherwise, I want you to be as silent as possible. If you notice anything unusual, wave an arm. Under no circumstances should you speak. We're going to walk up the hill and back down the other side."

After their ordeal with the stuck car, the climb was easy, steep but short. When they reached the bench that marked the top of the trail, Wächter motioned them to stop. He stared at the lone bench and then slowly turned to take in the view. To the west and southwest was the broad Havel River. Just to the north was the summit ridge, on slightly higher ground. Wächter looked up into the trees for anything unusual.

Just beyond the ridge, Becker was pocketing his false passport and some cash when he heard the footsteps reach the bench area and then stop. From the sound, Becker wasn't sure whether there was one person or more. But the footsteps were idling here.

Becker held his crouching position and waited. He reached in his jacket for his Luger . . . but it wasn't there!

Scheisse! It must have fallen out while I bent over digging! He also had two the Mausers, one in his pocket and one strapped to his chest. But they were still untested.

Without moving his body, he craned his neck to look in the three holes he had dug in the snow. He could see all the way to the bottom of two of them. The gun was in neither. The third hole was two yards away. Becker dared not move for fear of making a sound. And the gun might lie buried elsewhere, invisible in the powdery snow.

A sudden snapping sound made Becker's heart stop. It was behind him, but loud enough for the hiking party on the path to have heard. Maria must have stepped on a branch. Becker squatted motionless, an easy target.

Wächter jerked his head at the noise. He pulled out his gun, and silently motioned his companions to do the same. They carefully climbed toward the ridge just twenty yards ahead.

Three pairs of boots approaching in the snow told Becker he was in terrible trouble. Keeping his eyes on ridge, he shifted his body slowly to the third hole. Empty! He frantically looked around the snow for signs of his gun. There it was, barely sticking out of the snow, ten feet away from him toward the ridge.

"*Hände auf!*" Hands up!

The shout fell on Becker's ears like a boxer's bare fists.

Three men's outlines rose above the ridge, with three guns bearing down on him.

Becker put his hands in the air.

"Stand up!" ordered the middle one.

Becker obeyed. The three figures walked to within twenty feet of him.

"Were you squatting to take a shit in that hole you dug, like some mongrel human-cat? Lift your head up so I can see your face under that hat."

Becker held his chin up.

"So! Johannes Becker! Good morning!" Wächter added in English, before continuing to German. "It took me nine days, but I've caught up to you. What's going on with all this digging? What brings you to Angel's Hill on a day like today?"

Becker gave no answer. His mind was racing. *Maria. . . . Churchill. . . . The Rhineland. . . .*

Wächter cocked his gun. "Answer me, damn you, or else!"

"Don't move!" called a woman's voice from the top of the ridge, behind a tree.

It was Maria! She aimed her gun straight at Wächter.

All three Gestapo men whirled around with their guns. Leim and Vogt both trained their barrels on Maria. But since she remained fixed on Wächter, they held their fire. The colonel turned back to face Becker.

Becker had used Maria's distraction to scramble forward and pull his gun from the snow. Wächter found himself looking into a gun barrel on this side of him, too.

The five of them faced off in a mortal stalemate. Only Leim and Vogt were not immediate targets; they both pointed up the slope at Maria. She in turn fixed on Wächter. Becker and Wächter targeted each other in an almost point-blank stand-off.

"Fräulein Geberich," said Wächter, still facing Becker, his back to Maria. "Directly behind me in your line of fire is Mister Becker, an English spy. I wonder if he told you about that? Lower your weapon, Fräulein Geberich, and you will be treated gently."

Maria didn't budge.

The only movement was Leim's frequent head jerk to look for any visual cues from Wächter, who ignored him.

"Vogt, what's she doing?" asked Wächter, still looking down the slope at Becker.

"She hasn't moved, Colonel Wächter, sir," he answered. "She's still aiming at you."

"Fräulein, you're outgunned," said Wächter. "I'm giving you one last chance to save yourself."

"On the contrary!" countered Maria. "I could shoot you right now, and Becker would kill your henchmen before they turned around."

"But you would be dead," said Wächter.

"But Becker would escape, and that's the last thing you want," she replied.

Wächter bristled. "Vogt, turn your gun on Becker!"

"Do it and I'll shoot!" threatened Maria.

"Colonel Wächter, sir?" Vogt asked for confirmation of the order after Maria's threat.

"You wretched, pathetic woman!" Wächter still pointed his gun at Becker. Vogt didn't move.

The standoff lasted for more than a minute. To Becker it seemed like an eternity. Fingers on their triggers, they could all kill each other in one instantaneous chain reaction. There was no obvious escape.

The first shot sparked all the others.

Becker wasn't hit. He returned Wächter's fire. Wächter fell, clutching high at his upper left chest. Inexplicably, he'd missed Becker from less than ten feet away.

Leim and Vogt both fired at Maria. The only one not to fire was Maria. She fell backwards, out of Becker's sight.

Becker was enraged that Maria was down. He shot both guards before they could turn around. Their bodies hit the snow with soft thuds.

Becker wondered how Wächter could have missed him with the first shot at such close range. He turned from the two dead guards to see Wächter's gun pointing right at him. Becker dove sideways into the snow, and the two men fired at each other simultaneously. Both missed.

Now Becker stole a quick glance at Wächter from behind a medium-sized tree. Wächter was about the fire again. But his target was in the forest, behind Becker to his left. Wächter fired before Becker could turn around.

"Ack!" gasped a woman's voice.

Anna Lande! Becker turned to see her holding her abdomen. She fell to her knees, her eyes glazed over, blood trickling from her mouth. Then her dead body tipped forward into the snow.

Anna! No! In a split-second Becker realized what had happened. Wächter's first shot had missed him because there had been no such shot. Becker simply fired when he heard the first shot. Now he realized that shot had come from behind him. Anna had shot Wächter.

Becker looked back toward the two fallen guards. No movement there. Nor behind them. Maria, too, was down. Was she just injured? Dead?

Becker fired once at Wächter, forcing him to scamper for cover. Becker dashed to the two guards, aiming at Wächter all the way.

Becker kneeled behind a tree with the two bodies in front of him. He tested his Mauser by firing one bullet into each of their heads, to be sure they were dead.

Then he reached into his pocket for more ammunition.

Wächter shot at him again. Becker lay low.

From here Becker could see Maria on the ground, staring blankly into the sky.

Tears welled instantly in his eyes.

Wächter jerked upward and dashed five yards to one of the big pine trees.

"You Nazi piece of shit!" Becker half-screamed, half-sobbed as he pulled the trigger.

Wächter fell, wincing and grabbing his left leg. He crawled quickly on two arms and one leg to the tree's shelter. From there he returned fire.

Becker belly-crawled to Maria's body, ready to fire again if Wächter came out from cover.

He looked at the blood on Maria's neck as he approached her.

Then she turned her head!

"You're alive!" he whispered.

"Yes," she whispered back. She faced him, winked, and gave a strained smile.

Wächter continued his barrage, but stayed in place, groaning in pain.

"I think I'm all right, Johannes," she said. "Just grazed on the neck. I faked the fall."

She looked emotionally shocked, but physically well. "Phenomenal showing, Maria." He kissed her forehead, and she smiled again. "Just phenomenal. It's time to get out of here. We'll take the regular path this time. Just scoot down this ridge a little bit while I cover you. Then stand up and run towards the path. . . . Wächter's on the far side of the ridge, and I hurt his leg bad. I'll distract him for a moment and catch up. . . . Your legs are good, right?"

She nodded.

"All right – go!" he said.

Maria scrambled down the gentle slope on all fours until the ridge fully blocked Wächter's line of fire. Then she took off running.

Becker moved sideways a few yards and stood up briefly to fire at Wächter again.

Wächter hadn't moved from behind the tree. He clearly wasn't going anywhere quickly.

Becker slid down the ridge until he, too, could stand up. On his feet, he took one look back and then ran. Maria was ahead of him on the path, and she paused to turn and look at him.

"Keep running!" shouted Becker.

Moments later, Wächter began to fire at them from fifty yards away.

"He'll never hit us running from that distance. Keep going!" Becker had almost caught up to her.

Running down the path through loose snow was easier than the climb, but still tough. Becker watched Maria's neck wound constantly, to make sure it didn't worsen. It was fine, just the grazing Maria thought. She seemed in great shape.

"Are you doing all right?" he kept asking her.

"*Ja*," she answered every time.

Near the bottom, they approached an older couple from behind. The two strangers looked terrified from the gunshots as they hurried to exit the forest.

Becker and Maria reached the last turn just twenty minutes after the gunfight.

"Oh my God, Johannes, look!"

Parked right behind them was Lodt's car! The driver's door was wide open.

Becker hadn't told Maria about Anna yet. Maria had been too far away to hear Anna's death gasp. Now Becker realized that all along it had been Anna following them in Lodt's car. Somehow she'd managed to steal the car and his gun.

Becker could imagine Anna's resourceful trickery. Gustav Lodt liked her, and he was the type to fall for an attractive woman's flattery. Anna must have made him loosen his guard until she'd suddenly jumped in his car with his gun. And she must have done it quickly, to catch up with them.

"Take cover behind this beech tree while I check out Lodt's car," said Becker. "I don't think it was Lodt driving this car, but someone friendly to us."

Maria turned her head towards him, her brow furrowed in confusion, while she trotted to the tree.

Becker abandoned the trail with his gun drawn. He ran towards the parked cars from the cover of successive trees. As he approached from the side he saw no one.

From five yards away he called, "Put your hands up!"

No response.

He walked closer. "Put your hands up right now, or I'll shoot at the first movement!"

Nothing.

Becker paused and jerked his gun around him. He jerked his head repeatedly from Lodt's car to its surroundings. Then he rushed forward and pointed his gun through the window. The car was empty.

Abruptly he turned to Janeck's car from behind, his gun still steady in both hands. Becker began to approach the Opel from the driver's side. Then he quickly switched to the passenger side and ran forward. This car was empty, too. He lowered his gun.

"Anna," he muttered to Lodt's empty car. "May your soul rest in peace."

"What is it?" Maria cautiously approached.

Becker stared back at Lodt's car. "It was Anna Lande in that car chasing us. It was she who fired the first shot up there. I never saw her coming behind me."

Maria's mouth dropped. She was speechless.

They got into Janeck's car. Becker cranked it up and turned it around on the road.

"Lodt had a gun and his wife was right there," he elaborated. "But somehow Anna got his car and followed us. I know Lodt was fond of Anna. He also has to be about the worst block leader in the Gestapo. Not a very clever man. She must have fooled him somehow. Then she followed us here. . . ."

Becker's voice trailed off as he drove toward the main forest road. He wondered why Anna had embroiled herself in this mess. He knew she'd admired him, but she'd always maintained a certain distance. She'd never struck him as an adventuresome heroine. Yet now he owed his life to her heroics. Her death saddened him profoundly. Another kind spirit snuffed out by the Nazis.

"She saved us up there . . . ," Maria realized.

Becker nodded. "I can't believe she got into this business. . . . Yes, she saved us."

"So you work for the English, like the man said?" she asked.

Becker thought for a moment. He was under strict orders not to discuss his connections, but lying now would be obvious, even counterproductive. After the past twelve hours, he thought Maria deserved to know. "Yes, I do."

He was driving slowly and carefully down the secondary road, trying not to get stuck.

"But you're German. How? Why?" she inquired.

"It's a long story. I'm German and English both. I even changed my name to 'John' and went to university there. I hate the Nazis. My nanny was a Jew. She and her teenage children were like a second family to me. They were even more patriotic Germans than my family! Now they suffer terribly under the Nazis, and I've had quite enough of it. . . . What's more, I lost my father in the Great War, for nothing but vain imperial glory. . . . Germany had a chance in the twenties. Things were getting better. Now Hitler's taking this country back toward war. Europe shouldn't have to go through that again."

"Here's Hüttenweg Path," he said. "We've got to get away from here fast. In this cold air, those gun blasts carried for miles and fell on thousands of ears."

CHAPTER TWENTY-FOUR

"They'll be looking for our car," Becker explained. "Lodt surely called it in, unless Anna killed him, which I doubt. But they changed police shifts at seven o'clock. Hopefully the morning patrols don't know about us. Still, keep a look out."

Maria looked around the snow-white Grunewald Forest. There wasn't a car or hiker to be seen.

"It's time to finish your new passport," Becker told her. He drove carefully. Dry snow cracked under the wheels. "Keep your photos from your old papers and give me the rest."

Maria carefully peeled off her photos. Then she placed the papers on Becker's lap.

Becker pulled the car to the side of the empty forest road. He got out and ran around the front of the car. At the road's edge, in a foot of snow, he buried Maria's papers and his Luger. He had much more ammunition for the Mausers.

He reached into his left coat pocket and pulled out the stack of passports he'd retrieved on Angel's Hill. He chose the two he wanted and buried the rest, including one blank passport he'd carried for Maria since Friday. The blank one from this morning best matched the false papers for himself.

Back in the car, he handed a passport to Maria and resumed driving.

"Now," he said, "you'll find some glue in Janeck's suitcase behind you. Use just a touch of it and close the passport carefully. Then sit on it to help it stick."

Maria began the work.

"We're going to Prague," Becker explained. "The border agents will be looking for us. Wächter must have forwarded our photos all over Germany by yesterday at the latest. We certainly can't enter a Berlin train station. And there's no way we should try to drive across the border. We'll drive to Dresden and catch the Berlin-Vienna night train there at seven minutes after midnight."

"It's not even noon now," observed Maria.

"We'll have to wait awhile in Dresden. . . . The tank is full. Say good-bye to Berlin. Study your new self: Frau Inge Augustana, maiden name Strauss. My passport is that of your brother, Herr Walter Strauss. We both live in Cologne, each of us married with no children. We are going to visit our brother Klaus in Vienna."

Becker began to elaborate their false story – sightseeing in Dresden, even the hotel where they stayed. The car reached the turn at Onkel-Tom Strasse, still in the forest. Becker pulled out one golden wedding band for each of them.

"Up there's where we exit the forest," he said. "Watch for anything suspicious."

"All I see," said Maria, "are those people walking to church up ahead."

"Perfect!" said Becker. "We're driving through town just when there's a spike of traffic to cover us."

As Becker drove, they both tried to look calm while watching their surroundings. Becker drove through the Zehlendorf district to the Berlin city border and into the countryside.

From southwest Berlin, Becker drove eastward to meet the Dresden highway. There the drive turned southward. The snow-covered fields reflected the morning sunlight straight into Becker's eyes.

As morning turned to noon, the sunlit snow became almost blinding. It lulled Becker into drowsiness. The snow still covered the highway, too. The two-hour ride over one hundred miles lengthened into four hours.

Maria slept for much of the trip. She kept her eyes closed against the sun for the rest of it. Becker tried not to think about the nap he would take in Dresden. It required a real force of will not to nod off now.

When they finally arrived in Dresden, Becker was exhausted. He parked the car next to many others in the business district. Shops were closed for Sunday, but many people were strolling and sledding in the snow. Maria agreed to stand guard in her seat while Becker slept in his. For an hour, he dozed in and out of sleep. At least it was something, he consoled himself.

The rest of the day was a stalling exercise. They couldn't risk a hotel. And if they stayed too long in any one restaurant or coffee house, some part-time Gestapo informer was bound to raise questions. So they walked and lingered with the crowds outside. After dark, this got harder to do. But by then, Becker knew the busiest strolling streets. Throughout the evening, at least a few other people were always around.

By 10:30 Sunday evening, even the stragglers were clearing the streets for the night. Becker decided it was time to collect their luggage and walk to the train station. Janeck's car would be discovered parked illegally the next morning.

When they reached the station, Becker steered them first to the large garbage disposal in the back. Earlier in the day he'd seen the station newsstand discard bundles of old papers here. They were perfect for filling the suitcase to normal weight . . . as long as it wasn't searched.

The Berlin-Vienna train was scheduled to arrive in Dresden at 23:56, and depart at 00:07, just after midnight. It would reach the Czechoslovak border at 00:38 and arrive in Prague at 03:44 in the morning. It reached its final destination, Vienna, almost six hours later.

Becker bought two round-trip tickets from Dresden to Vienna. When they disembarked in the middle of the night in Prague, the German authorities wouldn't be around to notice the discrepancy.

Becker wanted a sleeper car. He didn't want Maria to spend half the night sitting upright in a regular compartment with four strangers. The Dresden ticket agent wasn't sure if any sleepers remained. This was, after all, the Berlin-Vienna line on a Sunday night, its busiest. Becker would have to ask the conductor on board for availability.

He and Maria joined the dozen passengers at the open-air bistro in the train station. The cold patrons huddled over their warm drinks. Maria took mint tea, and Becker had black.

Most people seemed to share the Prague or Vienna destination. A few had just arrived on regional lines, getting a drink before heading home in Dresden. Occasional train whistles and calls echoed across the wintry, cavernous train station.

Gradually, the Prague-Vienna travelers migrated to the platform where their train from Berlin would stop for eleven minutes before resuming its journey. Becker and Maria followed.

Becker paused to study the departures schedule. He looked through the station's massive steel arches to the starry night sky. Then he shifted his gaze to the rail lines, well above ground level.

"*Meine Damen und Herren,*" announced the speakers overhead, "in a few minutes, the Berlin-Prague-Vienna night train will arrive on Track 8."

Maria and Becker walked under the rails and approached the staircase up to Track 8. A young policeman stood at the bottom of the staircase. He nodded good evening to passengers as they climbed to the platform. Then he stopped one young couple to check their papers. He quickly waved them up the stairs. The fugitives were next.

"I can't wait to hear Klaus play the piano again," Becker told Maria in a casual tone.

"Besides Klaus himself, that's the thing I miss most about him, too," said Maria.

The police officer lifted his hand slightly, telling them to stop for questioning. "Good evening, Herr . . . ?"

"Strauss," answered Becker.

"Herr Strauss. And Frau Strauss?" asked the officer.

"No," Maria chuckled, "This is my brother. Augustana is my name."

"Frau Augustana. Excuse me. May I see your papers, please?"

"Of course," replied Becker.

The young policeman seemed barely twenty years old, if that. He stared at both of them intently, turning his head nervously back and forth between them.

"Cologne – Goethe Strasse, very well. And you ma'am?" the officer asked Maria.

Maria handed over her own false papers.

"Also Goethe Strasse." The officer raised his eyebrows. "Very convenient!"

The young man hesitated, seeming unsure what to do. He strained his eyes to focus on each of them, looking back and forth again.

The awkward pause grew longer. Other passengers passed to the right and climbed the stairs. The train could be heard entering the station, and the overhead speakers announced it.

"May we?" Becker gestured up the stairs.

"Yes, of course." The policeman blinked his eyes and looked away for a moment. "I'm terribly sorry. It's late you know. Good night."

"Good night," replied both Becker and Maria.

The young man tipped his cap. Maria and Becker climbed to the boarding platform. They did not look back or speak to each other.

At the top, Becker took the standard survey of both directions of the platform. In his peripheral vision he glanced toward the officer down the stairs. He was gone!

Becker took Maria's hand into his arm. Then he pulled her to the right, down the platform toward the back end of the braking train.

"That policeman disappeared as soon as we left him," Becker spoke into Maria's ear, over the sound of the train's breaks. "Be prepared to follow my lead."

As he looked down at Maria, he glimpsed behind her at the station floor below. Their policeman was talking with two plainclothesmen – Gestapo! – and pointing straight at them! All three started to move briskly toward the staircase.

"Quick, climb into this storage car!" he told Maria.

The train had just stopped. Becker unlatched the car door and wheeled it open in its tracks. Inside were piles of furniture. He all but threw Maria into the train car, then the suitcase. He jumped in himself and pulled the door shut behind him. He knew a few passengers on the platform had seen this quick move. But the police hadn't reached the top of the stairs yet.

Within seconds, Becker heard boot heels slamming on cement. The Gestapo agents were dashing down the platform towards their car!

Maria stared at the sliding door between them at the Gestapo agents.

"We're leaving the suitcase here," Becker said. "Follow me."

Becker leaped over a large office desk. He crawled over chairs to the end of the storage car, next to the caboose. He practically carried Maria as he helped her. Then he opened the door to the small landing between their car and the caboose. He pulled Maria out and closed the storage car behind them.

To their left, just three feet away on Track 7, another train slowly pulled away. It was headed back in the direction of Berlin. Becker led Maria down the landing stairway facing the departing train.

"You don't mean to jump onto that moving train?!?" she objected.

"I don't mean to stay here!" he replied.

Suddenly they heard the Gestapo roll open the storage car door.

One angry voice bellowed out, "Braun, watch underneath the train! Make sure they don't jump down on the tracks!"

Before Becker could throw Maria to the staircase of the departing train, she launched herself. All he could do was to push her upward. This added enough height to her jump that she landed on the bottom stair and avoided getting crushed on the tracks below.

Becker watched Maria pull away on the train.

Her purse! She doesn't have her purse and papers! Her photo there was crystal clear. Her gun was still fully loaded. Both were now lost.

Becker jerked his head leftward to look for the next entry staircase on the departing train. The end of the train was right on him! He dove forward.

His foot hit the bottom step and slipped. His whole body slid down past the step. His right foot hit one of the turning wheels, which kicked his whole leg and body up to the right. With his left hand, Becker grasped the staircase handrail. His feet scraped the railroad ties, jerking him now leftward.

"Did you hear anything, Braun?" called the voice in the storage car. Becker couldn't make out Braun's response, but it sounded dismissive.

The departing train accelerated on airborne rails some twenty feet above ground level. Becker dangled above the street below, clutching the handrail for his life. He kicked his feet repeatedly toward the bottom stair. Finally he landed one foot, and pulled himself to the top of the staircase.

He looked for people below and then in the station behind. No one watched him. Perhaps he had gone unnoticed. He and Maria now stood one car apart on a train pointed back into Germany, away from Prague.

Becker saw the car between him and Maria was yet another storage car. He picked the padlock open, dashed past large mail bins, and opened the door to the noisy, open-air landing between cars.

He startled Maria. She was freezing in the winter wind of the train ride.

"You're here!" she exclaimed. "Oh, thank goodness! My purse . . . . We're headed back to Berlin! We were so close to the border! I lost my papers – the gun – I have nothing!"

"Come in here and let's get out of sight," said Becker. They retreated into the mail car and shut the door. It was cold and drafty, but not windy.

"Actually, this train isn't headed to Berlin. I noticed it on the departures schedule in the station. We're on a slow overnight regional train to Leipzig. It's mostly a freight train, with one passenger car at the front end. If they didn't see us board this train, they might not stop it right away."

"Leipzig?" worried Maria. "What are we going to do from there?"

"I need to think about that," he said. "Our papers were finished anyway, since that young policeman checked them."

"I guess we won't get much sleep tonight," observed Maria.

"We can rest in these mail bins," he replied.

"But they'll know to check this train, won't they?" she asked.

"Almost certainly," he replied. "Let's get a little rest first. There's a half-full mail bin in the dark right here beside us. Can I give you a hand?"

Maria put her arms around Becker's neck, and he lifted her in. Before climbing in with her, he lifted a handful of letters from the bin and went to a crack in the car siding. By the streetlights of a Dresden suburb, Becker read the mail address lines: Leipzig, and villages nearby. This was good. Their mail bin, if not the whole mail car, would travel to Leipzig without disruption. Then he climbed in beside Maria.

"I'll think of a way out of this . . . ," he promised. The Gestapo could be relied upon to search this train thoroughly before it arrived in Leipzig early Monday morning. Becker knew he'd think of something.

They approached their first stop at 00:28. The train's steel wheels screeched for five minutes of intermittent braking.

Maria was terrified they were stopping so soon. Becker was mildly surprised when the mail car door rumbled open in its tracks. Two or three men – he wasn't sure – lifted one more mail bin into the car and rolled the door shut behind it. The train slowly pulled out of the station.

Becker tried to reassure Maria their bin was safe all the way to Leipzig. By the third such mail loading, at 01:22, she was merely scared.

Becker knew their time was short. The mail deposits weren't the problem. At any of these short stops, though, the Gestapo could stop the train and search it. The search might not come in the first three hours. But he was sure it would come after that.   .

The night train was scheduled for an hour-long wait in the middle of nowhere, from 03:14 until 04:26. The little train stop didn't even have a place name. It was just "Saxony Rural Station No. 2." He didn't tell Maria yet about the long stop.

By 03:14, they would need a plan to escape this train. Becker had less than two hours to come up with one. Sooner would be better. He was sleepy. He regretted not finishing his tea back at the Dresden train station. Coffee would have been even better. He was beginning to get a headache.

After the stop at 01:22, Becker climbed out of the bin and told Maria he was looking around. Then he crawled around looking for any loose floorboards.

He pulled a steel clasp off a nearby bin and began his search in one corner. He finished about one-quarter of the floor, he guessed, with no loose boards to work with. The train began to brake for another mail stop. He leapt back into their bin.

With another quick departure he resumed his search. Another fifteen minutes finally produced a single loose floorboard. It was easily removed. Becker used the clasp to pry up adjacent boards until he had a space wide enough to pass through. He replaced the boards just in time for the next mail stop, at 02:35.

When the train accelerated this time, Becker rushed to remove the boards. He wanted to look underneath the train while he had a little light from the last station. There were several large bars and fixtures near his hole, Becker observed. He repaired the floor and returned to Maria to describe their escape route.

Becker's body clock told him their train skipped a mail stop. Next would be Rural Station No. 2.

When the train began screeching its brakes at 03:10, Becker and Maria climbed out of their large mail bin. Becker pulled up the floorboards and stacked them neatly. He would have to replace them from underneath the train.

Next he stood at the edge of the car's right-side sliding door and waited for the little train station to appear. Maria followed him.

The train stop had only one gaslight, a small shed for shelter, and no platform. Rural "station" wasn't the right term. It was more like a bus stop. Two men waited in uniform, one Reichsbahn engineer and one conductor. It must be a shift change, thought Becker. He glanced toward Maria. With a little light from the crack, he could just make out the contours of her face. The train screeched its loudest just before halting.

"It's good to see you!" called a voice approaching from the head of the train.

The engineer from Dresden, thought Becker.

"More than you know," answered one of the men waiting. The next shift. This second voice stood still, about twenty yards away from the mail car. "You don't want to deal with what's headed this way . . . all the way from Reichsbahn Headquarters in Berlin. They sent orders for you two to stay and help watch the train. We make sure no one gets on or off until the police arrive."

Becker heard Maria swallow a gasp. He looked towards her in the near darkness.

They obviously couldn't jump to the ground here. They'd have to try to cling to the bottom of the train.

Becker whispered to Maria, "Back to the hole in the floor. Take steps only when you hear them talking, so they don't hear any sounds."

"Understood," she replied.

The four Reichsbahn employees talked intermittently. Maria and Becker took a step or two each time. Becker waited for another spark of conversation outside to lower himself to the floor. Then he put his head through the hole and looked underneath the train.

They were in luck. The bottom of the train here had one long bar that should support him, and a narrow ledge where Maria would fit. He lifted his head to whisper to Maria again.

"There's a ledge under here for you to lie on," he motioned to the right of the hole. "I'll be on a big bar over here," he whispered, motioning to the left.

Time was wasting, Becker knew. The Gestapo was on its way.

"Look down there and nod if you see your ledge," he continued.

Maria bent, looked, and nodded.

"All right," he whispered. "I'll hold your ankles while you crawl under there."

Maria hesitated before lowering her whole body under the train. Becker could tell from the way she moved that she was lying flat on her back. He saw her arm extended tight to hold a small fixture and brace herself in. He also saw her skirt drooping dangerously low, perhaps visible from the side of the train.

He pointed desperately at the skirt. Then he watched her pull the skirt's shadow to the train's underside.

Now Becker lowered himself into the hole. As his feet and hands searched for grips, he was reminded of climbing trees as a boy in the Black Forest. Once he was secure, he pulled the floorboards neatly into the hole above him.

In the nighttime, Becker could not see Maria's face from just a few feet away. But the waning moon had now risen to brighten the sky. He could see Maria's arm, a few folds in her clothes, and a little hair hanging loose.

He hoped she was more comfortable than he was. He'd given her the flat ledge, the much better space. His single, narrow bar instantly pressed into his flesh that rested on it. Becker felt the length of his back bruising already. Within minutes, the pain was tremendous..

Every few minutes, Becker shifted his weight slightly. But soon every angle was exhausted. Every available strip of flesh on his back was damaged. Deeper in his body, his nerves and blood vessels were pinched with damaging force. Becker knew they had about an hour until departure. Over that time, he risked partial paralysis from nerve damage and loss of blood to his muscles.

After fifteen minutes of this, Becker heard two automobiles arrive in a rush.

"*Heil Hitler!*" shouted the new arrivals.

"*Heil Hitler*," answered the four Reichsbahn employees.

"Get out of the way, you idiots!" yelled the Gestapo commander. "Your whole damn Reichsbahn failed us at the last stop. Any sign of them yet?"

"No, sir," answered the new shift's engineer.

"Oh, forget it," continued the Gestapo officer. "Your passengers could be wearing the hammer and sickle, and you guys would never notice the difference. As long as their tickets are in order. . . . Kopf, Falke – Look around the train for any suspicious footprints in the snow, especially a woman's. . . . Peters – Go down the tracks for a mile toward Dresden, and watch for footprints along the way."

"Yes sir, Obersturmführer Bauer," answered Peters.

Lieutenant Bauer continued, "You Reichsbahn men, continue standing guard. How long until the train is scheduled to depart?"

"Forty-five minutes, sir," answered the fresh engineer.

"That should be enough. But you don't pull out until you have my go-ahead. Who has the keys?"

"I do, sir," answered the Dresden conductor.

"Come with me."

The Gestapo lieutenant began to search the train from the back to the front. At the back entrance to the last car, he noticed the open padlock. "Is that supposed to be open?" he asked the first shift's conductor.

"No, sir," answered the conductor.

"Who was supposed to lock it?" asked Bauer.

"I locked it sir," replied the conductor. "Back at the Dresden station. I'm quite certain about that."

"You locked it before departure?"

"Yes, sir," answered the conductor.

Becker shuddered at the progression of this conversation.

"Well let's have a look," said the Gestapo lieutenant.

The mail car's side door rumbled as they opened it.

"Leaving mail unattended without a lock is a criminal felony," started Bauer.

"I locked it up, sir, I swear," answered the conductor. He tried to lock the padlock shut, but it wouldn't catch. "It's been picked broken, sir." He sounded relieved.

The Gestapo officer looked at the padlock. "Then they've been here!"

Becker heard boots enter and roam the mail car overhead. Bauer tripped right above the loose floorboards!

"Damn floorboard!" he yelled. "Get me some light!"

The conductor lit the car's gas lamp.

"Look at the condition of this thing!" exclaimed the lieutenant. "Someone knew enough to replace part of the floor, but why not all of it?!? Before you go home tonight, you call your command and tell them to keep their mail cars in better shape."

"Yes, sir."

"Now, search the mail bins," ordered Bauer.

The conductor started to object. "But sir, postal regulations state—"

"I am the authority here! Now do as I say!"

Two Reichsbahn officials spilled all the mail on the floor.

"Damn, damn, damn!" exclaimed the Gestapo officer. "They've been in here and gotten away."

"Kopf and Falke, you find anything?" The two men had just presented themselves.

"*Nein*," they answered together.

"You two search the rest of the train, top to bottom," he barked.

Becker lay in silent pain, just inches under Obersturmführer Bauer. Becker was afraid even to shift his body around for temporary relief. He could feel his muscles going numb, down into his right leg. He knew the bruises would be debilitating if he couldn't move soon.

Finally, after two more minutes, the Gestapo and Reichsbahn men moved to other cars. Becker allowed himself to shift again. The relief didn't last long. He shared the painful damage in turns all across his back. For more than thirty minutes, the train search continued.

Footsteps suddenly approached the mail car. Bauer's voice bellowed, "Peters, escort the mail car to the postal officials in Leipzig."

Becker could hear Peters approach their car, then his boots pacing in the space above them.

"What a mess," muttered Peters.

Becker knew that if he could understand Peters mumbling, then he and Maria had no chance to speak below unnoticed from above.

"Obersturmführer Bauer, it's 04:25," called the fresh conductor down the tracks from them. "May the train depart on time?"

"Go ahead," answered Bauer.

The whistle blew and the regional train began its slow acceleration into the snowy night.

Becker feared his legs were already damaged. He couldn't keep his weight on this thin bar any longer – not even for a few more minutes of jostling. He couldn't hold himself with his arms for three hours. And there was nowhere else to rest his body.

Earlier tonight, he'd noticed the railroad ties were covered with snow, glimmering with a layer of ice on top. The day's sun had melted the top snow. He hoped the ice was thick.

The train was a hundred yards underway. Soon it would be too fast for him to survive the fall intact. The railroad ties already passed too quickly to count.

With Peters guarding above, Becker could not tell Maria anything. He hoped she was looking toward him. Only the crescent moon's light on the snow gave him any hope that she would see what was about to happen.

Becker slipped his body off the bar and hung on by his hands and feet. He swung his body to show Maria his intention of jumping. Then suddenly he let go and twisted around. He hid his head behind his folded arms as he dove into the speeding railroad ties.

Snow and ice absorbed much of his fall. His body slid forward to a stop. He was bruised but intact. He lifted his head to watch the train speeding away, with Maria on it.

CHAPTER TWENTY-FIVE

Becker lay low on the railroad ties. He was banged up, but nothing felt broken. His face stung. Then the stinging faded to a chill. He realized his face was covered with snow. Unlike the rest of him, it was barely bruised. Nothing felt broken, and he could move all his limbs.

The departing train's noise seemed to violate the peaceful landscape. In empty fields all around, light from the stars and crescent moon reflected off the ice-glazed snow. Becker could see the small clouds of his panting breath in the still air.

He carefully turned his head back toward Rural Station No. 2. There was nothing . . . neither Gestapo nor railroad officials . . . only the lone platform light, hours before dawn. No one had noticed his fall from the train.

He turned back toward the vanishing train. Only twenty yards away, looking back at him, was Maria. She knelt on the tracks and clutched her left shoulder in pain.

Becker rose to a hunched position and scurried down the tracks to meet her. At the same time, he looked to the train for any sign of suspicion. The train chugged on toward Leipzig.

"My shoulder, Johannes, it's mangled." Maria bit her lower lip, rocked back and forth, and reached her right arm across her chest.

Becker gently removed her coat. He examined the shoulder and saw the problem. "It's dislocated. That happened to me once in a rugby match. Lie down and I'll see if I can fix it."

Becker remembered the counter-intuitive fix. Instead of trying to push the arm into the shoulder, he needed to pull it forward. That would bring the ball back into its socket. With Maria on her back, he lifted her arm straight up and gave it a tug.

Maria gasped. Then she looked curiously surprised.

"Very sorry," he said. "Does that feel any better?"

"My gosh, yes," she replied. "It's still sore, but like a bruise or something. I thought it was broken. Wow, was that a quick fix. Thank you!"

"Are you hurt anywhere else?" he asked.

"Just bruises, I think," she answered.

"I'm sorry about the surprise jump," Becker apologized. "I couldn't hold on any longer. There just wasn't enough space, and I risked losing use of a leg. With that Gestapo guy above us, I had to stay silent."

"I couldn't believe you did that! I thought the train would kill you. But you made it. I forced myself to let go before I could think about it." Maria looked exhilarated and fatigued at the same time.

"I had no idea the railroad ties were iced over so smoothly," she said. "I thought they'd kill me."

"Do you think you can walk up the tracks to that stand of trees?" pointed Becker. "It looks about half a mile away."

Maria slowly stood up. "Walking won't be a problem," she replied.

Becker led the way down the tracks. They walked on a frozen stream from the rails to the tiny wooded refuge, surrounded by snow-covered fields. When they found a spot sheltered from sight, they sat down to rest. They were only about thirty yards from the tracks, but a small rise in the little forest blocked the view.

"How will we get to Prague from here?" asked Maria.

"We won't," he answered. "That would be too obvious. They'll be looking so hard, we couldn't even stowaway on a train. We'd never make it in a stolen auto. We have to go the other way. To France."

"All the way across Germany?" Maria asked in disbelief.

"As train stowaways, yes. The hardest part is getting out of here. Then we play hobo from Leipzig to Munich. From there we take a night train to Paris. And I'm fairly certain I could break into a sleeper car for that – no more spending the night in a mail car!"

Maria chuckled. "By now, I wish we'd been left the whole night in that one!" It wasn't even five in the morning yet, and they'd been interrupted with mail loading every half-hour.

"At the French border, they might check the train very thoroughly," Becker continued. "If we have to get off – without jumping this time! – we can row across the Rhine River in the night. Out of curiosity, I once scouted that out. There's a handy rowing club just down-river from the railway bridge."

Maria sighed. "Tell me it can't get any harder than this."

"We haven't been caught," was his best answer.

"So how do we catch our next train?" she asked. "We're in the middle of nowhere. We'd be hard-pressed to find a parked auto, much less steal it."

"We jump the train," he said. "It will have to be dark outside. And we can't arrive too late in Leipzig, because we'll have no place to stay. The best thing is to arrive in Leipzig at morning rush-hour, having boarded here by cover of night."

"A train like the one we were on," she said.

"Precisely," he replied. "We wait twenty-four hours and board the same train."

That would be Tuesday morning. Churchill would be assassinated Wednesday night, if Becker didn't get the news out by then.

"That's your best idea?" she asked.

"I'm open to suggestions," he smiled.

"I wish I had one," she replied. "I don't know how in the world I'm going to jump onto a moving train."

"You did it last night in Dresden," he said.

"Yes, but not from the ground."

"I'll lift you when it passes," he replied.

"We'll see."

Becker thought ahead to later stages of their escape. He considered other options besides the French border. The Gestapo surely kept watch over the British consulate in Munich, and they would know his photo well. They would whisk him into a car before he could so much as shout a warning to the consulate windows. And then Maria would fall prey to the Gestapo.

Switzerland and Austria were closer than France. The Gestapo would be looking harder for him at their borders and British consulates.

France was his best bet. Becker expected to arrive there Wednesday morning. He might be able to travel personally to London in the time for Churchill's concert that evening. That was cutting it close. It was better to rely on British intelligence at the passport office in Paris, if only he knew someone there he could trust.

Gestapo Colonel Wächter arrived at his office at six-thirty Monday morning. The night's report lay on his desk:

SUMMARY of Overnight Field Reports
Sgt. S. SCHUMACHER
Monday, 17 Feb., 06:00

Just after midnight Monday morning, a twenty-year-old policeman in Dresden interviewed the two fugitives, Johannes BECKER and Maria GEBERICH, in Dresden Train Station, traveling with forged passports. He confirmed their identity when presented with photographs thirty minutes later.

The fugitives boarded a storage car on the Berlin-Vienna train, but they immediately disappeared. The train was delayed by one hour for a full search that yielded: a suitcase with spilled peroxide; and a purse with a loaded Bolo Mauser, and with false identification in the name of Frau Inge Augustana, née Strauss, with Fräulein GEBERICH's photograph.

The most likely escape route was a departing train for Leipzig. Dresden Gestapo agents believe the fugitives almost certainly took this train.

The Reichsbahn failed to stop this train through five mail pick-up stops, until three hours later, at a remote station, Saxony Rural Station No. 2. There the train underwent a thorough search. Despite evidence of the fugitives' stowaway, they were no longer to be found.

Sgt. S. SCHUMACHER

Again they got away! Wächter pounded his oak desk so hard, he wondered for a moment whether he'd broken his fist.

Wächter had spent Sunday afternoon getting his gunshot wounds bandaged at the Berlin Military Hospital. He'd gone to bed at five o'clock in the afternoon and slept for twelve hours. He'd been eager for news until he read this report.

He called Scharführer Schumacher to his office.

"Get these orders out immediately," started Wächter. "First, tell the guards at all Czech border points to be even more cautious than before, searching every corner of every train. Second, spread the message to all rail, road, and ferry crossings out of Germany. Third, in the next twenty-four hours, thoroughly search every train on the Dresden-Leipzig line, both directions. . . . Finally, yesterday we posted Gestapo guards outside public and clandestine British offices in Berlin to look for the fugitives and arrest them on the spot. Now, extend that order to all German cities with British consulates or other representations. And get our agents abroad to man the streets outside

British consulates in Prague, Vienna, Zurich, Berne, and Paris. . . . If anyone gives you trouble, cite General Heydrich's authority. . . . Now get these orders dispatched!"

"Yes sir!" answered Schumacher. *"Heil Hitler!"*

"Heil Hitler," answered Wächter.

Schumacher briskly retreated to carry out his assignment.

Maria fell asleep quickly in the dark, snowy woods where she and Becker would hide for the next twenty-four hours. She even slept through the next train to pass by, at six-thirty Monday morning.

Becker tried to sleep and couldn't. He was cold. Maria had the warmer coat, he could see. Around seven o'clock, he could no longer suppress his shivering teeth. The sound awakened Maria.

"Johannes, you poor thing!" She started to remove her scarf.

Becker managed a meager smile through his clacking teeth. "No thanks."

"If you don't wear it, no one will. I refuse. Take it," she insisted.

"Thanks," he accepted.

Maria pulled him from beside her to a position leaning back against her chest. She held him tight.

"Strong arm," he observed. "The shoulder?" Still freezing, he spoke in clipped phrases.

"Still sore, but that's all," she replied. "Try to get some sleep."

He finally did. His dreams were an intense collage of the past ten days. Every dream ended the same way, in Wächter's interrogation chamber. Whether the dream was about swimming in the canal, learning of Clara's death, Nadine spying on him, or the shootout in Grunewald Forest, it always ended badly.

The sun was high in the sky when he awoke and glanced at his watch. Noon.

"You slept very deeply," said Maria. "But with many nightmares."

Becker wondered whether to comment on that. Nadine had heard him speaking English sleeping on tranquilizers. What had Maria heard now? She already knew he was a British spy. He decided to let it pass. Maria didn't elaborate.

The rest of the afternoon and into the evening, one or the other of them was usually trying to sleep. They didn't do much talking. Both their stomachs grumbled. They ate a little snow for moisture. In this state, Becker found it impossible to sleep more than thirty minutes straight. He had no concern about sleeping through the night. Their train would arrive a half-mile away around three-thirty in the morning and depart an hour later.

At two o'clock in the morning, Becker decided it was time to prepare themselves. Maria was awake, too.

"That train doesn't arrive for another hour and a half," he started. "The train stop is probably abandoned right now. It's time to move into position. . . . The tracks rise above the fields enough for us to hide on this side, opposite the road. After the Dresden engineer gets off the locomotive, we'll come in closer. By the time of departure, the Dresden guys will be long gone. No one will be on the ground to see us stand up. We'll jump aboard the mail car while it's barely moving. . . . Like I said before, I'll hold you up so you can easily step onto the stairs."

"No," said Maria.

"What?"

"You have to get on first, Johannes."

"And risk you not making it? Never," he said.

"No, I insist you get on first," she repeated. "I'll wait up the tracks a bit and you can pull me up when you pass. I can't let you miss this train because of me. You've come too far, with too much at stake."

"I can't let *you* miss the train," he insisted.

"If you don't board the train first, I won't either. I'm not giving you a choice. . . . You need to get out of Germany. I'm slowing you down. You're trying to get me out, too. Maybe you can. Maybe you can't. I won't leave our little forest here unless you give me your word of honor that you will stay on the train, no matter what."

Becker paused. "All right. You have my word of honor. I will do everything I can to get you on that train. But I'll also make sure I get on it and stay on it. . . . One thing, though."

"Yes?" she asked.

"You must at least try to get on the train. If you're planning some kind of martyrdom here, forget it. If you don't seriously try to get on that train, I'll jump right back off. Do we have an arrangement?"

"Oh, I'm jumping! Don't worry about that," Maria laughed. "I don't plan on missing it. But I know it's possible. If that happens, you have to stay on. If I miss and you jump off, I'll turn myself in immediately. You'll be on your own then anyway. Don't miss the train for me. I'm dead serious."

Becker shook his head. "I don't like it. But you win. You're a tough negotiator."

They left their small patch of woods and returned to the tracks. It was another crisp starlit night. The waning crescent moon was starting to rise, and the snow amplified visibility remarkably.

Becker and Maria crawled on the dark rail tracks that hid their shadowy figures. Only when they got about fifty yards from Rural Station No. 2 did they climb down the short railway rise to the foot-deep snow below. Their tracks would be unmistakable by morning. By then Becker planned to be beyond Leipzig.

Becker noticed a small boulder ahead, about twenty yards from the train stop. It was closer than he wanted to get. But the rest of this area was wide open. It would be hard to hide from the locomotive's sight out there. The boulder was big enough to hide them both. But that brought their footprints in closer range.

"Try to step in my footprints from here to that rock ahead," he told Maria.

They moved forward, standing nearly upright while they focused on minimizing their tracks. Then they settled in behind the boulder, with the train stop out of sight.

About half an hour before the scheduled arrival, they heard the pre-dawn shift arrive at Rural Station No. 2. Then right on time at 03:10, they heard the screeching train brakes in the distance. Becker anxiously awaited the conversation between the old shift and the new one.

The train came to a stop. Becker could certainly hear the voices, but not the words. Unlike last night, the Reichsbahn workers didn't sound agitated.

Less than ten minutes after the train's arrival, Becker heard an auto crank started and pull away – the first shift leaving. Everything was going as planned. He peered around the rock and saw the new engineer and conductor in the shelter. They spoke intermittently and paid no attention to the train.

"When the locomotive passes our boulder," Becker explained, "I'll run to the back car and jump on. You climb up the small slope to the tracks here. That's where I'll get you."

They had an hour to wait, and they slumped in fatigue. After forty-five minutes, the crew of two emerged from the shelter and began preparing their departure.

Becker knew he and Maria faced a moment of truth. A train engineer perched in the locomotive and looking for footprints would see them. Becker took short, staccato breaths and held each one a long time. Five minutes on, there was no sign of any suspicion. It was now 04:17 by his watch. Less than ten minutes to go.

Finally the slow preparations for departure entered their last steps. The perfunctory whistle heralded the slow acceleration away from Saxony Rural Station No. 2.

Maria and Becker both poised to rise as soon as the locomotive passed. The seconds seemed like hours.

When the locomotive passed them, Becker whispered, "Now!" He scrambled up the incline and bolted to the back of the train, toward the station. He wanted as much space between him and Maria as possible. That would leave him time to prepare to lift Maria.

Before he reached the mail car, Becker turned around and jogged with the train. When the leading end of the mail car reached him, he ran a few steps with it and leapt on. Within two seconds he was stabilized. He stretched out his hands to meet Maria's.

Maria began her run before Becker reached her, just as she should. She kept looking back to gauge the distance. She looked more terrified than he had ever seen a human being. She would give it all up if she didn't make it here. The moment arrived. Becker's stairs reached Maria. She lifted her arms. Before she could jump, Becker pulled her onto the train.

Maria sobbed, safe on the landing. "I made it. I made it. That was going to be the end of me. I made it."

Becker's own eyes welled up in sympathy. They clutched each other in relief and congratulations.

The train accelerated further and the cold wind pushed them to shelter.

They settled into the mail car from Dresden to Leipzig. On this leg of the daily mail run, though, there were no more mail deposits. Becker and Maria sat unmolested in a large mail bin for all three hours.

They arrived in the crowded Leipzig train station at a quarter till eight Tuesday morning. Becker shepherded them safely out the wrong side of the train, onto the next set of tracks, up to the next platform, and into the train station's main hall. They both wore their hats low to hide their faces. They were famished.

Becker and Maria walked to the in-station bistro. The line wasn't long. Becker imagined he could eat every breakfast roll and pastry available.

At their turn, he said to Maria, "You order for yourself, and I'll get enough for everyone else."

Maria took two butter rolls and a coffee. Becker ordered his own coffee, half a dozen butter rolls, half a dozen jelly pastries, and dozen apples.

On the main thoroughfare, Becker checked the departures schedule. The next train to Munich left at eight-thirty. Excellent timing! They'd arrive in Munich at one-thirty, with hours to spare before the night train to Paris.

The Munich train already sat at its platform. No passengers were around Track 4, so Becker led them to the busy Track 3, a regional train that sat next to the Munich train. This was perfect.

Tickets were sold on board the regional train, so they could board with nothing, not even identification. Becker guided them to a passenger car parallel to a storage car on the Munich train.

They climbed the stairs to the regional train. Then they walked across its entryway and descended the stairs on the other side. Just a few feet away, across the ties and ground below them, sat the Munich train.

They quickly boarded the train to Munich and hid from view. Becker began to work at the storage car's lock when he saw it was open. The car was full of skis and sleds. It was packed tight, which meant no one would load or unload it until Munich. It was a great place to hide.

Becker read the tags on one of the sports bags: "Garmisch-Partenkirchen." Some kind of ski club from Leipzig was traveling to the Winter Olympics slopes. That's right, Becker remembered, the Olympics just ended on Sunday.

They hid on the floor in the middle of the car, out of sight of any door. For the first time in thirty-two hours, they ate and ate.

After an uneventful half-hour of waiting, the Munich train began its journey.

Wächter arrived at his office Tuesday morning at his usual six-thirty, well before most others. In mid-February that meant another hour before daybreak.

This morning Wächter's desk was bare. Becker was slipping away from him.

Wächter's temporary command of nationwide Gestapo resources was straining the limits. Border patrols were still on alert for the two fugitives. But Wächter wasn't permitted any more large searches unless new evidence presented itself.

At half past noon, he got a call from the field reports office at Columbia-Haus. A perceptive train engineer noticed footprints outside Saxony Rural Station No. 2. The engineer was sure they hadn't been there on Monday. An area search revealed an abandoned hiding place in the woods nearby.

Wächter wanted to pepper the field reports office with questions, but they were just forwarding information. He hung up and dialed outgoing dispatches. Becker was back within his grasp!

"Dispatches, this is Colonel Wächter. I'm ordering more train searches based in Leipzig and Dresden. Any train that left either station since 06:00 this morning must be thoroughly searched for the fugitives. And I mean thorough. The earliest trains first. . . . By my Reichsbahn schedule here, that makes the Leipzig-Munich train top priority. Remember, we want them alive. Instruct field agents to report their results immediately and directly to Columbia-Haus." Wächter got confirmation of the order and hung up.

Becker and Maria made it to Nuremberg with no surprises. That was the last stop for an hour, until their Munich arrival.

When the train suddenly stopped fifteen minutes out of Nuremberg, Becker was concerned.

"This is an unscheduled stop," he told Maria.

Then he listened. They were only one car away from the passenger cars. Angry young men shouted orders, and German shepherds barked furiously. Protesting passengers gave way to searches.

"Something's wrong," he whispered. "Even crossing the border to Prague, they're never this thorough."

The search lasted three quarters of an hour. Becker could hear teams of Gestapo agents up and down the train. The dogs never stopped barking.

Suddenly right outside their car they heard: "What do you mean, check the storage car?!? This thing hasn't been touched since Leipzig."

Another voice answered, "Precisely the point. Now open it!" A nearby German shepherd started barking ferociously.

Suddenly, the long panel loading door unlocked and rumbled open in its tracks, slamming at the end.

"But the train will be late, sir," protested the first voice.

"Shut up!" answered Rottenführer Gruber. "Look at all these skis! There's hardly room to walk."

Becker had positioned himself and Maria in the middle of the car. That was far from the small doors on either end. But they were right in front of the large side loading door. He looked straight at the Gestapo corporal, afraid to move so much as an eyelid.

Outside the car Becker saw snow-covered hilly farm fields. The noonday sun nearly blinded him. They'd stopped this train in the middle of nowhere.

Becker and Maria were about to be caught. Gestapo agents were teeming around the train. Escape was impossible. At least it would bring quick death. But that would abandon Maria to a painful one.

Rottenführer Gruber advanced into the over-sized luggage car.

"Ahhhh!" He screamed, startled to see Becker squatting right in front of him. He aimed his gun. "It's you! Fugitive Becker! *Hände auf!* Hands up! . . . Sergeant Welter! I can't believe it! We got him! . . . Hands up, Becker! Stand up slowly."

Becker slowly rose, his hands above him. He accidentally knocked over a few skis with his legs. Gruber almost shot him at the surprise.

Sergeant Welter leaped into the railway car. "Corporal Schukl, are you done looking on that other end of the car?"

"Just about, sir," answered Schukl from the far side of all the skis and sleds. "Yes, sir, that's it. Nothing else."

"Good," said Welter. "Come over here and help us."

Welter, too, aimed at Becker and cocked his gun. "I wouldn't want to be you right now. I'd like to shoot you myself, but they won't let me. . . . There are supposed to be two of you. Where is she?" Welter demanded.

Becker stared back mutely from the midst of all the skis.

"All the worse for you that you don't answer," said Welter. "Schukl, search this side."

Schukl moved to a long row of skis leaned against the wall. "Here she is! It's the woman! That's exactly her! Hands up, lady! Now!"

"All right, all right," answered Maria as she emerged with her hands held high. "What's going on?"

"You're asking us?" replied Sergeant Welter. "You're under arrest, Gestapo orders." He looked back and forth between Becker and Maria. "*Ja*, no doubt about it. You're the ones!"

"Damn!" launched Maria. "You've blown the whole thing! Deputy Führer Rudolf Hess will be furious. Do you know what you've done?!? This Englishman was supposed to escape carrying false information to London. He is . . . he *was* worth much more to us alive than dead. Now he's finished. Damn it all to hell! Dammit! Who sent you here? Was it that striver Wächter? Hess warned me the Gestapo might mess this all up."

Becker's jaw dropped in disbelief. Maria was a different woman. She was so convincing, he no longer knew the truth.

"Who are you, woman?" ordered Welter.

"I'm a lot of things," answered Maria. "That needn't concern you. Just call Hess, he'll tell you. Ask him about the 'Holy Mother.' I report directly to him."

"You talk tough, lady," answered Welter. "I don't believe it."

He pointed his gun at Maria while the other two trained on Becker.

"Go ahead," she challenged him. "Arrest me. See what happens."

Welter was stuck in the dilemma she presented. He paused to consider his response.

"All right, lady, prove it," he replied. "You turn your back to our gun barrels and take this gun and shoot him. . . . Don't kill him, mind you. We need him alive. Just shoot him."

"I'll shoot him," she answered. "Gladly! But before I pull my gun on him, you need to disarm him and order him to the back of the car. He's fast and strong. I don't need him coming at me from point-blank range."

"All right, Herr Fugitive," ordered Welter, "get to the back of the car. . . . Move it!"

Becker backed carefully to the wall, his hands held high while his feet maneuvered around the ski equipment. He was trapped.

"Now turn your back to us," Welter ordered Becker. "With your left hand only, and very slowly, pull out your gun and toss it out of reach. Any sudden moves and you're finished."

Becker did as told.

"You have any other weapons on you?" asked Welter.

"A knife," Becker replied.

"That too, then. Left hand."

After Becker's hands were back in the air, Corporal Gruber moved forward to collect the weapons.

"Keep your back toward us, Becker," said Welter. "All right, Fräulein, fire away."

Maria repositioned herself between the Gestapo agents and Becker. She lifted Welter's gun and aimed at Becker's feet.

"Becker," she cackled, "turn your sorry self around and face me. I don't do this to a man's back."

Becker slowly turned, hands still in the air. His brow furrowed as his mind raced to decide which Maria was the real one. His eyes widened when he saw her unlock the safety and then twirl the gun around her finger.

Maria laughed and aimed at Becker. "And you thought you taught me how to hold a gun!" she said to Becker.

"It's my turn to give you a lesson. . . . John Becker, born Johannes, your time is up. You didn't really think you'd escape the country with such an intelligence coup, and bag a new mistress in the process? Did you?"

She scowled at Becker, and he remained silent. "All you could manage to arm us with were those old Bolos. A professional would have secured the new Walther PPK, like these Gestapo guys gave me here." She fired a single shot.

Becker winced as a matter of reflex and then reached down to the wounded left foot. He flexed the foot and realized his smallest toe was grazed and bleeding, but nothing more.

Maria fired a warning shot to the side. "Hands back up, you wretch!"

"You conniving bitch," Becker fumed.

She fired a third time.

"Ahhhh!" Becker bent leftward to shelter his shattered left shoulder.

"Another word and I'll blow out your knees, you womanizing bastard!" shouted Maria. "You'll never see another woman, anyway."

She lowered the gun and turned to Sergeant Welter. "Enough? The jig is up anyway. Two years of work ruined by you guys. We may as well pack it in for Columbia-Haus."

Welter looked nervously at his two corporals. "That's enough, mystery woman. Impressive shooting. The gun, please," he held out his hand. "Thank you. . . . You're coming with us, too, of course. We'll call to confirm your story. Until then, you'll be chained to the prisoner."

They cuffed Maria's right wrist to Becker's left and then helped them both off the train.

Becker was in awful pain. He mostly avoided Maria's glare.

"Your sloppiness got Rupert into this mess, too," she hissed at him. "You killed my brother!" She spat in Becker's face.

Welter started to say something, but thought better of it. "Get in the car. We're headed to the Nuremberg airfield. We'll call Hess's office from there, Fräulein Geberich . . . or whoever you are."

Four of them climbed into the black Mercedes-Benz Pullman-Limousine. Schukl sat at the wheel, and Becker in the middle of the back, with Maria to his left and Gruber to his right. Gruber handcuffed his left wrist to Becker's right one.

After a few minutes Welter returned from consulting with the other agents searching the train. He took his place in the passenger's seat up front.

Maria turned to Becker, who stared straight forward. "You want to know what did you in, you pathetic excuse for a spy? I know both sides. Of many things. That's what did it. Those burns on my neck, they're not from some interrogation. They come from a communist lover I had back in '29. That bastard tied me up one night and abused me in a drunken orgy of perversion. None of his communist friends would help me turn him in. I've hated the lot of them ever since. Good riddance, is what I say to the Führer's purge of them. . . . And now, if there's one thing I can't stand, it's political lovers." She slapped his cheek hard.

"So a week later, I turned him in to the Nazi Brown Shirts. The bad lover was gone like that," she snapped her fingers and grinned. "Eliminated, along with four of his friends."

Becker scanned his memory of every conversation he'd ever had with Maria. Nothing she said now contradicted any of the rest, except for the cigarette burns. That was first lie he'd missed in years, evidently. The opponent sitting next to him was formidable indeed. He turned to look at her.

"Face forward, you scum," she ordered. "And don't make a move. I cannot tell you how steaming mad I am that Wächter's Gestapo men spoiled everything. Now my brother died for nothing. Damn! That wasn't supposed to happen. . . . I warned him to stay out of it. . . . You'll pay for this with your life, Becker, and I'm going to watch you die in misery. If you so much as blink wrong along the way, I'll send them after your mother in England."

Go after his mother? Of all their hideous acts. . . . Becker obeyed in studied silence. He looked straight ahead as the small limousine started toward the airport.

CHAPTER TWENTY-SIX

"If it's not Tweedle Chamberlain and Tweedle Halifax," gibed Churchill.

He'd been lounging and drinking in the House of Commons smoking room for hours. Neville Chamberlain and Edward Halifax had just entered. All the other parliamentarians present paused and watched, even those from the opposing Labour Party.

"Seeking another opportunity to appease the fascists, I presume," continued Churchill.

"You'd have our country at war!" retorted Chamberlain.

"And you'd sooner surrender to Hitler five years from now than raise arms today," countered Churchill.

"Hitler's only trying to defend Germany," insisted Chamberlain.

"Neville, you're a fool!" growled Churchill.

Before Chamberlain could respond, Churchill turned to the powerful onlookers surrounding them. "His Majesty's servants, mark my words! Today, that Nazi dictator is a weak man. A month from now will be a different picture. Hitler has all but announced his plans to remilitarize the Rhineland. We can stop him. We can rid Europe of the Nazis. We'd take some losses, but it would be over quickly. If we fail to act, we allow Hitler to strike when and where he chooses in the future. That insatiable beast will one day hunger for Britain. We must stop him now, gentlemen! The short fight now will prevent an unimaginable catastrophe on the horizon." Churchill pounded his fist on the oak counter. "The peace of Europe lies in our hands!"

Churchill's critics gave up the fight and left.

Becker rode toward the Nuremberg airport with Maria and the three Gestapo agents. His eyes were still adjusting to the early afternoon sun, after hours hiding in the dark train car.

Maria had never made sense to him. Her story always seemed to be missing something. Now he faced this. He wanted to ask her a thousand questions. There was so much he still didn't comprehend.

He wondered how he could have walked into Maria's trap. They'd sought her out, he'd thought, not the other way around. Unless . . . Michael McBride?!? The man who recruited Becker, a German double agent? McBride was a Protestant from Northern Ireland. He was supposed to be unquestionably loyal. Was McBride an Irish nationalist? Becker was dizzy at the prospect. His gunshot left shoulder made it worse.

If Maria was working with Rudolf Hess, then the Hossbach documents were fakes. Hitler wanted Britain to think he was weaker than he was. Why? To lure the British Army into a trap?

Becker wondered about the Churchill assassination. He had that news almost by accident, from another source. At least that must be real. The assassination was only thirty hours away. London still didn't know.

These low-ranking Gestapo agents would get in trouble for not frisking him, Becker thought. Rather, their posthumous reputations would suffer. They presumed he had only one gun, and that Maria knew everything.

But Maria hadn't seen him clip on the second gun back in at Janeck's apartment. Wächter's expanded border surveillance obviously stretched Gestapo resources. These guys were new to this, and it showed.

Becker could kill the three of them in a few seconds. Maria was a problem. He wanted to get more information from her, not kill her. If the Hossbach document was a fake, she might know the real Army numbers and plans.

And he didn't want to kill her. He knew this was a weakness he had, trouble killing the bad gals, too, not just the bad guys.

Becker rode in silence for ten minutes. He had to get far enough from the train, so the Gestapo swarm there wouldn't hear the gunshots. He also needed a straight stretch of road, to help control the car after he shot the driver.

His right hand lay on his leg, handcuffed to Gruber. Becker knew the guard would easily be overcome. He rested his left hand on his other leg, cuffed to Maria's wrist.

Becker chose his moment, and his first two victims barely perceived it. He slammed his handcuff's metal bracelet into the bridge of Gruber's nose. The shattered nose knocked Gruber out. Perhaps it killed him, Becker couldn't tell at first.

In the very same motion, Becker then whipped his right hand into his shirt for the extra Mauser. Just when Sergeant Welter began to turn his head at the sounds of all this, Becker put a bullet through his brain.

Despite the excruciating pain in his left shoulder, Becker moved his handcuffed left hand behind his body. With his legs against the right side of the car, he pushed his back into Maria. This blocked her from interfering with his shooting.

Gruber was still knocked out to his right. Becker glanced at the road and at Corporal Schukl's indecision. The driver couldn't decide whether to drive on or to pull his gun on the captive. Becker didn't wait. He shot Schukl in the back of the neck.

Finally Becker looked at Maria. She seemed surprised but not afraid. He marveled at her steely nerves.

Even if Maria would cooperate with their handcuffs, Becker wouldn't be able to drive the car with Gruber hanging off his right arm.

Suddenly the car hit a bump in the road that sent it swerving off to the snowy field on the right. The limousine descended a short incline and crashed at the bottom.

The car was turned on its right side. Becker lay facedown on Gruber's body, and Maria lay unmoving on his back.

"Maria?" he asked.

No answer. She didn't move. Becker felt a drop land on his neck. It was warm . . . blood, Maria's blood.

Becker's shoulder pain was beyond description. He slowly turned around, out from underneath Maria's limp body. He stood on the down-turned right side of the car. His two handcuffed arms now crossed to the opposite bodies beneath him.

He hunched over Maria. A tiny stream of blood ran from her nose. She was still breathing, though irregularly. It looked like a serious head injury.

"There was once good in her, too," he mumbled in German. He couldn't imagine that one Communist lover's beating had made a Nazi out of her. There had to be more to the story.

The amateurish organization of British intelligence had failed him, almost killed him. Lax screening had allowed McBride, or someone else, to sabotage him. He'd be demanding in return. He'd insist they document her full biography. It wouldn't make any difference to anyone else. But they owed it to him. Even if she died today from her head injury, Becker's curiosity would itch until he solved the mystery of Maria Geberich.

He reached down for the handcuff keys on Gruber's belt and freed both his hands. At last he no longer felt like a contortion artist. He climbed out the left car door towards the blue sky.

Without Maria, Becker had more options. He had an hour at most before the Gestapo figured out he'd escaped.

He was much farther from the Czech border than he'd been in the morning. A stolen car would not likely make it that far. . . . But it should get him to Munich.

He climbed the few feet to road level and stood on the side of the road away from Nuremberg. He wasn't sure where the small road led, except that it passed the isolated place where they'd searched the train. Becker tried to look as unruffled as possible. He walked back toward Nuremberg. He hoped a driver would see him before the Gestapo's car wreck.

The first car didn't approach until fifteen minutes later. Becker saw the figure of one driver with no passengers, and he waved desperately to the car. The green two-seater Opel 4/14 slowed down. Becker's hand rested on the gun in his coat pocket.

The driver rolled down the passenger window. He wore Bavarian farm clothes. His face was round, and he had dark hair and a moustache. "Where you headed?" he asked.

Becker kept his left shoulder out of view, with the bullet hole and traces of blood on his coat. "Anywhere you can take me," he answered. "There's been an accident."

The driver looked but didn't see a car. Becker was at least a half-mile away from it.

"It's up the road," Becker explained.

"Is anyone hurt?" asked the driver.

"Yes," replied Becker. "Bad. We need to get help."

"Climb in," said the driver.

Becker took his seat and feigned a state of shock. The driver was very similar in size, Becker observed.

"Let's head back into town." The driver started to turn around toward Nuremberg.

Becker pulled his Mauser and pointed it at the driver. "Let's not. Get us to the Munich highway." Becker knew he wouldn't use the gun on the innocent driver. But he had to seem like he would.

The driver's jaw quivered. "P-, p-, please don't hurt me! I have kids, a wife, a mother. . . ." His gaze darted back and forth from Becker to the road.

"Watch the road. Just do as I say and you'll sleep safe at home tonight." Becker saw this man wouldn't make any trouble.

"*Ja, ja*, anything you say, sir," said the driver.

They drove past the wrecked Gestapo Mercedes. No one moved inside. Any survivors would freeze to death if they weren't rescued before nightfall.

"The people who drove that Mercedes disobeyed me," threatened Becker. "They're dead now. Get the picture?"

The driver nodded and started crying. Becker felt sorry for him.

"You from Nuremberg?" asked Becker.

"No, I'm a farmer. I was just driving home from the winter market in Nuremberg."

"You know the road to Munich?" asked Becker.

"Certainly. It's just a few miles from here. No problem."

"Good," said Becker. "Drive toward Munich. Don't talk. I'll tell you what to do."

The driver nodded vigorously.

After thirty minutes on the road to Munich, Becker asked the driver, "Do you know this road coming up?"

"No," he replied.

"Turn right," ordered Becker. This was as desolate a stretch of road as he was likely to find.

They drove about five miles on the side road, and Becker ordered the driver to turn left on a country lane that had barely been driven upon since Saturday's snow. After another two miles, he ordered the car to stop.

"This is where you get out," said Becker.

The driver almost leaped out of the car.

"Wait, wait," said Becker.

The driver froze.

"Show me your papers," said Becker.

The driver obeyed.

Becker looked them over. "That'll do, thanks." He put them in his pocket.

"Next, Herr Egger, we're going to change clothes," said Becker.

For a moment, the farmer just stared back blankly. But when Becker got out of the car and started to undress, the farmer followed suit on his side.

Becker now wore the clothes of a Bavarian farmer: work boots, dark brown canvas pants, a yellow flannel shirt, a field green felt coat with silver buttons, and a gray felt alpine hat with four gray cords tied around it in place of a band. He put Egger's papers in the coat pocket. The outfit would work fine in Munich. Paris was a different question.

Becker hadn't worn anything like this since he was a boy in the Black Forest. The styles were somewhat different but similar enough to evoke Becker's memories. The farmer's clothes reminded him of Sunday walks in the country with his father. Even on Reinhold Becker's two short home leaves during the Great War, he had taken young Johannes on long walks almost daily. His father had loved him tenderly.

Reinhold died in the last days of the war only because old aristocratic generals dragged out a lost cause. These were the same generals who later put Hitler in power.

"Get home any way you want, Herr Egger. But don't tell anyone about me. Don't show up at home before eight o'clock this evening. And don't report this car stolen, or the wreck we passed, until tomorrow morning. Then, and only then, go to the police and report both, even tell them about me."

Becker knew the farmer would anyway, so it was better to put a timeline on it. "I better not run into any trouble from you today. If I do, first I'll take care of whoever is onto me, and then I'll come to your house. . . . Have I made myself understood?"

"Yes, sir, *ja ja, ja ja, ja ja* . . . ."

Becker was afraid he'd driven the farmer to a nervous breakdown. Hopefully the man would recover quickly when he realized Becker was out of his life. Becker drove away, abandoning Herr Egger to the sunny white Bavarian countryside. He continued his drive southward.

A half-hour later, Becker was driving in Munich. There was still plenty of time to catch the Paris night train. Becker even had Egger's papers. But they didn't resemble each other much, especially because of Egger's moustache.

It was four o'clock in the afternoon when Becker parked Egger's car in front of an optometrist's shop. This was a few blocks from the Munich train station, where Becker headed first. He identified the next train to Switzerland, departing in twenty minutes, picked out the postal car, and then entered the adjacent train on the parallel tracks. Becker crossed the foyer of one of this train's cars, descended the opposite staircase and then climbed the ladder on the Zurich train's postal car. He had to pick the padlock, and then he quickly slid the door open to let him in and then shut behind him. He waited a few moments for his eyes to adjust to the near total absence of light.

Perfect! The expected international cash transfer safe was in the corner, welded to a steel plate extension of the car's frame. Becker cupped his hand against the safe's door, and listened to the combination lock's tumblers. On the first try, Becker thought he got it, but the lock didn't open. But on the second try he got it. The safe overflowed with cash, but all Becker needed were one stack each in Reichsmarks, Swiss francs, and French francs. Then he closed the safe, left the car, and exited through the parallel train, undetected and ready to spend.

Back at the glasses the shop, Becker found a pair of simple rimless glasses. The lenses were round and the frames silver-colored. This had been the basic style twenty years ago in the rural Black Forest. He hoped it would pass with his new clothes.

He only wanted bifocal lenses, for reading. The rest should just be glass, he explained. Could they fill that order this very afternoon?

No, they couldn't, came the reply.

Would an extra hundred marks speed things up? Becker asked.

Two hundred was the counter-offer. They had just those lenses in stock, with only a little cutting needed to match Becker's frames.

Becker accepted. He worried a little whether the shopkeeper might report the transaction as suspicious. But the optometrist seemed delighted at the deal. He wasn't likely to jeopardize his little afternoon windfall.

While Becker waited for the glasses to be finished, he found a large pub nearby and waited there an hour. Next he purchased a large suitcase. He hesitated whether to buy a change of clothes, something that would look right in Paris. By now, the Gestapo had probably found the wreck and presumed he'd headed for Munich. Becker decided not to visit a clothing store. Instead, he half-filled his suitcase with newspapers, but new ones this time, from an unclaimed bundle sitting at an alley corner.

Just before six o'clock, he claimed his new glasses. They fit perfectly, and the bifocals didn't bother him much, especially by night.

He headed for the train station. Becker knew from the posted schedules in Leipzig that the Munich-Paris line departed daily at 18:35.

The Gestapo would be looking for disguises. Egger's clothes and the new glasses would help. But they wouldn't change his face.

Becker ambled through the station in his farm clothes. He cocked his hat forward over his forehead. The brim was smaller than on his fedora. His face was still very exposed.

Becker was glad to see the train. He strolled down the platform amidst the other passengers. He watched for any inquisitive stares. The conductors must have been warned about him – but not the farm clothes and glasses. No one seemed to notice. He chose a car with no conductor on it and boarded.

The night train from Tuesday to Wednesday would be one of the least crowded of the week. Of the three sleeper cars marked for Paris, one entire car was completely closed to passenger use. It seemed unlikely to open at later stops between Munich and Strasbourg. It was the perfect place for Becker.

When he was sure no one was looking, he entered the closed sleeper car. All the two-person sleeping compartments were unlocked.

He wouldn't be able to lock himself in. Otherwise, the "*Besetzt*" sign would show on the lock's dial, "Occupied."

He picked a compartment toward the middle of the car and slipped inside it. He climbed to the top of two bunks, and lifted his suitcase over the entry, where it couldn't be seen from the hallway.

After spending much of last night awake in the snow by Saxony Rural Station No. 2, Becker remembered how sleepy he was. He checked his gun and ammunition. Before the train even left the station, he allowed himself to fall asleep.

Until the first stop in Augsburg, Becker's sleep was deep and unguarded. He woke up there when it sounded like a conductor got on his car. Becker was scared stiff, but nothing happened.

After that, Becker's sleep was adequate but with open ears. From his bachelor life in noisy London, Becker had learned to sleep with background noise. Like a baby's mother, he'd also trained his sleeping self to recognize which noises were important enough to wake up for. In this state of conscious sleep, Becker rested until they stopped in Stuttgart.

As they neared the Rhine River border, Becker was wide awake. These were his last hours in Germany. The Gestapo had last spotted him on his way to Munich. They'd be checking Munich's international trains very closely at the borders.

He looked at his watch. They were fifteen minutes from the Rhine River border crossing. Becker had been wondering whether to jump off the train, or to try riding it over the border.

Suddenly Becker heard someone running furiously down the corridor, from one end of the sleeper car to the other. Just seconds after the first runner, a second one followed. The feet pounded the floor. These weren't the sounds of Reichsbahn officials rushing to some emergency. They were the sounds of life and death. They set Becker on edge.

His heart was racing. Did he dare open his compartment's door to the corridor for a look? He waited a couple of minutes. In just a few minutes more, the train would start braking for the border check. Becker decided to wait for the train's deceleration.

The first screech of the brakes came at exactly a quarter after midnight. At first, the engineer hit the brakes every fifteen or twenty seconds. But after a couple of minutes, he started to work them more. Becker could feel the train slowing down.

He was still undecided whether to jump off the train or ride it out. He was ready to jump if trouble arose. He decided to risk a look into the corridor.   More than ten minutes had passed since the frantic running past his compartment.

Becker partially opened his door.   Cold air drafted in through the narrow crack.   He could hear that the sliding door would be noisy.   It was better to open it quickly and get it over with.   He yanked the door open and looked right, where the feet had run.

His eyes met the soul-less glare of a huge man in plain clothes.   To Becker, the next minute seemed much longer.   The man's hands rested empty at his sides.   Becker decided not to fire.   But he had to flee. Both men started running at the same moment, Becker down the corridor to his left, and the large man coming after him.

When Becker reached the train car's entryway, he tried to tear open the right-side door.   It was locked.   The man was bearing down on him.

Becker darted to the far side.   This door opened.   The winter wind pushed Becker backwards, and he held the handrail to stay in the doorway.   His pursuer's racing steps were closing in.

The train was still traveling about twenty-five miles per hour.

Becker rushed down the entryway stairs and jumped off the train. He wanted to protect his damaged left shoulder.   Yet if he lost use of his right arm, he would be too lame for much of anything.   So in mid-air, he turned his body and landed on his upper left side.

The pain was awful.   The only way Becker held his silence was by turning his head to the right and biting into the arm of Farmer Egger's coat.   He left his fake glasses on the ground and looked back at the train.

The large man stood leaning off the train's entry stairs.   But he wasn't jumping, at least not yet.   Becker had to move.

He looked at the border stop down the rails, just before the river bridge.   It was about three hundred yards away.   Its lights drowned the stars on the western horizon.

To Becker's right was a small access road and an intersection.   One road followed the tracks.   Another pointed into the snowy fields on the north side, and down the slope toward the river.

Becker thought he saw some handlebars protruding through the snow, and he tried them.   The bicycle's tires were completely flat.   He had no choice.

He carried the bicycle to the road and began peddling, metal rims on packed snow, past the fields, on a slow arc to the river . . . to the boat house.

Sloping gently downhill, Becker coasted to a good clip.   He had only his right arm for steering.   He fell once and got right back on.

Now he could see the boathouse ahead of him, at the bottom of this road. He raced the bicycle to the boathouse door and let it fall into the snow.

Becker slid open the unlocked door. Dozens of boats stared back at him, most of them for four or eight rowers. Finally he found one for two.

There was no question of carrying it. His shoulder wouldn't bear it. He didn't want to slam the thing around and have it spring a leak in the middle of the river. It was all he could do to pull it to the ground with one arm.

With his right arm, he pulled the boat to the shoreline. The river, too, smelled of snow, but also of the earth and rock it sliced through, and of the chemical plants upstream in Switzerland.

He looked half a mile upriver at the railroad bridge over the Rhine, the border between Germany and France. He saw the train locomotive parked at the Kehl border station on the German side.

A spotlight searched the riverbank for him. Then the light hit him! Several seconds later came the sounds of shouting and then a few gunshots.

Becker ran back to the boathouse, got an oar, and slipped the boat into the water. He was many minutes from France, too many. The other side was over two hundred yards away.

The river's mighty current carried him farther downstream from the bridge. He fitted the oar into its rigger. With only one arm rowing, Becker's crossing would be slow. His back faced France, and he watched the German bank slowly recede.

Then he saw car headlights headed down the hill to the boathouse. In only a minute or two, they'd be in the water behind him.

Becker pulled the oar frantically in the dark water. He sucked the humid, cold air for every bit of oxygen he could muster. He watched the black water beside him, not the Gestapo agents at the boathouse. He turned his head around to gauge his progress. He was only a third of the way across, not yet at the unmarked French border midstream.

Then he heard the first gunshot from the shore and his heart skipped a beat. He turned back to the German side. A team of Gestapo agents would easily out-row a one-armed man.

There astern the two pulsing rowers sat Maria, her smoking gun pointed right at him!

CHAPTER TWENTY-SEVEN

Becker rowed furiously under fire. His right arm strained at the water and his left arm hung limp. He needed every second he could get. Rowing backwards, he watched the gun-toting Maria guide her two Gestapo rowers into the water.

He was about thirty yards from the middle of the Rhine River, the French border. The Gestapo boat was on the German shore seventy yards away. Both boats floated downstream with the strong current, even as they made their way across. The Gestapo's four oars against his one – the math worked out against him.

Suddenly he heard a bullet plunge into the river on his right. Maria had him in range.

Becker was surprised to hear a loudspeaker crackle behind his back, across the river: *"Vous vous approchez à la frontière française,"* You are approaching the French border.

"Achtung, Achtung," Attention, continued the loudspeaker, now in Alsatian-accented German. *"Das fliehende Boot erreicht gleich das souveräne Frankreich,"* The fleeing boat is about to enter sovereign France.

Bullets starting tearing into the water on his left side. Becker was ready to stop rowing and return fire. It was his only chance.

The loudspeaker continued, *"Sie haben kein Recht, auf französisches Territorium zu schiessen,"* You have no right to fire onto French territory.

Just when Becker dropped the oar to pull his gun, Maria's firing stopped. Becker still wasn't halfway across. He looked at the Gestapo's boat.

Maria held her smoking gun to her side, pointed into the river. Her boat drifted only thirty yards away, starting to point downstream. The two Gestapo agents slumped dead in their seats, both shot by Maria.

Becker's jaw dropped at the sight. Still uncertain about Maria, he pulled out his gun but held it at his side.

Maria stared at him for several seconds. Then she made a show of putting her gun down. Next she pushed aside one of the bodies and took up two oars to row. Her back now faced Becker.

Becker simply watched, drifting downstream. Maria was rejoining him. If she'd really wanted him captured or killed, she wouldn't have killed the Gestapo rowers.

Maria got close enough that he could hear her strained breathing as she paddled. "I'm still on your side, Johannes," she called over her shoulder. "I always have been."

Maria reached Becker's boat. She rose to step into it and asked, "Would you prefer to take my gun from me?"

She was granting him continued suspicion, he realized. She held Becker's first Mauser.

"That lousy Bolo?" he joked. "Bring it aboard."

He still felt a trace of uncertainty about her. But she could have finished him off if she'd wanted, he kept reassuring himself. The aching shoulder she'd shot at Nuremberg told him to remain wary.

As Maria entered Becker's boat, she commented on his rustic attire. "Nice clothes."

"Thanks," Becker replied. "How on earth did you make it from Nuremberg to here?" Becker wanted to know.

"I was on the same train as you," she said. "I'll explain more after we get to the other side. Back on the German side, they'll figure out very soon what I did. We should expect they'll try to follow us into France."

Becker nodded. He watched her move to the seat behind him. She took up a pair of oars and started rowing to the French bank. They had a lot to talk about.

While Maria rowed, Becker nursed his shoulder. He turned to face her and the French shore behind her. He made out three French border guards. They could provide safety from any Gestapo agents who tried to follow.

Their boat still had over a hundred yards to go. The Rhine pulled them farther downstream with each stroke. Becker shifted his gaze from the French guards to the shoreline downriver.

The French guards stood at the end of a wharf peninsula. Becker's boat would miss it by far, landing at least a half-mile away. He looked back to the German side for a second wave of pursuers. There were none so far.

It wasn't so bad to miss the French guards, Becker knew. It was after midnight, early Wednesday morning. The Churchill assassination was at the end of the same day. If Becker got caught up in some French borderland bureaucracy, he would struggle to get the news to London. No, it was better to bypass the guards. Becker would take the message to Paris in person. Or to London, if he had time.

Becker and Maria were being watched at a distance by the French guards across a wide canal that separated them. Their boat landed next to several moored houseboats.

As they pulled themselves ashore, Becker explained his situation to Maria.

"Those gendarmes will slow me down," he said. "My news from Berlin must reach London immediately. I must try to re-board the Paris train before it leaves Strasbourg. I'll resettle in the empty sleeper car. If you'd prefer to go with the French gendarmes, I'll certainly understand. It would be safer and calmer. And I could return for you in a couple of– "

"I'm coming with you," she interrupted. "You're close to useless on your own, with that shoulder. But how will we catch that train?"

"We borrow a car to the Strasbourg station." He nodded toward a parking area in front of them.

Of the three closest automobiles, Becker first tried the middle one. The key was actually in the ignition.

Becker revved the engine and Maria got in. While they drove away, Becker would see the French guards across the canal, jumping up and down in outrage.

Right behind Becker, in his mirror, he noticed a sleepy man stumble out of one of the houseboats. The man started running after their car and shouting. Becker sped away. He and Maria were fugitives again, this time in France.

He drove into Strasbourg and followed the main roads and signs to the railroad station. It sat on the far side of town.

The train was still there! From a distance, Becker and Maria both recognized the train from Munich. It was the only long train full of Reichsbahn markings. The other trains were short and French.

"We can make it!" Becker exclaimed.

He raced the car to the station. On the empty side of the train, Becker pulled to a quiet stop. The French rail and border officials stood on the platform, on the opposite side of the train. Becker had no idea how soon it might depart.

He and Maria got out of the car. They closed its doors softly and incompletely behind them. Next they jogged towards the tracks. When they reached the noisy rail yard gravel, they slowed to a walk.

Becker led Maria to the empty sleeper car. They approached the stairs to climb aboard.

Suddenly they heard voices in the very same car!

"You have no right to take us out of the train!" A German man spoke in heavily accented French.

"By international contract," answered a French guard, "this train is under French authority the moment it crosses the border."

"That we're German is no reason– "

"Get off now or I'll shoot the gun you feel in your back!" shouted the guard.

Becker peered around the train wheels and under the train car, to the platform on the opposite side. The protesting Germans and two French guards stumbled out. Becker recognized the man who'd chased him off the train! This was doubtless some Gestapo tandem. Now the train was clear of them.

"The inspection's finally done," the guards said to the conductor on the platform.

The French conductor instantly called aloud, "All aboard!" The whistle blew, doors slammed shut, the engine cranked up, and the train began to move.

"Now!" mouthed Becker to Maria in the train's shadows. With his right arm, he lifted her up the staircase and pulled himself aboard. They quickly found their way to a sleeper compartment for two.

Becker peeked through the off-white curtains to the platform outside. Except the arrest of the Germans, all was normal. He and Maria could rest easy for awhile. French authorities would find and link the stolen car to this train, but perhaps not until morning.

He leaned against the black wall of the unlit sleeper compartment. Only the slightest light entered through the corridor curtain. The train swayed gently as it accelerated out of Strasbourg.

Maria still stood at the compartment entrance, with the door shut behind her. Then she rushed at Becker.

"Thank you, Johannes!" She hugged him tight and pulled his head down to kiss both cheeks. "I'm free! Thank you!" She hugged him again. Then she let go and clutched her hands together in silent exhilaration.

Becker watched her and clutched the shoulder she'd shot twelve hours ago and squeezed tight just now.

Maria soon calmed down. She sat on the deep burgundy covers at the foot of the lower bunk.

She lifted her dark eyes to Becker's soft blue ones. Her disheveled brown hair covered some of her face. Even in the dark, her eyes and mouth still sparkled from excitement.

Perhaps she'd saved them by shooting Becker back at Nuremberg, he thought. Maybe she distracted the Gestapo from frisking him for his second gun. She hadn't known about the second gun, though. Perhaps she and Becker could have made it without her shooting Becker twice. They'd never know, he acknowledged to himself.

At the very least, she'd deceived him by omission.

"Where did you learn to shoot?" he asked calmly.

Maria pursed her lips regretfully. "I'm so sorry. . . . I can't tell you how sorry I am about that." She looked at his shoulder. "It's a long story."

Patrick O'Hagan sat in the basement of Queen's Hall. His only light came from a streetlight through the clouded window glass.

When he heard the supervisor locking the doors from outside, he knew he was alone. It was the middle of the night. Tuesday's night's concert was finally all cleaned up.

The IRA's London hit man moved into action. O'Hagan uncovered the bomb he'd smuggled in earlier that week. He set the twenty-four-hour timer for 19:30 Wednesday, half an hour into the concert. Without setting up the fuses, he carefully carried the bomb upstairs.

Many of the passageways were pitch black. O'Hagan walked slowly, quietly, deliberately. After years working here, he knew every step by heart. He didn't need his flashlight.

He reached Churchill's box seats in the dark concert hall. Everyone at Queen's Hall knew where Churchill would sit, joined by his wife and a few other politicians and their wives.

O'Hagan stepped down to the front row of Churchill's box. His hands counted seats in the dark until he reached Churchill's.

He unscrewed the seat bottom and removed the seat's padding. Next he turned on his flashlight and set up the fuses. The bomb was activated. He turned off the flashlight.

O'Hagan carefully placed the bomb's hard case into the seat. Then he replaced some of the padding over it and screwed the seat bottom on.

He had to test the seat. There was no way around it. His forehead beaded with sweat. He sat down forcefully. He barely felt the bomb case, even knowing it was there. That was as good as it could get.

Inside the seat, the clock ticked the hours to Churchill's assassination.

For once, Colonel Wächter was silent in his fury. His rage had driven him to smash his desk lamp against his office wall in Gestapo headquarters. The latest news still boiled up inside him. He had to contain it and function for now.

Just half an hour ago, Becker had literally been within the Gestapo's grasp. Wächter's men were about to grab Becker on the train at the Kehl-Strasbourg border. Becker escaped with a lucky jump – no injuries, and a bicycle right there.

Then the treachery of Maria Geberich fooled his men for the second time. Hadn't the Kehl guards gotten the warning about her? Evidently not. What idiots Wächter had working the case. Dead idiots – one car full, one boat full. They were smart enough to find a suspect, but too incompetent to keep hold.

Wächter picked up the phone. "Get me Tempelhof Airport. . . . Colonel Kurt Wächter here, Gestapo. Have a plane ready for me in fifteen minutes. It must be civilian, preferably diplomatic. Paris-bound." He hung up the phone before any objections could be raised to his improbable demand.

He placed the next call. "Gestapo Intelligence. . . . Colonel Wächter here. I have a message for the Paris station chief. Remind them about the two fugitives' photos I sent on Monday. I want every single Paris agent at our meeting point outside the train station, Gare de l'Est, in two hours. We'll intercept the Munich train. I'm headed to Orly airfield right now. . . . I don't give a damn how that will look! We have these people so we can use them. Just do it!" He slammed down the phone.

"If it's a long story, it can wait," Becker told Maria. "You should get some sleep." He'd slept on this train from Munich to Stuttgart. He didn't know about her.

"No, thanks," she replied. "I'll sleep later. I owe you an explanation for your shoulder . . . for everything."

"As much as you can talk, I can listen," he replied. Becker sat down at the head of the bottom bunk in the dark compartment. His eyes had adjusted to the minimal light from the sleeper car's corridor.

By the faint light from the hallway, Becker could just make out Maria's facial features. He'd always found her attractive. He'd never seen her so athletic-looking and so electrified as now. She was gorgeous. She'd shot his shoulder to pieces that afternoon. Now he wanted to share her bed.

"My story is long," started Maria. "But the main explanation is simple. . . . I am an actress by profession. In the countryside near the Babelsberg studios, we dabbled in all sorts of things. That's where I learned shooting. I can also play cards, ride a charging horse, and blow rings of smoke." She made an "O" with her mouth and smiled.

Becker nodded slightly. If Maria was an actress, things might make sense. He should have guessed such a possibility when Maria shot the Gestapo oarsmen, if not sooner.

"I first tried film. This was before the talkies. The directors always said I was too short and dark. So I became a personal assistant to the stars. I even helped Marlene Dietrich in a few films. Gradually, I took on stage roles in the Berlin cabaret scene. I can't tell you how much I miss the singing and dancing. The stuff we did, the Nazis shut down right away. Or at least they shut it officially. They still wanted their private showings. I quit the business immediately. When I refused the private shows, some SS officer got mad and dragged me in. That's when I got the neck burns, by the way. The rest about my brother Max is true, though."

Becker listened with fascination.

"Anyway, I developed quite a name for myself. I wasn't Maria, of course. I was billed as Lola Montez."

Becker was stunned. Lola Montez! They still talked about her in Berlin and even London.

"You've heard the name?" she grinned. "To my knowledge, no one at Kristner Engineering knew who I was. I buried that life. I had offers to move to an Austrian cabaret company. But I didn't want to leave Rupert. He needed me, as insecure as he was. I felt like I was the only thing resembling a moral anchor that he had. I thought things in Germany couldn't get any worse." She paused and sighed.

"So there's your explanation. I won't blame you if you can't believe me. Ask me anything you want. . . . I learned to shoot at the film studios. I learned to improvise on the stage. . . . And from you, Johannes, I learned to hope again." Maria's eyes welled up with tears. "Thank you." She reached out tentatively and held his knee. "Thank you." She wiped the tears from her eyes and smiled.

Becker held out his right hand and pulled her to his gentle embrace. He kept patting and rubbing Maria's back, not just to comfort her, but also to give him time to think. Part of him believed her wholly. Part of him was naturally suspicious of anyone who could have shot him only twelve hours earlier. Part of him loved Maria. Part of him wanted to sleep with her. He told himself to ignore this last impulse while he thought about the others.

His whole life, Becker had relied on his uncanny ability to distinguish lie from half-truth from truth. Even with Maria he'd always been right. Or almost. He'd always sensed he was missing part of her story. He'd just failed to imagine what it really was. In the minutes after she'd shot him, though, she'd concocted the story about Nazis rescuing her from an abusive communist lover. When she'd said that, he couldn't decide what to believe. She'd just turned on him and shot him badly.

His old instincts told him she was telling the truth now. This is where he had to suppress his baser desires. He wanted to believe Maria, for the pleasure of her company tonight and beyond. Even when he acknowledged that, though, he found her believable. Every piece of the story fit what he knew of her biography. Every nuance of her voice conveyed sincerity.

"Let's—" started Maria.

"Just a moment," he said. He wanted a few more seconds to assure himself of his conclusion. Yes, he was convinced, he finally had the whole story of Maria Geberich.

Maria had never known such generosity of spirit before. She loved him the more for it. She couldn't entirely believe Becker when he decided to trust her. In his place, she didn't think she could be so trusting so quickly.

Maria had been in the acting business so long, she sometimes hadn't known anymore herself what her real personality was. She knew what she stood for in life – kindness and fun. But as an actress, she'd mastered so many different ways to live by her principles.

Once the Nazis closed the public cabarets, Maria decided to reinvent herself. She wanted to recultivate her own personality. She wanted people to know her only as Maria, not as a woman of the stage. And after years of carousing, she deliberately chose her chaste independence.

For two years under the Nazis, Maria's resolve of chastity went untested. But from the moment Becker arrived at Kristner, she'd felt drawn to him. In public, she allowed herself to be friendly with him. Whenever Becker approached her alone, she intentionally froze up and froze him out. She wasn't ready to lose her independence then, and she wasn't sure she ever would be.

In retrospect, she decided she'd withheld her past too long from Becker. After three years of this, change wasn't easy. But their adventures of the past week were so extraordinary. She'd instinctively responded to their real-life dramas with dramatic improvisations to match.

After the forest shoot-out, Becker had even vaguely confided his purpose to her. Still, it hadn't seemed crucial to share her own past with him . . . until Nuremberg. She improvised her way out of that tight spot. It worked, but only because Becker had an extra gun.

If only she'd told him about the acting before Nuremberg, he might not harbor lingering suspicions. She certainly didn't blame him now if he did. She was eternally grateful for his protection after the Hossbach break-in, when she was of no further use to him. The past days brought her more deeply in love than she had ever been.

"Let's have a look at your shoulder," she said. She slid off the bed to her knees beside him. Then she began to unbutton his farmer's coat. "How bad is it?"

"Frankly, it's awful," he answered. "I don't know if it will ever heal right. We'll have to hear from the doctors about that. For now, the whole left arm is completely useless."

Maria sighed. "At least I can bandage it up for you, give it more support." She looked around, stood up, and took a sheet down from the top bunk. She began ripping it into strips.

Then she kneeled down again and finished removing Becker's shirt. "Could you lean forward so I can get this around your back? . . . Good."

"How did you get from Nuremberg to the border?" he asked.

"I followed the path you said you'd take," she replied. "When I woke up in the Gestapo's car crash outside Nuremberg, you were gone. The three agents there were all dead. I cleaned my bloody nose and took back your Mauser Bolo, since you've got ammunition for it. . . . Up on the road, I got the first driver to stop. With the gun, I made him drive me to Munich and give me the car. As soon as he was out of the car, I left Munich to cover my trail. I drove to the next stop for the Paris train. That was Augsburg."

"That was you I heard get on my sleeper car? . . . this sleeper car?" he asked.

"I suppose so," she said. "I got in the second berth at the forward end."

"We rode together for hours. . . . Did you have anything to do with those two agents racing down the corridor over by Kehl?"

"I don't know. They caught me in the corridor after the train stopped at Kehl on the Rhine. I used exactly the same story as near Nuremberg. I said you were my agent, and they had to help me unless they wanted to get in trouble. It helped that we knew Wächter's name from the shootout in the Grunewald Forest. It also helped that I knew to look for you by the boathouse. When we saw you down there, they believed me. . . . The rest, you saw."

"So here we are, on the run together again!" he quipped.

"Mm-hmm," she smiled.

Maria wrapped an entire sheet's worth of bandages around Becker's shoulder and upper body, tucking and tying the strands together.

"Did you learn that at the studios, too?" he asked.

"As a matter of fact, yes," she answered. "The actors' assistants learned everything." She made the final adjustments to his bandages.

Maria slowly leaned over Becker's chest. Just short of his mouth, she pulled up slightly to look into his eyes through her dark dangling hair. She pulled all her hair back and tied it in a loose bun. Then she closed her eyes and rested her lips on his. She pulled her head up again to look at him.

"Do you believe me?" she asked.

Becker nodded slightly, with a slow blinking of his eyes.

Maria smiled and whispered, "Thank you." She kissed him again, slowly stroking his body with the fingernails of her left hand. Becker lifted his legs to the length of the bed. He placed his right hand on the side of her back. Maria finished tying up his shoulder bandage.

Then she climbed to his right side. She propped herself on her elbow and pulled the sheet and covers over them both. She undressed first herself and then Becker. Attentive to his shoulder, she pressed her firm flesh on top of his.

Their lovemaking was gentle at first, passionate at the end. Maria rested on Becker's body. He cradled her head with his right arm. Soon she fell asleep. He listened as her slow breathing found its rhythm with the train's rattling wheels.

CHAPTER TWENTY-EIGHT

Maria still slept on Becker's chest when he woke up. He didn't think he'd slept for long. But it was too dark in the sleeper compartment to read his watch.

He thought about Wächter's Gestapo network. They'd already followed him to two different borders. They wouldn't give up now. He knew they'd be waiting for this train's arrival in Paris.

Becker hesitated to wake up Maria. But he had to move to read his watch. He waited a few minutes. Then he shifted Maria's body onto the bunk.

"Mmmm," she groaned cheerfully. Her fingertips brushed his body as he pulled himself from the bed.

Becker pulled back the corridor curtain just a fraction. His watch read 01:53.

"It's almost two o'clock." Becker spoke softly. "The train was scheduled to arrive in Paris at 07:10. The border delays will put us in later, probably around eight o'clock."

Maria propped herself on her elbows and let the sheet fall from her chest. "Come back to bed." As Becker moved towards her, she lay on her back and opened her arms to him.

Becker carefully lowered himself, protecting his left shoulder.

"Don't worry," she said. "You can put your weight on me."

Becker rested his body on Maria's. He curled his right arm under her left one. He felt her breasts underneath him. They made love again.

This time they lay awake next to each other.

"What moves you, Johannes?" asked Maria. "I mean, you're an English spy, but you speak German like a native. You risk your life for this business. Why?"

"Many reasons," he replied. "I love England. It's been my home since I was a schoolboy. Some things about Germany I love, too. Others I abhor. The Nazi regime is an abomination. Hitler's treatment of the Jews is despicable. My childhood nanny, Esther, suffers more every month. I'd do almost anything to hurt the Nazis. . . . There's something else, too."

Maria listened closely, interested in every detail about the man she loved.

"My father died back in 1918, in the last days of the World War," he continued. "He thought Germany was guilty of starting the war. But he had to fight for four years. Four years shooting at Englishmen, whom he admired so much. As a twelve-year-old, I hated the German generals for marching my father to his death. I still hate them, even though that generation is dead. I can never take revenge on them. So I aim at the Third Reich. Hitler wants the same thing, you know. Another massive war, millions more killed. I'll never get my father back. But I can fight the warmongers in Berlin. I'll pour my life's blood into it, if that's what it takes!"

Maria embraced Becker and put her head back on his good shoulder. "You poor thing. I lost my parents to accidents. That was tragic, but no one's fault. My brother Max . . . ," her voice broke and she paused. "My brother Max . . . was lost to the demons you're fighting. I hope with all my soul your mission does some good."

"We're just hours from pulling it off!" Becker's voice anticipated a great victory over Nazism.

"I hope so. . . ." Maria's voice trailed off.

They held each other awhile in silence.

"Are you going to arrive in Paris wearing Bavarian farm clothes?" asked Maria.

Becker laughed. "That's a problem, isn't it? No. I'll have to find some gentleman on board with clothes to spare."

"In the middle of the night?" she asked.

"There's a large clothes closet in every sleeper car. I'll just look until I find something my size. . . . I need to start that shortly. I might have to keep watch awhile to avoid the conductors."

Becker kissed Maria's forehead and then stood up to get dressed.

"I'm afraid I can't dress myself alone, with my shoulder," said Becker.

"Of course, sorry!" Maria laughed as she rose naked from the bed to help.

Back in his farmer's garb, he was ready to hunt for more cosmopolitan clothes.

"This shouldn't be difficult. If for some reason I don't come back, just get off in Paris three minutes after the train stops. Then go straight to the British Embassy and explain everything . . . including that Churchill is scheduled to be assassinated at his concert tonight."

"What?!?" she exclaimed.

"That's right," he replied.

"How do you know?" she asked.

"I know," he said. "I'll be back soon. Don't worry." Becker opened the compartment door and shut it quickly behind him.

The search for the clothes went smoothly. He walked through the adjacent sleeper car to the one after that. On the near end he found the clothes closet and opened it. Inside he found a dark gray, three-piece suit, his height, for a somewhat heavier man. He pulled it off the rack and replaced the garment bag. The bag had two other suits in it. They were matched with two pairs of shoes, and Becker took one of them.

He hoped his new outfit wouldn't be missed before the train's arrival in Paris. He returned to the closed sleeper car where Maria was.

"That was easy," he told her when he reentered their compartment. Only fifteen minutes had passed since he'd left. "I've got a nice gray suit, and a gray fedora to match. The shoes are one size too big, but I can manage that."

"Let's see!" Maria urged him. She sat up in the bottom bunk, pulling the sheet to her body.

Becker removed the farm clothes and put on the suit.

"It looks marvelous in the shadows!" she said.

"It's too big in the waist and chest. But not enough to get me a second look most places. It'll do." Becker hid his farm clothes in the luggage space above their compartment's doorway.

"I regret to deliver some bad news," he said.

Maria inhaled a short gasp.

"I'm afraid you should get dressed now," he continued.

Maria got off the bunk and took a playful swipe at him. "You! You scared me stiff."

Becker laughed and kissed Maria. She grinned through the kiss and laughed with him while she dressed.

"Hopefully we can get a little sleep," said Becker. "I'm sorry to ask you to sleep in your clothes. But we should be ready for any unscheduled stops."

Maria nodded. "I'll take the top bunk." She climbed up. "I'm not injured. And you're better prepared to deal with any intrusion."

"Thanks," Becker replied.

"Will we wake up in time for a smooth exit?" she asked.

"I'll only be half-asleep," he answered. "You can sleep soundly. I'll wake you up."

"Sleep should be easy," she said. "I'm exhausted from two nights away from any bed. I know you must be, too." She leaned out to kiss him. "Sweet dreams, Johannes."

"Sweet dreams, darling." Becker lay down into his bunk.

Becker re-entered his state of semi-consciousness. It was almost three o'clock in the morning. They could rest for four hours.

In his half-sleep Becker dreamed incessantly. It was always the Gestapo firing at him. He dreamed the Gestapo found them on the train and unleashed a hail of bullets into their sleeping bodies. He dreamed they shot at him in the Gare de l'Est train station in Paris, killing dozens of innocents before mowing down him and Maria. He dreamed the Gestapo stopped the Paris Metro and executed him and Maria in front of the other underground riders. He dreamed the Gestapo chased them up and down the train to London, finally catching them on the ferry ride over the Channel. In that dream, he had to watch Maria fall dead overboard before they got him. He dreamed they were shot down at Waterloo Train Station in London, and finally again at the entrance of Queen's Hall. In his dreams, he never got the news to Churchill.

Through all of this, half of Becker's mind knew he was still in the sleeper car. He listened to a thousand refrains of the wheels' double-click on the tracks. Sometimes those clicks were the gunshots in his dreams.

Every few minutes he woke up, his heart racing, his body cold, his mind uncertain of the time.

After three hours, Becker pulled the curtain enough to check the sky. It was still dark. He checked again every twenty minutes. The third time he saw a tinge of gray. He got out of bed to check his watch by the hallway light.

"What time is it?" Maria asked from the top bunk.

"Seven o'clock," he answered. "Have you been awake long?"

"No," she replied. "Just now."

"Sorry for waking you."

"No worries," she assured him.

Becker gave her a quick kiss.

"I can't wait for this nightmare to be over, Johannes."

"We're just hours from London," he replied.

"How do we get there?"

"We'll try to catch the 08:20 train to Calais. We'll have to run to the Metro underground to make it."

"If we don't?" she asked.

"Then I decide who in Paris is most trustworthy. I don't personally know any of the Embassy staff or even the intelligence people. I know where to find them, though.   I can forward the news about the assassination. But some of those British intelligence blokes are too keen on Hitler. They might not be kind to us. Or more to the point, to you. I'd rather get us to London."

Becker watched through a crack in the window curtains for the first sign of suburban Paris. It finally came at twenty minutes till eight. The train began a long, slow deceleration into the French capital.   A regional train approached Paris on parallel tracks. It was just a hint slower than their train from Munich. Becker knew that any attentive passenger on the parallel train might notice the slightest movement of his window curtain. He gave up his vigil at the window.

"We'll try to disembark in Paris with the other passengers," he told Maria. "That means getting out of this closed sleeper car into the next one. Let's go."

Maria climbed down from her bunk. She tried to straighten her clothes and hair.

Becker picked up the suitcase and led the way down the corridor.

They paused on the landing between the two sleeper cars. It was loud, cold, and drafty. Becker peered in the window to the foyer of the next car. He could see only one old woman standing impatiently with her luggage. He motioned to Maria and they entered the foyer.

The old woman barely gave them a second glance. She seemed oblivious to the fact they'd come from a closed section of the train.

Becker was more concerned about the conductor. If the conductor noticed unfamiliar passengers, there could be trouble.

The old woman was positioned to get off the train as soon as she could. She looked like she must know which side of the train would open to a platform exit. Becker positioned himself across the foyer, by the exit door they wouldn't use. He kept watch out the windows above the old woman's head.

At 07:52, the train braked for its final approach into the Gare de l'Est. Other passengers filled the foyer. By now they were crowded enough that a passing conductor was unlikely to notice two new faces.

Then Becker saw the neighboring tracks fork out. They were seconds from the station. Their car was near the front of the train, so they'd travel over a hundred yards down the platform before the train stopped.

Their track took the right fork at the first wedge of the long platform. All the way out here stood a lone man watching the train above the edge of his newspaper!

The Gestapo! They're waiting for us! Dammit!

Thirty yards farther down stood another idle man, this one pacing casually.

Becker gave Maria a nervous glance. She was clearly aware something was wrong. They had to melt into the crowd. He pulled his fedora's brim even lower.

He looked at his watch. "We'll have to take a cab." He tried to speak casually. He could hear the shaking of his own voice. Could others?

They passed at least two more plainclothes agents on the platform. Pacing around these were two uniformed gendarmes. Not the regular Parisian police – these were members of the French national police force. French authorities were obviously tracking their train. The policemen clutched their gun handles. They looked ready for another war.

All because of Becker. He didn't have a spare moment. He had to escape both sides.

The train wheels screeched to their final stop. The doors opened to the press of exiting passengers. Becker and Maria hung back for a minute.

Soon Becker saw passengers walking past from exits farther back in the train. This lead car would be empty in a couple of minutes. It was time to get off and blend in.

Becker lifted the suitcase and stepped forward. Maria followed him. Neither one could dare look for Gestapo observers. They kept their heads as low as possible.

Becker moved rightward with the crowd, towards the station hall. Maria simply followed him. He tried to look like a native familiar with the station. He did know it well. Becker allowed his peripheral vision to seek any gendarmes could he identify.

For a moment he locked his eyes on a policeman in front of him. The policeman was clearly watching one of the Gestapo agents behind Becker. The gendarme furrowed his brow at something strange.

Suddenly the policeman spun toward Becker, and then looked back again at the agent behind him and Maria. The Gestapo agent must be watching Becker!

Just in time, Becker looked away from the policeman. He feigned dropping something to the ground. This allowed him a quick rearward glance.

Unmistakably, the German agent had identified Becker. The agent was moving in. He silently motioned to his colleagues down the platform, their object was here.

At the same instant, Becker's left ear was seized with pain. It was the loud whistle of the French policeman near him.

"*Arrêtez!*" Stop! The gendarme lunged at the Gestapo agent behind Becker.

A dozen more whistles sounded across the station hall. Gendarmes came running to the Munich train platform.

Becker understood the gendarmes had been watching the Gestapo agents all along. When the Gestapo started to move, the gendarmes stopped them. They might round up all the Gestapo men in the station, if Becker was lucky. Chances were, though, at least one or two would escape.

The first French gendarme caught the agent behind Becker. The others started to block off all the passengers from exiting the platform. At the same time, they scanned the crowd for the agents who'd lingered before the train's arrival.

Becker and Maria were the last ones to escape the platform before the gendarmes closed it off completely. A number of other passengers pushed unsuccessfully to follow. The first gendarme was too busy with his prey to point out Becker to his colleagues. Becker and Maria escaped at a quick clip across the station floor.

The sights and sounds of morning rush hour greeted them as they exited the station. The cab area sat empty before them. White clouds dotted the blue sky. The air smelled of burning coal and car exhaust. By the time they reached the curb, a cab pulled up for them.

Becker and Maria nearly dove into back seat, pulling the door shut behind them.

"Gare Saint-Lazare," said Becker. He put on his best English-accented French. "We have a very tight train connection."

"The London train?" asked the cabbie.

"Yes." Becker pulled out some Swiss francs from his pocket. He dropped a 100-franc note onto the front seat. "Will you take Swiss francs?"

The driver glanced briefly at the large sum. "Certainly."

"There's another hundred if we make it by 08:18." They all three looked at the Gare de l'Est station clock. It read 08:05.

"It's not likely in this traffic," replied the driver. "But I'll try my best, sir." He was already lurching through fits and starts of the morning rush hour.

Thirty seconds later the driver frowned into his rearview mirror. "I believe two men are following us in another cab, sir."

Becker resisted the urge to turn his face toward the back window. "Don't let them catch us!" He threw another hundred francs into the front seat.

"Yes, sir! Don't you worry. I know that driver. He'll be easy to beat."

Their cab careened westward through heavy traffic. The driver swore up and down in his guttural Montmartre accent. He took a side street to a parallel avenue that was less congested.

"I think we've lost them, sir."

"Bravo!" replied Becker.

Three minutes later, the cab driver took another side street. They came out onto Boulevard Haussmann. Not thirty seconds after that, they watched the cars in front of them pile up in a sequence of three crashes.

The driver slammed his brakes. "*Merde!*" He looked frantically for a way out. The lane to their right was also stopped. The one on their left flowed steady with oncoming traffic. The driver's string of French curses seemed endless.

Becker realized they weren't going to make the Calais-London train. He'd have to risk some other communication with London. Then he could find safe shelter for himself and especially Maria.

"Listen, cabbie," he started. "We're not going to make the train. Here's Plan B. You think you can turn around in this traffic?"

"I'll find a way, sir."

"Good," said Becker. "Take us out to Orly airfield."

Becker watched Maria raise her eyebrows in surprise. He smiled mischievously at her.

"Yes, sir," answered the driver. He waited nearly a minute before finding a gap in the oncoming traffic. Then he jerked the cab into a u-turn, away from the pileup.

The taxi crossed Paris southward. They drove over the Seine, through the Latin Quarter, around the Place d'Italie, and onto the Avenue de Choisy. The traffic was much lighter now, headed out of town.

At that moment they heard a crash about thirty yards behind them. The driver looked in his mirrors.

"Sorry, sir. I think we've been followed for quite awhile without me noticing. I see the same two men getting out of the cab that just crashed. Their driver was shifting lanes to stay behind another car, and he hit someone else beside him."

"What!" Becker and Maria both looked out the back window.

"Not to worry, sir. They just crashed, without a replacement cab in sight." He sped on toward the airport.

Kurt Wächter's plane taxied in at Orly airfield. He'd been delayed for hours because of fog in Paris. Finally he'd been able to leave Berlin. But he missed the Munich train's arrival across town. He was eager for news.

Before the propeller even stopped, Wächter was climbing out of the plane. Hauptsturmführer Blei was there to meet him.

"I've been here the whole time," reported Blei. "I've just had a phone call from one of my men."

Wächter sensed disappointing news. He glared at Blei until the captain lowered his gaze.

"We, uh, . . . ," stammered Blei. "We identified the suspects disembarking from–"

"You didn't take them on the spot?!?"

"We were ambushed. The French gendarmes were waiting for us. It was a disaster. They arrested all but two of my men. Our Paris operations are devastated."

"What?!?" bellowed Wächter.

"There is some good news," added Blei.

"Out with it!"

"My men followed Becker across town until their cab crashed. It was quite clear they were headed this way. Our men just called. Becker will be here any minute."

CHAPTER TWENTY-NINE

"Have you place in your garage?" Wächter asked in broken French. He didn't know the word for hangar. He was sleep-deprived and angry. He didn't care if he sounded rude.

Just inside the hangar, a man cleaned a private white airplane. Its name was painted in royal blue, "*Pinceau des Cieux*," Paintbrush of the Heavens. The Couzinet 70 was the most popular trimotor passenger plane in France.

What a pathetic name for an airplane, thought Wächter.

The man ignored Wächter. Or he hadn't realized Wächter was addressing him.

"Have you place in your garage?" Wächter repeated. His tone was even harsher the second time.

"Who are you?" answered the man.

"German diplomacy. You are Monsieur . . . ?"

"Pierre. . . . And your answer is, Hell no, Kraut. Not without a reservation. Get lost."

Wächter was furious. He stomped back to his plane. He instructed his pilot to park the German plane next to the airstrip.

After the train station incident, Wächter knew French authorities would be on full alert. With most of the Paris Gestapo cell arrested, he had little support. He had to be careful.

"How well do you know the airfield, cabbie?" asked Becker as they approached Orly. "What a lovely morning for flying," he said in English to Maria.

"It's not a very big place," answered the driver. "There's usually a few folks at this time of day. It's quite a club of dandies out there. They blow family money on flying lessons and the latest planes."

Maria couldn't understand the French conversation. She knew to keep her German mouth closed. Becker was acting English.

She thought she understood "flying." It was one adventure after another with Becker, she smiled inwardly. A long time ago, a film producer had taken her up in a biplane outside Berlin. She would love to fly again!

The taxi raced toward the small cluster of buildings by the airstrip.

"Can you drive us over to the hangar?" Becker asked.

"No problem."

"Good. . . . How about that guy over there? You think he's a pilot?"

"Yeah," the driver replied. "He's always out here. He's one of the instructors. He doesn't have his own plane, but he tends to several of them. He pilots that small passenger plane he's cleaning, the *Pinceau des Cieux*."

"Perfect. Pull up to him," Becker instructed.

Wächter stood by his German plane and watched Becker's taxi approach the hangar. He was glad his plane was parked pointing toward Becker. The German markings wouldn't be visible.

Wächter ordered Captain Blei to stay back. Then he started walking behind a service building toward the back of the hangar. His fingers gripped his Walther PPK. He couldn't wait to slap Becker around a bit, before hauling him to Berlin.

"Any pilots around here available for a private ride?" asked Becker, again in English-accented French.

The French pilot walked out to greet Becker. "That depends."

"I pay well." Becker showed a small stack of Swiss franc notes.

Pierre nodded. "Where to?"

"London."

"Out of country. . . . That'll be extra."

Becker pulled out more bills.

"You got two thousand there?"

"I'll pay fifteen hundred."

"Eighteen."

"Deal."

Wächter entered the back of the hangar and watched the negotiation. Then he darted behind the row of airplanes toward the Couzinet 70.

Pierre reached out for the money, and Becker pulled it back.

"Half up front." He handed it to the pilot's eager hands. "And half upon arrival."

"Agreed." Pierre grinned from ear to ear. "Let's get going!" He walked back toward the hangar, contemplating different planes.

Becker and Maria got out of the taxi cab. Becker paid the driver another hundred francs and began to walk away.

"Sir, you forgot your luggage!" the driver called.

Becker looked to Pierre and then back to the driver. "Oh heavens. Thank you!" He took the suitcase and led Maria into the hangar.

Becker patted the first plane, the *Pinceau*. "Is she ready to go? We're late."

The pilot looked at his watch, then at a single engine plane down the line. "I'm not supposed to take that one out today. . . ." He looked again at his watch. "Ah hell, let's take her. Climb aboard."

Behind two pilot seats, three pairs of passenger seats sat empty. Becker threw the suitcase into the middle row, and motioned Maria to the back.

"All right if we sit here?" he asked Pierre.

"Absolutely. Stretch out and relax. It's a beautiful, sunny day, after that fog we had last night." Pierre was visibly thrilled to have Becker's business.

"Say, sir," the pilot addressed Becker. "Do you have any idea of the weather in London this morning?"

"Sorry, no," replied Becker.

Pierre cranked up the engine. He checked his instruments and taxied to the two-story control tower. He left the plane idling and ran inside.

A couple minutes later, the pilot returned and took his seat. "The controller says the Channel looks good. I can't exactly tell him I'm going to cross it. The approval process would hold you up. Hopefully there's no fog in London. We're good to go."

"We're ready back here," said Becker. He and Maria smiled at each other. They would soon be in England.

The pilot rechecked his instruments while he taxied to the end of the airstrip. "Here we go!"

The Couzinet 70 rumbled down the strip. Suddenly the aircraft lifted it into a steep, smooth climb. Becker and Maria had a fantastic view of Paris in the morning sunlight. Then the plane turned to the northwest.

"Beautiful, isn't it!" Pierre glanced back with enthusiasm.

Becker nodded politely. Then he rolled his eyes at Maria for the over-enthusiastic commentary.

After fifteen minutes, the pilot leveled off the altitude. They watched the north French countryside roll by peacefully. Inside the plane it was cold and loud.

Maria smiled silently and reached out her left hand.

Becker smiled back and took it.

Half an hour later, the English Channel came into view on the horizon.

"I'll have to wait until we're over Britain, sir, to radio London. Don't want to give authorities on either side a chance to turn us back."

Becker nodded.

"Ow!" Becker nearly screamed as his shattered left shoulder pulled backwards with his whole arm. "What the–?!?"

He felt a firm grasp on his wrist and heard a click. He looked down to see himself shackled to his seat.

"Everything all right, sir?" asked the pilot.

"Answer him," whispered Colonel Wächter. He glared at Maria and held a gun to Becker's temple.

"Yes, just an old problem," Becker called up front.

"Hands behind your back, you wench," Wächter whispered to Maria.

Maria obeyed. Wächter handcuffed her hands together. Then he pulled her past Becker to the left side of the plane.

Becker observed the sinister Death's Head ring on Wächter's left hand. It marked Wächter as one of Himmler's elite SS guards.

"What's going on?" asked the pilot.

"Tell him to turn back," ordered Wächter in German.

"Change of plans," shouted Becker in French, over the din of the engines.

Pierre glanced back into the cabin. "You! Who the hell *are* you?!?" Pierre saw both of his passengers in handcuffs.

Wächter's scowl changed the pilot's expression from irritation to fear.

"He's in charge, now," Becker told the pilot. "Turn around and go back to Paris."

Pierre focused on the gun, and his face went ashen gray. "Yes, sir," he said. "Back to Paris."

The plane arced southward into a slow semi-circle.

"Don't move or your interrogations will be even worse," Wächter addressed his captives in German. "You're coming back, both of you. Back to Berlin with me, for a full . . . debriefing, shall we call it." Wächter pulled a sinister grin. "General Heydrich is very curious to know all about you."

Wächter handcuffed Becker's remaining hand to the middle armrest. "Johannes Becker, this time I have you, Fatherland traitor."

Wächter jerked Maria forward to the front row. He re-handcuffed her to the front right seat leg. The cast iron leg was bolted to the floor. "Where's your gun, Fräulein?" demanded Wächter. "Don't worry. Unlike your English abuser here, I do not intend to take advantage of you."

Maria spat in Wächter face.

Wächter slapped her. "Where's the damn gun?"

"On my waist, you bastard," she replied.

He delicately felt for it and pulled it out. "Now, now, Fräulein. No need to get testy. Not yet . . . ," he laughed.

"Can you translate for me, Fräulein?"

Maria shook her head.

"*Vous*," he addressed the pilot in halting French. "We not go to London, not Paris. We go to Köln." Wächter turned to Becker in German, "Ask him if he understands, ask him if he can find it."

"Can you find Cologne?" Becker asked Pierre.

"I think so," the pilot stammered. "I've never been there. But I'm sure I can find it on the Rhine, if the weather's all clear there."

Wächter pointed to the fuel gauge. "*Assez?*" he asked in French. Enough fuel?

"Yes, sir," answered Pierre. "I just filled her this morning. As long as we don't take any more detours. We'll have to fly over Belgium. . . . w-, w-, will I still get paid?"

"You idiot, I ought to smack you," Wächter shouted back in German. "The way you spoke to me back at the hangar. . . . Count yourself lucky to be alive right now. You're not indispensable – I can fly this thing myself."

Becker tried to read Wächter's claim. He thought there was some truth to it. Becker told the pilot, "He says, he flies planes and count yourself lucky to be alive."

Wächter continued in German, "Now I'll sit right here next to you. Don't you try any tricks! Understand? . . . Tell him, Becker!"

Becker duly translated. Pierre nodded so vigorously, nervous sweat flew from his chin.

"Excuse me, sir," the pilot addressed Wächter. "Could you please get out the Germany chart there?" He pointed to a pouch under the copilot's seat.

Wächter kept his gun ready in his right hand. He reached under his seat with the left. He leafed through several charts before he found the one labeled "Allemagne."

"I need the general coordinates from Lille to Cologne," said the pilot.

Wächter looked at the plane's compass. Then he read the map. "Almost straight to the east from Lille. Just a little north of that."

Becker translated for the pilot.

"All right," Pierre looked at his compass. "We should fly over Lille in about twenty minutes. Then we'll move into Belgian airspace. And finally we'll reach Cologne." He looked at the fuel gauge. "Remember, we don't have fuel for anything else."

Pierre took a quick rearward glimpse of his handcuffed passengers.

"Keep your eyes forward, dammit!" said Wächter. "They are of no concern to you!"

"Look straight ahead," translated Becker.

The pilot stared ahead. Sweat dripped from his palms as he gripped the controls.

Suddenly the plane fell into a nosedive. The pilot lunged for the cabin wall. Becker looked and saw two escape parachutes hanging there. Pierre got his hands on one.

Wächter fired at Pierre. The pilot ducked and clutched his parachute. Wächter left the cockpit of the plunging airplane and cornered the pilot. One point-blank shot was all the more it took. The pilot's body slid to the floor. Wächter dashed back to the controls.

"*Scheisse! Scheisse!*" shouted Wächter.

Becker saw that Wächter knew what he was doing.

Wächter pulled the plane level. Then the engines stalled out! In eerie silence, the plane glided far above the wintry farms below, slowly losing altitude.

Now Wächter broke into a sweat. He fumbled desperately to restart the engine. It puttered but failed to catch.

Wächter looked back at the parachutes. He paused and collected himself. The interlude would also avoid flooding the engine.

"One more time . . . ," he muttered to himself.

The engines sputtered and sputtered, then roared to life. Wächter smiled at his handiwork. He pulled to regain altitude.

Becker exhaled in nearly irrational relief. Sudden death was surely preferable to the Gestapo's tortures.

CHAPTER THIRTY

Colonel Wächter leveled off the plane and looked at the compass. He guessed they were way off course, probably somewhere over Belgium. He steered the plane eastward, far to the right, back toward Cologne.

Becker's cold hands strained at his handcuffs. The whole plane was cold. Becker was trapped in the last of three passenger rows. Maria lay out of sight, in front of the first row. He wanted to make eye contact with her.

Finally Becker managed to twist his body across the seat to his right. The movement tugged painfully at his wounded left shoulder. He looked under the seats ahead of him.

There was Maria's back. Her hands were cuffed behind her back, around a cast iron chair leg, itself bolted to the floor.

Maria shuffled her body position.

"Stop moving around!" Wächter yelled over the din of the three engines.

Becker jerked upright. Wächter was turning from the controls to look at Maria. He wasn't concerned with Becker. As soon as Wächter looked ahead again, Becker bent down.

He could see Maria's fingers probing up and down the chair leg for any place her handcuffs might slip through. All of a sudden she clutched the iron leg. Then she let go. Then she clutched it again. She repeated this several times. Becker wondered what it was all about.

"Don't try anything, Fräulein!" Wächter yelled again. "I'm fully aware you can kick me from there. Don't even think about it."

Maria didn't budge.

"You still conscious back there, Becker?" asked Wächter. He hadn't heard from Becker since the nosedive. Standartenführer Wächter wanted his prey alive.

Becker sat up again. "Yes," came his unenthusiastic response. He waited a moment and bent down again.

Now Maria's fingers probed the base of the iron leg behind her back. Suddenly her whole upper body winced and she jerked back her fingers.

Her finger just got pinched. . . . That means the leg is loose! Becker realized. The plane's earlier jostling must have done it.

Carefully Maria felt around the base again. Her fingers stopped on one bolt, and then the second one. She tugged at them quickly and vigorously. If she could get them off, she could free herself from the chair leg. Then she could move around the plane, though still in handcuffs.

Maria was almost done removing the first bolt when the seat began to vibrate and rattle against the floor. She instantly grasped the leg to stop the noise. Wächter said nothing, seemingly oblivious. Maria screwed the first bolt halfway back in.

Her fingers moved to the second bolt. It wouldn't budge. She kept trying. It still didn't move.

Becker sat up again, for another twenty minutes. He didn't dare try to get Maria's attention now. He mustn't do anything to draw Wächter's attention to her. He wondered if they were over German territory yet.

When Becker looked under the seats again, Maria had made no progress with the second bolt. She retried every minute or two. It still wouldn't budge. Finally she risked loosening the first bolt again. When the seat started vibrating on the floor, Maria held the leg still. She left the bolt almost all the way out.

After two more minutes, she tried the second bolt with her other hand. It turned as easily as a child's spinning top! Now it was rattled loose, too. Maria frantically tightened the first bolt halfway. Then she removed the second bolt completely.

Becker could hear the slight buzz of the loosened chair base against the floor. He nervously anticipated Wächter's response. So far, their captor didn't notice.

Finally Maria unscrewed the first bolt all the way with one hand, while holding the leg with the other.

The buzzing got louder. It was beyond Maria's control. As the bolt came out, the buzz became a loud rattle.

In no more than two seconds, Maria pushed the seat up with her back, jerked her handcuffs under the chair leg, stood up, and pulled her handcuffs forward under her legs.

Wächter turned his head. "What's—"

It was too late. Maria stood behind his seat and pulled her handcuffs against Wächter's neck.

Wächter's only sound now was gagging. He removed his hands from the plane's controls and tugged at Maria's wrists.

The strength of his arms was no match for Maria's legs, as her feet pushed against the back of the pilot's seat. She pulled the full weight of her body into the chain at Wächter's throat.

Wächter reached for his gun and fumbled to aim it behind him. Maria kicked it out of his hands. It landed next to her and fired upward, putting a hole in the plane's roof.

With the same foot, Maria kicked Wächter in the groin. He couldn't gag any more. His throat was completely closed by Maria's handcuffs. He removed his hands from Maria's wrists and reached for his bruised groin.

Maria wrapped her legs around the pilot's seat and Wächter, holding his arms to his sides. She leaned backwards, pulling all of her upper body weight and strength into Wächter's neck. He flailed his forearms around helplessly. He was unable to reach even the plane's controls.

"Ahhhhhh!" Maria screamed.

Becker heard both extreme exertion and delight in her voice.

Wächter went limp.

"Don't let go!" screamed Becker. "It's a trick!"

"Hehhhh!" sounded Wächter's quick inhalation. He jerked his hands toward the loosened chain on his neck.

Maria pulled back again. She'd lost control of Wächter's arms.

He tore at her hands with his fingernails. The scratches drew blood. But his nails weren't long enough to gouge her deeply. Wächter was unable to pull the chain loose.

The plane flew on, unguided, pitching slightly downward.

"For my brothers, you son-of-bitch!" yelled Maria. "And all the rest of them!" Maria arched backwards and screamed again. She pulled the chain even harder into his throat. In the back row, Becker could hear Wächter's cartilage crunching.

Wächter flailed his arms over his shoulders, kicking his legs wildly. A bone snapped. He went limp again.

Maria kept pulling and pulling. She stopped only when her wrists felt Wächter's warm blood oozing out of the trench she had gouged in his throat.

"Hurry, Maria!" shouted Becker. "We may already be over Germany! Get his keys and unlock us! We're losing altitude!"

Maria fumbled toward Wächter's belt. Then she thought to lift her chained hands over his head first and come down on his right side. She rushed the keys back to Becker.

Her hands trembled mightily. She managed to unlock Becker's right hand. He took over and unchained Maria and then his own left hand.

The plane started to veer to the right and downward. Becker looked forward and saw Wächter's corpse slumped over the controls. Becker dashed up front. He threw Wächter's corpse into the copilot's seat and pulled the controls straight again.

Then he darted back to the parachutes. He handed Maria the clean parachute on the wall. For himself he took the bloodied parachute still in Pierre's hands on the floor.

Becker started putting his on when he saw that Maria was trembling too much to make any progress. He put her parachute on her shoulders. Then he finished putting on his own.

The plane began to pitch forward again. Becker reached into the cockpit for Wächter's and Maria's guns.

"Quick!" he said. "There's no time. Hold me around the waist, right below the draw cords. I'll hold your waist, too. My other arm's useless. Five seconds after we jump, I'll yell to pull, and you pull the chute's cords. Got it?"

Maria nodded. She clutched so hard, Becker felt the breath go out of him. He used his one good arm to open the escape hatch. Then he held Maria.

"Here we go!" he shouted over the freezing wind.

Maria followed his jump so well, they could have been longtime dance partners.

Five seconds later, Becker gave the word and Maria pulled his cord. The parachute opened perfectly.

"I've got you, Maria. Don't let go, but I've got you." The steady cold wind in their ears seemed quiet and natural after their horrific plane ride. "We'll be down in just a minute or two."

Becker looked down to a semi-rural landscape. It was dotted with small towns and villages. They quickly approached the ground.

Damn! he thought. *This looks more like Germany than Belgium. . . . All those flower boxes. . . . We'll see.*

Suddenly they heard an explosion. The plane crashed about a half-mile away.

"Wow," muttered Maria. "Look at the smoke."

"Uh-oh. . . . That'll draw attention from miles away. At least it wasn't near any buildings. But people will be looking to the sky right away. . . . Here comes the ground. Hit it running!"

Maria jumped from Becker right before landing and rolled into a slide on the snow.

When Maria jumped off Becker, her arms caught his right leg and pulled it outward. He had only his left foot to break the fall. He landed and collapsed in pain.

"My ankle . . . ." Becker stood up and tried to walk. The pain was sharp. His ankle was perhaps broken, at the very least badly sprained. The injury would really slow him down. He sat down and removed his parachute.

"Go ahead, Maria. Save yourself – run for cover. We don't even know what country we're in. . . . Stay low. Someone might have seen our parachute."

"I'm staying with you," she replied. "Look over there. There's a forest across the road, about a half-mile away. That's the opposite direction from the plane."

Becker turned his head around. The fields were mostly snowy, but the roads were visibly clear this Wednesday morning. The sky was blue, but the winter air was humid with a slight fog.

"That'll give us some cover," he agreed. "But I'll be very slow. Please go ahead. I'll catch up." He looked back to the plume of black smoke rising from the plane crash.

Maria stayed by his side.

They heard sirens approaching the crash. Becker could see a few people walking toward it on the horizon.

He lifted himself to his feet and eyed the distance to the small forest. Then he placed his right arm around Maria's waist. "Stay low. I'll go as fast as I can."

Their line to the small forest crossed a road. As they neared the road, they crouched even lower. At the sound of an approaching car, they fell to the ground. The car drove by.

After two minutes, they resumed their walk. Becker looked to the left and read the village clock tower: ten-thirty, Wednesday morning. With the time difference, only ten hours remained until Churchill's concert! Becker imagined the bomb that killed Tsar Alexander.

Becker limped across the road with Maria's help. He read a sign with the village's name, Gillrath.

"Gillrath – a German name!" he quietly exclaimed. "After all that, we're back in Germany! No!"

They walked towards the woods, not very far from the road. Once inside the forest perimeter, they kept walking.

A hundred feet into the forest, out of the road's sight, Becker finally collapsed.

"I've got to rest. My ankle's killing me. You go on."

"I told you I'm not leaving you," she said. "You stayed with me when I slowed you down. Now it's my turn. I'll scout around the forest while you rest your ankle."

"Be careful. . . . Here, take your gun. We'll skip the shooting lessons this time," he smiled.

Maria laughed as she tucked the gun into her skirt. "Get some rest," she said. "I'll see what's around."

Becker nodded and waved. Maria trudged deeper into the forest.

She was a greater asset to his mission than he'd ever imagined. Perhaps she could join Dansey's spy network in some capacity if they made it to London. He'd certainly recommend it, if she wanted.

As Becker's thoughts drifted farther from the present, they turned into dreams of a deep slumber.

First he dreamed of the flight with Wächter, except that it ended with him and Maria crashing to their deaths. Next he dreamed of his kind and loving father, on long, listless Sunday afternoons. Then came Becker's mother, Amalie, weeping over her husband's death in the World War. The dreaming shifted to Becker's London childhood, and family vacations in Jamaica. The memory of the tropical sun warmed his spirits. Next he saw the image of Amalie Becker in a concert hall, sitting next to Winston Churchill. And Churchill sat on an assassin's ticking time bomb. The dream's explosion sounded more like a gunshot.

"*Auf! Auf!*" Get up!

Becker opened his eyes to see three local policemen, one of them holding a smoking gun. Maria lay handcuffed and bloodied at their feet.

"Johannes . . . ," she whispered. "Johannes. . . ."

Becker turned to the policeman tapping his right cheek. But instead of the policeman, he saw Maria.

He opened and closed his eyes several times in sheer disorientation. He shook his head and took a deep breath. Now he was sure he was awake. It was just Maria waking him up, not the police.

"Oh . . . Oh . . . . What time is it?" he asked.

"About one o'clock, according to your watch," she replied.

"Wow," Becker shook his head back and forth to wake up. "It feels like just minutes ago that you left. I'm exhausted. It'll take a few minutes to get myself oriented."

"While you're doing that, let me tell you what I found," said Maria. "These woods are about a mile wide and two miles deep. There are a few small lakes amid the fields on the far–"

"Over here!" called a boy's voice in the distance. It sounded about ten-years-old. It also sounded like it might be onto Maria and Becker.

"Oh no, Matthias," said a second boy's voice. "Don't follow those footprints by yourself! Let's go get the police!"

"No way," said the first voice. "I'm going in."

"Well then I'm coming with you!"

Maria helped Becker up quickly. "There's a small stream just over here. It'll be almost impossible to follow tracks in that."

Becker clutched Maria's waist with his good arm. They plunged deeper into the forest. Becker was so jolted by the German boys that he momentarily forgot his sprained ankle. The first step reminded him. After a few minutes, the ice-cold stream soaked his ankle and numbed it slightly.

The boys' voices followed behind at about the same, slow trot, close enough for Becker and Maria to hear.

"Here's another footprint, Karl!" said the first voice.

"Wow. Hey, Matthias, I can barely see the road anymore. Are you sure this is a good idea?"

"Of course! . . . I've lost track of them. They're not on the trail. They'd better not run onto Farmer Limburger's land!"

Both boys laughed.

"Yeah," answered the second voice, "He's enough to scare anyone back into the forest, screaming owls and all."

"Maybe these footprints aren't even from today, Matthias. What do you think?"

There was a pause in their conversation. "Did you hear that?" said the first voice.

Becker tugged at Maria to stop.

"What?" said the second boy's voice. "No, I didn't hear anything."

"It sounded like a breaking stick. No animal here is that big."

"I'm scared, Matthias. I want to go back."

The boys' conversation paused again. Then the first voice said, "Yeah, I guess maybe we should."

"But now the whole village will come in here after us," whispered Becker. "I have got to get to a phone by sunset. It's worth any risk.

They'll surely be screening overseas calls, and even calls to the British Embassy in Berlin. But I have to try it. There's no choice. When the time comes, you need to go your own way and save yourself."

"There's another village on the far side," said Maria. "Maybe it will be less concerned with our plane . . . and easier for you to place your call."

They plodded farther into the forest. Occasionally they glimpsed farm fields beyond the forest's left flank.

"The woods take a strange turn up here," said Maria. "It looks like it curves to the left, but then it cuts back sharply to the right, where the lakes are. Come look past the far edge and see where you think we should go."

It took Becker almost an hour to limp the length of the woods. From the western edge, he and Maria could see the lakes and fields and villages on the far side.

"Look on the other side of the lakes, Maria, about two or three miles away. That's not a village, it's a small town. And over there, there's another one. That's odd. . . ."

Suddenly they heard frantic dog barking. The dogs were distant. But there could be no doubt they were tracking fugitives, Becker and Maria.

"Those towns are too far for me to outrun the dogs on this ankle," said Becker. "Not even to the next forest across the field here. Go, Maria! Save yourself!"

She ignored him and looked upward and around. "Look at that pair of birch trees over there. C'mon." She pulled Becker up the small hill behind them, and began to climb the tree.

"Use your good arm and leg," she said. "You have to do it. There's no other way."

"Sure, I'll manage here while I can. But get out of here, Maria! Go!"

Maria began climbing one of the trees.

Becker followed. He wedged himself between the two trunks until they reached branches several feet above the ground. As the barking drew closer, he and Maria settled on branches twelve feet high. In front of them were fields and small lakes, more woods, and towns. Behind them, in the forest, were the fiercely barking dogs and whoever commanded them.

Ten minutes later, three German shepherds approached from within the woods. They ran all the way to the edge of the field, past their hiding place above. The dogs' masters were not yet in sight.

Becker considered shooting the dogs, but he thought better of it. He had nowhere to go, and the dogs hadn't found him and Maria. They continued barking, but with less conviction. Gunshots would draw attention from miles around, especially so soon after the plane crash.

After twenty more minutes, two men's voices came trotting around the base of the hill to the dogs. The German shepherds still sniffed for the lost trail.

"The dogs lost the trail," said one of the men. "And with this hill angled toward the sun, there's not much snow left for footprints."

The two men, both bearing guns and dressed in gray, looked around for the fugitives' tracks.

Without warning, the sound of a small avalanche terrified Becker. A bucketful of snow showered to the ground from the end of the branch where he sat.

An owl called out from a nearby tree, disturbed from its daytime slumber. The bird flapped his considerable wings and flew off. The scared owl gave Becker a second start.

Maria's own surprise was more noticeable. She scraped loudly against a small branch as she shifted her look first to the falling snow and then to the owl.

The dogs resumed their frantic barking.

"Look up there!" shouted the first pursuer.

"*Grenzschutz!*" shouted the second, pointing his gun clumsily upward. "Get down from there immediately!"

Border Guard?!? thought Becker. *We're near the border? On the wrong damn side of it!*

Becker looked to the towns across the field. On the road about a half-mile away stood two small figures, with their own dogs. The figures were dressed in blue rather than gray.

Three quick shots exploded from Maria's gun. She felled the first guard.

The second guard fired two shots into the trees. His second shot hit the trunk next to Becker's head.

Becker killed the second guard with one shot. He wounded one of the dogs with a second shot.

The two unwounded dogs whimpered and retreated quickly into the forest.

Becker looked back across the field. One of the men was waving broadly. Their two dogs kept jumping at their leashes.

"That's got to be the border over there, Maria. We can make it!" Becker half-slid, half-fell, section-by-section, down the tree trunk. Maria descended gracefully behind him.

Becker aimed at the wounded dog's head and put it out of its misery.

"That's the border!" rejoiced Becker. "Run for it!"

Becker held Maria's upper arm as they half-sprinted across the field. The soil was mostly frozen, covered with a thin layer of snow. Each of them slipped occasionally.

The two border guards on the other side beckoned them vigorously.

Becker ran all the faster. He felt his ankle bleeding. The pain was indescribable. He rested more of his weight on Maria. She bore him with unexpected strength. On his right leg, Becker hopped his way across the remainder of the field. His arm clutched Maria for balance, but he placed as little weight as possible on her.

Just beyond earshot of the blue-uniformed guards, an exhausted Becker panted to Maria, "Nothing . . . about England until . . . I say it. . . . Belgium is trying . . . to play neutral in all of this."

Maria nodded.

Becker looked behind them. No one followed. They were going to make it!

The two policemen smiled broadly as Becker and Maria made it onto the road. *"Welkom in Nederland!"*

"Niederlände?!? Können Sie Deutsch?" asked Becker.

"I speak a little, yes," answered the shorter one. "Welcome to the Netherlands!" Many Dutchmen spoke German, a closely related language.

"Thank you! Thank you! Thank you!" cried Maria. She collapsed to the ground in sobs. Becker kneeled down to embrace her.

"Where will you take us?" he asked.

"To the police station, naturally," answered the policeman. "We've never had a refugee crossing here before. We'll have to review the protocol. Don't worry, though. You'll be well taken care of. . . . Right this way, please."

Becker and Maria stood up and followed them to their car a few dozen yards away.

Churchill. My phone call.

"What's the name of this town?"

"Brunssum. You were in the Staher Heide, on the German side. . . . You were in that plane?"

"That's right," answered Becker.

"You're very lucky."

"Indeed."

"No, more than survival. Our radio monitoring just picked up traffic on the other side. The Gestapo is activating over there. Berlin seems very interested in that plane. . . . Where are you coming from?"

"Paris. Well, Germany and Paris. We got side-tracked." Becker looked at Maria, who now rested her head on his chest.

"Our police chief will really enjoy meeting you." The four of them crowded into the small car and drove into town.

Safe out of Germany, seated in the car, Becker again felt the days of sleep deprivation behind him. His muscles loosened. His head and eyes felt very heavy.

He looked at the church clock as they passed it. Two-thirty. Six hours until Churchill's concert.

They pulled into the small station and got out of the car. A third officer came out of the station to greet them.

"Come inside, please," the German-speaking driver beckoned Becker and Maria. "Chief Verweij, this was the cause of all that commotion. Brunssum's first refugees!"

"Welcome! Welcome!" the chief addressed them in German. "Come in and get warm. We will get you coffee and food."

"Thank you," answered Becker.

"Is the woman French?" asked the patrol officer.

"No, I'm not, just exhausted," came Maria's answer. "Sorry to be an ungrateful guest."

"Not at all," answered the chief. "Please sit down at my personal table, Herr . . . ?"

"Becker. Johannes Becker."

"Herr Becker and . . . ?" Chief Verweij looked at their wedding bands.

Maria seemed unsure how to answer.

The chief left it at that. "And Frau Becker, then. Please have a seat. My wife will be bringing some nice warm stew and coffee in just a few minutes. Is there anything else I can get for you?"

"A bed," answered Maria.

"I would like to let my relatives in England know that I'm out," Becker replied.

The room was some kind of break area, not a prisoners section. The air was warm and the furniture comfortable. It was enough to send Maria and himself into a good slumber.

"Of course, of course. . . . We'll have to get permission from The Hague for an out-of-country phone call, though. So how about a nice meal and some rest first, no? You look exhausted. . . . Ah, here's the food!"

Both Becker and Maria were famished. But they were so tired, they could only eat slowly and deliberately.

"Your limp looks bad, Herr Becker. We should take you to the hospital over in Maastricht to get that looked at."

"Yes, it may be broken," replied Becker. "But it's really important that I make that phone call as soon as possible, actually."

Maria remembered the Churchill assassination plot. Knowing the high stakes, she admired Becker's restraint and smiled lovingly at him.

"It sounds urgent," said the chief. "Let me get on the phone to The Hague right away. Excuse me for a minute, please." Chief Verweij left to make his phone call. Becker and Maria continued their meal.

Verweij returned with an update.

"They've got the regular lines tied up until seven o'clock this evening. We're allowed to call after that."

"It would be much better if I could call sooner," said Becker. "That's really cutting it close, if I may say so." With the time difference, that left only one and a half hours for London to respond.

"I'm terribly sorry, Herr Becker. It's just not possible. If they say seven o'clock, it's got to be seven o'clock. Hopefully the lines will function swiftly for you then."

"Hopefully," sighed Becker.

He and Maria finished their meal and moved to a sitting area. Becker had forgotten his mild headache until the chief's coffee began to improve it. Maria drifted off to sleep. Becker observed to himself again how beautiful she was.

Winston Churchill settled into his box seat at Queen's Hall. The gallery bells summoned concertgoers to their seats.

"That's funny," Churchill grinned, "I didn't think my hind quarters had lost any padding. You and the doctors must be starving me, Clemmie!" Churchill shuffled around until he got comfortable in his seat.

"It's about time we saw Arturo Toscanini conduct," Clementine Churchill said to her husband.

"An Italian conducting German music in London. . . ," remarked Churchill. "Toscanini's as anti-fascist as they come, though. And Beethoven only happened to be German. He's above us all. Not like

Wagner and his German fairy tales. Beethoven's Fifth, now this is music for the ages."

Struggling to stay awake, aching profoundly in both his ankle and shoulder, Becker anxiously marked the minutes and hours to seven o'clock . . . six o'clock in London.

At ten minutes till seven, he started pressing to make his call.

"In just a few minutes, sir," answered a new policeman, Officer Kuypers.

Maria opened her eyes at the conversation, and then went back to sleep on the sofa.

At precisely seven, the officer placed the call to The Hague. "They're working on the connection to London now," he reported to Becker.

The minutes ticked by. Now it was seven-fifteen.

"It seems the European lines into London are overloaded, sir. The Hague says they'll keep trying."

Becker nodded and gave a pursed smile.

Another quarter of an hour passed . . . . It was seven-thirty Dutch time, just one hour before the seven-thirty concert in London.

"What are they telling you?" asked Becker.

"I can hear their constant attempts, sir. They're very impressed by your escape from the Gestapo. They really do want to help you."

Maria woke up and felt the tension. She sat up and watched.

Becker was losing patience. If there were no progress by eight o'clock, he would commandeer the police station's radios by force and contact British Intelligence himself on open channels.

After another half-hour, at eight o'clock, Becker started to reach for his gun.

"They've made the connection, sir!" announced Kuypers.

Becker patted his chest, faked a cough, and lowered his hand.

He involuntarily clenched his fists. He only had thirty minutes until the concert started. This was cutting it way too close.

"Do you speak English?" asked Becker.

"No, don't you?" replied Kuypers.

"Yes," said Becker. "Should I take the phone?"

"Of course." Kuypers handed the phone to Becker.

It was five minutes after seven in London. Only twenty-five minutes remained.

Becker listened.

"Hello? Dutch Embassy London here. Hello?"

"My name is John Becker," he said in English. "Please put me through immediately to 54 Broadway."

"Broadway House? Secret Intelligence?" asked the Dutch embassy official.

"It's a matter of urgent national security! I'll wait on the line if you need me to.   Tell them it's John Becker, calling from the Netherlands, it's supremely urgent."

"That sounds improbable, sir," answered the official. "But your guard there says you've been through a lot. I'll give it a try."

Becker waited through ten minutes of assurances. It was seven-fifteen in London. "This is a national emergency!" shouted Becker.

"I understand, sir," answered the patient Dutch officer on call.

"If you can't get Broadway, get Scotland Yard!" Becker preferred to talk with Secret Intelligence, where they knew him and would take him seriously immediately.   There was no time to review his credentials.

Five minutes later, a new voice came on the line, this one native English. "Broadway House," the on-duty officer answered. "Hello? Hello?"

It was seven-twenty.

"Yes, is the chief available?" asked Becker.

The voice at Broadway chuckled. "At this hour? He's at an evening concert with the Churchills. What can I do for you?"

"The seven-thirty concert?" asked Becker.

"The concert started at seven o'clock."

The concert was underway! Seven-thirty must be the assassination time. Only ten minutes away! Becker was desperate.

"I just got out of Germany hours ago.   The Germans plan to assassinate Mr. Churchill in ten minutes' time. Get him out of there!!! Stop the concert! Get everyone out!"

For a moment Becker heard no response. He wondered if the line were dead.

"The intelligence section confirms, Agent Becker. We're calling the bomb squad right now."

Seven-twenty-two.

Wailing sirens raced toward Queen's Hall from all directions. Police and ambulances and fire crews would all be on hand. The crucial bomb squad was the second car to arrive.

Seven-twenty-seven.

Several police cars skidded to a stop before the first policemen were in the building. They burst into the grand entryway, in red velvet wallpaper, gold trim, and crystal chandeliers. The final movement of Beethoven's Fifth pulsed frantically through the concert hall doors to the entry gallery.

"There's a bomb!" shouted the first officer in the building. "Get everyone out!" He rushed to the auditorium doors. Three thousand people sat inside.

"Where's Churchill's box?!?" shouted the first bomb expert, behind him.

A quick-thinking young usher pulled the bomb expert by the arm. They ran to a side staircase, before the hallways became packed with fleeing concertgoers.

The first officer entered the auditorium. The last movement of Beethoven's Fifth Symphony was approaching its final crescendo. Toscanini conducted a fast Fifth, and this was his fastest ever.

"There's a bomb!" shouted the officer over the orchestra. "Everyone leave immediately! It's a bomb!"

Screams and closing chairs and then a stampede ensued. The officer was now stuck at the back of the hall, blowing his whistle into the mayhem.

Orchestra players shuffled at the commotion. Screams of "Bomb! Bomb!" were unmistakable. Toscanini glanced back at the audience, without stopping his conducting. He stared at the orchestra players and fiercely drove them to the symphony's conclusion. Every last player obeyed the legendary maestro. The concert hall around them was in chaos.

The bomb expert reached the box just as Churchill's party was leaving it. Before exiting to the hallway, Churchill stepped aside for the expert to enter.

"Where's your seat, sir?" asked the expert.

"Second from the right in the front row," answered Churchill.

The expert went straight to Churchill's seat and surveyed the box from there. He saw enough irregularity in Churchill's own seat to attack it immediately.

The orchestra was reaching the symphony's end with unheard of speed and frenzy, under Toscanini's incredible discipline.

Seven-twenty-nine.

Thousands of concertgoers packed the exits. No one was trampled yet. But the desperate shouts and cries rose up with the symphony's finale.

Someone cried from the concert hall floor, "It's in Churchill's box! Look!" People pointed at the bomb expert above the left front of the hall.

Dozens of gentlemen shouted a cacophony of orders. More women screamed. A thousand audience members ran and stumbled from one side of the hall to the other, to escape the bomb.

The bomb expert removed Churchill's seat cushion with his knife. He slowly lifted the bomb case and brought it to the floor. His coolness reflected nothing of Beethoven's dramatic climax or the pandemonium in the hall. If anything, the music steadied his hand. He opened the bomb case. There lay the bomb and its silently ticking clock.

Only ten seconds till detonation!

The bomb's wiring was simple but tiny. The expert carefully pinched the regulating fuse.

Four seconds, three . . . .

As Toscanini struck the Fifth Symphony's final chord, the bomb was defused.

CHAPTER THIRTY-ONE

Thursday, February 20

Becker left Maria at the Earl's Court debriefing house. She was comfortable in the library. The fire was blazing and thousands of books beckoned, even a few in German. After their exquisite lunch, she told him she felt like napping.

Becker needed help getting in the car. His left ankle was badly sprained from his parachute landing the day before. Since he couldn't manage crutches with the gunshot left shoulder, the doctors ordered him a wheelchair.

Churchill's secretary drove Becker to Churchill's flat in Morpeth Mansions. With help, Becker hopped from the car into his wheelchair. They rode the lift to Number 11, entered the front room, and waited. Once his wheelchair was locked in place, Becker elevated his left leg.

Becker had met Churchill once before. Several years earlier, the veteran politician was a guest at an importers' party co-hosted by his Uncle Jochen. That brief encounter seemed like a lifetime ago. Becker looked forward to meeting him again.

His wheelchair rested between two blue velvet chairs on one side and a matching sofa on the other. A fire roared and crackled in the fireplace. The room's white walls sparkled with daylight. A close-up view of Westminster Cathedral took Becker by surprise. The walls were studded with small paintings of the English countryside. Two floor lamps supplemented the daylight and firelight.

"You caused quite a stir, Becker!" said Churchill, entering the front room from the opposite side, cigar in hand. "A most tumultuous concert. My wife and I are forever indebted."

"England couldn't do without you, sir." From his wheelchair, Becker returned Churchill's solid handshake.

"I believe you've met Colonel Dansey," said Churchill. Becker and Dansey exchanged greetings. Not two weeks ago they'd met in Prague.

"Have a seat, Dansey," said Churchill. "Becker, your doctors are impressed by your body's healing powers. I can't say I blame you for refusing to spend the next week in the hospital. I found privacy much better after my New York accident five years ago. Can we help make you more comfortable?"

"No thank you, sir," replied Becker. "I'm quite comfortable."

Dansey and Churchill sat down on either side of Becker.

"Before we get into your discoveries," said Churchill, "Dansey has some news for you."

"I've heard the summary of your ups and downs with Miss Geberich," said Dansey. "We've confirmed her cabaret act as Lola Montez. We're checking out the rest of her story."

"She'll check out," Becker stated matter-of-factly.

Dansey continued. "We've apprehended the assassin, one Patrick O'Hagan. He's worked at Queen's Hall for years, evidently IRA from the start. He swears he knows nothing about the German connection. We're already cornering O'Hagan's thuggish friends in Dublin."

Churchill added, "The IRA's not too fond of me, you might know. The Protestants in Northern Ireland wanted to remain with the United Kingdom back in twenty-two, and I was glad to oblige."

Dansey turned to the next topic. "On another front, yesterday's events in Paris bore remarkable fruit. As a by-product of your escape, you did tremendous damage to the Gestapo there. . . . Your dramatic Rhine River crossing was picked up within hours by intelligence headquarters on both sides. By morning at the Gare de l'Est, as you saw, the Gestapo and French intelligence were both out in full force, waiting for your train. You escaped, but the Gestapo team did not. The French rounded them up. They got all of those on the station platform. Then later in the morning, they tracked down the Gestapo's Paris station chief and a couple more, out at Orly airfield. French interrogation methods confirm the damage to the Germans. You cleaned out Paris – an unexpected bonus."

Becker smiled at this additional triumph.

"Becker, I offer my congratulations," said Churchill. "I'm sorry we can't give you the ceremony you deserve, not now. Time is against us. So on to our main business. . . . We need to know every relevant detail you've stolen from Berlin. It's barely a secret that Hitler plans to move his army into the demilitarized Rhineland. Every government in Europe knows it. I'm trying to push ours to intervene. The French foreign minister is begging us to help. Their generals are afraid to act, but several French Cabinet ministers are afraid not to act."

Churchill pulled his cigar out of his mouth and leaned forward. "You say your mission was successful. So what is it? Hitler's going to remilitarize Germany's western border. Does his army have the firepower to hold that? Or is it an empty shell? In short, is Hitler bluffing?"

"In short, yes," replied Becker. "And he knows it. . . . A week ago yesterday, on Wednesday, February 12, Hitler met his chiefs of staff to lay out plans for remilitarizing the Rhineland. He explicitly expects Britain and France to stand aside. Here's the biggest news: They all agreed the German Army is much too weak to withstand an Allied attack. The contingency plan is to retreat across the Rhine. If we don't resist, Hitler said, quote, 'with the Rhineland secure, Germany could prepare to defeat France and destroy Poland,' unquote. Those are the exact words, sir."

"Then it's World War!" said Churchill. "That murderous demon! . . . What else do you have for us?"

"There was more to the meeting minutes, but I was forced to flee without them," replied Becker.

Churchill paused in uncharacteristic silence and looked into the fire. Then he turned to Becker. "It's most solemn news you bear. And not in the least surprising. Yet we've never had documentary proof until now. Astonishing work, Becker. Astounding. . . . Dansey, have a secretary type all this up. Make it look good and official. The appeasers will be skeptical. We know we can trust Becker, but they'll try to discredit him."

Becker understood what Churchill meant. It was clear to all three of them that Hitler must be stopped. Others would disagree. They fell for Hitler's assurances that he didn't want war. The evidence against them was Becker's memory, not the actual German document one could put in the newspapers. Voters would never know about the evidence. And after the Great War, they'd need a lot of convincing to go to war again. Churchill faced a tough political struggle ahead.

"I'm sorry I didn't get a copy of the document," said Becker. "I was interrupted at gunpoint."

"You've done a top job, Becker," said Churchill. "You nearly got yourself killed, many times over. The extended leave coming to you is not equal to your sacrifice. . . . We wish you a speedy recovery. Let us know if there's anything we can do for your convalescence."

"Actually," said Becker, "there is one thing."

The apartment of Becker's adolescence was part of Uncle Jochen's large red brick house in tidy Hampstead, London.

"Oh Johannes, look at you! How could your ski trip have gone so wrong?" Amalie Becker still spoke German with her son. She stood in her doorway looking down at John, bandaged in the wheelchair. She hadn't seen him in fifteen months. She reached down and embraced him.

Amalie wore a yellow and red flower-print dress and a thick gray cardigan. Her long gray hair was pulled in a bun behind her head. Her soft face bore few wrinkles yet, since she weighed twenty pounds more than in younger years. Her blue-gray eyes scrutinized her son sharply.

"The ski broke," replied Becker. "Poor craftsmanship, and my bad luck." Becker hated lying to his mother. He wanted to steer the conversation elsewhere.

"And this must be the young woman you told me about," smiled Amalie.

"Muti, meet Maria Geberich," said Becker.

"Welcome to London," smiled Amalie. She took Maria's right hand in both of hers. "Welcome."

"It's a pleasure to meet Johannes' mother," said Maria.

"I'm sorry, Muti," said Becker, "that it has taken me so long to visit."

"I know how things go, Johannes. You're fortunate to have a good job in these hard times. I'm grateful for that. How have you been? It must be frightful under the Nazis. I've had to end many old correspondences, so fanatical have they become over there."

"It is beyond imagination, Muti," said Becker. "Even some everyday experiences are too frightful to recount."

"Thank you," said Amalie. "Yes, please, spare me. . . . Come in, come in! I've got tea ready."

Becker introduced Maria as a business associate as well as his special companion. He had rarely brought a woman home. His mother thought he should marry and start a family. He could see she was pleased to meet Maria.

"You got into town last night?" Amalie asked her son.

"Yes, very late," answered Becker. "Uncle Jochen is paying for accommodations. Given my condition, that's been most helpful."

"I wish you would stay with me," said Amalie. "You couldn't get any better nursing than mine! You can have the downstairs bedroom."

"That would be wonderful," replied John. He knew nothing could make his mother happier. "I'll come home, then, after my dinner meeting. I'll stay all three nights that remain, if that's all right."

"*Wunderbar!*" beamed Amalie.

After an hour more of conversation, Becker and Maria left for more debriefing at Earl's Court.

"Will she ever learn about your real work?" asked Maria.

"Not from me," he said.

Four mornings later, Maria and Becker arrived with their bags at the foggy London docks. Becker now walked with a cane. A porter was ready to help with their luggage. The cold fog was thin enough to reveal patches of blue sky above.

Their small liner, the *Odyssey*, would leave in an hour. The porter picked up their bags.

"Becker! Miss Geberich! A moment of your time, please!"

Becker motioned for the porter to put the bags down. "Look at this!" he whispered to Maria.

The short but solidly built Winston Churchill strutted from his limousine in fine clothes, smiling as usual. Becker and Maria stepped away from the porter, out of earshot.

"Mister Churchill," Becker said, "we cannot thank you enough. It would have taken us more than twice as long to travel to my uncle's estate in Jamaica. I don't know how you managed to reroute this vessel for direct delivery. We are most grateful."

"A trifle compared to the lives you saved last week," said Churchill. "And to the information you brought from Berlin. . . . I wish I could say more people were moved by it."

"Oh?" said Becker. He knew it could have been much worse. Some day soon, Britain would have to fight the Third Reich. If Churchill had been killed, the Chamberlains and Halifaxes might surrender instead. Becker had faith that Churchill would pull it out in the end.

"I've been pressing Chamberlain and the others to use your information and repel Hitler from the Rhineland border areas after he moves. There can be no doubt Hitler's army is a figment. But the prime minister won't call Hitler's bluff. They won't stop him. I should say, they won't do it now. For in the end, they shall have no choice. You proved Hitler has plans to conquer France and Poland, even beyond. . . . You've set the ball in motion here, Becker. The appeasers may hold power today. But your information has steeled the nerves of others for the war that awaits us. Sooner or later, we'll oust the appeasers, and lead our nation to victory. . . . I've talked with every one of the appeasers that I could corner since last Thursday. Only one of those conversations yielded the slightest satisfactory results."

"Who was that?" Becker felt Churchill's news clouding his mission's successes.

"My Conservative colleague, Lady Astor," said Churchill. "She rejected my pleas like the rest of them. 'Winston,' she said, 'If you were my husband, I'd poison your tea.' 'Madame,' I replied, 'If I were your husband, I'd drink it!'" Churchill grinned and chomped his cigar.

Becker and Maria burst out laughing.

Late winter on Jamaica's north shore was enough to fade any memory of the German winter. Jochen Becker's estate sat on a private strip of white-sand beach. Shallow turquoise waters extended a hundred yards to the reef, teeming with fish in reds, yellows, and blues. The villa above offered a breathtaking view under the sunny blue sky.

The first week here had been wonderful. Becker and Maria talked for hours on end about anything and everything. They ate together, walked the beach together, and slept together. The next three weeks would fly by, Becker knew. Perhaps he could extend their stay.

They finished a breakfast of fruits, bread, and coffee. A steady, pleasant sea breeze complemented their sweet pineapples and mangos. They watched the palm trees rustling across the lawn.

For the first time in days, they heard a car pull up the long driveway on the other side of the house. Becker wasn't expecting anyone.

He stood up. "I'll just see what they want. . . . I'll be right back."

Maria nodded and took a sip of coffee. Becker's limp barely showed as he walked through the house.

The delivery was a telegram from Dansey: "MARIA CLEAR COMMA STATES SOPADE STOP."

Becker smiled. He hadn't doubted Maria's story, though Dansey had. Dansey found a connection with the German Socialist exiles, Sopade, to confirm Maria's long-term political activism and her hatred of the Nazis.

The telegram continued: "JANECK GREETINGS PRAGUE STOP."

So Herr Janeck's story was true. He'd escaped to Sopade headquarters, the German Socialists in exile in Prague.

"CONFIRM YOU RECRUIT MARIA STOP BEST WISHES END."

With Maria's story confirmed, they gave Becker the go-ahead to recruit Maria into Dansey's network. They'd discussed this in London, pending confirmation of Maria's anti-Nazi credentials. Churchill and his intelligence friends admired and valued Maria's performance in their escape from the Third Reich.

Maria stared out across the Caribbean. She knew Becker was waiting for London's confirmation of her story. She believed his assurances that he already believed her. She wouldn't have blamed him for doubting her. She certainly didn't blame British Intelligence. They had to be careful against the conniving Nazis.

In her acting days, Maria had faced two main challenges. The first was to convince her friends and acquaintances that she wasn't acting when she was off-stage. The second was to convince herself. Finding her own character after immersing herself in a stage character was harder than the actual acting.

After the Nazis took over, she declined offers to move to Vienna. This was in part for her own sanity, after so many years between acting like others versus being herself. The virtue of settling into herself, however, made her miss the thrills of the stage. Her adventures with Becker had rekindled old delights. Once again, she'd found herself swinging from one persona to the next. For a practiced actress, it was a kind of vertigo of the spirit, and she liked it.

Maria saw Becker walking back through the house, paper in hand. She returned his smile.

"They say I'm all right?" she asked.

Becker nodded.

"Now they want me to work for them, as you predicted?"

He nodded again and sat down. "Will you?"

Maria smiled. "Of course. Anything to damage the fanatics that destroyed Rupert and so many others." As a British agent, she'd be returning to the stage, though a very different one.

"There's plenty of work to do," he said.

She smiled and reached her hand across the table to his. "You still have plenty of resting to do. And playing. . . . Are you ready for our morning swim?"

"As ever."

HISTORICAL NOTES

Lieutenant Colonel Claude Dansey was in and out of British intelligence service his entire adult life. With fascism on the rise in 1930s Europe, and with the official British intelligence agency ignoring the dangers, Dansey established a semi-private intelligence organization comprised especially of businessmen paying for their own part-time espionage. Dansey took the code name Colonel Z, and his ultra-secret group was the Z Organisation.

On March 7, 1936, Hitler remilitarized the German Rhineland, his border with France and Belgium. By his own account years later, no other step along his path to war ever made him so nervous. He worried that the Allies might respond by invading Germany as easily as France had invaded the German Ruhrland in 1923. In that event, Hitler's Army had secret orders for immediate withdrawal. Hitler knew that German armed forces would be overwhelmed if the French alone intervened, not to mention with British help. To scare them off, Hitler told the Allies that the German Army was several times larger than it actually was. If the Allies feared German numbers, they might not invade the Third Reich. Hitler bluffed.

The elderly, ultra-conservative generals of the French High Command believed Hitler. And they were anyway more interested in fighting French communism than German fascism. Some French politicians and junior officers wanted to fight Hitler in 1936, but they were too dispersed to challenge the generals' inertia.

British officials were mostly skeptical of Hitler's boasts. But like the French, most British leaders and public opinion had little taste for even a minor war with the Third Reich in 1936. Contrary to their own country's 1919 Treaty of Versailles, Neville Chamberlain and other Conservative Party leaders thought that Hitler should have the right to arm and defend Germany territory. And they, too, feared communist threats from Russia and even from within France.

Although Churchill's Conservative Party ruled Britain, Churchill himself was confined to the back benches of Parliament, out of favor in the country and within his own party. However, since his Cabinet service during the First World War and the 1920s, Churchill's long-term security clearance to top-secret intelligence information remained in place, and he followed and admired Claude Dansey's Z Organisation.

In 1936, even Winston Churchill needed persuading to intervene against Hitler. If a spy like John Becker had produced proof of Hitler's short-term bluff and long-term war plans, London and Paris could have acted. War against Hitler in 1936 would have been much easier than in 1939-40, when it finally came.

German remilitarization of the Rhineland in 1936 is perhaps the most underappreciated turning point on the road to Hitler's war. Other turning points were yet to come.

Jeffrey Vanke holds a Ph.D. in European history from Harvard University. He lives in Roanoke, Virginia.

2/13 2014-0 ___ *

Made in the USA
Lexington, KY
19 December 2012